Praise for Emma M

"A sweet tale."
—*RT*

"There is warmth to the characters that will leave readers looking forward to seeing more."
—*RT Book Reviews* on *A Match for Addy*

Praise for Marta Perry and her novels

"Set within the Amish community, with a strong, sympathetic heroine at the center of a suspenseful plot, Perry's story hooks you immediately."
—*RT Book Reviews* on *Home by Dark*

"Perry's strong writing, along with loads of suspense, will keep you turning the pages."
—*RT Book Reviews* on *Danger in Plain Sight*

Praise for Diane Burke and her novels

"A fascinating story of hidden identities and forbidden love, creating a page-turning mystery."
—*RT Book Reviews* on *Double Identity*

"Burke's solid mystery has characters who are easy to empathize with."
—*RT Book Reviews* on *Midnight Caller*

Praise for Kit Wilkinson and her novels

"This excellent story builds an intriguing mystery around a developing romance in the fascinating world of competitive steeplechase."
—*RT Book Reviews* on *Sabotage*

"Plenty of action, a heartwarming love story and a good mystery make this a compelling read."
—*RT Book Reviews* on *Protector's Honor*

Emma Miller lives quietly in her old farmhouse in rural Delaware. Fortunate enough to have been born into a family of strong faith, she grew up on a dairy farm surrounded by loving parents, siblings, grandparents, aunts, uncles and cousins. Emma was educated in local schools and once taught in an Amish schoolhouse. When she's not caring for her large family, reading and writing are her favorite pastimes.

Marta Perry realized she wanted to be a writer at age eight, when she read her first Nancy Drew novel. A lifetime spent in rural Pennsylvania and her own Pennsylvania Dutch roots led Marta to the books she writes now about the Amish. When she's not writing, Marta is active in the life of her church and enjoys traveling and spending time with her three children and six beautiful grandchildren. Visit her online at martaperry.com.

Diane Burke is an award-winning author who has had six books published with Love Inspired Suspense. She is a voracious reader and loves movies, crime shows, travel and eating out! She has never met a stranger, only people she hasn't had the pleasure of talking to yet. She loves to hear from readers and can be reached at diane@dianeburkeauthor.com. She can also be found on Twitter and Facebook

Kit Wilkinson is a former PhD student who once wrote discussions on the medieval feminine voice. She now prefers weaving stories of romance and redemption. Her first inspirational manuscript won a prestigious Golden Heart® Award. You can visit Kit at kitwilkinson.com or write to her at write@kitwilkinson.com.

EMMA MILLER

Anna's Gift

&

MARTA PERRY
DIANE BURKE
KIT WILKINSON

Danger in Amish Country

HARLEQUIN® LOVE INSPIRED®

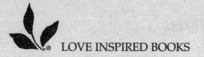

LOVE INSPIRED BOOKS

Recycling programs for this product may not exist in your area.

ISBN-13: 978-0-373-83900-1

Anna's Gift and Danger in Amish Country

Copyright © 2017 by Harlequin Books S.A.

The publisher acknowledges the copyright holders of the individual works as follows:

Anna's Gift
Copyright © 2011 by Faulkner, Inc. and Judith E. French

Fall from Grace
Copyright © 2013 by Martha Johnson

Dangerous Homecoming
Copyright © 2013 by Diane Burke

Return to Willow Trace
Copyright © 2013 by Kit Wilkinson

www.Harlequin.com

Printed in U.S.A.

CONTENTS

ANNA'S GIFT

Emma Miller

For Mildred,
for the delight her beauty brought to my world.

Let your beauty not be external…
but the inner person of the heart,
the lasting beauty of a gentle and tranquil spirit,
which is precious in God's sight.
—1 Peter 3:3–4

Chapter One

~❧

Kent County, Delaware... Winter

Anna Yoder carried an open can of robin's egg-blue paint carefully through the big farmhouse kitchen, down the hall and into the bedroom across from her mother's room. Her sister Susanna trailed two steps behind, a paintbrush in each hand.

"I want to paint," Susanna proclaimed for the fourth time. "I can paint good. Can I paint, Anna? Can I?"

Anna glanced over her shoulder at her younger sister, and nodded patiently. "Yes, you can paint. But not right now. I'm cutting in and it's tricky not getting paint on the floor or the ceiling. You can help with the rolling later."

"*Ya!*" Susanna agreed, and her round face lit up in a huge smile as she bounced from one bare foot to the other and waved the paintbrushes in the air. "I'm the goodest painter!"

Anna chuckled. "I'm sure you are the *best* painter."

Susanna was nothing, if not enthusiastic. Of her six sisters, Susanna was the dearest and the one toward which Anna felt most protective. Sweet, funny Susanna was the baby of the family and had been born with Down syndrome. Their Dat had always called her one of God's special children; at eighteen, Susanna still possessed the innocence of a girl of nine or ten.

Fortunately, for all the tasks that came hard to Susanna, such as reading, sewing or cooking, the Lord had blessed her with a bottomless well of special gifts. Susanna could soothe a crying baby better than any of them; she always knew when it was going to rain, and she had a rare ability to see through the complications of life to find the simple and shining truth. And sometimes, when things weren't going well, when the cow had gone dry or the garden was withering for lack of rain, Susanna could fill the house with laughter and remind them all that there was always hope in God's great plan.

Still, keeping track of Susanna and running the household was a big responsibility, one that Anna felt doubly, with Mam off to Ohio to bring Anna's grandmother, great aunt and sisters, Rebecca and Leah, home. Susanna and Anna would be on their own for several days. Their sister Ruth and her husband, Eli, who lived just across the field, had gone to a wedding in Pennsylvania. Irwin, the boy who lived with them, had accompanied their sister Miriam and her husband, Charley, to an auction in Virginia. Not that Anna didn't have help. Eli's cousin was pitching in with the milking and the outside chores, but Anna still had a lot to do. And not a lot of time to get it all done.

Anna had promised Mam to have the house spic-and-span when she returned home, and she took the responsibility seriously. Having both Miriam and Ruth marry and move out in November had been a big change, but bringing Grossmama and Aunt Jezebel into the house would be an even bigger change. Grossmama was no longer able to live on her own. Anna understood that, and she knew why her mother felt responsible for Dat's aging mother, especially now that he was gone. The trouble was, Grossmama and Mam had never gotten along, and with the onset of Alzheimer's, Anna doubted that the situation would improve. Luckily, everyone adored Grossmama's younger sister, Jezebel; unlike Grossmama, Aunt Jezebel was easygoing and would fit smoothly into the household.

"We're paintin' because Grossmama's coming," Susanna chirped. Her speech wasn't always perfect, but her family understood every word she said. "She baked me a gingerbread man."

"*Ya,*" Anna agreed. "She did." Susanna was the one person in the household who her grandmother never found fault with, and that was a good thing. If Grossmama could see how precious Susanna was, she couldn't be that bad, could she?

Once, when she was visiting years ago, Grossmama had spent the afternoon baking cookies and had made Susanna a gingerbread man with raisin eyes, a cranberry nose and a marshmallow beard. Susanna had never forgotten, and whenever their grandmother was mentioned, Susanna reminded them of the gingerbread treat.

Grossmama had fallen on the stairs at her house the previous year, fracturing a hip, so Mam hadn't wanted her climbing the steps to a second-floor bedroom here. Instead, they'd decided to move Anna and Susanna upstairs to join Leah and Rebecca in the dormitory-style

chamber over the kitchen. Grossmama and Aunt Jezebel could share this large downstairs room just a few
feet away from the bathroom.

It was a lovely room, with tall windows and plenty
of room for two beds, a chest of drawers and a rocking
chair. Anna knew that Grossmama and Aunt Jezebel
would be comfortable here...except for the color. Anna
couldn't remember which of her sisters had chosen the
original color for the walls, but Grossmama hated it.
She'd made a fuss when Mam had written to explain
the new arrangements. Grossmama said that she could
never sleep one night in a bed surrounded by fancy
"English" walls.

By saying "English," Anna understood that her
grandmother meant "not Plain." To Grossmama, white
was properly Plain; blue was Plain. Since the ceiling,
the window trim, the doors and the fireplace mantel
were white, blue was the color in Anna's paint can.
Actually, Anna didn't see anything improper about the
color the room was now. The muted purple was closer
to lavender, and she had a lavender dress and cape that
she really loved. But once Grossmama set her mind on
a thing or against it, there was no changing it.

Standing in the bedroom now, staring at the walls,
Anna wished Ruth was there. Ruth was a good painter.
Anna prided herself on her skill at cooking, perhaps
more than she should have, but she knew that her painting ability was sketchy at best. But, since the choice
was between Susanna or her, Anna knew who had to
paint the room.

Of course, she'd meant to get started sooner, but the
week had gotten away from her. Susanna had a dentist appointment on Monday, which took all afternoon

by the time they had to wait for the driver. On Tuesday, there had been extra eggs, which needed to go to Spence's Auction and Bazaar. Normally, they didn't go to Spence's in the winter months, but Aunt Martha and Dorcas had opened a baked-goods stand. Anna had taken the opportunity to leave Susanna with their oldest sister, Johanna, so that she could go with Aunt Martha to sell her eggs and jams.

Now it was Wednesday. After Mam left at dawn, Anna and Susanna had spent the morning scrubbing, dusting, polishing and setting her yeast dough to rise. Now there were no more excuses. Anna had to start painting if she wanted to be finished on time. Because they were alone, Anna wore her oldest dress, the one with the blackberry stains, and had covered her hair—not with a proper white *kapp,* but with a blue scarf that Irwin's terrier had chewed holes in.

Knowing that Susanna would be certain to lean against a freshly painted wall, Anna had made sure that Susanna's clothing was equally worn. That way, if the dresses were ruined it wouldn't be a waste. Anna's final precaution was to remove her shoes and stockings and ask Susanna to do the same. Paint would scrub off bare feet. Black stockings and sneakers wouldn't be so lucky.

Gingerly setting the can on the little shelf on the ladder, Anna climbed the rickety rungs, dipped her brush in the can and began to carefully paint along the wall, just below the ceiling. She'd barely gone two feet when Susanna announced that she was hungry. "Wait a little," Anna coaxed. "It's still early. When I get as far as the window, we'll have some lunch."

"But, Anna, I'm hungry *now.*"

"All right. Go and fix yourself a honey biscuit."

"'Fff…*thi*rsty, too," she said, struggling to pronounce the word properly.

"Milk or tea. You don't need my help."

"I'll make you a biscuit, too."

"*Ne.* I'll eat later. Don't wander off," she cautioned her sister. "Stay in the house." Susanna was capable of taking care of herself on the farm, but it was cold today, with snow flurries in the forecast, and she didn't always remember to wear her coat. It wouldn't do for Mam to come home and find Susanna sick with a cold.

Anna continued to paint. The blue covered the lavender better than she thought it would. It would need a second coat, but she had expected as much. As she carefully brushed paint on the wall in a line along the ceiling's edge, Anna began to hum and then to sing one of her favorite *fast tunes* from the *Liedersammlung.* She liked to sing when she was alone. Her voice wasn't as good as Johanna's or Ruth's, but singing made her feel bubbly inside. And now, with only Susanna to hear, she could sing as loudly as she wanted. If she was a bit off-key, her little sister wouldn't complain.

"Anna? Maybe we come at a bad time?"

Startled by a deep male voice, Anna stopped singing midword and spun around, holding onto the ladder with her free hand. "Samuel!"

Their nearest neighbor, the widower Samuel Mast, stood inside the bedroom holding his youngest daughter, Mae, by the hand. Mortified by her appearance and imagining how awful her singing must have sounded, Anna wanted to shrink up and hide behind the paint can. Of all the people to catch her in such a condition, it had to be Samuel Mast. Tall, broad-shouldered, handsome Samuel Mast. Anna's cheeks felt as though they were on fire, and she knew she must be as flame-colored as a ripe tomato.

"I remembered what you said." Susanna hopped from one foot to the other in the doorway. "I didn't go outside. Let Samuel and Mae in." She beamed.

"You're busy," Samuel said, tugging on Mae's hand. "We can come back another—"

"*Ne,*" Anna interrupted, setting her brush carefully across the paint can and coming down the ladder. "Just...you surprised me." She tried to cover her embarrassment with a smile, but knew it was lopsided. *Samuel.* Of all the people to see her like this, in her patched clothing and bare legs, it had to be Samuel. Her stomach felt as though she'd swallowed a feather duster. "It's not a bad time," she babbled in a rush. "I'm painting the room. Blue."

"*Ya,* blue. I can see that." Samuel looked as uncomfortable as she felt. Anna had never seen him looking so flustered. Or untidy, for that matter. Samuel's nut-brown hair, which badly needed cutting, stuck out in clumps and appeared to have gobs of oatmeal stuck in it. His shirt was wrinkled, and one suspender hung by a thread. Even his trousers and shoes were smeared with dried oatmeal.

"Something wrong?" Anna glanced at Mae. The child was red-eyed from crying, her nose was running, her *kapp* was missing, and her face and hands were smeared with dried oatmeal, too. Anna's heart immediately went out to the little girl. She'd left her aunt's only two weeks ago, to live with her father for the first time, and Anna knew the move couldn't have been easy for her. "Are you having a hard morning, pumpkin?"

Mae's bottom lip came out and tears spilled down

her cheeks. "Want...want Aunt L'eeze. Want...want to go home! Want *her!*"

Anna glanced at Samuel, who looked ready to burst into tears as well, and took command. "Mae—" she leaned down to speak to her at eye-level "—would you like to go with Susanna into the kitchen and have a honey biscuit and a cup of milk?"

Mae nodded, her lower lip still protruding.

Anna stood up. "Susanna, could you get Mae a biscuit?"

"*Ya,*" Susanna agreed. "And wash her face." She smiled at Mae. "You look like a little piggy."

For seconds, Mae seemed suspended between tears and a smile, but then she nodded and threw her chubby arms up to Susanna.

Samuel sighed as Susanna scooped up Mae and carried her away. "I don't seem to get anything right with her," he said.

Anna smiled. "Best to *feed* children porridge and *wash* them with soap and water. Not the other way around."

Samuel returned a hint of a smile, obviously embarrassed. "It's...been hard...these last weeks," he stumbled. "Having her home. She's been four years with my sister, and I'm...we're strange to her. She doesn't know me or her brothers and sisters."

Sensing that it might be easier for Samuel to share his concerns if she continued with her work, Anna climbed the ladder again and dipped her brush into the can.

Aunt Martha had been telling Mam the other day that Samuel was finding it difficult to manage his farm, his house and to care for five children, and that it was just a matter of time before he realized it. "*Then* he'll start looking for a wife," she'd said. "Something he should have done three years ago."

"When Frieda passed, little Mae was only two months old," Samuel continued. "I had my hands full, so Louise thought it better if she took the baby home to Ohio until…until…"

Anna knew *until* what—until Samuel finished mourning his wife and remarried. Usually, widowers waited a year before looking for a new partner, but sometimes, when there were small children, the waiting period might be much shorter. Samuel's widowerhood had somehow stretched to four years.

In all those years, Samuel had made no formal attempt to court anyone, but most of Kent County suspected that he was sweet on Mam. Despite their age difference—Mam was eight years older—it would be a fine match. Samuel was handsome, a deacon of the church, and would make an excellent provider for an extended family. Not only did their farms run side-by-side, but Samuel had one of the finest dairy herds in the state.

Everyone liked Samuel. It wasn't just that he was a good-looking bear of a man, with his broad shoulders, a sturdy build and warm brown eyes, but he was hardworking, funny and fair-minded. It was clear that he and Mam were good friends, and Samuel spent many an evening at their kitchen table, drinking coffee, talking and laughing with her. Why he hadn't formally asked to court her, Anna couldn't guess. But that was okay with Anna. It was hard for her to imagine having Samuel for a stepfather. She'd secretly dreamed about him, although she'd never said a word to anyone other than her cousin, Dorcas. Even now, just having him in the room with her made her pulse race and her head go all giddy.

Anna knew, of course, that Samuel Mast, probably the catch of the county, would never look at her. Anna considered herself sensible, dependable, hardworking and Plain. But among the pretty red-haired Yoder sisters, Anna stuck out like a plow horse in a field of pacers. A healthy mare, her Aunt Martha called her, but no amount of brushing her hair or pinching her cheeks could make her pretty. Her face was too round, her mouth too wide, and her nose was like a lump of biscuit dough.

Her mother had always told her that true beauty was in the heart and spirit, but everyone knew what boys liked. Men were attracted to cute girls and handsome women, and it was the slender *maedles* with good dowries who got the pick of the best husband material.

No, Anna wasn't foolish enough to consider ever marrying a man as fine and good-looking as Samuel, but it didn't keep her from dreaming. And it didn't stop her from wishing that there was someone like him somewhere, who could see beneath her sturdy frame and Plain features, to appreciate her for who she was inside.

"Don't worry," Aunt Martha always said. "Any woman works as hard as you do and cooks *hasen kucha* like yours, she'll find a man. Might be one not so easy on the eyes out West someplace, or a bucktoothed widower with a dozen sons and no daughters to help with the housework, but someone will have you."

Anna knew she wanted a husband, babies and a home of her own, but she wondered if the price might be higher than she wanted to pay. She loved her mother and her sisters, and she loved living in Seven Poplars with all the neighbors and friends who were dear to her. She wasn't certain she would be willing to leave Delaware to marry, especially with the prospects Aunt Martha suggested would be available to her.

"Anna?"

"*Ya?*" She glanced back at Samuel, feeling even more foolish. While she'd been dream-weaving, Samuel had been saying something to her. "I'm listening," she said, which wasn't quite true.

"My Frieda is dead four years."

Anna nodded, not certain where the conversation was going. "She is," Anna agreed. "Four years."

"And two months," Samuel added. "Time I...made plans for my family."

Suddenly realizing what he might be talking about, she grasped the ladder to keep it from swaying. "I'm sorry you missed Mam." Her voice seemed too loud in the empty room. "I'm not sure when she'll be home. A few days. It depends on the weather and how Grossmama is feeling."

"I...didn't come...didn't come to speak...to Hannah." Each word seemed to come as a struggle.

She paused, resting her brush on the lip of the paint can, giving him her full attention. If he hadn't come to talk to Mam, why was he here? Was he sick? Was that why he looked so bad? "Do you need help with something? Charley should be back—"

"*Ne.* It's you, really, I want to talk to."

"Me?" Her mouth gaped open and she snapped it shut. Her stomach turned over. "Something I can do for you?"

"*Ya.* I want..."

Anna shifted her weight and the wooden step under

her left foot creaked. "You want…" she urged, trying
to help.

"If you would…" He took a deep breath and straightened his shoulders.

He was a big man, so attractive, even with his
scraggly hair and oatmeal on his clothes. He filled the
doorway, and staring at him, Anna couldn't stop the
fluttering in the pit of her stomach. "*Ya?*" she coaxed.
"You want…"

"I want to court you, Anna," Samuel blurted out.
"I want that you should give me the honor to become
my wife."

Anna froze, unable to exhale. Surely he hadn't said
what she *thought* he said. She blinked as black spots
raced before her eyes. Abruptly, she felt her hands go
numb. Her knees went weak and the ladder began to
sway. An instant later, paint, ladder and Anna went
flying.

Chapter Two

"Anna!" Samuel rushed forward in an attempt to catch her, and they went down together in a crash of wood, entwined arms and legs, and what seemed like gallons of blue paint. Samuel slid rather than fell to the floor and ended up with Anna in his lap, his arms securely around her middle. Somewhere in the jumble, the paint can hit the wall and bounced, spraying paint everywhere.

Samuel peered into Anna's startled face. Her eyes were wide, her mouth gaped, but the only sound she made was a small, "Oh, no."

"Are you hurt?" he asked, letting go of her when he realized he still held his arms tightly around her. He tried to rise, slipped in the river of paint and sat down hard, a splat rising from around his britches. As they fell a second time, Anna's arms instinctively went around his neck, bringing her face only inches from his. She was so close, he could have kissed her full, rosy lips.

"Anna?" he said, out of breath. "Are you all right?"

She gave a gasp, wiggled out of his embrace and scrambled up, her back foot slipping. Throwing both arms out for balance, she caught herself before she went down again.

Samuel knew he had to say something. But what?

Anna sucked in a gulp of air, threw her apron up over her blue-streaked face and ran through the doorway, nearly running into Susanna and Mae, and out of the room.

"Anna," he called, trying to get to his feet again, but having less luck than she had. "Come back. It's all right." He dropped onto all fours and used his hands to push himself up. "It's only paint. Anna!"

But Anna was gone, and the only evidence that she'd been there was the warm feeling in his chest, and a trail of bright blue footprints across the wide, red floorboards.

"You spilled the paint." Susanna began to giggle, then pointed at him. "And you have paint in your beard."

"Beard," Mae echoed, standing solemnly beside her newfound friend.

Samuel looked down at his blue hands and up at the two girls, and he began to laugh, too. Great belly laughs rolled up from the pit of his stomach. "We did spill the paint, didn't we?" he managed to say as he looked around the room at the mess they'd made. "We spilled *a lot* of paint."

"A lot," Susanna agreed.

Mae stared at him with her mother's bright blue eyes and clutched the older girl's hand. The fearful expression in his daughter's wide-eyed gaze made him want to gather her up in his arms and hug her, but in his state, that was out of the question. Two painted scarecrows in one house was enough; the hugs would have to wait until later.

"Susanna, could you go and see if your sister is hurt?" Samuel asked. His first instinct was to follow Anna to see for himself that she was okay and to assure her that she had no need to be embarrassed. Anyone could have an accident, and the wooden ladder had obviously seen better days. But he'd heard her run up the stairs, and it wouldn't be seemly for him to intrude on her. With her mother out of the house, he had to show respect and maintain proper behavior. If he was going to court Anna, he was going to do it right and behave the way any man courting her would be expected to.

"*Ya,*" Susanna agreed. Still giggling, she trotted off with Mae glued to her skirts.

Turning in a circle, Samuel exhaled and wiped his hands on his pants. The way he'd been swimming in the paint, they were a total loss anyway. He rubbed a bruised elbow and the back of his head as he studied the floor, the wall, and the broken ladder. How, he wondered, had so much paint come from one gallon?

This was a fine barrel of pickles.

After putting it off for so long and practicing his proposal of marriage to Anna over and over in his head, it had gone all wrong. It couldn't have gone worse. He didn't know what he'd expected, but he certainly hadn't thought the statement of his intentions would frighten her so badly that she'd fall off a ladder, or drop into his arms—although that had been a pleasant interlude. He didn't know why sweet Anna had been so surprised, or why she'd run away from him. He hoped that it wasn't because the idea of marrying him and instantly becoming the mother of five children was so preposterous.

Samuel picked up the paint can and set it upright— there couldn't have been more than half a cup of paint left in the bottom. The room was a disaster. He decided he'd better get a start on cleaning it up before the paint began to dry. If he was lucky, maybe Anna would come down and join him and they could talk. He would need rags, a mop and maybe even a shovel to start wiping up the excess paint, but he didn't have the faintest idea where to find them.

The first thing he needed to do, before he went looking for the supplies, was to take his shoes off so he didn't track paint through the house. Setting the ladder upright, he sat down on the lower rung and began to unlace his brogans.

Samuel wondered if he'd gone about this all wrong. The custom was for the suitor to ask a go-between to talk to the girl's family before a proposal of marriage was formally offered. But with Anna's father dead and not a single brother, that left Hannah as the sole parent. Samuel supposed he could have approached Anna's uncle by marriage, Reuben Coblentz, but that would have involved Reuben's wife, Martha. Reuben didn't scratch until Martha told him where he itched. Plus, Hannah and Martha didn't always see eye to eye, and Hannah had made it clear that she didn't care for her late husband's sister interfering in her personal family matters.

That left speaking directly to Hannah before he approached Anna, but he'd decided against that because he was afraid that Hannah might have misconstrued his previous regular visits to the Yoder farm. There wasn't any doubt in Samuel's mind that most of the community thought that he was courting Hannah, or at least testing the waters. It could well be that Hannah thought so, too, and he didn't want to make matters worse by embarrassing her, maybe even hurting her feelings. Samuel liked Hannah, and he always enjoyed her company, but there was no comparing the warm friendship that he felt for her to his keen attraction to Anna.

What Samuel and his late wife, Frieda, had had was a comfortable marriage, but his father and her family had arranged the match. Samuel had been willing because it seemed such a sensible arrangement. He thought Frieda would make a good wife, and he'd always been reluctant to go against his father's wishes.

He'd been just nineteen to Frieda's twenty-three when they wed. Everyone said that it was a good match, and he could remember the excitement of their wedding day. Neither of them had expected romance, but they'd come to respect and care for each other, and they both adored the children the Lord sent them.

When Frieda's heart had failed and he'd lost her, he'd genuinely mourned her passing. But Frieda had been gone a long time, so long that he sometimes had trouble remembering her face. And he was lonely, not just for a helpmate, not just for a mother for his children, but for someone with whom he could open his heart.

If he was honest with himself, Samuel reckoned he'd been attracted to Anna for at least two years. Just seeing her across a room gave him a breathless, shivery thrill that he'd never experienced before. Oh, he wasn't blind. He knew what the other young men in the community thought about Anna. She wasn't small or trim, and she didn't have delicate features. Some fellows went so far as to make fun of her size. Not where Anna could hear, of course, or him either. He would have never stood by and allowed such a fine woman to be insulted by foolish boys who couldn't see how special she was.

In his heart, Samuel had always admired strong women. Other than Frieda, who'd been the exception, every girl he'd ever driven home from a singing or a young people's gathering had been sturdy. His mother, his sisters and his aunts were all good cooks and mothers, and all of formidable size. Like Anna, they all had the gift of hospitality, of making people feel welcome in their homes. And regardless of what anyone else thought, he appreciated Anna Yoder for who she was. "Big women have big hearts," his father always said, and Samuel agreed.

For longer than he wanted to admit, Samuel had been watching Anna and trying to convince himself that it was just his loneliness. After all, how fair was it for a man with five children and the responsibility of a large farm to propose marriage to a beautiful young woman like Anna? So he'd put off the decision to do anything about his feelings. As long as he didn't speak up, he was free to imagine what it would be like having her in his house, sitting beside him at the kitchen table, or bringing him a cold glass of lemonade when he was hot and sweaty from working in the fields. Month after month, he'd waited for her to reach the age of twenty-one, but when she had, he still hadn't found the nerve to ask.

What if she rejected him out of hand? So long as he didn't speak up, he could keep on going to Hannah's house, sitting at their table, savoring Anna's hot cinnamon-raisin buns and chicken and dumplings. But once he brought up the subject, if Anna refused him, Hannah might have no choice but to discourage his visits.

He hoped he was a truly faithful man, a good father and a good farmer. He'd been blessed by beautiful children, caring parents and a loving family. The Lord had provided material goods, land of his own and a fine herd of dairy cows. He served on the school board and helped his neighbors. His life should have been full, but it wasn't. He longed for Anna Yoder to be his wife.

It had taken his sister Louise to finally put an end to his hesitation. She'd brought Mae home, handed her over, and told him that it was time he found a new wife and a new mother for his children. He had to agree. It was past time. But now that he'd made up his mind and chosen the right woman, he'd made a mess of things.

What must Anna think of him? No wonder she was embarrassed. He'd had his arms around her, had her literally *in his lap,* and they'd both been doused in blue paint, like some sort of English clowns. He wanted to court her honorably, to give her the love and caring she deserved, and instead he'd made her look foolish.

In his stocking feet, Samuel stepped over a puddle of paint, taking in the room again.

After the mess he had made, it would serve him right if Anna never spoke to him again.

Anna stood in the shower in the big upstairs bathroom and scrubbed every inch of her skin. She knew that she should be downstairs cleaning up the terrible mess she'd made, but she couldn't face Samuel. She'd probably have to hide from him for the rest of her life.

How could she have been so clumsy? Not only had she fallen off the ladder, but when Samuel had tried to catch her, they'd both gone down in a huge pool of blue paint.

She wished she could weep as her sisters did, as most girls did when something bad happened. But this was too awful for tears. Not only had she embarrassed herself and Samuel, but she'd probably ruined things between her mother and Samuel. She'd be the laughing stock of the community, and Samuel would probably never come to the Yoder farm again. And all because of her foolish daydreaming. What a silly girl she was, thinking Samuel had said he wanted to court her. She probably needed to clean out her ears. She had obviously misunderstood.

"Anna!" Susanna cracked the bathroom door. "You made a mess."

"Go away," Anna ordered.

"Samuel told me to come see if you were all right."

"He didn't leave yet?" her voice came out a little shrill.

"Nope. He told me to come see if you—"

"I'm fine," Anna interrupted, hugging herself. Emotion caught in her throat at the sheer mention of Samuel's name. "Just go away, please."

The door opened wider, and her sister's round face appeared. Anna could see her through the filmy, white shower curtain.

"Are you blue, Anna? Will the blue come off? Will you be blue on Sunday? At church?"

"Susanna! I'm in the shower." Eli had promised to fix the lock on the door a few weeks ago when he'd put the doorway in between the room over the kitchen and the upstairs hallway in the main house, but he hadn't gotten to it. She'd have to remind him because right now there was no privacy in the upstairs bathroom. "I'll be out in a minute."

"But Anna…"

"Anna," repeated little Mae.

Susanna had brought Mae to the bathroom! Anna

took a breath before she spoke; there was no need to take this out on Susanna. It was all her own fault. "Take Mae back downstairs to her father. See them out. And give them some biscuits!"

Without waiting for an answer, Anna turned the hot water knob all the way up and stood under the spray. *Give Samuel biscuits?* Had she really said such a thing? Was there no end to her foolishness? Samuel didn't want her biscuits. After the way she'd embarrassed him, he'd probably never again eat anything she baked.

Anna could hear Susanna and little Mae chattering in the hall and she felt trapped. If Mae was still in the house, Samuel had to be. She couldn't possibly get out, not with him still here.

"She has to go potty," Susanna piped up over the drone of the shower. "Mae does. She has to go bad."

Gritting her teeth, Anna peered around the shower curtain. The water was beginning to get cool anyway. They had a small hot water tank that ran on propane, but there wasn't an endless supply of warm water. "All right. Just a minute. Close the door and let me get dried off." She jumped out of the shower, grabbed a towel and wrapped it around herself. "All right, Susanna. Bring Mae in."

Susanna pushed open the door. "There's the potty, Mae."

"Do you need help?" Anna asked the child.

Mae shook her head.

Anna wrapped a second towel around her head. "When she's done, wash her hands, then her face. Clean up her dress and bring her into the bedroom. We can fix her hair." She smiled down at the little girl. "Would you like that? I never pull hair when I do braids. You can ask Susanna."

"Anna does good hair braids," Susanna agreed. "But I fink she needs a bath," she told Anna. "She looks like a little piggy."

A quick examination of the little girl convinced Anna that she wasn't all that dirty, she'd just lost a battle with her breakfast. "We don't have time for a bath. I'm sure Samuel needs to be on his way."

Susanna wrinkled her nose as she looked at the little girl. "You spill your oatmeal this morning?"

"*Frowed* it. It was yuck," Mae said from her perch.

Susanna's eyes got big. "You *throwed* your oatmeal?"

"*Ya.* It was all burny." She made a face. "It was lumpy an' I *'frowed* it."

On her father as well, Anna realized, suddenly feeling sympathy for both father and daughter. "Well, don't do that again," she admonished gently, tightening the big towel around her. "It's not polite to throw your breakfast. Big girls like Susanna never throw their oatmeal."

"*Ne,*" Susanna echoed, helping the little girl rearrange her dress. "Never." She turned to Anna. "Are you going to court Samuel?"

Anna gasped. "Susanna! What would make you ask such a thing?"

"Because Samuel said—"

"Were you listening in on our conversation, Susanna?" Anna's eyes narrowed. "You know what Mam says about that."

"Just a little. Samuel said he wants to court you."

"*Ne,*" Anna corrected. "You heard wrong. Again. That's exactly why Mam doesn't want you listening in."

That, and because Susanna repeated everything she heard, or *thought* she heard, to anyone who would listen. Obviously, she had misheard. They'd both heard wrong. That was why Anna had lost her balance and fallen off the ladder. She'd misunderstood what Samuel said. There was no way that he wanted to court *her*. No way at all. She was what she was, the Plain Yoder girl, the healthy girl—which was another way of saying fat. But was it really possible that they had both misheard?

More possible than Samuel wanting to court her!

Anna hurried out of the bathroom. "Bring her in as soon as I'm decent."

She dashed down the hall to the large bedroom over the kitchen and quickly dressed in fresh underclothing, a shift, dress and cape. She combed her wet hair out, twisted it into a bun and pinned it up, covering it with a starched white *kapp.* A quick glance in the tiny mirror on the back of the door showed that every last tendril of red hair was tucked up properly.

The few moments alone gave her time to recover her composure, so that when the girls came in, she could turn her attention to Mae. *Please let me get through this day, Lord,* she prayed silently.

When Susanna and Mae came into the bedroom, Anna sat the child on a stool and quickly combed, parted and braided her thin blond hair. "There. That's better." She brushed a kiss on the crown of Mae's head.

"She needs a *kapp,*" Susanna, ever observant, pointed out. "She's a big girl."

"*Ya,*" Mae agreed solemnly. "Wost my *kapp.*"

"Find me an old one of yours," Anna asked Susanna. "It will be a little big, but we can pin it to fit."

In minutes, Mae's pigtails were neatly tucked inside a slightly wrinkled but white *kapp,* and she was grinning.

"Now you're *Plain,*" Susanna said. "Like me."

"Take her downstairs to her father," Anna said. "Samuel will be wondering why we've kept her so long."

"You coming, too?" Susanna asked.

Anna shook her head. "I'll be along. I have to clean up the bathroom." It wasn't really a fib, because she did have to clean up the bathroom. But there was no possibility of her looking Samuel in the eye again today, maybe not for weeks. But she couldn't help going to the top of the stairs and listening as Samuel said his goodbyes.

"Don't worry, Samuel," Susanna said cheerfully. "Anna wants to court you. It will just take time for her to get used to the idea."

"Court you," Mae echoed.

What Samuel said in reply, Anna couldn't hear. She fled back to the safety of the bathroom and covered her ears with her hands. She should have known that her little sister would only make things worse. Once Susanna got something in her head, it was impossible to budge her from it. And now Samuel would be mortified by the idea that they all thought he wanted to court her instead of Mam.

Anna stayed in the bathroom for what seemed like an hour before she finally got the nerve to venture out. She might have stayed all morning, but she knew she had to clean up the paint before it dried on Mam's floor. She would have to mop up everything and get ready to start painting again tomorrow, after she and Susanna went into town to get more paint. The trip itself would take three hours, beginning to end.

Anna wasn't crazy about the idea of going to Dover alone in the buggy; she liked it better when Miriam or Mam drove. She didn't mind taking the horse and carriage between farms in Seven Poplars, but all the traffic and noise of town made her uncomfortable.

By the time Anna got downstairs, she'd worked herself into a good worry. How was she going to get all the painting done, tend to the farm chores and clean the house from top to bottom, the way she'd hoped?

Calling for Susanna, Anna forced herself down the hall toward Grossmama's bedroom. She pushed opened the door and stopped short, in utter shock. The ladder was gone. The bucket was gone, and every drop of paint had been scrubbed off the floor and woodwork. The room looked exactly as it had this morning, before she'd started—other than the splashes of blue paint on the wall and the strip she'd painted near the ceiling. Even her brushes had been washed clean and laid out on a folded copy of *The Budget*.

Anna was so surprised that she didn't know whether to laugh or cry. She didn't have to wonder who had done it. She knew. Susanna could never have cleaned up the mess, not in two days. Anna was still standing there staring when Susanna wandered in.

"I'm hungry," she said. "I didn't get my lunch."

Anna sighed. "*Ne*. You didn't, did you?" She glanced around the room again, trying to make certain that she hadn't imagined that the paint was cleaned up. "Samuel did this?"

Susanna nodded smugly. "He got rags under the sink. Mam's rags."

"You mustn't say anything to anyone about this," Anna said. "Promise me that you won't."

"About the spilled paint?"

"About the spilled paint, or that I fell off the ladder, or the mistake you made—" she glanced apprehensively at her sister "—about thinking Samuel wanted to court me."

Susanna wrinkled her nose and shifted from one bare foot to another. "But it was funny, Anna. You fell on Samuel. He fell in the paint. It was funny."

"I suppose we did look funny, but Samuel could have been hurt. I could have been hurt. So I'd appreciate it if you didn't say one word about Samuel coming here today. Can you do that?"

Susanna scratched her chubby chin. "Remember when the cow sat on me?"

"*Ya,*" Anna agreed. "Last summer. And it wasn't funny, because you could have been hurt."

"It was just like that," Susanna agreed. "A cow fell on me, and you fell on Samuel. And we both got smashed." She shrugged and turned and went out of the room. "Just the same."

Exactly, Anna thought, feeling waves of heat wash under her skin. *And that's how Samuel must have felt— like a heifer sat on him.* Only, this cow had thrown her arms around his neck and exposed her bare legs up to her thighs like an English hoochy-koochy dancer.

If she lived to be a hundred, she'd never forgive herself. Never.

Chapter Three

The following morning proved cold and blustery, with a threat of snow. All through the morning milking, the feeding of the chickens and livestock and breaking the thin skim of ice off the water trough in the barnyard, Anna wrestled with her dread of venturing out on the roads. She needed to buy more paint, but she didn't know if it was wise to travel in such bad weather. The blacktop would be slippery, and there was always the danger that the horse could slip and fall. And since she didn't want to leave Susanna home alone, she'd have to take her, as well.

Anna considered calling a driver, but the money for the ride would go better into replacing the paint. If only she hadn't been so clumsy and wasted what Mam had already purchased. She wondered if she could find some leftover lavender paint in the cellar. If there was any, maybe she could cover the blue splashes, and put the room back as it had been.

But the truth was, Grossmama would be angry if she found her new bedroom *English purple,* and Mam would be disappointed in Anna. Anna had caused the trouble, and it was her responsibility to fix it. Snow or no snow, she'd have to go and buy more blue paint.

What a noodlehead she'd been! Was she losing her hearing, that she'd imagined Samuel had said that he wanted to court her? She tried not to wonder how Susanna could have misheard, as well. It was funny, really, the whole misunderstanding. Years from now, she and her sisters would laugh over the whole incident. As for Samuel, Anna thought she'd just act normal around him, be pleasant, pretend the whole awful incident had never happened and not cause either of them any further embarrassment.

After the outside chores, Anna returned to the house, built up the fire in the wood cookstove, and mixed up a batch of buttermilk biscuits while the oven was heating. Once the biscuits were baking, she washed some dishes and put bacon on. "Do you want eggs?" she asked her sister.

"*Ya,*" Susanna nodded. "Sunshine up." She finished setting the table and was pouring tomato juice in two glasses, when Flora, their Shetland sheepdog, began to bark. Instantly, Jeremiah, the terrier, added his excited yips and ran in circles.

"I wonder who's here so early?" Anna turned the sizzling bacon and pulled the pan to a cooler area of the stove.

Susanna ran to the door. "Maybe it's Mam and Grossmama."

"Too early for them." Thank goodness. Not that she wasn't eager for Mam to get home. Her younger sisters had been away for nearly a year, with only short visits home, and she'd missed them terribly. But Grossmama would make a terrible fuss if her room wasn't ready and the walls were still splashed with blue paint.

Susanna flung open the door to greet their visitor, and the terrier shot out onto the porch and bounced up and down with excitement, as if his legs were made of springs. Coming up the back steps was the very last person on earth Anna expected to see. It was Samuel, and he'd brought his three daughters: five-year-old Lori Ann, nine-year-old Naomi and Mae, all bundled up in quilted blue coats and black rain boots. They poured through the door Susanna held open for them. The two older girls carried paint rollers, and Samuel had a can of paint in each hand.

"It's Samuel!" Susanna shouted above the terrier's barking. "And Mae! And Naomi! And Lori Ann!"

Anna's stomach flip-flopped as she forced a smile, wiping her hands nervously on her apron. "Samuel." She looked to Naomi. "No school today?"

She pushed her round, wire-frame glasses back into place. "My tummy had a tickle this morning, but I'm better now."

"I think we were missing our teacher," Samuel explained. "I let her stay home. She never misses. Do I smell biscuits?" He grinned and held up the paint cans. "We didn't mean to interrupt your breakfast, but I wanted to get an early start on those walls."

Confused, Anna stared at him. "You wanted to get an early start? You bought paint?"

"Last night." He smiled again, and mischief danced in his dark eyes as he set the cans on the floor. The girls added the rollers and brushes to the pile. "I just took my shirt along to the store, and they were able to match the color perfectly."

"Good you brought paint," Susanna announced. "Now we don't have to take the buggy to town."

"I don't know what to say." Anna gripped the front of her apron. "It's kind of you, but you have so much to do at your farm. We'll pay for the paint, of course, but—"

"I smell something burning." Naomi peered over her glasses and grimaced.

Anna spun around to see smoke rising from the stove. "Oh, my biscuits!" She ran to snatch open the oven door, and used the hem of her apron to grab the handle of the cast-iron frying pan.

"Be careful," Samuel warned.

A cloud of smoke puffed out of the oven, stinging Anna's eyes. She gave a yelp as the heat seared her palm through the cloth, and she dropped the frying pan. It bounced off the open door, sending biscuits flying, and landed with a clang on the floor. Anna clapped her stinging hand to her mouth.

Lori Ann squealed, throwing her mitten-covered hands into the air, and the terrier darted across the floor, snatched a biscuit and ran with it. In the far doorway, the dog dropped the biscuit, then bit into it again, and carried it triumphantly under the table. Flora grabbed one, too, and ran for the sitting room with her prize.

"They're burned," Naomi pronounced, turning in a circle in the middle of the biscuits. "You burned them, Anna."

"Never mind the biscuits, just pick them up," Samuel said. Somehow, before Anna could think what to do next, he had taken charge. He crossed the kitchen, retrieved the cast-iron frying pan from the floor using a hand towel, and set it safely on top of the stove. "How bad is the burn?" he asked as he put an arm around her shoulders, guiding her to the sink. "Is it going to blister?"

"I'm all right," Anna protested, twisting out of his

warm embrace. Her palm stung, but she was hardly aware of it. All she could think of was the sensation of Samuel's strong arm around her and the way her knees felt as wobbly as if they were made of biscuit dough.

Samuel gently took her hand in his large calloused one, turned on the faucet, and held her palm under the cold water. "It doesn't look bad," he said.

"Ne." Anna felt foolish. How could she have been so careless? She was an experienced cook. She knew better than to take anything out of the oven without a hot mitt.

"Let the water do its work." Samuel said, speaking softly, as if to a skittish colt, and the tenderness in his deep voice made Anna's heart go all a-flutter again. "The cold will take the sting away."

"Does it hurt?" Susanna asked.

Anna glanced at her sister. Susanna looked as if she were about to burst into tears. *"Ne.* It's fine," Anna assured her. Susanna couldn't bear to see anyone in pain. From the corner of her eye, Anna saw Mae raise a biscuit to her mouth. "Don't eat that," she cautioned. "It's dirty if it's been on the floor."

Samuel chuckled, picked up a handful of the biscuits and brushed them off against his shirt. "A little scorched, but not so bad they can't be salvaged," he said.

"In our house, we have a five-second rule," Naomi explained, grabbing more biscuits off the floor. "If you grab it up quick, it's okay."

"Mam says floors are dirty," Susanna said, but she was picking up biscuits as well, piling them on a plate on the table.

Anna knew her face must be as hot as the skillet. Why was it that the minute Samuel Mast walked in the door, she turned into a complete klutz? She hadn't burned biscuits in years. She always paid close attention to whatever she had in the oven. She wished she could throw her apron over her face and run away, like yesterday, but she knew that she couldn't get away with that twice.

"Don't put them on the table," Anna said. "They're ruined. I'll feed them to the chickens."

"But I want biscuit and honey," Mae pouted, eyeing the heaped plate. "Yes'erday, she…" She pointed at Susanna. "*She* gave me a honey biscuit. It was yum."

"Shh," Naomi said to her little sister. "Remember your manners, Mae."

"I can make more," Anna offered.

"Nonsense." Samuel scooped up Mae and raised her high in the air, coaxing a giggle out of her. "We'll cut off the burned parts and eat the other half, won't we?"

Anna took a deep breath and shook her head. She was mortified. What would Mam think, if she found out that she'd served guests burned biscuits they'd picked up off the floor? Pride might be a sin, but Mam had high standards for her kitchen. And so did she, for that matter. "Really, Samuel," she protested. "I'd rather make another batch."

"Tell you what," he offered, depositing Mae on the floor and unbuttoning his coat. "I came here to offer you a deal. Maybe we can make biscuits part of it."

"I… I l-l-like b-biscuits," Lori Ann said shyly. "A-a-and I'm hungry."

"He made us egg," Mae supplied, tugging on Anna's apron. "Don't like runny egg." Anna noticed that she was wearing the too-large *kapp* that she and Susanna had put on her yesterday, while her sisters wore wool scarves over their hair. Mae's *kapp* was a little worse for wear, but it gave Anna a warm feeling that Samuel had thought to put it on her today.

"Hush, girls," Samuel said. It was his turn to flush red. "They don't think much of my cooking. Naomi's learning, but she's only nine."

"Naomi's eggs is yuck," Mae agreed.

Naomi stuck her tongue out at her sister.

"We don't criticize each other's work, and *you* shouldn't make ugly faces," Anna corrected. Then she blushed again. What right did she have to admonish Samuel's children? That would be Mam's task, once she and Samuel were husband and wife. But it was clear that someone needed to take a hand in their raising. Men didn't understand little girls, or kitchens for that matter.

"Listen to Anna," Samuel said with a grin. "It's cold outside, Naomi. Your Grossmama used to tell me that if I stuck my tongue out at my sisters my face might freeze. You don't want your face to freeze like that, do you?"

Susanna giggled. "That would be silly."

"And we're not outside."

Samuel gave Naomi a reproving look.

"Sorry, Mae." Embarrassed, Naomi looked down at her boots. Puddles of water were forming on the floor around them.

"For goodness' sakes, take off your coats," Anna urged, motioning with her hands. "It's warm in the kitchen, and you'll all overheat."

"I'm afraid we tracked up your clean floor with our wet boots," Samuel said.

Anna shrugged. "Not to worry. You can leave them near the door with ours." She motioned to Susanna. "Get everyone's coats and hang them behind the stove to dry. I have bacon ready, and I'll make French toast. We'll all have breakfast together."

"What—what about b-b-b-biscuits?" Lori Ann asked.

"Let me give you a hot breakfast, and I promise I'll make a big pan later," Anna offered.

Lori Ann sighed and nodded.

Samuel looked at his daughters shrugging off their wet coats, then back at Anna. "We didn't come to make more work for you. We ate. We don't have to eat again."

Anna waved them to the table. "Feeding friends is never work, and growing children are never full." She opened the refrigerator and scanned the shelves, choosing applesauce, cold sweet potatoes and the remainder of the ham they'd had for supper the night before. "Susanna, would you set some extra plates and then put some cocoa and milk on to heat?"

"I—I—I l-l-like c-c-cocoa," Lori Ann stuttered. Lori Ann had pale blue eyes and lighter hair than either of her sisters. Anna thought that she resembled the twin boys, Rudy and Peter, while Mae looked like her late mother.

Mae, in her stocking feet, scrambled up on the bench. "Me, too! I wike cocoa."

"If you're sure it's not too much trouble," Samuel said, but his eyes were on the ham and bacon, and he was already pulling out the big chair at the head of the table.

Anna felt better as she bustled around the kitchen and whipped up a hearty breakfast. She liked feeding people, and she liked making them comfortable in Mam's house. When she was busy, it was easier to forget that Samuel was here and Mam wasn't.

"I want honey biscuit," Mae chirped. When no one responded, she repeated it in *Deitsch,* the German dialect many Amish used in their homes.

"Be still," Naomi cautioned. "You're getting French toast or nothing."

"She speaks both *Deitsch* and English well for her age," Anna said, flipping thick slices of egg-battered toast in the frying pan.

"Louise has done well with her. I know many children don't speak English until they go to school, but I think it's best they speak *Deitsch* and English from babies on."

"*Ya*," Susanna agreed, taking a seat between two of the girls. "English and *Deitsch*."

"Mam says the same thing." Anna brought cups of cocoa to the table for everyone. "She says young ones learn faster. I suppose we use more English than most folks."

"She's smart, your mother," Samuel answered. "The best teacher we've ever had. The whole community says so."

Anna smiled as she checked on the browning slices of fragrant French toast. This was good, Samuel complimenting Mam. Maybe Anna hadn't ruined Mam's chances with him, after all.

"This is a real treat for us." Samuel sat back in Dat's chair and sipped his cocoa. "The neighbors, and your mother especially, have been good about sending food over, but I can't depend on the kindness of my friends forever."

Anna brought the heaping plate of French toast to the table to add to the other plates of food and sat down. Everyone joined hands for a moment of silent prayer, and then the silence was filled with the sounds of clinking silverware and eating. Conversation was sparse until the six of them finished, and then Samuel cleared his throat. "Anna—"

"Oh!" Anna popped out of her chair. "Coffee. I forgot. Let me get you a cup of coffee."

Samuel smiled and shook his head. "The hot cocoa is fine. But I wanted to ask you about that trade I mentioned."

Anna tucked her hands under her apron and looked at him expectantly.

"Gingerbread c-c-cookies," Lori Ann supplied.

"Yesterday, the kids got it in their heads that they wanted cookies. I thought we could do a deal. You make cookies with my girls, and I'll paint the bedroom. I'd be getting the better end of the deal," he added. "With breakfast *and* cookies."

"Dat brought ginger and spices," Naomi supplied. "They're in my coat pocket."

"We were out of flour and just about out of sugar. I can't get the hang of shopping for staples." He shook his head. "No matter how often I go to Byler's store, I always come home without something we need."

"Like baking powder," Naomi chimed in. "We don't have that either."

Anna chuckled. "Well, lucky for us Mam has three cans. When you go home, remind me, and you can take one with you."

"C-c-can we make—make c-c-c-cookies?" Lori Ann asked, her mouth full of French toast.

"Of course, I'll be glad to make cookies with you," Anna said, "but I can't let you paint the bedroom, Samuel. That's my job, and—"

"Ne." Samuel raised a broad hand. "It's settled. You'll be doing me a real favor. What with the bad

weather and being stuck in the house, my ears are ringing from the chatter these three make. Having you bake
with them will be a treat for them and a nice change for
me. Besides…" He grinned as he used the corner of a
napkin to wipe the syrup off Lori Ann's chin. "Maybe
I'll even get to take some cookies home for the twins."

Anna sighed, gracefully giving up the battle. "If you
insist, Samuel. I have to admit, I much prefer baking to
painting, and I won't have to climb back up on a ladder to do it."

"Nobody's getting back on *that* ladder until I've had a
chance to repair it," he said. "I brought another one in the
back of the buggy." He rose from the table and rubbed
his stomach. "Great breakfast. Best I've had in months."

What a good man he is, Anna thought, as she
watched Samuel put on his coat to go outside for the
ladder. *And he's a good father.* Mam would be lucky
to have him for a husband. Any woman would. Having
him here at the table, enjoying a meal together like a
family, had been wonderful, but she had to remember
who Samuel was and who she was.

"Potty," Mae said loudly. "I haf' to go potty. Now!"

"Susanna, could you take her?" Anna asked. "And
if you two would wash your hands and help me clear
away the breakfast dishes, I'll get Mam's recipe book."

"I can read the ingredients," Naomi offered. "I like
to read."

"What we need to do is find aprons just the right size
for Lori Ann and Mae," Anna mused.

Now that Samuel had left the kitchen, she felt more at
ease with the girls. She and Samuel's daughters would
bake cookies, biscuits and maybe even a few pies. And
while the oven was hot, she could pop a couple of chick-

ens in the back to roast for the noonday meal. It would
take hours for Samuel to finish the bedroom walls, and
all that work would make him hungry again. She began
to calculate what would go best with the chicken, and
how to keep the little ones amused while she taught
Naomi the trick to making good buttermilk biscuits.

As Samuel crossed the porch, he could hear Anna
talking to his girls. She had an easy way with them,
and Naomi liked her, he could tell. It wasn't fair that
Naomi had had to take on so many household chores
since her mother had passed. If Anna agreed to marry
him, Naomi could be a child again for a few years.

Maybe he'd been selfish, waiting so long to look for a
wife again. He knew there were plenty who would have
taken him up on an offer, but it was important that his
new partner be able to love his children and teach them.
It would take a special woman to fill that role, and he
couldn't think of a better one than Anna Yoder, even if
she was shy about giving him an answer.

He went down the steps, into the icy yard. They'd
gotten off on the wrong foot yesterday, but despite the
burned biscuits, today seemed different. Sitting at the
table with Anna, seeing how kind she was to Mae, Lori
Ann and Naomi, he wanted to court her all that much
more. He was glad he'd worked up the nerve to come
this morning.

Even though Anna hadn't said anything about the
courting, she hadn't shut the door in his face. That was
a good sign, wasn't it? Maybe she wanted more time to
think about it. It was a big decision, taking on him
and his family.

He paused beside the buggy and closed his eyes,
breathing deeply of the cold air, letting the wet snow-

flakes pat against his face and lodge in his beard. He knew a father had to put his children's welfare first, but the memory of the way Anna had felt when he put his arm around her made his throat tighten and his pulse race. How good she'd felt! And she'd smelled even better, all hot biscuits, honey and, oddly, a hint of apple blossom.

She had pretty hair, Anna did, and he couldn't help wondering how long it was. Those little curls around her face meant that it would be wavy, even when she brushed it out. Anna was a respectable woman, a faithful member of the church, and it would be wrong to think of her in any way that wasn't honorable. An Amish woman covered her hair in public and let it down only in the privacy of her home...for her husband to see.

He swallowed, imagining what it would be like to touch those red-gold strands of hair, to watch her brush it out at the end of the day, to have the right to be her protector and partner.

The sound of the porch door opening behind him jerked him from his reverie. "Samuel? Do you need help with the ladder?"

He chuckled, glanced back over his shoulder and shook his head. "*Ne,* Anna. It's not heavy. I can get it." He looked at the gray sky. "But I'll put it on the porch and take the horse to the barn. It's too nasty a day to leave him tied outside."

"Turn him into the empty box stall," she called. "And throw down some hay for him."

"*Ya,*" Samuel agreed, smiling at her.

He was rewarded with a smile so sweet that he was all the more certain that he and Anna were meant to be man and wife. The only thing standing in his way was Anna.

Chapter Four

Careful not to disturb her sleeping sister, Anna crept from her bed in the gray light of early dawn, and hurriedly dressed. Sometime after midnight, Susanna had left her own bed and slipped under the blankets with Anna, complaining that she was cold. Anna thought it more likely that she was missing Mam and hadn't become accustomed to sleeping in the room over the kitchen yet. In any case, Anna hadn't the heart to turn Susanna away, and she'd spent the rest of the night trying to keep Susanna from hogging all the covers.

The house was quiet. Usually, even at this hour, Mam would be bustling around downstairs, one of Anna's sisters would be snoring and someone would be banging on Irwin's door, calling him to get up for milking. When Anna went to a window and pulled back the shade, she understood the silence that went beyond an empty house. The ground was covered with snow, and large flakes were coming down so thickly that she could barely make out the apple trees in the orchard.

Snow… Anna smiled. Delaware rarely saw snowfalls more than just dustings, but this year had been colder than normal. She wondered if Johanna would cancel school. Her oldest sister had offered to fill in for Mam while she was in Ohio, but not many parents would send their children out to walk to school on such a morning.

Anna smiled as she padded down the hall to the bathroom in her stocking feet. Although she loved her big family dearly, it was nice to have the house quiet and not have to wait to brush her teeth or to get into the shower. And it was better yet to be able to think about everything that had happened yesterday and remember all the details of Samuel's visit, without being interrupted.

Having Mam's suitor here two days running was a wonder, and although she'd enjoyed Samuel's company, Anna wasn't certain that it was quite right for him to spend so much time here with the family away. True, Susanna had been here, but Susanna wasn't what one would call a perfect chaperone, or at least not one her Aunt Martha would approve of. Anna couldn't hold back a chuckle. There wasn't much that Mam and Anna's sisters did that pleased her aunt. Aunt Martha meant well, but in Anna's opinion, she spent far too much time worrying about the proper behavior of her relatives and neighbors.

Having Samuel at the table yesterday had been very enjoyable, so enjoyable that it made her feel all warm inside. He'd been still painting at one o'clock when she called him for dinner. Despite her earlier disasters, that was one meal that Mam would have been proud of. The biscuits weren't burnt, the chicken had browned perfectly and the rest had turned out the way it was supposed to. And Samuel had given her so many compliments that she'd been almost too flustered to be a good hostess.

A quick stop at the bathroom and Anna was downstairs to build up the fire in the woodstove before going outside for morning chores. They didn't need the woodstove to heat the house anymore because they used propane heat, but Anna loved baking in it and loved the way it made the kitchen cozy on cold mornings. Flora and Jeremiah wagged their tails in greeting, and the little terrier dashed around her ankles as Anna took Dat's old barn coat off the hook and put it on.

"Come along," she called to the two dogs, as she tied a wool scarf over her head. Although she never shirked her share of what had to be done, Anna had never been fond of outside chores. Pigs and horses made her nervous, but cows were different. Cows were usually gentle, and there was something peaceful about milking. Anna had always found it a good time to pray. She had asked Mam once if it was irreverent to talk to God in a barn. Mam, in her wisdom, had said that since the baby Jesus had been born in a stable, she could see no reason why His Father in heaven would be put out.

With Irwin gone to the auction with Miriam and Charley, Tyler, from down the road, was helping her this week. The red-cheeked twelve-year-old had already fed the horses and filled their water buckets. Both Bossy, the Holstein, and Polly, the Jersey, would be calving in the spring and had about gone dry. Tyler offered to milk them off while Anna milked Buttercup, the new Guernsey. Buttercup was as sweet as her name. She'd had a late calf and still produced lots of milk.

"Good girl," Anna crooned to the fawn-and-white cow with the large brown eyes. "Nice Buttercup." She washed the cow's udder with warm soapy water that she'd carried from the house, poured a measure of feed into the trough and settled onto the milking stool. The snow falling outside, the fragrant scents of hay and silage and the warmth of the animals made the barn especially cozy today, making Anna content. As she rested her head against Buttercup's side and streams of milk poured into the shiny stainless steel bucket, Anna's heart swelled with joy as she thought of all the gifts the Lord had bestowed on her.

She had a wonderful mother and sisters, a home that she loved and the security of a faith and community that surrounded her like a giant hug. Even the grief of her father's death more than two years ago had begun to ease, so that she could remember the good times that they'd had together. They all would have wanted Dat to live to be a hundred, but it wasn't meant to be. No human could hope to understand God's ways, least of all her. What she *could* do was work each day to appreciate the bounty He had blessed her with.

Silently, Anna offered prayers for her mother's and sisters' safe return from their journeys, and for the health of Grossmama and Aunt Jezebel. As she prayed, the level of the milk rose in the pail, smelling sweet and fresh, drawing the barn cats to patiently wait for her to finish.

She asked God to heal Samuel's sorrow for the loss of his wife and give him the wisdom and patience to tend his children. Above all, she prayed for little Mae, so far from the only home and the only mother she'd ever known. She finished, as always, with the Lord's prayer and a plea that He guide her hands and footsteps through the day to help her serve her family and faith according to God's plan. She was about to murmur a devout amen, when one last prayer slipped between her lips.

"And please, God, if it seems right, could you find someone to marry me, someone with a heart as good as Samuel's?"

"Ya?" Tyler called from a stall away. "You said something to me?" He stood up from behind Bossy. "Not much this morning from her."

"Ne," Anna replied quickly.

She pressed her lips tightly together. She hadn't meant to trouble God with her small problems, and she certainly hadn't meant for Tyler to hear. Her eyelids felt prickly and moisture clouded her eyes. She hadn't meant to be selfish this morning, but since she had uttered her deepest wish, maybe the Lord wouldn't take it amiss.

She blinked away the tears and closed her eyes. *This is Anna Yoder again, Lord. I know that I'm not slim or pretty or particularly smart,* she offered silently, *but I think I would make a good wife and mother. So if You happen to come across someone who needs a willing partner, remember me.*

"Anna?"

Jerked from her thoughts, Anna realized that Tyler was now standing beside her. At twelve, he was losing the look of a child and starting to shoot up, all long legs and arms, but he still retained the sweet, easygoing nature that he possessed since he'd been a babe.

"Sorry," Anna said. "I didn't hear—"

Tyler grinned, his blue eyes sparkling with humor. "Falling asleep on the milking stool, I'd say." He held out his pail. It wasn't even half full. "All I could get from the two of them." He set the bucket on a feed box. "I'd best be getting to school."

"You better stop by the chair shop and see if your Dat's heard anything about school. Be sure Johanna hasn't cancelled."

"That'd be nice." Tyler grinned even wider. "Then I can go sledding." He pulled thick blue mittens from his jacket pocket. "You need me tomorrow?"

"*Ne*," Anna replied. "Miriam, Charley and Irwin should be back today." Anna patted Buttercup, lifted her bucket away from the cow and got to her feet.

"Unless this turns into a blizzard and they're stuck in Virginia. Irwin's lucky, getting out of school all week."

"Don't worry. Mam will see that he makes up every last math problem. And you know how he *hates* homework." After a rocky start when Irwin had first come to Seven Poplars, he and Tyler had struck up a fast friendship. Anna was glad to see it. Irwin needed friends, and he couldn't pick a better pal than steady Tyler.

"I'll see to the chickens on the way out," Tyler called over his shoulder.

Anna turned Buttermilk into a shed with the others, and then started for the house with a milk pail in each hand. She was halfway across the yard and planning what to cook for breakfast, when the two dogs suddenly began to bark, and abruptly Samuel and all five of his children came around the corner of the corn crib. Anna was so surprised that she nearly dropped the milk. Samuel? Again, this morning?

She scrambled for something to say that wouldn't sound foolish, but all she could manage was, "Good morning!"

Samuel had one girl—it appeared to be Lori Ann—clinging to his back and he was pulling another on a sled. They were so bundled up against the cold that it was hard to tell the two smallest ones apart. The twins, Rudy and Peter, trudged behind him, and Naomi trailed behind them. "Good morning to you, Anna!" Samuel called cheerfully. Lori Ann echoed her father's greeting.

"You walked," Anna said, which sounded even more foolish. It was obvious that they had walked. There was no buggy in sight and Samuel was pulling the sled. They had probably taken a shortcut across the adjoining fields rather than coming by the road.

"School is closed," Naomi supplied.

"C-c-closed," chimed Lori Ann.

"I came to finish the room," Samuel explained. His wide-brimmed felt hat and his beard were covered with snow, and it seemed to Anna as if the snowflakes had gotten as large as cotton balls since she'd gone into the barn. "To give it a second coat," Samuel finished.

"Oh." Had they eaten breakfast? What could she offer them? Anna wondered. She and Susanna had planned on oatmeal and toast this morning. The thought that Samuel had caught her at less than her best again flashed through her mind. She was wearing Dat's barn coat and her hair wasn't decently covered with her *kapp*.

"You don't have to feed us this morning," Samuel said, as if reading her mind. "I fed them all before the oldest went off to school."

"But Johanna sent us home," Rudy said. "The radio said we're getting eight inches."

Peter added hopefully, "Maybe there won't be any school next week either."

Samuel's ruddy face grew a little redder. "I have a battery radio," he said. "Not for music, but so that I can hear the news and weather. I just turn it on when it appears that there might be an emergency. Something that might affect the school or the trucks that pick up my milk."

Anna nodded. *"Ya."* Mam had a radio for the same reason, but it wasn't something that Samuel needed to know. Radios weren't exactly forbidden, but they were frowned upon by the more conservative members of the church. Of course, that didn't keep some of the teenagers and young people from secretly having them and listening to "fast" music. "That makes sense."

"We brought a turkey," Naomi said. "For dinner."

Samuel shrugged. "I'm afraid it's frozen. I wasn't expecting to bring the three oldest with me today, but I don't know how long the painting will take, and—"

"Why are we standing out here?" Anna said. She'd covered the tops of the milk buckets with cheesecloth, but any moment the melting snow would be dripping into the milk. "Come into the house. And not to worry about the noon meal. You didn't have to come back to do a second coat. I could have—"

"And another reason," Samuel said, following her toward the house. "A phone call to the chair shop, from Hannah. Roman came over to tell Johanna, at the school. Your mother won't be headed home until Sunday or Monday. Their driver is waiting to see how bad this snow is before he starts for Delaware."

Anna nodded. She missed Mam, and she knew that Susanna had hoped Mam would be returning by tomorrow. But having Samuel finish the painting would be a Godsend. That would leave her free to make the rest of the house shine like a new pin.

And having Samuel all to herself again, that would be fun, too...wouldn't it? Anna shook off that small inner whisper. Samuel was a friend and a neighbor, and was soon to be Mam's suitor. He'd come to help out for her mother's sake, no other reason. And just because she'd foolishly mistaken what he'd said about courting Mam, she had no reason to spin fancies in her head.

Then the little voice in the far corner of her mind spoke again. *But you could pretend that this was your family.... What harm would that do? Just pretend for today....*

"It would be wrong," Anna said.

"What would be wrong?" Samuel asked. "It seems to me that waiting to see if the weather's going to grow worse before starting such a long drive is good sense. You wouldn't want them to go into a ditch somewhere between here and Ohio, would you?"

"Of course not," Anna protested. "I was thinking of something else, nothing important. You come in and get warm."

"We want to stay out and play in the snow," Rudy said. "Dat said we could."

"Just the boys," Samuel said. "Girls inside."

"But Dat," Naomi protested. "I want to make a snowman."

Samuel's brow furrowed. "I need you to watch over your sisters. Anna has more to do than tend to mischievous children."

"*Ne,* Samuel," Anna put in gently. "Let her enjoy the snow. Lori Ann is a big girl. She can help me bake pies, and I have Susanna to tend to Mae. We see so little snow in Kent County. Let Naomi play in it."

Naomi threw her a grateful look. "Please, Dat," she begged.

Lori Ann was beaming.

"Well, if Anna doesn't mind. But you're getting past

the age of playing with boys. Best you learn to keep to a woman's work."

Anna rolled her eyes, but when she spoke, she kept her voice gentle and soothing. "Soon enough she will take on those tasks, Samuel, and joyfully, from what I can see. She's been a great help to you these past four years."

"I can see I'm outnumbered," he answered. "But I'll not have you spoil them beyond bearing. And little Mae is a handful, as Naomi can vouch for."

Mae giggled.

Anna bent and lifted the child from the sled. "Nothing to laugh at," she admonished. "You must respect your father. You're not a baby anymore. Watch Lori Ann and see how good and helpful she is."

Lori Ann's eyes widened and she nodded, pleased by the praise. "*Ya,*" she said. "You—you must mind Dat and—and not pull t-the c-c-cat's t-tail."

Anna opened her mouth in mock astonishment. "You didn't hurt kitty, did you, Mae?"

Mae clamped her lips together and shook her head.

"Did so!" Peter said. "What she needs is—"

"What she needs is to get inside out of this cold," Anna broke in. She eyed Peter, letting him know they didn't need his two cents' worth. "Come along, Lori Ann. Let's see if Susanna is awake yet."

Samuel followed after her, not certain that Anna and the girls hadn't bamboozled him into letting Naomi stay outside against his wishes. It wouldn't be easy to court Anna with five children hanging on his shirttails, but they were his life and Anna had to know they were a "package deal," as the Englishers liked to say. As much as he loved his children, he didn't want to allow them to become lazy or disrespectful. Naomi was nine, after all. He tried to remember his sisters at that age. Had they been running wild with the boys at nine?

They stepped up onto the porch and stamped their boots to knock most of the snow off. Then Anna got a broom and handed it to him. Slipping out of her galoshes, Anna carried Mae inside, leaving him to help Lori Ann.

"I—I—I l-like Anna, Dat," Lori Ann whispered in his ear as he leaned down to pull off her boots.

"I like her, too," he agreed, but he had to admit that he was somewhat troubled by what had just happened. The thought that if he married, his wife would actually have *more* influence on his children's behavior than he would crossed his mind. It was right, of course, but he'd been used to doing things his way ever since Frieda had passed on. He supposed there would be adjustments he'd have to make, adjustments that he hadn't thought about. And Anna would have to make adjustments, as well. After all, the man was the head of the house, and Anna would have to learn to respect his wishes.

Not that she was the bossy type. Not his sweet, sweet Anna. Even now, when she'd gone against him, it had been asking, not telling. He wouldn't let her spoil them, for certain, but he wanted to be a reasonable man. He didn't want to give Anna the wrong impression that he was like her Uncle Reuben, who hopped every time his wife, Martha, said jump. But neither did he want to scare Anna off. After all, he was a lot older than she was—sixteen years, give or take some months. It wouldn't do for her to think he would be a stern and unyielding husband.

Susanna held the door wide. "Come in," she called in her high, singsong voice.

Anna's little sister was smiling, as always, and Samuel smiled back. Of all of Hannah's girls, Susanna was the easiest. In some ways she was as wise as an old woman, and in other ways as innocent as Lori Ann. But no matter which Susanna greeted them, she always made him feel good inside.

"I'm going to get right to that painting," he said to Anna, "but if these two give you a minute's problem, you call me or Naomi to deal with them."

"*Ya,* Samuel, I will," Anna said softly.

He set the frozen turkey in the sink, removed his outer garments and hung his gloves behind the stove to dry. "Sorry the bird isn't thawed. Roman brought it from the freezer at the chair shop. I didn't think about how long it would take to—"

"I'll manage," Anna assured him. "Leave it to me."

Samuel started right in on the second coat, and by the time Anna called him for dinner, he had finished three quarters of the room and his stomach felt as if he hadn't eaten for days. As he came into the kitchen, he walked into a wave of delicious smells: cinnamon, hot bread, chicken and dumplings, apple pie and more.

All of his children were already seated at the table, faces shining clean, hair slicked back and cheeks as red as cranberries. "No turkey," Peter informed him.

"Chicken and dumplings," Rudy said. "Turkey tomorrow."

"Not that I expect you to come back tomorrow," Anna hastened to say. "But I'll set it to roast tonight, and by morning it will be done. If you send the boys to fetch it, you can—"

Samuel felt his face grow warm. "I'll be back tomorrow," he confessed. "Rather, some of us will. That bedroom floor and the hall need a fresh coat of that dark red. I've got a few gallons left from when I painted my place, and I was planning on—"

"I can't let you do all this work here," Anna said. "You must have chores at home."

"Not so many. Not this time of year, and I've got the two hired boys to keep busy. I'll be back to finish up tomorrow, unless you…" He hesitated, not knowing what more to say, not willing to hear her say she didn't want him here.

"*Ya*," Susanna pronounced. "Make nice for Mam and Grossmama and Aunty Jezebel."

Anna put a huge bowl of mashed potatoes in the center of the table. "I don't know what to say," she protested.

Susanna beamed. "Say thank you."

"Th-thank you," Anna repeated.

"Good. That's settled," Samuel said, taking Peter's hand for grace. "Now, I'm starving. Let's get to this good food before it gets cold."

Dinner was every bit as good as the previous day's. He was a man who liked his food and Anna was one of the best cooks he'd ever known. Eating like this every day would be one of the real pleasures of having her as his wife. Not that he was marrying her for her housekeeping or her cooking skills, but a kitchen was the heart of the house, like a wife was the heart of the family.

By late afternoon, Samuel had finished painting the walls and gathered his brood for the walk home. The snow had tapered off, and there was not quite eight inches, but a good six, and it was so cold that it wouldn't melt anytime soon. Playing in the snow had tired his three oldest, and it seemed that Anna had kept the two little ones occupied in the kitchen all day. They were going home almost as heavily laden as they'd come, with a gallon of vegetable soup, biscuits and cinnamon buns for supper.

The following day, the three oldest stayed home to do chores and play in the snow, leaving Samuel with just the two youngest girls to carry along to Anna's house. To his relief, Anna and Susanna seemed just as pleased to see him, Lori Ann and Mae as they had before. And the house smelled of roasted turkey, just as Anna had promised. "I don't want to impose on you," he said as they entered. "It's just that it's a lot to leave them with Naomi when she has work to do."

"Nonsense," Anna said. "You know we love to have them. Lori Ann was a big help with the cinnamon buns yesterday. And today she can help me with raisin pies."

Lori Ann nodded excitedly.

"Mae's a little cranky," Samuel said. "I think she needs to go back to bed. She had nightmares again last night, and she was awake for hours."

"Not to worry," Anna assured him as she gathered Mae in her arms. "Susanna will make her feel better."

"Don't want a nap," Mae grumbled.

Samuel quickly escaped to his painting, leaving Anna to handle Mae. Getting his youngest adjusted was harder than he'd expected it to be. He loved her dearly, but it was hard to *like* the child when she whined and fussed half the time. And when she dissolved in tears, crying for his sister Louise, he felt completely helpless. It was so much easier to leave her to Anna and Susanna.

About an hour into his work on the floor, Anna came in with a steaming cup of coffee and a cinnamon bun.

He smiled at her and took a sip of the coffee. It was strong, just the way he liked it. "You're a wonder, Anna Yoder," he said.

She stood for a moment, tall, her cheeks rosy, twisting her hands in her apron. "Samuel, I don't know what…" She trailed off, then looked up at him through thick lashes. Anna's eyes were beautiful, wide and brown and sparkling with life.

She looked vulnerable, so sweet that he wanted to gather her in his arms as he'd seen her do with his little daughter. He wanted to taste her lips, to smell her hair. He wanted to claim Anna as his wife before God and his church.

Wanting her so badly gave him courage. "Have you thought any more about what I said before, about courting—"

"Courting Mam," she said, answering so quickly that he didn't get to finish.

"What?" He blinked, unsure what to say. Surely, she didn't think…

She nibbled at her lower lip. "Mam. You said you want to court Mam. Before… Didn't you?"

"Hannah?" His face flamed. "*Ne.* Not Hannah. What would give you that idea?"

"But you said—"

"It's *you* I want to court, Anna Yoder," he said in a rush. "Not your mother. Not any other woman in Kent County. Just you."

Chapter Five

Anna's eyes widened as she backed up to lean against the freshly painted wall of the bedroom. "Oh." She felt as though she might faint. "Oh, my. I… I misunderstood. I was sure you said…but then…" She paused to catch her breath. "I thought I was mistaken…about what I heard."

"You were, if you thought I said it was Hannah I'd come to court." Samuel balanced the paintbrush carefully on the edge of the can, and came to stand in front of her. "Anna, I didn't mean to give anyone the wrong idea…but…it's been you all along I've been interested in."

She couldn't wrap her mind around what he'd said, yet there was no doubt what he'd meant. *Samuel Mast had said that he wanted to court her.* Was she awake or asleep and dreaming?

"Anna." He reached out to take her hand and she drew it back and shook her head.

"Give me a moment," she said. First she hadn't been able to catch her breath, now she felt like she was breathing too fast. "It's…it's a surprise."

Samuel folded his arms across his broad chest. The expression in his eyes grew serious and she saw his Adam's apple constrict. "A good surprise or a bad one?"

"I'm not sure." She felt silly with him standing here towering over her, but she felt so addled that if she stood up she might faint—not that she ever had before. Samuel reached for her hand again and childishly, she tucked it behind her and shook her head. If he touched her, she knew she'd lose all ability to think clearly. "Why me?"

"Why not you, Anna? I'm older than you, that's true, but you're of legal age."

"But all this time… I thought…everyone thought that you and Mam were going to—" She could feel herself choking up, knew she was going to cry. She never cried, but suddenly she couldn't stop the tears from welling up in her eyes.

"Don't cry. Why are you crying? I thought you'd be happy."

Anna covered her face with her hands. He'd been so happy this morning, and now she feared she'd angered him.

"I like your mother," he persisted. "I admire her, but I've been thinking about you for a long time. I think we would make a good match."

Samuel was saying words she wanted to believe, but her heart told her they weren't possible. She was what she was—the third daughter of a widow…the Plain Yoder girl…the *sturdy* girl. How could Samuel Mast choose her? He was handsome. He had a fine farm, and he was a solid member of the community, a deacon in the church. Any family would be proud to have him marry one of their daughters or sisters. He could pick and choose from all of the unmarried girls and young widows of Kent County, or any other Old Order Amish settlement in the country. Why would he pick her?

"But, your wife…" she stammered. "Your Frieda was beautiful."

"*Ya.* She was. But she's gone, Anna, and I'm alone. Too long, I think. The children…sometimes they're more than I can manage."

She looked up at him, barely able to string four words together. "I see why you need a wife. Everyone in Seven Poplars sees. But why me, Samuel?"

His face reddened. "We are both hard workers. You're a good cook, a good housekeeper." He cleared his throat. "And…and a faithful member of our church. I think you would make me a fine wife."

"I see." *Good cook. Good housekeeper.* Honest words, so why did they cut into her like sharp thorns? Had she expected Samuel to declare his love for her?

"Tomorrow is church," he said stiffly. "I want to…" He swallowed again. "Can I come for you and Susanna to drive you to service?"

"*Ne.*" She shook her head. If they arrived in Samuel's buggy, everyone would notice. There would be talk. "*Ne,* Samuel," she repeated, recovering some of her composure. "Not for everyone to see. You must give me a few days to think and pray about this. Church is at Roman and Fanny's. Not far for us to walk."

He looked hurt. "You don't want to go to church with me?"

She wanted to squeeze his hand, to reassure him, but she was afraid to touch him. She couldn't trust herself. "Best if we keep this idea between us for a while," she said. "To be sure it's what we both want."

He took a deep breath and the lines around his eyes

crinkled. "*Ya.* I can see that might be wise," he said, "if you are not certain." Disappointment puckered his mouth. "But not too long."

So that he can choose someone else if I refuse him, she thought. "Marriage is a big step," Anna said, feeling better, but still not completely herself. "I need to talk with my mother."

Samuel looked at the floor, then at her again. "So you will speak to Hannah about my proposal?"

Anna nodded. "Who knows me better than Mam?" She tried to smile, but was unable to cover her nervousness. "You have to try to understand. My doubts are not of you, Samuel, but of myself." Her mouth felt dry. "It's just that it is so sudden."

He nodded. "So you have said." He turned, as if to return to his painting, but then stopped and turned back to her. "It's not my age, is it? I'm not a raw boy, but—"

"Anna! Anna!" Susanna shouted from the hall. "Come quick. Miriam and Charley! And Irwin!"

Jeremiah began to bark, and Anna heard the sound of voices in the kitchen. "Smells like roast turkey," Irwin said.

Anna looked at Samuel meaningfully. "Just between us?"

He frowned and nodded. "Go and greet your sister and her husband," he said. "I will finish this."

With a sigh of relief, Anna hurried from the room. With Miriam and Charley back, the house would echo with good talk and laughter. They would be full of news of the auction and the people they'd seen. She would think about Samuel's request for permission to court her later. She would have time to think and to decide what was best for her and for him. She would need to pray harder than she ever had before.

If she said yes to Samuel, her whole life would change in more ways than she could imagine. She would leave her home to go to his…to be his partner and help-mate—to mother his *five* young children. It would be hard, but she would do it willingly, if only she knew for certain that he wanted her for the right reason. But the fear that he didn't pressed hard on her heart.

Marriage was forever. The Englishers might separate or divorce, but never the Plain folk. If she said yes, she would be bound to Samuel and to his will so long as they both drew breath.

Again, his words echoed in her head. *"You are a hardworker."*

What he was saying was that theirs wouldn't be a love marriage like Miriam and Charley's, or like Ruth and Eli's. What if Samuel would be marrying her for her strong back and skill in the kitchen? Again, she thought of Johanna, her relationship with her stern husband, and the tears her sister shed when she thought no one was looking.

Anna didn't know if she could exist in a marriage like that. It would be like settling for half a loaf when she wanted the whole, hot and fragrant from the oven—when she wanted it so bad she could taste the sweet goodness of the bread on her tongue.

"Anna!" Her twin sister, Miriam, shook the snow off her coat, dropped it onto a kitchen chair and threw open her arms. "I've missed you," she cried.

"And me?" Susanna demanded. Samuel's two youngest clung to her hands, giggling. "You missed me, too?"

"*Ya,*" Miriam agreed, hugging first Anna and then

Susanna. "The auction was fun, and I saw lots of cousins and friends. But Charley and I were ready to come home yesterday. We couldn't find a driver who was willing to head out late in the day, not with the weather."

"And we bought three horses," Irwin said excitedly. He had Jeremiah in his arms, and the little terrier was licking his face. "One is for me. Charley bought a horse for me."

Anna looked to Miriam. "A horse? Charley bought Irwin his own horse?"

"More colt than horse," Charley supplied. "He's a two-year-old, and he needs work, but if Irwin is willing to work with him, he'll come around and make a good driver." He grinned. "Is that turkey I smell? We left early and didn't stop for lunch on the road."

"Plenty for all of us," Anna assured him. "Samuel brought the turkey. He's been helping out by painting, getting the bedroom ready for Grossmama and Aunt Jezebel."

Miriam's brows went up. "Samuel? Samuel's been here painting?"

"*Ya*," Susanna said. "Anna broke the ladder and spilled the paint."

"Shhh," Anna said. "Remember what I told you."

Susanna nodded. "You said not to tell about—"

"Later," Miriam said, interrupting Susanna's tale. "I think these men are hungry. We should get dinner on the table and share our news later."

"Amen to that," Charley agreed. "I could eat a whole turkey, feathers and feet."

"You usually do," Miriam teased. Smiling, she shooed Susanna and the little girls toward the china cabinet. "Set the table," she said.

Anna mouthed a silent *thanks* to her twin. Another second, and Susanna would have spilled the beans. The last thing she wanted was for Charley and Irwin to hear that Samuel wanted to court her. Irwin was as bad as Susanna for telling things a person didn't want told. She supposed little brothers were like that, and although Irwin wasn't really kin, since he'd come to live with them he'd begun to feel more and more like he was one of them.

But what was there for anyone to tell? Samuel had asked to court her, but she hadn't agreed, and she wasn't ready to share her secret yet—not even with Miriam.

The following day, Anna sat in the midst of her three sisters, closed her eyes and let the peace and beauty of the familiar hymn enfold her. Not everyone in the community had made it to services, due to the icy roads, but Roman and Fanny's small house was still packed to the walls with worshipers. Ruth and Eli had returned from their travels. Now only Mam and Grossmama, Aunt Jezebel and her youngest sisters, Leah and Rebecca, were absent.

Although, had the whole family been here, Anna didn't know where they would have found room to sit. The congregation was certainly growing, and that was a blessing. But if the church grew too large they would have to split, and Anna couldn't imagine not seeing Samuel and his children, all of her sisters, the Beachys, or all of their closest friends at services every other Sunday.

Bishop Atlee was offering the sermon this morning with the assistance of Preacher Uri Schwartz, visiting from Tennessee. Preacher Uri told about the Good

Samaritan and used the story to elaborate on the importance of getting along with the Englishers while maintaining a distance from the outer world.

Anna shifted on the bench and tried not to look in Samuel's direction. Lori Ann had started off sitting with Susanna, but had tired of playing with her handkerchief dolly and had wiggled through the row of men to sit on her father's lap. Mae was in the kitchen with Johanna and another young mother, and Naomi was seated between Susanna and Miriam. Samuel's twins, always a handful, sat directly in front of him, so that he could keep an eye on their mischief.

As much as she wanted to concentrate on Preacher Schwartz's sermon, Anna's thoughts kept drifting back to Samuel and their conversation the previous day. She'd slept only fitfully last night, for thinking about him. What was she to do? She wanted to accept his proposal; it was a dream come true to most girls. But was it just that? Something not real? A dream…or a mistake on Samuel's part? Whatever reason had caused him to seek her out, Samuel would soon come to his senses and see that it was a bad choice. That he could do better.

There must be a half-dozen other young women he could choose from in Kent County alone, all of them more attractive than she was. Sitting in the row behind her were Mary Byler and Amy Troyer, both unmarried and of courting age. Either of them would be suitable, and either would be thrilled to have Samuel propose to them. And they were both pretty.

It was all well and good for Mam to say that "true beauty comes from inside," because her mother was beautiful. Her mother loved her, Anna knew that, but

Hannah Yoder had never looked out at the world from Anna's eyes.

The congregation rose for a hymn and Anna stood with them. As she opened her book, she glanced at Samuel, only to find his gaze on her. Her breath caught in her throat, and she felt tingles run from her fingertips to her toes. Immediately, she averted her eyes and stared down at the Old German text, but moisture clouded her vision and a single tear drop fell onto the page.

Lord, help me, she prayed silently. *Help me to be strong, to consider Samuel's proposal with both my head and my heart.*

Susanna's off-key voice rose beside her and Anna reached over and squeezed her hand. Obviously, God hadn't meant for Ruth to remain home with Mam and Susanna, as Ruth had once believed. But maybe God meant for Anna to sacrifice having a family of her own to help her mother. She could be happy, living with her mother and her little sister, and tending to Grossmama and Aunt Jezebel, as well. She didn't need a husband and children of her own to fulfill her life, did she? Not all women were given the gift of children; her sisters would give her nieces and nephews to love and care for.

A final prayer ended the service. Men and boys began to file outside while the women flowed toward the kitchen to prepare to serve the communal meal. This was one of the best things about church Sundays. Anna loved making and serving good food to those she loved. She felt most at ease in the kitchen, and it never failed to make her feel useful to see that others were well fed.

"Anna," her cousin Dorcas called. "Come down to the cellar with me and help fetch up the macaroni sal-

ads. Fanny ran out of room in the kitchen for all the
food."

Anna nodded and followed Dorcas through the narrow door off the hall and down the steep steps. The
basement was dim. The only light present was the weak
winter sunlight filtering through several windows at
ground level. Downstairs, Roman had fashioned a spacious storage area for Fanny to place her rows of home-
canned tomatoes, green beans, sauerkraut and corn.
Naturally cool but unlikely to freeze, this area was perfect for keeping baskets of potatoes, sweet potatoes,
apples and pears through the winter months.

A long table covered with newspaper held pies, cakes
and four giant bowls of macaroni salad, potato salad,
three-bean salad and pasta salad. "Do you think we'll
have enough to eat?" Anna teased.

"I sure hope so," Dorcas said, going along with the
joke. "My father can eat all of this and ask for seconds."

"*Ya,* he does like to eat," Anna agreed, "but my
question is, where does it all go?" Uncle Reuben was a
stringbean, tall and lanky. No matter how much he ate,
he never seemed to gain a pound.

Dorcas giggled and used a plastic fork to scoop up a
bite of the potato salad. "Johanna's," she pronounced.
"I like the way she makes her dressing."

Anna nodded. "She's a good cook, my big sister."

Dorcas captured another bite. "Umm. Can you manage more than one bowl, or should we make two trips?"

Anna hesitated. She'd promised Samuel she wouldn't
say anything to anyone but Mam, but her secret was
rubbing like a blister on her heel. Her mother hadn't
gotten home yet, and if she didn't share her problem

with someone, Anna thought she would burst. "Can I tell you something?" she said impulsively.

Dorcas shrugged. "You tell me stuff all the time."

Anna put a finger to her lips. "This is different. A secret…"

Dorcas giggled. "You've decided to turn English and buy a motorcycle like Eli used to have?"

"*Ne*. Be serious. I need to ask you something important."

Dorcas picked up the bowl of four-bean salad and studied it. "Lydia's, I think," she said. "She puts too much vinegar in her sauce." Then she realized that Anna was watching her intently and shrugged. "So what is this big secret?"

"Samuel Mast asked if he could court me," Anna blurted. There, it was out. She'd said it, and the house hadn't fallen in around them, and the stars hadn't fallen from the heavens. She felt better already.

"Mmm-hmm," Dorcas agreed. "Sure he did." She chuckled. "You wish."

"*Ne*. True. Yesterday. Well, actually, before that, but—"

"Your mother's beau suddenly decided he wants you instead?" Dorcas grimaced. "Bad joke, Anna."

Anna shook her head. "Not meant to be funny. He asked me. At first I thought that he was asking about Mam…you know, if I minded. But that wasn't it. He told me he never intended to ask Mam to marry him. He says he wants to marry *me,* Dorcas."

"Not possible."

"That's what I thought, but he means it."

"And your mother? What will she think—that you

stole her beau while she was in Ohio fetching your grossmama?"

"No, you don't understand. We were mistaken. Mam and me. All of us. Samuel said he thinks of Mam as a friend, but that it's me he wants."

Dorcas pursed her lips. "You think maybe he asked her and she said *ne?*"

Anna swallowed. "It's possible, I suppose, but I think Mam would have told me—told us. He didn't say anything about asking her. I don't think he did." She hesitated. Dorcas was sampling another salad. "So what do you think?"

"I think it's a better match than you could hope for. Samuel's nice, and he's got a big farm. But are you willing to take on five stepchildren?" She pointed with the plastic fork. "That won't be easy. And that youngest is a handful."

"I think I could, with God's help. I really do. They are such sweet children, especially Lori Ann."

Dorcas rolled her eyes. "And the twins? Rudy and Peter? *Sweet?*"

Anna shrugged. "They're eleven-year-old boys. Full of themselves."

"*Ya.* Those two are. Tried to burn down the school, didn't they? Not to mention your barn."

"Not on purpose," Anna said. "Samuel's done a good job, but the children really need a woman—a mother— in the house."

"Maybe." Dorcas hesitated, swallowing another mouthful. "Are you sure, Anna? Are you sure you're not mistaken, not wishing so hard for someone that you've…"

"Made all this up?" Anna felt hurt. "It's true. Samuel

asked me if he could court me. I wouldn't tell you if it wasn't. I thought you would be happy for me."

"I *am* happy for you." Dorcas shrugged. "I just wouldn't want you to be mistaken."

"I'm not mistaken," Anna said firmly. "And Samuel wants an answer, but I don't know what to say."

"Do you like him?"

"'Course I do. Who doesn't like Samuel?" But she didn't tell the entire truth about how he made her feel. Not even to Dorcas could she admit that she more than liked him. She couldn't explain how just watching Samuel made her heartbeat quicken or how the sound of his voice made her feel like she'd bitten into a ripe Golden Delicious apple. "It's just… I don't know why he would pick me," she finished in a rush.

Dorcas nodded. "You know I love you, Anna. It doesn't matter to me if you're…you know."

"Fat?"

"Sturdy," Dorcas supplied, "But you know you aren't one of the cute girls. Neither am I. So you have to wonder if he asked you because your mother owns the farm next door or maybe because you cook so good."

The backs of Anna's eyes prickled. What Dorcas was saying was no more than what she'd thought herself, but it still hurt hearing it out loud. "He's looking for a housekeeper and someone to watch his children," she murmured.

"Maybe he loved his Frieda so much that he doesn't want to feel that way about a second wife." Dorcas's mouth turned up in a crooked smile that showed her broken tooth. "What you have to decide is if it matters. If having Samuel as your husband is more important than marrying someone who adores you—like Eli does your sister Ruth. Not everybody can have that."

Anna sighed and she nibbled at her lower lip.

"I didn't mean to hurt your feelings." Dorcas put down the fork. "You asked me, and I—"

"*Ne.* You didn't hurt my feelings," Anna said. "I wanted the truth, and I knew you'd tell me exactly what you thought. It's what I thought, too, that maybe he was thinking more of the house and his kids than what *he* wanted."

"I'd take him anyway," her cousin said. "Having a husband like Samuel any way at all, has to be better than being an old maid."

"Maybe so," she agreed. It would be an answer to her prayers, wouldn't it? Having Samuel to cook and sew for…maybe, if the Lord was willing, maybe having babies with him.

"It would be enough for me," Dorcas whispered, reaching for one of the big bowls of salad. "So you grab him and hold onto him if you can. Because if he looked in my direction, I'd take him up on the offer in an Englisher's minute."

Chapter Six

Outside, in Roman's long, open carriage shed, the men of the congregation gathered. It was a time to relax after the long and thought-provoking sermon. Neighbors shook hands, exchanged news about the various families' health, talked about the weather and what they would plant in the spring, and waited for the women to call them to the communal meal.

Samuel and Charley were discussing the merits of the new stock Charley had purchased at the Virginia auction. Samuel was keeping a sharp eye on Rudy and Peter when Shupp Troyer sauntered up and stuck out his hand.

"Awful cold for January, ain't it?" Shupp grabbed Samuel's hand and pumped it.

Samuel nodded. "This is when we generally get a warm spell before February hits." He was still watching his twins, who, for once, seemed to be on their best behavior. The boys were standing with Lori Ann amid a crowd of children at Roman's back porch, where Anna and Miriam were handing out apples, buttered biscuits and small meat pies that would tide the little ones over until they got a chance to come to the table.

Samuel could remember how hungry he used to get, waiting for the elders and guests, all the men and older boys, and finally the women and babies to eat before it got to the children's sitting. As usual, Anna Yoder had remembered the children and their growing appetites. He felt a surge of pride that she had such a good heart. He knew that if she accepted him, she'd make a good mother.

"Weatherman calling for more snow tomorrow." Shupp droned on as he scratched his chin. "Don't usually get snow when the temperature drops this low. Makes it hard to tend to the animals. And makes my sprung back ache like a toothache."

Not that you do much tending of anything around the farm, Samuel thought. He'd never seen Noodle Shupp Troyer work a full day since he'd come to Delaware, and that was before his two daughters married and brought strong sons-in-law into his house to pick up the slack. Noodle could always be depended on to have some ailment to complain about at any gathering. Luckily for him, his girls had taken after his wife, Zipporah, and were as industrious as honey bees.

"Heard you was doing some work for Hannah," Noodle said slyly. "Been traipsing up there a lot this past week, ain't you?" He raised one side of his bushy eyebrow. Noodle had a single eyebrow that extended in a thick line from the far corner of his left eye, over his nose, to the corner of his right eye. It was so wooly that Samuel once took it for a knit cap under the man's hat. "Guess there was need, with Hannah still away."

"I did some painting for the Yoders," Samuel admitted. "What with Jonas's mother coming to stay." He was an easygoing man, and this was the Sabbath. It wouldn't do for him to let Noodle's gossiping ways get under his skin or cause him to have uncharitable thoughts.

"Some of Hannah's girls home to watch the farm, ain't they? That big one, Anna?" Noodle chuckled and elbowed Samuel. "Now, she'll make an armful for some man."

Samuel gritted his teeth and forced his voice to a neutral tone. "Anna's a good girl," he said. "And there's no better cook in the county, for all her being but twenty-one. You've no call to poke fun at her."

Noodle tugged at his eyebrow, pulling loose a few gray hairs and dropping them into the straw underfoot. "No offense, but sayin' that she's hefty ain't no more than the honest truth. 'Course…" He grinned at Charley. "Once Samuel here makes the widow his wife, it's natural he'll be scramblin' to find that one a husband—seein' as how she'll be his stepdaughter."

Charley's normally genial expression darkened. "Anna may be bigger than most girls, but her heart's big to match."

"Never meant no…"

The clang of Fanny's iron dinner triangle signaled the first seating. As a deacon of the church, Samuel was one of those so honored, and for once, he didn't mind leaving Charley and the younger men to join Reuben and Bishop Atlee and the others. If he stayed here any longer with Noodle Troyer, he'd say or do something that wouldn't set a good example for the younger people on a Church Sunday. He was a peaceful man, but he had his limits.

Noodle wasn't the brightest onion in the basket, and

Samuel doubted he meant any harm, but he was slighting Anna with his loose talk. He had to knot his fists to keep from tossing the man into the nearest horse trough.

Lots of people would be sticking their noses in when he and Anna started officially courting, but that was their shortcoming. Anna and he were right for each other. Her size wasn't a problem for him, and it shouldn't be anyone else's concern. He thought she was perfect, in a homey and comfortable way that a wife ought to be, and she had the most beautiful eyes. He was glad that Charley had stuck up for Anna, and he wished he'd said more. But it wouldn't be right to tell Noodle or anyone else what he figured on doing, not until he and Anna settled things between them.

As he crossed the snow-covered yard toward the house, he looked up and caught Anna watching him from the back step. Her basket, once full of foodstuffs, was empty, and the children had scattered to eat their prizes, but Anna still stood there, tall and fine in her starched *kapp* and best Sunday dress. It made him go all warm inside at the thought that she was watching him.

He smiled at her, but she didn't smile back. Her eyes went wide like a startled doe, and she darted back inside and slammed the door. Instantly, the good feeling in his chest became a cold hollow.

What if Anna didn't care for him in that way? What if she thought of him only as a neighbor and a fellow church member? What if he'd laid his heart open and she wouldn't have him? What then?

It was after three, when everyone had eaten and the young men were packing the benches into the church wagon, but Samuel still hadn't had a minute alone with

Anna. She'd stayed in the kitchen, instead of serving at the tables, as she usually did. Now, when he had all five of his children gathered up and waiting in the buggy, he went to find her.

Fannie met him at the back door, and Samuel could see the kitchen was still crowded with chattering women cleaning up the last of the dishes and stowing leftover food. "Could I speak to Anna?" he asked.

"Anna Yoder?" Mischief sparkled in Fannie's eyes.

What Anna did she think he meant? The only other one he knew that was here today was three years old. "*Ya,* Anna Yoder."

All the women in the kitchen were staring at him through the open kitchen door, and he felt his face grow hot. Growing up with older sisters, he'd always felt that women were so different from men that they might have been a different breed altogether. They always seemed to have secrets; and put two women together, and no matter how much he liked them, a man always felt tongue-tied.

Like the other day, when Anna had asked why he wanted to marry her, his brain had frozen and he'd mumbled something about hard work, when that hadn't been what he wanted to say at all. He *did* admire Anna for her cooking and her skill at sewing and such, but he would have wanted her if she couldn't boil water or thread a needle. It was her quiet way he loved most, her gentle nature and her generous heart. Any man ought to be able to see that Anna shone like wheat in a basket of chaff, and should be honored to have her walk out with him. But saying those fancy love words out loud were more than he could manage.

"Samuel?"

He blinked. He'd been daydreaming and not seen Anna until she was standing right in front of him. Susanna was right behind her; her little round face peered around Anna, full of curiosity.

"Like to take the two of you home," he managed. "Maybe more snow. Sun be going down soon…get your feet wet." His stomach knotted and he broke out in a cold sweat beneath his heavy coat. What was wrong with him, that he couldn't speak to Anna easy-like, as he had a thousand times since she was a young girl?

"Going with Charley and Miriam." Susanna peeked around her sister. "In Charley's buggy."

"Our things are already loaded," Anna said. "They're coming to Mam's for coffee and evening prayer."

"Ah. So you won't need a ride?" His heart sank. He'd hoped to drive her home, maybe go in for coffee and visiting.

"*Ne.* It's thoughtful of you to ask." She smiled and closed the door while he stood there, leaving him feeling both disappointed and a little hurt.

He tried not to let any of his emotions show as he made his way to his buggy, but when he went to climb up in the front seat, his mouth dropped open in astonishment. Sitting there was not his little Mae or Naomi or even Lori Ann. Martha Coblentz was planted solidly on the bench, her feet against the kick board, her mouth tight and her shoulders stiff beneath her black wool cape.

"Martha?" He did a double take, wondering for a moment if he'd started to get in the wrong carriage. But, no, this was his horse, Smoky, his buggy, his five kids giggling in the back. *What was Martha doing here?* "Is there a problem?" he stammered. "Is your horse lame?"

"'Course not," Martha said. "Don't talk foolishness, Samuel. I've been wanting to have a good talk with you for a long time, but you're a hard man to catch up with." She waved her hand. "Well, don't just stand there. Get in."

"Am I driving you to your house?"

She shook her head. "Reuben will be along to bring me home. Drive on to your farm, Samuel. You're blocking Lydia and Norman in."

With a sigh, Samuel did as he was told. No good could come of this. He didn't need to be a smart man to know that. Martha, sister to Hannah Yoder's dead husband, and Reuben's wife, was full of advice, and he was certain he was about to receive a good measure of it, whether he wanted it or not.

"I feel it's my duty to talk sense into you," Martha said as they crossed the blacktop road in front of the chair shop. "You know that Frieda and I were close."

Not that close, Samuel thought, but he held his tongue. Frieda had once confided to him that she thought Martha should keep her nose in her own affairs, but... He stifled a groan. Frieda would have also been the first one to caution him about uncharitable thoughts on the Sabbath.

"She was a good wife, a good mother, a faithful member of the church," Martha intoned. "Your Frieda was one of the best. You'll not find her equal."

Samuel nodded and kept his eyes on the horse's rump. The road was icy, so he didn't want to drive fast and take a chance on the animal slipping. "She was and is still dear to me and the children."

"But she's gone on to a better place," Martha continued. "Frieda's with God. And you're here. With five children to raise. A house and a farm to run. You have responsibilities, Samuel, big responsibilities."

He nodded again. Did she think he didn't know that? That he didn't pray for guidance every day—that he didn't worry about his children? That he wasn't lonely for a woman's smile and soft word?

"It's common knowledge that you've been calling at Hannah's regularly for the past two years," Martha said, turning to look at him over her spectacles.

Samuel passed the lines from one hand to the other. The wind was blowing full into their faces, and he felt sorry for the horse. Luckily, they didn't have far to go, just past the schoolhouse to his lane, and that had trees on either side, to shield them from the icy blast. "Hannah's lost her husband," he said, "and she's been a good neighbor. It would be less than my duty to neglect her."

"I'd say nothing bad about Hannah," Martha went on. "Wasn't she my own dear brother's wife? But you're a young man, still in your prime. You've a big farm, and you need more sons to help in the fields. Hannah's too old for you, Samuel. There. I've said it to your face."

"Hannah's hardly over the hill."

"She's a grandmother. And too old to give you more children. You need a young woman, and I know of one who's secretly had affection for you for a long time."

Suddenly understanding why Martha had approached him, Samuel straightened in the seat and began to smile. Relief eased the hard knot in his chest, and he didn't feel the cold anymore. Martha hadn't come to lecture him. She'd come as a go-between for Anna, her niece.

"You understand, I never intended to court Hannah," he admitted. "We're friends, nothing more."

"That's good to hear." Martha didn't sound entirely convinced.

Smoky turned into the lane so fast that the buggy skidded sideways. The girls shrieked and Martha clutched the edge of the seat. Samuel reined the animal to a walk. "You'll be in the barn soon enough," he soothed. Roman's place was close, no more than half a mile. Had it been just him and the two boys, they would have walked over to church, but it was too bitter a day for his daughters.

"My, but that gives a body a start," Martha said, still clutching the seat. "We could have turned over."

In the back of the buggy, the squeals had turned to giggles and whispering. Samuel decided the best course was to ignore them.

"*Ne.* We were in no danger. Just the lane's slippery." More snowflakes were beginning to float down, large, lacy ones that reminded him of meringue on one of Anna's lemon pies. The sky was already dark in the east, and the air smelled of snow. They might get a few more inches before it was done. He decided to keep the cows inside tonight. "It eases my mind, you telling me this," he admitted. "I was wondering whether she was favorable toward me or not."

"Oh, she favors you well enough, but she's modest, as an unmarried girl should be. But she thinks of you a lot, enough to make a chicken pot pie for your supper tonight. I tucked it into the back of the buggy, wrapped in toweling to keep it warm. Along with some potato salad and apple cake. You'll not have to do a thing. I'll put the food on the table and Naomi and the girls can set out the dishes and flatware while you're doing your chores."

The house came in sight, and behind it the barns and sheds that housed his animals, wagons and machinery, all quickly becoming frosted in white snowflakes. As it was the Sabbath, no work was permitted by the *Ordnung,* but the chickens and ducks, the pigs, the horses and cows still had to be fed and watered, and there was still a night milking to do.

"It's thoughtful of you and of her."

"It's the least I can do, seeing how much I loved your poor Frieda. You've been a widower too long, Samuel. People have been wondering why you haven't remarried. It's your duty to your children and to your community. There always seem to be more available girls than prospective husbands."

"I thought maybe I was too old for her—that she'd want a younger man, someone closer to her own age."

"Then you're wrong. The best marriages are those where the man is older and more settled in his ways. You can guide her both spiritually and in her daily responsibilities. Young husbands are flighty, by my way of thinking. A proper husband needs to be the authority in the house."

A small smile came to Samuel as he pondered who was the authority in the Coblentz house. He guided Smoky around to the back of the house. "Help your sisters out," he ordered the boys.

"Oh, it's snow—snowing," Lori Anne cried.

"Snow," Mae echoed.

"Take the little ones inside," Samuel said to Naomi. "The door's unlocked. And keep Mae away from the stove." As the children hurried toward the house, Samuel turned to face Martha. "I want you to know that Anna and I were properly chaperoned when I was there painting. I'd do nothing to cast suspicion on her name or mine. Susanna and my children were with us all the time."

"I'm glad to hear it. Rumors are easier to prevent than to erase, once they've begun. It behooves a man in your position to always be above criticism."

He climbed down and helped Martha out of the buggy. Peter came to take hold of Smoky. "Unharness him and turn him into his stall," Samuel said. "Then change your clothes before starting the chores." He glanced around, half expecting to see Reuben's carriage. "You did say that Reuben was coming for you, didn't you?" he asked Martha.

"I wasn't sure how long our talk would take. He'll be along. I'll just make a pot of coffee and see to it that the girls are doing their evening chores. They need guidance as much as boys, you know. They've been too long without a mother's direction."

"I suppose," Samuel agreed. He took Martha's arm as they went up the steps to the open porch. "You can take off your boots inside," he said. There was a utility room just inside, with benches to sit on and hooks for winter coats and hats. "Just make yourself to home."

Inside, the house was warm, and Lori Ann's tiger cat was pleased to see them. Purring, it curled around Martha's ankle as she pulled off first one wet boot and then the other. "Reuben doesn't hold with animals in the house," she said. "Hair and dirt. Animals belong outside."

"I'm afraid I spoil my children," he admitted. "And the cat's a good mouser." He pointed to a pair of Frieda's old slippers on the shelf. "You can put those on. Warmer on your feet than just stockings." He excused himself to go and change into his barn clothes. Having Martha in the house felt a little awkward. He knew what a snoop she was, but she'd come to bring him the great news today, and he would never treat her unkindly. "Coffee's over the stove," he called over his shoulder.

As he padded down the hall in his stocking feet, he could hear Martha giving sharp orders to his girls. There was a basket of laundry on the floor near the table, left there since yesterday. He wished he'd folded and put away those clothes last night. Martha would be sure to notice that and the breakfast dishes still standing in the sink. She was right, he supposed. He did need a helpmate. Soon he'd be ready for unexpected company anytime.

When he returned to the kitchen, he found the coffee pot simmering and his two older girls busy setting the table for a light supper before the children went to bed. Mae was under the table hugging the cat, and her eyes were red, as if she'd been crying. "What's wrong?" he asked, holding his arms out to her.

"She's wet her drawers," Martha fussed. "A big girl like her, nearly four. She should know better. I told her to just sit a while in them and see how it felt."

Samuel frowned. He'd changed his share of diapers and wet underthings since Frieda died. Martha might know best. Such was usually women's business, but it didn't seem right to him, to punish a little girl for an accident. "She's still not settled in here yet," he defended. "Accidents are bound to happen. Naomi, could you take your sister and see that she's dressed in dry clothing?"

Naomi nodded. "Come on, Mae," she said, extending a hand. Sniffing, the little one crawled out, took hold of her sister and shuffled after her, out of the kitchen.

Lori Ann stopped, mouth open, a plate in her hand and stared longingly at her sisters.

"What? You want to go with them?" Samuel asked. She nodded, and he took the plate and motioned her away. "Go on, then."

Martha took down two mugs and set them on the counter with a loud thump. "You make their new mother's task no easier," she said. "Spare the rod and spoil the child. My Dorcas will have her hands full."

It was Samuel's turn to stare, gape-mouthed. "Dorcas? What has Dorcas to do with anything?"

Martha cleared her throat. "You're not usually so thick. Who do you think I've been talking about all the way from Roman's? My daughter, Dorcas, the girl you'll soon be walking out with."

"Dorcas?" He shook his head. "But I didn't..." He dropped into a chair, suddenly feeling as if his head might burst. "There's some misunderstanding, Martha. I never intended to court your Dorcas."

"Nonsense. Who else would you choose? She's unwed, nearly twenty-five, and has been brought up to know her duty." She made a sound of disbelief. "Sometimes I think men are blind. Of course, Dorcas. She's exactly right for you, and now that I've brought it to your attention, Reuben and I will expect you to begin making formal calls on her within the week."

Rudy banged open the kitchen door. "Reuben's here, Dat. He says for Martha to hurry. Snow's getting worse, and he wants to get home before dark."

"I didn't intend to court Dorcas," Samuel repeated. Was it possible that he'd completely misunderstood? That it was Dorcas that Martha had come to speak for and not Anna? "Dorcas made the chicken pot pie for me?"

"I said so, didn't I?" Martha snapped. "Honestly, Samuel, I don't know what to think about you. You always seemed so sharp-witted to me, not a man that had to be hit over the head with a thing before he saw the right of it." She followed Rudy out into the utility room, plopped down on a bench, and began to pull on her left boot as his son vanished through the outer door.

Samuel caught a whiff of something unpleasant, and Rudy's quick exit set off a warning alarm in his head. "Don't—" he began.

Martha jammed her foot into the boot and let out a scream. She leaped to her feet and began to hop on her right foot, yanking at the left boot. "What have they done?" she shrieked as she stared at her filthy black stocking and the unmistakable smell of wet cow manure permeated the room. "Monsters!" she accused. "Your sons are monsters!"

Chapter Seven

The following day, at four in the afternoon, Anna's mother, grandmother, great aunt and two younger sisters arrived in the hired van. Instantly, the house, which had been relatively quiet with only Anna, Miriam, Ruth and Susanna in the kitchen, rang with laughter and eager chatter. There was a great deal of hugging, stamping of snowy boots, exchanging of news, talk of the snowy roads and thankfulness that the long winter trip had been completed without mishap.

"We saw a terrible accident near Harrisburg," Leah said as she squeezed Susanna for the third time. "A bus overturned."

"There were police and ambulances," Rebecca added. "But our driver spoke to one of the firemen who was directing traffic. He said that he didn't think anyone was killed. We prayed for them."

Aunt Jezebel nodded. Anna hadn't seen her Gross-mama's younger sister in years, but she didn't look a day older than the last time she'd visited Delaware, and she certainly didn't appear to be a woman in her sixties. She was small and neat with an Ohio-style *kapp,* a rose dress with long sleeves and cape, black stockings and black lace-up, leather shoes. Aunt Jezebel's glasses were thin silver wire rims, which often slid down to perch on the tip of her small nose; and her hair, once red like Anna and her sisters', had faded to mousy-brown with silver streaks.

According to Mam, Aunt Jezebel wore only rose-colored dresses, never any other color, even on Church Sundays. She was shy and only spoke amid close family, and then as quiet as a mouse's squeak. Anna didn't believe that Aunt Jezebel was touched, as some people whispered, no matter how odd some of her habits were.

Johanna had once confided that Aunt Jezebel had been courted by a boy from Lancaster when she was seventeen. Her parents had felt that Jezebel was too young to marry and had refused to agree to the match until her next birthday. She had waited patiently, but on the day of her wedding, her bridegroom never arrived and no one ever saw him again. What happened to him was a mystery; some people thought he'd run away to become English, others suspected something worse had befallen him. Regardless, Jezebel never recovered from the shock, and had remained single all these years. Anna thought it all very tragic and romantic.

Now, amid the noisy welcome, Aunt Jezebel perched on a chair in the corner of the room like a small rose-colored sparrow. She watched Grossmama, Mam and Anna and her sisters with bright blue eyes, waiting for someone to tell her what to do next. Aunt Jezebel would do anything you asked of her, and she was a tireless worker, but she never seemed capable of deciding what needed to be done on her own. Usually, it was Grossmama who gave the orders, and Aunt Jezebel carried them out with quiet efficiency.

"It's cold in here." Grossmama, a tall, imposing woman with big hands and a stern countenance, made a great show of sniffing loudly. "I knew that we should have waited for spring. I took a chill in the van and my neck hurts. The driver put on her brakes so hard when we stopped at that Englisher food-fast for lunch that I twisted it." She rubbed her back and glared at Mam. "You should have packed more sandwiches. That chicken was tough—and expensive. Three dollars for a little dry chicken on bread. Ridiculous." She rapped her cane on the floor. "Jezebel. Find my shawl."

"Here it is, Grossmama," Leah said, draping a black wool shawl around the old woman's bony shoulders.

Grossmama picked at the weave of the shawl. "Not this one. It itches. Jezebel! Where's my gray shawl?"

Behind Hannah's back, Rebecca grimaced and rolled her eyes for Anna's benefit. *It's starting already,* Anna thought. Their grandmother was nothing, if not consistent. Nothing ever pleased her, least of all their mother.

"I'll fetch it, sister," Aunt Jezebel said obediently. She hurried across the room to sort through a large, old-fashioned zippered bag. "Here." Removing the offending black shawl, Aunt Jezebel placed another around her sister's shoulders, a wrap that appeared to Anna to be identical to the first, other than its color. Aunt Jezebel folded the black shawl neatly and tucked it into the bag, carrying the satchel back to her chair and standing it by her feet before taking her seat again.

"My stomach isn't right," Grossmama proclaimed. "Is there any clear broth?" She peered at the clean white tablecloth, as if hoping to find a stain.

"I made chicken soup," Anna said. "I remembered that soup was always easy on your stomach when you were unwell. It's on the back of the stove. Shall I dip some out for you?"

"Chicken soup? Does it have noodles?"

Anna nodded. "Egg noodles."

"Are they store-bought? Store noodles give you worms. They have bugs in them. I never eat store noodles." She turned her gaze on Susanna. "The Englishers put bugs in them."

"Ne." Susanna shook her head. "Anna rolled the noodles. I cut them." She beamed.

Grossmama nodded. "Well, at least someone is thinking of my health." She patted Susanna's chubby hand. *"Danke,* Susanna. You should've come to Ohio, instead of those two." She waved a hand at Leah and Rebecca. "Silly as hens, both of them. Fancy girls. Trying to act English. Take after you, Hannah."

"Now, Lovina," Hannah soothed. "I'm sure that Rebecca and Leah did their best to help you." Mam never called Grossmama mother, always by her name. Grossmama had insisted on it years ago, when Mam had wed Dat. She'd said pointedly that Mam was not a daughter, but a daughter-in-law, and that she shouldn't be pretending blood kinship where there wasn't any.

"Hmmp," Grossmama grunted. "That one." She indicated Leah with a bob of her chin. "She's not Plain. She draws boys like flies to honey. Comes of you giving her such an outlandish name—an Englisher name."

"You're tired," Hannah said, ignoring the last remarks.

Anna knew that there was no sense in Mam pointing out to Grossmama that "Leah" was from the Bible, and that it wasn't her fault that she'd been born beautiful. It was true; everyone noticed how pretty Leah was, and boys especially noticed. Leah's picnic baskets had always been the first one auctioned off at community fundraisers, and had usually brought in the most money.

Secretly, Anna had wondered if her sister had gotten both of their shares of looks. Not that she was jealous of Leah. She wasn't. Leah was her sister, and she loved her. God had made Leah as she was, as God had made her, and their grandmother was wrong to accuse Leah of trying to be English because she had a pretty face. Dat always said that Grossmama was hard on Leah because she'd been a notoriously Plain child and a Plain woman. It had been the Lord's will that Anna take after Dat's side of the family and not Mam's.

"And I want those little crackers, the ones with no salt," Grossmama said. "Salt will kill you."

Anna looked at Rebecca, who shrugged. "Water crackers, I think," her sister said. "We bought them from the big supermarket in town…in Ohio. I've never seen them here."

"I should never have come," Grossmama whined. "Jezey, didn't I tell you we should never have come? I don't like Delaware. I never have. I'm going home tomorrow."

"She needs…she needs her rest, I think," Aunt Jezebel whispered to Anna. "Such a long trip is hard on her, and her arthritis pains her."

"Exactly right," said Mam, who had excellent hearing. She glanced at Ruth. "If you and Miriam could get her into bed, I'll have Susanna bring her the chicken noodle soup and some of those sweet white peaches we canned last August."

Grossmama headed toward the back door and Ruth took her shoulders, gently turning her in the right direction. "This way to the bedrooms, Grossmama."

"I know which way," Grossmama insisted. "And I don't want chicken soup. Bring me toast with honey. And herb tea. Blackberry. And some meat. Scrapple. I don't suppose you have any decent scrapple. Jonas likes it crispy with ketchup. You never could get the recipe right, Hannah. You were hopeless when it came to scrapple. Jonas always says so." She narrowed her eyes and looked around. "Where is he? Why isn't he here?"

Mam sighed. "Jonas is in the barn, Lovina. Milking the cows."

"*Ne,*" Susanna said. "Dat's not in the barn. He's—"

"In God's hands, as always," Mam interrupted. "You'll see him later." She gestured to Ruth and Miriam, and they led Grossmama out of the kitchen and down the hall toward the newly painted bedroom.

Anna could hear Grossmama fussing. "Jonas likes his scrapple just so. The way I make it. Hannah…"

"But Dat isn't milking the cows," Susanna protested. "He's in…in—"

"He's in heaven," Anna said. "But Grossmama forgets."

Susanna looked puzzled.

"Dat was her son," Mam explained. "And your grossmama is old. It's all right if she pretends that your father is alive. You don't want her to be sad, do you, Susanna?"

"*Ne.*"

"Sometimes she remembers," Aunt Jezebel whispered. "And then Lovina cries and cries." She got to her feet to follow the others to the bedroom and nearly tripped over Grossmama's bag. She gave a little yip, turned around three times, sat down and got up again. Anna knew that was one of Aunt Jezebel's odd habits, and everyone but Susanna pretended not to notice as she hurried out of the kitchen after her older sister.

Anna glanced at Rebecca, who just shrugged. It was simply Aunt Jezebel's way, and they'd all have to get used to it.

Hannah hugged Anna and Susanna again. "I've missed you all terribly. How is everything? Did the school have to close for snow?"

"Just the one day," Anna answered. "Has Grossmama been like that for the whole trip?"

Hannah chuckled. "Worse. But it must be difficult for her, having to leave her home, not knowing if she'll ever return. And your grossmama has many aches and pains. You must all do your best to welcome her and make her feel wanted."

Mam accepted a mug of coffee from Susanna and settled into a chair at the table. "I've had enough traveling for a while. I can tell you that. And I was gone less than a week. I don't know how Leah and Rebecca managed for so long without being homesick."

"We were," Leah said, coming to sit beside her mother. "We missed all of you terribly."

"Me, too?" Susanna asked.

"You most of all," Leah assured her.

"You're lucky you got that one home," Rebecca teased, indicating her sister. "There were four boys who wanted to marry her."

Leah smiled, making her beautiful face as rosy as an angel. "Not four boys," she corrected. "Two boys and two men."

"One was fifty," Rebecca confided. "Can you believe it? He had a long, scraggly beard and he chewed tobacco." She wrinkled her nose. "Yuck."

"I'm not getting married for years and years," Leah said. "I've missed you all too much. And I wouldn't want to be so far away. When I marry, I'll pick someone from Kent County, so we can still come for Anna's dinners."

Four suitors, Anna mused. And Leah wouldn't be twenty-one for two months. "I cooked enough for a crowd," she said to her mother. "I imagine Johanna will be over with the children as soon as she hears—"

Irwin opened the kitchen door and Jeremiah ran in. The little dog barked and ran in circles before darting under the table. "Company," Irwin announced. He grabbed a biscuit off the tray on the gas stove and left the kitchen so fast that he didn't stop to take off his heavy denim jacket.

"Johanna?" Mam asked. Her question was answered as Aunt Martha and Dorcas appeared in the doorway. "Come in." Mam rose to her feet. "It's good to see you."

"My duty." Martha shed her coat and the scarf she wore over her *kapp.* "What with Mother arriving." She handed the coat to Dorcas. "Do something with this."

"Ruth and Miriam are getting her into bed," Hannah said. "We fixed up the room across from mine for her and Aunt Jezebel. You can go in and see her if you like."

Aunt Martha turned her scorching gaze on Leah. "You're not wearing paint, are you? Your cheeks look awfully red."

Rebecca smiled. "No, Aunt Martha. Leah's cheeks are red from the cold. And it's good to see both of you, too."

"Hmmph." Aunt Martha looked pointedly at the coffee pot.

Anna caught the strong scent of bleach. Aunt Martha always smelled of bleach; and when she was small, Anna had wondered if she bathed in it every night. She hurried to pour her aunt and Dorcas a cup. "Two sugars, Aunt Martha?" she asked. "And milk?"

"Cream. I always use cream. It's good for my stomach condition."

"No cream or sugar for me," Dorcas said. "Just the coffee."

"Thin as you are, a little sugar and cream would do you good," Aunt Martha said as she took Dat's seat at the head of the table. "I'll give Mother a chance to get into bed. Too much excitement isn't good for a woman her age."

"I hope Reuben is well," Hannah said.

"Toothache. Been bothering him all week. He's in the carriage. No sense in him coming in. We're not staying," Aunt Martha said in her piercing nasal voice. "Just doing my duty as a daughter. Mother and I will have lots of time to visit, and I don't want to tire her on her first day home."

"Maybe I should—" Anna began.

"*Ne.* You stay right where you are. It's only fair that you hear what I have to say. I don't like to drop this on you when you've hardly caught your breath, Hannah. But you have a right to know."

Mam sighed. "*Ya,* Martha. What is it I should know? Miriam hasn't been riding motor scooters again, has she?"

Susanna's eyes grew huge. "Miriam has a scooter?"

Aunt Martha sat up to her full height and tightened

her thin mouth. "Samuel Mast has been making noises about wanting to court your Anna. It's ridiculous, of course. You need to put a stop to it before Anna gets her heart broken or becomes a joke."

"Anna?" Rebecca asked incredulously, turning her gaze on her sister. "But I thought Samuel and Mam were...were..."

Anna felt her face flush.

Martha turned around in her chair to address Rebecca. "Am I talking to you, girl? I'm talking to your mother, and it would behoove you to hold your tongue and show some respect."

Anna's stomach turned over as she gripped the back of one of the kitchen chairs. She opened her mouth to protest, but no sound came out. She glanced at her mother to see Mam's questioning look, and felt her face grow even hotter. She'd had no chance to speak to Mam, yet; she hadn't expected Aunt Martha to bring the news so quickly. She never should have talked to Dorcas before talking to Mam.

"I don't know what's gotten into the man. Has he buckwheat for brains? Probably his frustration with his poorly behaved children. They're out of control, I tell you."

"Ne." Anna bristled. "Samuel's children—"

"I'll not have you defend them. They are monsters," Aunt Martha declared. "Those twins put fresh, runny cow manure in my boots last night. Can you believe it? Ruined a pair of perfectly good boots. I'll never get the stink out of them. Samuel's buying me a new pair. You can be certain of that. But don't tell me that the lot of them are better than wild little animals."

"Cow manure?" Susanna echoed.

Leah coughed, put a hand over her mouth, and fled the kitchen. Rebecca and Dorcas were hot on her heels.

Cowards, Anna thought. She looked back at Mam. She wasn't smiling.

"If they did that, they certainly deserve punishing," Mam said. "I'm sorry about your boots, but what does that have to do with Anna and Samuel?"

"Dorcas tells me he wants to court Anna. Samuel's gone soft in the head, I tell you. I told Reuben to speak to the bishop. You know Samuel can do better than Anna."

"And how could he *do better than Anna?*" Mam asked. Her voice was low, her eyes cool.

Anna knew that look, and knew that this was no place for Susanna. Quickly, Anna moved to the stove, dipped a bowl of chicken noodle soup, added a spoon and pushed it into her little sister's hands. "Take this to Grossmama," she ordered.

"But she wants crackers," Susanna said.

"Soup first," Anna said, and Susanna did as she was asked.

"Why is that so strange, that Samuel should want to take my Anna to wife?" Mam asked, folding her arms over her chest and taking a step toward Aunt Martha. "What is wrong with Anna?"

Anna's chest felt tight. Tears stung the backs of her eyelids. She was ashamed, and she didn't know why. She wanted to run after her sisters, but she wouldn't leave her mother to face Aunt Martha's sharp tongue alone. If she didn't have the nerve to defend herself, she would at least stand with Mam.

Aunt Martha's face turned the color of lard and her

mouth pursed. "Not wrong, maybe," she said. "Just not…not proper."

"How not proper?" Mam persisted. "My Anna is a good girl." Mam now glared at Aunt Martha with a gaze hot enough to fry eggs. "Why wouldn't Samuel want her?"

"Well, because she's…"

"I'm Plain, that's what she means," Anna whispered. She felt sick. "Too Plain for a man like Samuel Mast." She blinked and sat down hard.

Unbidden, a bad memory came back to her, a memory that haunted her dreams. She'd been in second grade, maybe third, but she was chunky then, the fattest girl in the school.

Someone had left a big section of pipe on the edge of the schoolyard. The boys started crawling through it at recess, and one day, Miriam did, too. Then, all the smaller girls wiggled through the pipe.

Anna refused to join them until the King boys started teasing her, shouting, "Fat, fat, the barn rat."

"She is not!" Miriam had protested. "You can do it, Anna. Show them!"

Against her better judgment, Anna had tried to crawl down the dark pipe, but at the end, where it got even smaller, she'd gotten stuck. She started to cry, and the teacher came running to see what was wrong. The only way they got her out was when Ruth crawled down the pipe and pulled her backwards by her feet.

In the process, Anna had torn her *kapp* and her stockings, and all the kids laughed. She was so upset that she'd thrown up all over her new blue sneakers in front of everyone.

"You see," Aunt Martha flung back, ripping Anna

out of her thoughts. "Anna sees it. She knows she's fat. You're blind, Hannah, blind to the faults of your girls."

"And how, exactly, is it Anna's fault if God has made her beautiful in a different way?"

"Not only her size…her looks. It's not…not appropriate," Aunt Martha stammered. "What with Samuel courting you for so long. People will talk."

Mam closed in on Aunt Martha. "Who says that Samuel was courting me?"

"Why…why, everyone. Everyone knows he was. Now, suddenly, it's Anna he wants. It might likely be Leah next week. Or Rebecca! It's not right. Not fitting."

"No matter what you think, no matter what *anyone* thinks, there was never an understanding between me and Samuel. He is my good friend, Martha. Nothing more. And if he wishes to court Anna, or Leah for that matter, both girls are of age to walk out with a decent man of our faith. And, who they choose to be with is none of your affair."

Aunt Martha grabbed her coat and threw it around her shoulders. "Dorcas!" she shouted. "Dorcas! We're leaving."

"You are always welcome in my home, sister," Mam said. "But only if you can refrain from insulting one of my girls."

"I came here out of the goodness of my heart," Aunt Martha flung back. "So that Anna wouldn't be shamed in front of the community."

"I thought you came to see your mother and Aunt Jezebel."

"That, too. Don't change the subject. You're too bull-headed to listen to common sense, Hannah. You always were." She planted both feet and settled her hands on her bony hips. "There are more appropriate choices for Samuel Mast, and he will soon come to realize that. He will never marry your Anna, no matter what you think."

"Anna," Mam said gently. "Would you show your aunt out?"

Anna swung open the door to the porch and a blast of icy air struck her full in the face. She gasped. Samuel was standing on the porch, his fist raised to knock. "Samuel?"

"Anna." He took a step forward onto the threshold and stopped, half in the kitchen and half out. "I came to speak to Hannah…and to you."

"Samuel." Martha sniffed. "I should think you would have a great deal to say for yourself—for your actions."

Anna turned to meet her mother's gaze.

"Come in, Samuel," Hannah said. "Martha was just leaving."

Samuel looked from Mam to Aunt Martha to her. "Anna, if I could talk to your mother… Say what I should have said…"

"Take my word on it," Aunt Martha pronounced. "You'll be sorry you didn't ask Dorcas. She'll not be available long!"

"Mother!" Dorcas, her face as red as a radish, cried. "Don't—"

"I'm the one voice of reason," Aunt Martha said. "You'll all come to see that." She pushed past Samuel and out of the house. Dorcas seized her coat and ran after her, looking as if she was about to burst into tears.

"Have I come at a bad time?" Samuel asked.

"*Ne,*" Anna said, taking down Dat's big brown mug and pouring him a cup of coffee with shaking hands. "I think you have come at *exactly* the right time."

Chapter Eight

Samuel stood there, frozen to the spot, until Hannah nodded. "Sit down, Samuel," she said, sitting down. "We do have much to talk about."

He sat at the table, holding his coffee mug between his big hands and wishing he were anywhere but here. "The last thing I wanted to do was make trouble for you, Hannah, or for your family."

Mam motioned toward the coffeepot, and Anna took her mother's cup and refilled it. Anna carried the steaming cup to Hannah and joined them at the table. "Mam…" she began.

Hannah shook her head. "I think we should let our guest tell us why he's come. It's a cold afternoon, with evening chore time coming on fast. It must be important, to bring Samuel here."

"*Ya,*" he agreed. "It is. But maybe you and me should talk, Hannah. Alone?" He glanced at Anna. She looked as if she had been crying, and he felt a stab in his gut. He'd never wanted to hurt Anna. But there were Hannah's feelings to consider, as well. Had he given the impression that he was courting her? If he had, he'd betrayed their friendship. And it wouldn't be right for him to begin courting Anna without settling the matter.

"My Anna is a grown woman and dear to me," Hannah replied. "Whatever you have to say, you may say to both of us."

He nodded. "All right." Stalling for time, he took a sip of the coffee. Somehow he swallowed wrong, coughed, and then choked, spitting coffee across the table and feeling like a total dumbkin. "Sorry," he blurted. "I didn't mean—"

Anna silenced him with a smile. "There is no need. It's easily fixed." She went to the sink, returned with a cloth and wiped the tabletop clean.

"Now, what has my sister-in-law in such a stew?" Hannah asked. Her expression was serious, but a hint of amusement lurked in her eyes.

Anna turned her gaze on her mother. "It's a long story, but while you were gone, Samuel came to paint and—"

"Never mind the painting," he said. "That's not important. I'm afraid I've... I've hurt your feelings, Hannah. Did you think I've been courting you these past two years? If I caused you to—"

Hannah held up a palm. "Hush, Samuel. What I might have wondered and what I was certain of are two different things. You never asked, and I never did either. You're too good a friend to me and to my daughters to let a silly misunderstanding come between us. The truth is, if you'd outright asked to court me, I would have refused. In my heart, I'm still Jonas's wife. Maybe my love for him will always come first, but I know that as much as I care for you, it was never in that way. You're a good neighbor, and we've shared laughter and tears together, but nothing more."

"So you're not angry with me for wanting to court Anna?"

"Ah." Hannah steepled her hands, and Anna made a soft sound in her throat. "So it *is* true? You two are walking out together? Without consulting me? Without asking my permission?"

Samuel rose to his feet, knotting his hands nervously. "I wanted to speak with you. I meant to, but..." He glanced at Anna, trying to figure what she was thinking, and then looked back at her mother. "You're right. I should have asked you." He exhaled. "None of my reasons seem all that good, now that I think on them."

"Sit down," Hannah said gently. "Drink your coffee. The worst is over. Now we can talk, friend to friend, *ya?*"

He still wasn't sure if he was welcome here. "Anna?" he said. "Do you want me to leave?"

She shook her head. "*Ne,* Samuel," she murmured.

She looked small and helpless, and he wanted to wrap his arms around her and hold her so tight that he could feel the beat of her heart, but he knew that was out of the question. Hannah might still refuse her permission, and then what would they do? Anna would never go against her family for him, would she? He wished he hadn't come. He wished that he'd waited until he could talk to Anna again, to see how she felt.

"Widowers with children often marry girls younger than them," Hannah said. "Clary and Moses Peachy? He had seven children."

"But Clary was in her thirties, with a child of her own," he said, taking his seat again.

Hannah studied her daughter for what seemed like centuries, but he knew it could have been only a few seconds. His chest felt so tight that he thought he would explode.

He cleared his throat. "Hannah, I ask your permission to court your daughter, Anna," he said woodenly. "In every way that is proper and according to our custom. And if we suit each other, I want to make her my wife and the mother to my children."

Hannah pursed her lips. "Was that so hard? Samuel, Samuel, you men make things more difficult for yourselves." She cut her eyes at her daughter, who was blushing. "Now, you must ask Anna if she wishes you to court her."

"He did," Anna managed in a small, breathy voice. "I told him that I wanted to talk with you first and pray on it. Then I made the mistake of confiding in Dorcas. She must have told her mother last night after church, after Aunt Martha stopped by to see Samuel." She looked at him. "I'm sorry, Samuel. I should have known Dorcas would tell her mother."

Hannah reached across and patted Anna's hand. "Who knew what or when they knew it isn't all that important. My question is, did you give him an answer? Do you want him to walk out with you or not?"

A lump rose in Samuel's throat. This was exactly why he had been putting off asking Anna. Because this was it...or could be. Right here at this kitchen table Anna could say she had no feelings for him, that she never could. And that would be the end of it. There would be no more dreams of cozy evenings in his kitchen with Anna...or sharing his warm bed with her.

Anna broke through his worries with a long sigh. Moisture flooded her beautiful eyes. "I haven't had time to think it out," she said.

"Have you prayed about this, Daughter?" Hannah asked.

"*Ya,* I have, but I'm still confused."

"Is there no chance for me, then?" he asked, his voice sounding shaky in his own ears. "Is there someone else you'd rather—"

"I told you," Anna said, all in a rush. "It isn't you. You're...wonderful. It's me I'm not sure about."

She thought he was wonderful. Relief turned his bones to warm butter. "I'm not too old for you?" he ventured.

Anna shook her head. "You're exactly the right age." She looked down at her clasped hands. "The boys my age seem so...so feather-headed to me sometimes. And you're different...more sensible."

"Does the thought of being mother to Samuel's five children frighten you?" Hannah asked, taking Anna's hand again and squeezing it. "It isn't wrong to feel that way. Better that you admit it, if that's how—"

"I love his...your," she corrected. "I love your children," she admitted shyly. "Even the twins, who find trouble like Irwin finds laziness. They are good, sweet children, all of them, and I can see how they need the care of a mother."

He drew in a ragged breath and his heartbeat quickened. "Then why won't you..."

Hannah raised her hand again. "Listen to her, Samuel. I think what Anna is saying is that she needs time to decide what is best to do...time to get to know you."

"But she's known me most of her life," he protested.

"But as Samuel," Anna put in. "I've known you as our neighbor, as our deacon, and as a member of the school board—not as...as..."

"Not as a beau," Hannah finished. "She's right, Samuel. You've dropped this on her quickly. Anna's not had much experience at riding in a buggy with a young man, or sitting with him on the porch swing."

"It's a little cold for porch swings, don't you think?" he asked.

"What I mean is, my Anna is not a flighty girl. I've kept her close at home, maybe more than I should have. She's always such a help to me."

"I know she is...must be. I mean to court her properly, but how can I, if she won't agree...if she's not willing?" He stood up and went to Anna's side and looked down at her. "This has not been a decision I've made lightly. I've thought about you for a long time...prayed for guidance." He gazed into her eyes. "Anna, I believe God intends you to be my wife."

"Lots of people *think* they know what the Lord intends," Hannah said. "It may be that this is right. But there can be no harm in waiting a little longer, so that Anna can be sure."

Anna averted her eyes, but he could see that she was trembling.

"I think my Anna would be glad to have the opportunity to consider your proposal, but she doesn't want to commit herself yet. Is that right, Anna?"

She nodded shakily. "That's it exactly, Samuel. I want time."

Disappointment made his reply gruffer than he intended. "How much time were you wanting?"

Anna cast a desperate glance at her mother.

"What if we say by her next birthday?" Hannah suggested. "She will be twenty-two on the twenty-fifth of February. Would that suit you, Anna?"

Anna nodded. *"Ya."*

"And you, Samuel? Is that agreeable to you?"

"Ya," he agreed. "I've waited this long, I can wait a few weeks more. But I hope that I can call on Anna… that we can spend time together before that."

"I think that would be lovely," Hannah said. "So long as she feels comfortable. Would you like that, Daughter?"

Anna nodded again, glanced up at him, and offered a tremulous smile. "I think I would."

"It's settled then," Hannah said, bringing her hand down on the table. "And we'll keep this between ourselves until the two of you come to a firm decision. No sense in giving Martha and the other gossips more fuel for the fire."

"Hannah!" An older woman's shrill voice sounded from the back of the house. "Where's my Jonas? He can't still be milking those cows."

Hannah rose to her feet. "Anna's Grossmama. She's tired from the trip and a little confused. I should tend to her." She smiled. "Anna, would you pour Samuel some more coffee?"

He shook his head, moving around to the other side of the table. *"Ne.* Best I be heading home. See what those rascals of mine are up to. Cows will need tending soon."

"No need to run off," Hannah assured him. "Stay and have another cup. I believe I saw a pumpkin pie in the refrigerator. You're welcome to a slice."

"I should be going," he said.

"You have time for pie." Anna got up. "I made four. There's a pear pie you can carry home to the children."

His mouth watered at the thought of Anna's piecrust.

He'd had a slice of Dorcas's chicken pie the night before, and the crust was soggy. Anna's were always good. And if Hannah was leaving them alone, there was something else he wanted to talk to Anna about. The bad thing about being a single father was that there wasn't anyone to share the responsibility of the children. He had to make all the decisions alone, and he was thinking that Anna might be someone he could talk to about what was worrying him. If she became his wife, he liked to think they would spend lots of time talking and making decisions together.

He nodded, and before he knew it Hannah had vanished down the hall, and Anna had slid a big wedge of pie in front of him. She went to the stove and came back with the coffeepot. "Go ahead. Dig in," she said. "I have to wait for the others for mine. After supper, I mean." She grimaced. "Not that I don't like pie. I do. You can see that I like just about everything."

He paused, a forkful of pear and flaky crust in midair. "I always liked a body with a good appetite," he said. "My Mam and my sisters. They like to eat."

She smiled shyly. "Sometimes I feel funny, eating in front of other people. They stare at my plate...you know. Like I must be a pig to be so big." She sighed. "But I was born big, Mam said, over nine pounds. And that wasn't anything I did wrong."

"Nine pounds." He washed the mouthful down with a sip of coffee. "The twins didn't weight that between them. Came out like scrawny little skinned rabbits. I was afraid they'd never live. Frieda had a time getting them to eat. Was months before they started looking like normal babies."

"But look at them now," Anna replied. "Healthy and

hale, praise God. Bright boys, too." She sat down at the table, close enough for him to make out the little specks of dark brown in her light brown eyes. He sighed, thinking what a fine figure of a woman she was.

"Those boys are a handful," he admitted. "And…"

"Is there something?"

He nodded. "It's what they did to Martha."

"The cow manure in her boots?" Anna asked. The corner of her full lips twitched in amusement.

"*Ya,*" he said. "That."

Anna clapped a hand over her mouth, but couldn't suppress a giggle, and before he could stop it, he began to laugh, too. "And she stepped in it?" Anna squeaked, before breaking into a full-bodied shriek of laughter. "Poor Aunt Martha."

He began to choke. She jumped up and slapped him on the back, and suddenly they were both roaring with laughter. Tears rolled down his cheeks as he remembered the look on Martha's face when she pulled her stockinged foot out of the boot and stared in disbelief at the manure. "And the stink!" He snorted, and they were both off in peals of laughter again.

"I wish I could have seen it," Anna said, when she'd gotten control of herself enough to speak again. "Poor Aunt Martha."

"Lord forgive us," he rasped, wiping his eyes with the back of his hands. "It was wrong of Peter and Rudy, rude and disrespectful."

"*Ya,*" Anna agreed. "Very disrespectful. But funny to see, I'm certain."

He burst forth with another chuckle, one so deep that it shot up from the pit of his belly. "And it's disrespectful for us to laugh at her misery. For a deacon of the church to—" And he was off again, choking with laughter.

"For which, I'm sure, we shall both ask forgiveness in our prayers," Anna said, in a properly meek tone. Her gaze locked with his, and he saw the twinkle in her eyes.

"Amen," he said, wiping his eyes again. "Oh, I haven't laughed like that in…in forever. Either you are very good for me or…"

"Very bad," she teased.

He looked at her with new respect. He'd never realized Anna Yoder had such a sense of humor about her, or the ability to bring out the child in him. There was a lot more to this bighearted girl than tasty pie and light biscuits. There was a deep well of fun and good-natured joy. "I have to punish them, of course," he said. "I can't let it go—such disrespect to an older person."

Anna nodded. "And a guest in your house. It was wrong of them."

"They take after my father, they do," he said. "Dat was always up for a good joke. Once he got up in the night and put something in his brother's cow dip, so when Uncle Harry started to run his herd through the water to kill the lice in their fleece, they turned purple. He had three purple cows before he realized what was happening."

"That, I would have liked to see," Anna said. "Purple cows."

"The bishop was not pleased. I can tell you," Samuel said. "He had people visiting from Lancaster, and they asked him if his church allowed such nonsense as purple cows. Dat was in hot water at the next services."

"So, your twins come by it honest."

"That they do. But…" He exhaled slowly. "When

Frieda was alive, the two of us used to talk out what should be done when the children needed a doctor or when they needed correcting. Usually, I wanted to talk to them, and Frieda was all for a good backside tanning. But my Dat was always light on the switching, and I never really got the hang of it. Now, with just me to make the decisions… I wonder if I'm too soft. If they get into even more mischief."

"Our Dat never spanked us. Aunt Martha spanked me once, but never Mam or Dat." Anna pulled a face. "I deserved it. Dorcas and I got into four plates of brownies that Aunt Martha had made for a quilting bee, and ate most of them."

"How old were you?"

"Nine." She wrinkled her nose. "We ate so many that they made us sick."

He chuckled. "So, what do you think? Should I spank Peter and Rudy? It almost seems like a spanking is getting off easy, considering how bad Martha felt. And her ruined boots. I gave her money for new ones, and I'll make the boys pay for it out of their own savings, but—"

"You're right, Samuel," she said softly. "It *is* getting off too light. They were disrespectful, and they need to learn a lesson. But I wouldn't spank them. All that proves is that you are bigger and stronger than they are, and that you have that right."

He put his elbows on the table and leaned toward her. "So what would you suggest?"

"Well…" She looked thoughtful. "Since it was manure that caused the trouble, it might be good to send them over to clean Aunt Martha's stable after school every day for a week. They should pay for the boots, and they should apologize to her. But hard work never hurt anybody. And spending time mucking stalls will be time they can spend thinking on how they can be better behaved children."

"Martha expected me to give them a sound thrashing. Reuben, too. They said as much when they left. 'Spare the rod and spoil the child', Reuben said. He is our preacher."

"True," Anna agreed. "He is, but *you* are their father. It is *your* responsibility to guide your children and teach them. You have to do what you think is right."

He nodded. "Cleaning out Martha's stable, that's a good idea. And maybe her henhouse as well. Two boys, two chores."

"And a proper apology," Anna reminded him. "They have to do that. It's important a boy learns to apologize for his failings. Learning as a child makes it easier as an adult."

He sighed audibly with relief. It was a good decision. "You are wise beyond your years," he pronounced.

Anna blushed as she reached for his empty plate.

"It makes me feel better, to hear what you think."

"But you knew a spanking wouldn't suit. You didn't need me to tell you that."

"I worry that my heart is too soft," he admitted. "And sometimes with boys, a man must be hard."

"But not too hard," she said with a smile.

"You see, this is why I think we should court. You and I, we make a good team. We would make a good marriage," he said, sitting up straight and looking into her eyes. "I won't change my mind."

"But I haven't said yes," she reminded him. "And I have until my birthday to come up with an answer."

"It will have to do," he answered. "And now, I should

get home. But you have helped me, eased my mind about Rudy and Peter."

She followed him to the door and stood there watching him as he walked to his buggy. Snow was falling again, and darkness was closing in on the farmyard. "The pie was good," he said.

"Danke." She smiled and waved, then closed the door.

As he drove down the Yoder lane, Samuel wondered if it had been the smartest thing for him to come by buggy. The road would be slick, and he would have to be cautious about traffic. Some of the Englishers drove like drunken chickens on ice, and not all knew how to safely share the highway with horse-drawn vehicles. He turned on his battery-powered lights and guided the gelding onto the blacktop.

Only two cars passed before Samuel drew alongside the chair shop. Near the mailbox, he caught sight of Roman clearing snow away from the driveway. Roman called out to him and waved. Samuel wanted to get home, but Roman was his friend, and he might need something.

"Some weather, eh?" Samuel said as he reined in the horse. He'd pulled into the parking area, well off the road. "Think we'll get much more tonight?"

"Ya." Roman leaned on his shovel. "Weatherman on the radio says maybe two inches."

"Not too much." He waited. Roman had something on his mind; he could tell. Roman wasn't one to keep a man from his evening chores without reason. "Something?" Samuel asked. "Is there a problem?"

"I don't know," Roman answered. "Word is, you're courting one of the Yoder girls. Noodle said—"

"Noodle Troyer talks too much."

"So you're not? Nothing to it?"

Samuel leaned forward and rested his elbow on the dashboard. "I want to court Anna, but she's not certain she'll have me."

"Anna, then, is it? Not Hannah?"

Samuel chuckled. "It was never Hannah. I think the world of Hannah, you know that. Who wouldn't? She's a good woman, but I'm set on Anna."

"It's a lot, asking a girl that young to take on a ready-made family." Roman leaned the shovel handle against the mailbox and came over to the buggy. "She's a hard-worker, Anna. None better. But the age difference between you might be too much. Those twins of yours are a handful."

Samuel stroked his chin. "Not something I haven't wrestled with, Roman. It's time I took another wife, and she seems to me to be the best fit. I'd treat her right, be good to her."

Roman looked thoughtful.

"You have problems with that?" Samuel asked. "You think I'm too old for her?"

"*Ne*. It's just that…" Roman tugged at his knit hat. "Frieda was a real looker, and Anna… Anna's a special girl. I wouldn't want to see her hurt."

Samuel tensed. "No more than I would. I wouldn't ask her if I thought to make her second-best. I've prayed over it."

"Have you thought of talking it over with the bishop?"

Samuel shook his head. "I have a lot of respect for Atlee, but I didn't pick his wife for him, and I'd not think to ask him about choosing mine."

A grin split Roman's face, and he nodded. "Fair enough. It's none of my business either, I suppose, but Jonas was my friend. If he was here, he'd be askin' these questions. No offense meant."

"And none taken. But in the end, it's between Anna and me."

"You spoke to Hannah, asked her blessing?"

"I made it clear to her how I feel about Anna. They didn't want anything said, not until Anna is sure, but it sounds like the whole community is already buzzing."

Roman chuckled. "Martha and Reuben are buzzin', for sure. Reuben told Noodle he thought you'd had your eye on his Dorcas."

"Nothing wrong with Dorcas, other than her mother, but she's not right for me. Anna's the one."

"And if she turns you down?"

"She won't," Samuel said with more conviction than he felt. "And if she does, I'll just have to talk a little harder to convince her to change her mind."

Chapter Nine

Three days passed, and Anna was no closer to coming to a decision concerning her dilemma. In truth, she hadn't had much time to think, because Grossmama's arrival had thrown the entire house into a tizzy. The Yoder household had gone from four members to eight overnight, meaning more laundry, larger meals and generally more confusion as to who would tackle which tasks. Not that it was all bad. Having Rebecca and Leah home again was wonderful, and they'd sat up until nearly eleven every night talking, so late that Susanna usually fell asleep before they got her to bed. There had been little quiet time for Anna to consider whether or not to allow Samuel to court her.

"This oatmeal is lumpy. And it has too much salt," Grossmama's piercing voice cut through Anna's musing as she carried a plate of blueberry pancakes to the kitchen table. "I think your mother is trying to poison me," Grossmama fretted.

"*Ne*," Aunt Jezebel soothed. "Hannah wouldn't do that, Sister. She's done everything possible to make us feel at home."

"Well, I'm *not* at home," Grossmama said. "My back hurts. That bed is too hard, and there's a bathroom next to it. All night long, the water keeps running. Swish-slosh. Swish-slosh. A body can't get a wink of sleep."

Anna laid a gentle hand on her grandmother's shoulder. "I know you must miss your own house, but Mam really wants you to be happy here with us."

"I'm happy." Susanna slid her chair over close to Grossmama's. "'Member when you made me gingerbread? When I was little?"

Anna's grandmother reached for a pancake and then another. Aunt Jezebel lifted the pitcher of syrup to pour it onto the pancakes, but Grossmama snapped at her. "*Ne*. I want honey on my cakes." She looked around suspiciously. "Did Hannah make them?"

"Anna," Susanna said. "Anna did."

Grossmama was already chewing. "Dry," she muttered. "Too dry."

Leah brought the honey jar. "You'll like this," she said. "Apple blossom honey from Johanna's hives."

"Don't be so sure." Grossmama took a noisy slurp of coffee. "Where's Hannah? She shouldn't be lazin' in bed at this hour."

"Mam's already gone," Anna said. "Remember? Mam teaches school."

"Where's my Jonas? Hannah should see he has a decent breakfast before she goes out visiting."

Leah arched an eyebrow. "Um, Dat's milking," she murmured, cutting her eyes at Anna.

"What? Speak up, girl!"

"Leah, why don't you grab some more plates? Johanna will be here soon with the children," Anna said.

"Johanna wants you to teach her how you make your

rugs," Aunt Jezebel explained to her sister. "Everyone thinks you make the best rugs."

"Better than Hannah's," Grossmama said. "That one by my bed is all uneven braids and loose stitches. Hannah is a slow learner. I don't know how Jonas puts up with her."

"Mam found a length of lovely blue cotton cloth at Spence's," Anna said. "It will go perfectly with the yellow that Aunt Jezebel showed me. Johanna wants to make a rug for Baby Katie's room."

"Hmmp." Grossmama snorted. "A fine thing, when your mother can go sashshaying off wherever she pleases and leave Jonas without his breakfast." She stabbed another pancake. "I'm going home to Ohio after dinner. The weather here is too cold for my arthritis."

"It was colder at home," Aunt Jezebel reminded her.

"I don't care. I'm going as soon as Jonas hitches up my buggy."

"You haven't even had time to visit with your family, yet," Anna said. "Aunt Alma and Aunt Martha and their families would be disappointed if you went home so soon."

Grossmama belched, pushing away from the table. "Those pancakes are dry as corn husks." She looked at Anna. "Why would I want to see them? Mean-spirited girls, both of them. If Martha smiled once, her back teeth would fall out."

Leah choked back a strangled giggle.

"Come sit in the rocking chair by the window and watch for Johanna, Grossmama," Anna suggested. "You can look at all the pretty snow."

"Nothing pretty about snow," she snapped, slowing rising from the table. "Makes my hands ache."

Anna sighed. There was a lot to do today. She wanted to bake a ham for the evening meal and make cookies for Samuel's children. She hoped that things would get easier with Grossmama after she settled in. Leah and Rebecca had kept her up late last night, telling her tales of their grandmother's outrageous behavior.

Sometimes Grossmama was almost pleasant and sharp in her mind, and the next minute she lost track of reality. According to Leah, Grossmama frequently hid her change purse or her belongings and forgot where she put them. Then she would insist that Aunt Jezebel was stealing from her. And even though Dat had been gone more than two years, Grossmama believed that he was still alive. At first, the sisters had tried gently to remind her of the truth, but Hannah had suggested letting the matter go. With Grossmama's mind as it was, each time she was told her son was dead, it was if she had to relive it all over again. Sometimes an unclear mind could be a blessing, Mam told them.

It hurt Anna when Grossmama said mean things about Mam, when she was always so good to her. The two of them had always rubbed each other like a blister in new leather shoes. Grossmama hadn't wanted Dat to marry Mam because she'd been raised Mennonite.

Ruth said that she doubted anyone would have been good enough to marry Lovina's only son. And Grossmama didn't get along any better with her own daughters. She certainly didn't make her sister, Jezebel's, life easy either, but Anna knew in her heart that there was good in her grandmother. Lovina had a lifetime of wisdom and experience to share, and no one made a finer braided rug.

Anna rested her hand on the back of the rocker as

Grossmama sat down, and she handed her a shawl. It was warm in the kitchen, but the shawl seemed to make Lovina feel safe, so Anna always kept it nearby.

Respect and caring for older people had been ingrained in Anna since she was a small child. She felt deeply that providing food and shelter and medical care wasn't enough. It was important to make Grossmama a part of the household, to show her that she was loved and wanted. The question was—how?

Church was held every other Sunday. This week, Sunday was a day of rest, a day for visiting with friends and family, for reading the Bible and for remembering the blessings that the Lord provided. Leah, Rebecca and Susanna were just clearing away the dishes from the noon meal when Samuel arrived at the kitchen door with his three girls.

"Come in," Mam said. "Anna, look who's here."

Anna offered Samuel a nervous smile. She could feel her face growing hot as Leah gave her a knowing look and Rebecca kicked her ankle under the table. Grossmama and Aunt Jezebel, still seated at the table, stared. Irwin scooped up Jeremiah and fled the kitchen for the back of the house.

"You've come to see Hannah?" Grossmama asked. "Not wise. She's not a good cook."

"Sister," Aunt Jezebel chided. "Hannah is a fine cook."

Lori Ann giggled and Mae pulled off a wet mitten and stuck her thumb in her mouth. Samuel took a deep breath, and his handsome face grew ruddy. "*Ne,* Lovina. I've come to see Anna."

"Anna? Why?" Grossmama asked.

Susanna piped up. "Samuel's courting Anna."

Anna rushed to take the little girls' coats. Samuel hung his on the hook on the back of the kitchen door. "Susanna," Anna said. "There's a new copy of *Family Life* that Naomi might like to read, and maybe you could take Lori Ann and Mae up to the attic and let them play with the Noah's Ark." She looked at Samuel, nervous, but a little excited, too. He'd come to see her, just her. This was one of the ways couples got to know each other when they were courting. And even though she and Samuel weren't courting, the idea caused a flutter in her stomach. "Would you like to sit in the parlor? Irwin made a fire in the stove this morning."

Samuel nodded, and Anna led the way to a small room that was only used when special guests came to call. A high-backed oak bench that had been made in Lancaster more than a hundred years ago, three cane-seat chairs and a larger mahogany Windsor chair were arranged around the cast-iron stove. The walls were a soft cream and the wide chair rail and molding were dove-white. More straight-back chairs lined the wall and the worn plank floor was clean enough to eat off.

On the dark oak table lay Dat's Old German Bible and a newer one belonging to her mother. Other hymnals, Bibles and histories of the Amish martyrs lined the shelves of a simple oak bookcase that Eli had built. Anna opened the interior shutters, so that light poured through the tall windows from Mam's flower garden and motioned Samuel to take the single armchair.

Instead, he pushed the heavy pocket door nearly closed, leaving only a few inches open, for propriety's sake, settled onto the bench and patted the seat beside him. "I think that you could sit beside me, Anna. Your mother, Grossmama and sisters are in the next room."

Hesitantly, she sat where he asked. "We're not doing a very good job of keeping this a secret," she said. Her voice came out so soft that it was a wonder Samuel heard her. Still, it wasn't unpleasant sitting so close to him.

"You don't have to be afraid of me."

"I'm not afraid." That wasn't exactly true. She was afraid, afraid that this would all come to nothing, that her deepest wish might be nothing more than a girl's silly daydreaming. Shivers ran under her skin and her heart raced and skipped.

"I know you asked for more time," Samuel said, "but—"

"Dat! Mae—Mae—Mae wet her pants." Lori Ann squeezed through the opening in the doorway. "She made a—a—a puddle on the floor. Sh-sh-she did."

Samuel started to rise, but Anna halted him with a hand on his arm. "It's nothing, Samuel. You don't have to worry yourself over a child's accident."

He relaxed, giving a hesitant smile. "Usually I do."

"Not here. We're used to such things." She waved to Lori Ann. "Ask Mam to come if Susanna can't find dry clothes for her." The little girl nodded and dashed off. Anna looked back into Samuel's face, thinking again how big he was, how handsome. "This is your day of rest, too. You should make the best of it."

He smiled and nodded. "Being with you is restful, Anna." He hesitated. "I… I told Roman," he admitted.

"Oh." She exhaled slowly.

"He's my friend. I wanted him to know that we were thinking of…" He reached for her hand and cradled it in his broad one. "I wanted him to know that I'd asked to court you—that I want you to be my wife."

Anna closed her eyes, savoring the warmth of his touch. She hoped that Samuel wouldn't think she was fast. Handholding was allowed between couples that were walking out together, which they weren't, but Samuel seemed so sure. And, as he had said, her mother was nearby. Her throat constricted. She wanted to ask what Roman had thought, but the words wouldn't come. Instead, she breathed in the clean male scent of Samuel, picturing in her mind him forking hay and hitching up the horse. All her life, she'd felt too big. Next to Samuel, she didn't seem nearly as tall or broad.

"Anna, I think maybe we—"

The door scraped against the floor. There was the tap-tap of Grossmama's cane, and the old woman shuffled into the room, followed by Aunt Jezebel. Grossmama stared at them for a long minute, then took a chair near the stove, directly across from Samuel and Anna, and blew her nose loudly on a big handkerchief.

"Sister wanted to join you," Aunt Jezebel said apologetically, as she took a seat in one of the cane chairs. "She insisted."

"You courting my Anna?" Grossmama demanded.

"*Ya,*" Samuel answered. He released Anna's hand and she tucked it safely under her apron. She saw by Aunt Jezebel's expression that she'd noticed, but Anna wasn't certain that Grossmama had seen them holding hands.

"*Ne,*" Anna said. "Maybe. We're not sure."

Her grandmother ignored her and looked hard at Samuel. "Good. She's a good girl. Make you a good wife." She frowned and blew her nose again. "But first you ask my Jonas for permission. Ask her father. My son."

A furrow appeared between Samuel's brows, and he glanced at Anna in confusion. Anna's eyes widened and she nodded.

"I will," he said.

"Is right. Proper," Grossmama said. "My Jonas is a bishop. He has a good farm. *Ya?*"

Samuel nodded. "A very good farm."

"Do you have a job?" Grossmama asked. "Do you work hard? Let me see your hands."

Dutifully, Samuel got up, walked over to her and held out his hands. Grossmama stared.

"Turn them over." When he did as he was told, the old woman nodded. "Strong hands. Not lazy hands. Is a good man, Anna. You take him." Grossmama twisted to look at Aunt Jezebel. "Well, are you going to read to me or not? I can't find my glasses. I think Hannah took them."

"I don't believe Mam took your glasses," Anna said, rising to her feet. She walked to Samuel and whispered, "This isn't going to work. Let's go back in the kitchen."

"What?" Grossmama demanded. She peered at Samuel. "He doesn't work? No good. How will he feed your babies?"

Anna felt a flush start at her chest and flash over her neck and face. Her cheeks were burning as she motioned toward the door. "Kitchen," she begged Samuel. And then to Grossmama she said, "Samuel has the farm behind ours. Where the school is. Fine fields and a big herd of milk cows. He can provide for a family."

"My Jonas is milking the cows," she replied. "Go ask him now, young man. It's only right."

Anna fled the room with Samuel on her heels. "Grossmama thinks—" she began when they were safely in the next room with the sliding pocket door closed behind them.

"Is all right. I have a great uncle who thinks he is married to two women." Samuel chuckled. "He's a hundred and two."

"Is he?" Anna asked. "Married to two women?"

"Uncle Jay? He was married four times, but all of them have passed on." His grin grew wider. "He insists he's married to his preacher's wife and an English woman who keeps the corner store."

"She doesn't mean harm," Anna explained, standing in the hall beside him. "Dat was her only son. I think it's easier for her to let her go on thinking he's still alive."

"Your grossmama doesn't frighten me," he said. "I like her. And she's a smart woman. She said I would be a good husband for you."

"I have not said yes, Samuel."

"But you will." He reached for her hand and she put it behind her. "It's just a matter of time. We will stand before the church together, Anna."

"We'll see about that." Her stomach felt as though she'd eaten an entire shoo-fly pie and then rolled down Charley's father's steep hill. Breathless, she led the way into the kitchen where Mam, Rebecca, Leah and Samuel's three girls were baking cookies. Irwin sat on the floor near the stove, pulling an empty spool on a string of yarn for Jeremiah to chase. Irwin had used a pen to make eyes on the spool, hoping the little terrier would take the toy for a mouse.

"Not much chance to talk alone with her, is there?" Mam asked with a chuckle. Samuel shook his head.

"Maybe the two of you should walk across the field to Ruth and Eli's. Visit with them. I'm sure Ruth has the coffeepot on and they'd appreciate the company."

"It would be nice to visit with Ruth and Eli and Miriam and Charley," Samuel agreed. "But I'm not sure I should drop in with all my girls."

Naomi laid the cookbook on the table and glanced back at her father. Her glasses were smudged with flour, but she was smiling. "We're making sugar cookies, Dat. They aren't ready yet, but Hannah said we could take them home."

"Why don't you go on?" Leah said. "We'll watch them. It will give the two of you a chance to talk."

"Alone." Rebecca giggled. "Since you're courting."

"We *aren't* courting," Anna corrected.

Samuel shrugged. "I'm courting her. We're just waiting to see if she—"

"You should take her to the taffy pulling at Johanna's Wednesday night," Leah suggested excitedly. "Anna's never had a fellow take her to a young people's get-together."

"Taffy pulling?" Samuel looked unconvinced. "Will it be all the younger folk?"

"Oh, Samuel, I meant to ask," Anna said, all in a rush. Suddenly she wanted to go to the frolic, and she wanted to go with him. "I would like that."

"Then it's settled," Leah said, clapping her hands together. "Anna should have fun, and you can always just watch, Samuel, if you don't want to pull taffy."

Mam was handing Samuel his coat. "Now you two go on. It's broad daylight. You can certainly walk to Anna's sister's house without causing talk in the neighborhood."

Samuel nodded. "If you're sure the girls won't be a trouble."

"The girls will be fine. I'm sure Charley will want to show off those new animals he bought at the auction. And you and Eli always get on well together."

"Anna?" Samuel looked at her, accepting his coat. "Do you want to walk to your sister's? It's cold out, and your feet—"

"I would like that, Samuel," Anna interrupted happily. "And I have new boots. I'm not afraid of a little snow."

Soon, the two of them were crossing the farmyard. Samuel's horse looked up from the shelter of the shed and whinnied. "I'll be back for you," he promised the animal.

"See you in an hour or so," Mam called from the porch.

Samuel waved and then he slowed his steps so that Anna could keep up. "I never thought this courting stuff would be so hard," he confided to her.

"Because you are older than me?" she asked.

He shook his head, stuffing his hands into the pockets of his sturdy denim coat. "Because I've never done it before. My mother and father and Frieda's parents arranged my marriage. We didn't have to sit in the parlor across from old grandmothers or go to taffy pulls."

She felt a stab of disappointment. "You don't want to go. It's all right. We don't have to—"

"Ne." He stopped and faced her. "We will go. You deserve to do these things, Anna. If this is going to work, we'll both have to make compromises. If you can, I can."

"Compromises." She sighed. "We need to make compromises."

"And I will keep praying. As I told Roman, if God wants this match, nothing can keep us apart."

Nothing but me, Anna thought, as all her old fears and feelings of inadequacy bubbled up inside her.

He looped her arm through his and they began to walk side-by-side down the lane. "You're the woman for me, Anna Yoder," he continued. "And I'll do whatever I have to, so that you will see the right of it."

Chapter Ten

Wednesday night's taffy pulling at Johanna's was every bit as uncomfortable for Samuel as he thought it would be. Giggling teenage girls and immature boys, like Elmer Beachy and Harvey Bontrager, did their best to attract attention with silly pranks and jokes. Donald Zook shook a bottle of soda pop and sprayed two of the girls, causing shrieks, and dashed around the kitchen, making Johanna threaten him with expulsion from the frolic if he didn't behave.

There were only a few young women of Anna's age. Leah, Rebecca, Miriam, Ruth and Susanna were present, but Ruth and Miriam were both married. Anna's cousin Dorcas was older than Anna, but she seemed no more an adult than the sixteen-year-olds. Although Samuel enjoyed every bite of the homemade donuts Anna brought, the entire candy-making evening seemed more suited to fun for his children than for teenagers.

It was little wonder that Samuel felt out of place. After all, he was a deacon of the church and an authority figure. It was obvious that the young people didn't want him here anymore than he wanted to be here. But

Anna didn't seem to notice that the kids were obviously subdued by his presence. She appeared to be having a good time, and that was why he had come. Why she'd wanted to be here, he didn't know. She seemed a woman grown next to these kids.

According to custom, Samuel hadn't brought her to the taffy pull, she'd come with her sisters. Usually, girls traveled to singings and frolics with their family members or friends. And if a boy asked a girl and she liked him, the two would quietly slip out of the house and ride home together.

Some Amish parents were liberal. Once they reached the girl's house, the pair might be allowed to sit up late in the parlor, talking or playing Dutch Blitz or other approved games. These dates were much less serious than courting, and were considered an accepted part of social life for those in their late teens.

Samuel was glad that he'd have a few more years with his own children before they entered their *running around* period. Other, more liberal churches allowed their young people a time of *Rumspringa,* when they were expected to experience some of the loose behavior of the English world. That was not the case here in Kent County. Thankfully, the bishops, preachers and congregation agreed that such freedom opened their children to too many dangers.

But as for himself, he was thirty-seven, a mature man with a family and responsibilities. And sitting at Johanna's table with buttered hands pulling taffy with Anna was a far distance from where he wanted to be. He'd long outgrown the taste for moon pies and popcorn balls, let alone the sweet bottled grape soda the kids seemed to favor.

Samuel wondered if he'd have been wiser to have simply refused to come. And for the first time, a small doubt crept into his mind. Maybe courting a younger woman would be more of a task than he'd thought. Would Anna expect him to keep her company at the young people's singings and game nights?

He wondered if Hannah would allow him to come in and spend time alone with Anna tonight—provided there was any privacy in the Yoder household. He wanted to relax, to talk over his day with Anna, to just sit and look at her without being watched and judged by her family. He had liked the feel of her smaller, warm hand in his, and he longed to put his arm around her and sit beside her with her head on his shoulder. He wanted to inhale the scent of her hair and stare into her beautiful cinnamon-colored eyes. Oh, he was smitten, no doubt about it. He wanted to take Anna as his wife. But so far she'd kept him hanging, and the longer she hesitated to give him an answer, the greater his feelings for her grew.

As soon as Anna's pieces of taffy were stretched thin enough to suit her and were ready for cutting, Samuel excused himself and went out to the barn. Johanna's husband was there in his workshop, and Samuel thought that he could better spend his time having a long-needed discussion with Wilmer. Wilmer worked long hours on his construction job and often was away for days at a time. Although working close to home was best, Samuel couldn't fault the man for providing for Johanna and their two small children.

As he approached the workshop, Samuel caught the smell of tobacco. Wilmer had originally come from Kentucky, where some of the Amish still grew tobacco as a cash crop. Again, Samuel didn't want to judge. He'd experimented with smoking a pipe as a young man before he joined the church, but the practice was generally frowned upon. His role in the community as a deacon was as advisor and counselor, but he couldn't insist that Wilmer give up his cigars. That was between Wilmer and his conscience.

"Run you out, did they?" Wilmer looked up from the chain saw he'd been oiling. "Never expected you to last this long with those crazy kids."

"I feel a lot more at ease here in the barn," Samuel agreed.

"Bunch of nonsense, I say, but Johanna would have it."

"You know how young folks are. They need a little clean fun now and then. And Johanna and her sisters are a good example for the girls."

Wilmer grunted and reached for his half-smoked cigar. He took a long puff and blew smoke through his nose. "I'd offer you a stogie, but I don't suppose you use tobacco."

"I gave it up a long time ago," Samuel answered. "Never missed it either."

"Well, to each his own, I suppose." Wilmer waved toward an overturned peach basket and Samuel sat down on it. "'Spose you're courting one of those Yoder girls. Can't figure any other reason you'd be out on such a cold night."

"I've a mind to have Anna."

"Anna?"

"*Ya,* Anna. We suit each other."

Wilmer made a sound of disapproval. "You'd do well to stay away from any of them, if you ask me. Hannah's too liberal. She spoiled the lot of them, and Jonas—when he was alive—wasn't much better. They don't know their proper place. Too mouthy for womenfolk."

"Not that I've seen. Hannah's always seemed sensible to me. She does a good job with her farm, and the school's never had a better teacher."

"That's what I'm talkin' about. The bishop shouldn't allow it. A widow's got no business workin' outside the house. She ought to have enough to do at home."

"She needs the salary from teaching to help support her family," Samuel defended.

Wilmer snorted. "Should have remarried…long ago. The Bible says that a man is the head of the house. You know what I think? I think Hannah Yoder likes fillin' a man's shoes. She wasn't born Old Order, you know. Raised Mennonite. She's not Plain, and never will be as far as I can see."

Samuel shifted on his basket. Talking about Hannah like this wasn't right, but Wilmer was family and he wasn't. Not yet, at least. Still, he didn't like what Wilmer had to say. He was beginning to think he was more uncomfortable in the barn than in the kitchen. He needed to turn the conversation to Wilmer, and he needed to do it without offending him. "Hannah is outspoken, that's true," he admitted, "but we've never had a cross word, and she's been good to my kids."

"You're not careful, she'll let them run as wild as she does Jonah when he's at her place. My girl, now, Katy, she's a sweet baby, but Johanna and her mother will ruin Jonah, given half a chance."

Samuel knew Wilmer and Johanna's boy, a sturdy, ginger-haired lad, somewhere between the age of his own Mae and Lori Ann. The child had always been

well behaved at church services, which was more than
he could say for his own kids. Maybe if Wilmer had
to father Rudy and Peter for a few weeks, he wouldn't
be so quick to fault little Jonah. But Jonah was Wilmer's boy, and telling a man he was too hard on his own
child wouldn't make Wilmer any more likely to hear
what else he had to say.

A single kerosene lantern gave off a yellow, wavering circle of light. Samuel noted that the bench was littered with tools and wire and bits of this and that. He
hadn't been in Wilmer's shop in two years, but it had
been a lot neater then. Wilmer had a lot of expensive
saws and woodworking equipment, but careless treatment had left many rusting and gathering dust.

"We missed you at services the last two church Sundays," Samuel said.

Wilmer concentrated on wiping the grease off his
chain saw with a dirty rag. "Had something more important to do."

"Nothing is more important than worship, Wilmer. If
your spirit's heavy, it's best to go and talk to someone."

"You?"

"Me. One of the elders, or maybe our bishop. Atlee's
a sensible man with the gift of sharing the Holy Word.
There's nothing you carry in your heart that can't be
eased by the Lord."

Noodle Troyer had told Samuel that he'd seen Wilmer
coming out of a package store last Sunday with a bottle
of what could only be spirits. And word was that some
had seen Wilmer driving his horse and buggy home
from Dover after dark on a work night in less than a
sober state. Samuel didn't want to mention the alcohol.
If Wilmer had a drinking problem, it was more than

a deacon could handle. It would take the preachers, Bishop Atlee and the elders to help him. But the matter of Wilmer not attending church services, that was Samuel's responsibility.

Wilmer turned to give him a long stare. "Sometimes a man has worries that plague him like mange on a dog. No matter how hard you try to ease it, the itch is still there."

"All the more reason to take it to the Lord in prayer," Samuel said. "And to reach out to the church elders for help. None of us can make it through the trials of this world alone."

"Easy for you to say, Samuel. Farm the size of yours, big herd of milk cows. You've always been a lucky man. Not me. I work hard, but everything I touch turns to empty husks."

"How can you say that? You've got a good wife, two healthy children, steady work and a community that cares about you."

Wilmer's eyes narrowed. "You notice the color of my baby girl's hair?"

"Brown?" Samuel didn't know what Wilmer was getting at.

"Real dark, dark like mine. And the boy's hair is red."

"Like Johanna's. All the Yoder girls are gingers like their father."

"Umm." Wilmer grunted again and turned back to his chain saw. There was silence for a few minutes until he glanced back. "She had to have one of those C-sections when Jonah was born. Where they cut the woman open to get the baby out. I expect I'll be paying off that bill until he's old enough to start school."

Samuel remembered Johanna's emergency delivery.

Since their people carried no insurance, like the English did, the church had rallied to help the young family with the expense of Jonah's medical bills. They'd held breakfasts and suppers and even a benefit auction. At the time, Samuel thought that the majority of the bill had been paid.

Maybe he was wrong. If it was money trouble that was worrying Wilmer, that was something that the community could do something about. Samuel would take it up with the bishop when next he saw him. Whether it was help for a barn raising or illness, the members of the church joined hands to assist their own.

"I'm sorry to hear that you're having a hard time," Samuel said. "You should have spoke up sooner." He stood up. The frolic would be winding down, and he wanted to get back in to Anna. "The church is here for you. I'm here for you."

"Are you?" Wilmer's tone was flat. "Heard you're killing hogs next week. If you want to help, send over one. My smokehouse is as empty as last summer's jelly jars."

"A pig?" Samuel nodded. "I'll be glad to let you have one. I'll send the boys over with the meat right after butchering."

"Obliged."

As Samuel walked away, he wondered why Wilmer's request made him uneasy. The gift of a hog to a neighbor in need was something that he'd done before without a moment's hesitation. Was it that he'd never particularly taken to Johanna's husband? The Bible said to love thy neighbor, but even a devout man couldn't be expected to like everyone. And he certainly didn't begrudge Johanna and the children a stock of winter's meat. He'd donate the pig and a front quarter of beef to the family, and he'd pray for Wilmer as well.

"He don't look nothin' like my girl," Wilmer called after him. "The boy. Jonah. Not like any of my kin."

Samuel shook his head and walked on. It wouldn't hurt to ask the Lord for a change in his own attitude. He needed patience and he needed to be more charitable.

Inside Johanna's house, Dorcas followed Anna into the bathroom and closed the door. The two washed the sticky candy off their hands, reached for the towel at the same time and laughed. "Share and share alike," Anna said.

"Are you riding home with him?" Dorcas asked in a low voice. On the far side of the door they heard one of the Beachy girls teasing Harvey and giggling.

"With who?"

"Who do you think? Samuel. That big barn of a man you had pulling taffy with you."

"*Ya,*" Anna admitted. "I like him, Dorcas. I like him a lot."

"I know you do," Dorcas whispered. "But it still worries me. I'm sorry that Mam did what she did, going to his house. She deserved what the twins did to her. Sometimes I'd like to do worse."

Anna had to work hard not to smile. "I think she means well."

"Maybe, but it doesn't seem like it to me." Dorcas hung up the towel. "She told Samuel that I'd be a better match for him—right in front of me. I could have sunk through your mother's kitchen floor."

Anna put her arm around Dorcas and hugged her. "Samuel would know it didn't come from you."

"I wouldn't want this to come between us, Anna. Even if you do marry him."

"It won't. You're my best friend and you always will be."

Dorcas nodded. "I still think this is a bad idea."

Anna swallowed, trying to dissolve the lump in her throat. "But you said…you said you'd jump at the chance to have someone like Samuel. Why shouldn't I let him court me if he really wants to? It would be wonderful, living close to Mam and my sisters, having my own home…taking care of Samuel and his family."

Someone banged on the bathroom door. "Just a minute," Dorcas said. She grabbed Anna's hand and squeezed it. "Do you think Samuel fit in here tonight?"

Anna's shook her head. "Not really. It was easy to see that he wanted to get away. Most everyone here is too young for him."

"Exactly. So why would he pick you? Have you thought that maybe he's still in love with his wife, that he's only asked you so he'll have someone to take her place, someone who's willing to work hard…and…"

"And what?" Anna asked. She'd been having such a good time tonight. She knew that Samuel had only come to please her. She was looking forward to having him drive her home in his buggy, maybe asking him in for coffee and a slice of her chocolate pie. But Dorcas's doubts brought her own back. Maybe her cousin was right. "You may as well say it all."

Dorcas took a deep breath. "What if he's marrying you because he knows he could never really love you? If he wants a companion, but not a wife in that way? If he thinks of you as…well, a sister?"

"A sister?" Anna bit her bottom lip. "You think Samuel thinks of me as a sister?" Suddenly a black hole seemed to open below her feet. "I…didn't think that a man like Samuel would ever want me," she murmured. "But he wouldn't take no for an answer. I prayed over it, and it seemed to me that it was the right thing to consider his offer."

"So you don't care *why* he wants to marry you?"

"Hurry up in there," came a boy's voice. "I drank three sodas."

"You hush that talk," Dorcas hollered. "We'll be done when we're done."

"Of course I care," Anna whispered. "I don't think of him as a brother." Had she been fooling herself? Anna turned back and looked into the small mirror, and the same, round pudding face stared back. *Why would he want a fat girl?* How did she know if this was the way it was done…how Samuel would act if he really cared for her? She'd never been courted before. "He tried to hold my hand on Sunday."

"Doesn't mean anything. Friends hold hands."

"Not men and women friends."

"Did you let him?"

"Ne." Anna choked on the lie. *"Ya,* but just for a minute."

"Hmm." Dorcas folded her arms over her chest. "I don't know what that means. Maybe he does like you." But Anna didn't think Dorcas sounded convinced. "Is he driving you home?"

"I think so. He hasn't asked me yet."

"Dorcas!"

"We'd better go," Anna said.

"Tell me everything tomorrow. Then we can decide what to do." Dorcas opened the door and Elmer Beachy rushed past them into the bathroom.

What do you mean "we"? Anna thought as they re-joined the others in the kitchen. She valued her cousin's advice, but Dorcas had never been courted either. This was all too confusing. If Johanna didn't have a house-ful, she might have asked for her guidance. Ruth and Miriam had both recently courted and married, but they hadn't married older men, as Johanna had. Actually, the difference between Johanna and Wilmer wasn't as great as that between her and Samuel, but Johanna might have some good ideas. She would listen to everything Anna had to say and give her opinion. And she didn't care if it was what you wanted to hear or not. Next to Mam, Johanna gave the best advice. And Anna really needed some. She'd been about to tell Samuel he could court her, and now she was more in a quandary than ever.

Chapter Eleven

A half hour later, Anna found herself bundled into Samuel's buggy with a sheepskin robe over her lap, riding down Johanna's driveway. Her sisters, just ahead of them, turned left toward home. Samuel guided the horse right.

"Where are you going?" Anna asked him. "Home is that way."

Samuel chuckled. "I think I know where you live." He grinned boyishly at her in the light of the carriage lamps. "The rules say that I'm supposed to drive my girl home. They don't say what route I have to take to get there."

"Mam won't be pleased," Anna ventured. Sitting beside him was wonderful, but the doubts and fears that Dorcas had raised made her apprehensive. She wanted to come right out and ask Samuel if this was a courting of convenience, or something more…but she couldn't be that bold. And if he said that he thought of her as a good companion and nothing more, she couldn't stand it.

Anna's stomach churned. She shouldn't have eaten that second popcorn ball or the whoopie pie. She should have stuck to the apple and celery slices that everyone was dipping in peanut butter. No wonder she was so fat and ugly. She always had a good appetite. And what man wanted a wife who could lift a hundred-pound bag of calf feed? She sank back on the seat and clutched the bag of taffy she was saving for Samuel's children.

"Are you going to invite me in when we get to your house?" he asked.

She didn't know. She hadn't decided yet. Instead of answering his question, she thrust the bag of candy toward him. "For your kids," she said.

"Danke." He took the taffy and thrust it into a compartment under the seat. "It's thoughtful of you. They love sweets. Homemade are best. They always beg for candies at Byler's store, but I don't buy much. I don't want them to have bad teeth."

Anna nodded. This was a much safer subject. *"Ya.* You are a wise father. You should see what some of the children bring to school in their lunch pails. Mam can't believe it. Cans of soda pop. Candy bars and potato chips. Not what she packed for us when we went there."

"Sandwiches and apples?"

"Sometimes. Usually cheese or meat, whatever she had on hand. Always fruit. And in the winter we had thermoses of hot soup. Mam was big on soup and raw vegetables. I ate so many carrots when I was little that it's a wonder my ears didn't grow like a rabbit's."

"But you have nice teeth. White. Even. I always liked your teeth."

In spite of herself, Anna felt a little shiver of excitement run through her. *He liked her teeth.* She'd always brushed after the noon meal, as well as night and morning. Mam was in her forties, but she still had all of her own teeth and not a single filling. Anna wanted to be like her when she was old, and she hoped it wasn't *Hockmut* to be proud of her smile. "Mam always took us to the dentist to have our teeth cleaned."

"That's important." He shook the lines over the horse's back and the stocky Morgan turned off the blacktop road onto a dirt lane that ran through Stutzman's woods.

"Oh." Anna swallowed. Trees closed over their heads, shutting out the pale winter sky. Some of the trees were pine, others hardwood. The oak and maple leaves had fallen, and the bare branches looked like ghostly fingers. "I don't like driving this way at night."

"You'll be fine. I'd never let anything or anyone harm you, Anna. Smoky's a good horse. He may not be as fancy-stepping as some of those thoroughbred pacers, but he knows his business."

Anna glanced from the scary trees to the Morgan, noting that Samuel had covered the horse's back with a warm, quilted blanket. Not everyone thought of their animals on such a cold winter night, and it pleased her that Samuel cared about Smoky's comfort as well as hers. He was a kindhearted man…a good man. But could they be happy together?

Even in the shadowy darkness, she could see how handsome Samuel was. Among the Plain People, looks weren't supposed to matter, but you rarely saw a good-looking man with a wife who had a face like hers. "Like to like," as Aunt Martha was fond of saying. "The Lord didn't mean for an apple tree and a paw-paw to make fruit."

Anna sighed. If Samuel was an apple tree, he'd be a Jonathan or a Yellow Delicious, and she was certainly

a paw-paw—big and shapeless, without much taste.
But still, a paw-paw could enjoy the sunshine and the
rain, too, couldn't it? Why couldn't she savor every moment of this night? What would it hurt to pretend that
Samuel was her beau? That he *did* love her, and that
he had chosen her above any other girl in the county
because he wanted her to be his wife in every way the
Lord intended?

The buggy wheels squeaked and squished in the
snow. The harness creaked and Smoky huffed and
puffed, sending plumes of white into the air in front
of his head. The woods smelled wonderful: all ever-
green, fresh and wintery. In some ways, the dark lane
was scary, but in others it was wonderful. With Samuel
beside her so tall and strong, what could hurt her? In
spite of what she'd said to Samuel earlier, she was now
glad he had taken the buggy this way. No matter what
happened, she would have this night to remember…the
night when, for a little while, she belonged to Samuel
and he belonged to her.

"I wanted to ask you," he said in his quiet way, "to
do me a favor."

"Anything."

"I have to go away on Friday. There's a farm auction
over to Sudlersville. I thought to take the boys, but after
what they did to your Aunt Martha, they don't deserve
a day off from school. Me and another fellow, we have
a ride in a van, but now I need someone to watch the
kids. Naomi and the twins will be in school, but I was
wondering if you would mind coming to the house and
staying with the little ones?"

Something rustled in the bushes. Unconsciously,
Anna slid closer to Samuel. "Of course I will," she said.

"I'll be glad to. I promised Grossmama to take her to Byler's in the afternoon, but if it's all right with you, I can take the two girls along."

It was easier for her when they talked about homey things like the children. She could almost shut out the feeling that the space between them was charged in the same way the air felt before a lightning strike.

"To Byler's." He snorted. "Those two could have the walls down around you, if they take a mind to."

"They will not," she said firmly, aghast at the very idea. "My sisters are going, and Leah can be quite firm. I think she learned it taking care of Grossmama."

"Fine by me if they go, if you think you can handle them. It will take a load off my mind having you keep them for the day. I hear there's a small horse-drawn cultivator for sale, and it will be just the right size for Rudy and Peter."

There was a comfortable silence between them for perhaps five minutes. That was a nice thing about Samuel, Anna thought. They could ride along without talking and feel at ease. He wasn't like Charley, who always had to be explaining something or asking questions or telling jokes, and he certainly wasn't like any of the silly boys who'd been at Johanna's tonight. Dorcas had called him a big barn of a man, and it fit. He was solid and dependable, not exciting, but real. She liked him, a lot, but she didn't know if that was love she was feeling. She wanted the joy that she saw in Miriam's eyes every time she looked at her new husband, Charley.

Something about what Samuel had said about the boys not deserving to have a day off and go to the auction tugged at her thoughts. "What about Naomi?" she said, almost without realizing she'd said it out loud.

"Naomi? What about her?" Samuel sounded surprised.

"Maybe she'd like to go with you. To the auction."

"A girl? What would Naomi do at an auction?"

"Follow you around. Have you buy her lunch. Spend special time with her father. Naomi works hard. She takes care of her little sisters. She tries to keep the house clean."

"Keep her out of school?"

"You were going to take the twins out for the day, and Naomi gets all A's on her report card. She's at the top of her class. She deserves a reward."

"I doubt there'll be any other girls her age there."

"But *you'll* be there. You don't love her any less than Peter and Rudy, do you?"

"Ne." Samuel raised his voice. "Of course, not. Why would you say such a thing?"

Anna lowered her head so that he couldn't see her smile. "I know that you love all of your children equally, but it's important that *they* know it—especially your daughters. And giving Naomi a special outing would make her happy."

"You don't approve of the way I raise my children?"

"Ya, Samuel, I do. I don't know of a better father." *Other than my own,* she thought, but didn't say. "You must do what you think right. It's only that…"

"Only what?"

She made her own voice soft and coaxing. "That a man has so many things on his mind, he may not remember what pleases a girlchild." Her father had always taken one of his daughters with him whenever he went somewhere, even if it was a trip to the dentist. And in a household of seven children, those special times with him stayed in her mind like treasures. "You know your Naomi best, Samuel, but I think she would like it."

"And other men? What would they think if I drag a girl along?"

Anna chuckled. "I think they will shake their heads and smile and hold their opinions, because I doubt few men would care to remark on what you do with your own children."

"Few men. But you would."

"I'm only a woman. My mind is on house and children. And I know that if you want to court me, you would have a woman who will speak her mind to you, not one who will bob her head like a nanny goat and say '*Ya,* Samuel, *ya.* Whatever you say.'"

He laughed. "I think there is more to you than I expected, Anna Yoder."

"More bad or more good?" she dared.

"That—" he smiled "—I'm sure, I'll find out."

As Samuel drove the horse and buggy into the yard, he saw that the only lights visible were those in the kitchen and a single kerosene lamp in an upstairs window. "Someone's up late," he said, pointing to the second floor.

"*Ne,*" Anna replied. "That's for me. Whenever one of us is away, we keep a lamp burning to welcome them home."

"Your sisters were in Ohio for most of a year. Did you leave a light in the window every night for them?"

Anna smiled in the darkness. "A Christmas candle that ran on batteries. Plastic. Susanna was in charge of replacing the batteries when they started to lose their power. She did a good job."

"I like that. It must make you feel good inside that someone would do such a thing." He climbed down and helped her out. The ride home hadn't gone as he'd expected. He'd enjoyed being alone with Anna, but she hadn't let him hold her hand. He'd been hoping for a kiss, but that wasn't going to happen either, so long as she hadn't agreed to seriously consider his proposal. "Are you going to ask me in?"

"*Ya.* I am. It's cold out here, and you need a cup of hot coffee before you start home. But we can only visit a little while. You have to be up early, and it's too nasty a night to keep Smoky standing out here."

"I thought I'd put him in the barn, out of the wind. I've a feed bag in the back. He can have some oats, although I'm sure he'd drink coffee if I offered it to him."

Samuel waited until Anna was safely on the porch before tending to Smoky. When he stomped his snowy boots off on the mat, shrugged off his coat and came into the warm kitchen a few moments later, he was enveloped by the odor of fresh coffee. Three mugs and a generous slice of pie waited on the table. Inwardly, he groaned. Seated at the end of the table was Anna's great aunt, Jezebel. Obviously, he and Anna would not be allowed to enjoy each other's company in private.

"Did you two enjoy your taffy pull?" Jezebel waved Samuel to the high-backed seat at the head of the table.

Samuel nodded and sat down.

"It was fun," Anna agreed. "Did the girls get home safe?"

"Your sisters? *Ya.* They went up to bed, seeing as how late it is." She pushed her glasses up off her nose and peered at Anna with a glint in her eyes. "Samuel's horse must be lame. It took the two of you a lot longer to come from Johanna's than it took your sisters."

"Oh, we came a different way," Anna said. "By the dirt lane." She glanced at Samuel. He was staring into his coffee cup and stirring hard with his spoon.

Her aunt nodded. "That explains it then. I took a long buggy ride or two in my day." She smiled and Anna smiled back, a little relieved Aunt Jezzy wasn't upset with her for dawdling with Samuel.

"Hannah, is she asleep?" Samuel took another forkful of the pie.

"Sound asleep," Aunt Jezebel said. "I'm the only night owl, beside you two youngsters. Thought I'd sit up and see how your evening was."

"I liked the candy making." Anna sat down at the table. "But some of the kids were silly, spraying soda pop and playing catch with popcorn balls. Johanna had to threaten to send some of the boys home early to get them to behave."

"And how did you put up with all that nonsense?" Aunt Jezebel looked pointedly at Samuel. He was scraping the last crumbs off the plate and washing them down with coffee.

"Anna wanted to go, so we went," he mumbled through a mouthful of pie. "It wasn't bad."

"I know just what you're thinking." The little woman peered at him through her glasses. "You're wondering why I'm still up and keeping you from visiting with Anna."

Anna was afraid of what to think her great aunt might say next.

Samuel started to protest, but Aunt Jezebel silenced him by simply raising a tiny hand. "You're thinking it's not fair," she said, "that most of those boys got to drive a girl home and sit with her in her house in privacy. I have to say what I have to say about the two of you courting and then you won't hear any more from me on the matter, either of you."

"We're not courting," Anna protested. "At least, not yet."

"I'm courting," Samuel said. "She's the one who's undecided."

"Then it's good I say this now." Aunt Jezebel toyed with her own cup, turning it around and around. Anna knew her aunt was fond of spinning things; she usually made three circles before she was satisfied. "I know you might think we're being overprotective of Anna. Maybe watching over her closer than her sisters might have been watched." She tapped a finger on the table. Three times. "I don't want you to take it personal, Samuel, but it's because you are a man grown, and in some ways Anna is still innocent."

Anna felt her face flame. She stared at her lap, rolling the hem of her apron into a tight ball. Was Aunt Jezebel really making a reference to what went on between a man and a wife in the privacy of their bedroom?

"Where you are used to living a married life," Aunt Jezebel continued, "our Anna is a good girl. We trust her."

"I'd never do anything to harm Anna or shame her, Jezebel. You need to know that about me."

Aunt Jezebel's pale blue eyes took on a piercing expression that Anna had never seen before. "I can see you'd never *intentionally* do anything to hurt our Anna, but we know that you are human, as are we all. We are frail, sometimes weak. And the call of the flesh can be strong."

Samuel nodded. "That's true enough, I suppose."

"Sanctioned by marriage, physical love is a beautiful thing," Aunt Jezebel continued, "or so the preachers tell me. I never married myself. It wasn't God's plan for me. But Anna's mother and her family would not be doing their job to protect her if they—if *we* weren't careful."

"I understand," Samuel said. "But like I said, you have nothing to worry about in me. I've nothing but honorable intentions concerning Anna."

"Good. Glad we've got that said between us." Aunt Jezebel hit the table lightly three times with the palm of her hand, and then motioned to Anna. "Now fetch Samuel another piece of pie and refill his coffee cup. He has a cold drive home, and he'll need to fortify himself."

"No need," Samuel said, rising. "As you say, it's late. I should go."

Anna walked to the porch with him. "You mustn't mind Aunt Jezebel," she said softly, so Aunt Jezebel couldn't hear her. "She's old-fashioned and—"

"She was fine," Samuel said. "She was just trying to make it clear that your family cares about you and wants what's best for you. I didn't mind." He smiled at her. "Even if I did hope to steal a kiss tonight."

Anna took a step back and pulled her father's old coat closer around her shoulders. "You'll get no kisses from me until we're joined in marriage—if we are. I'm still not at peace in my heart about this, Samuel. I'm honored by your asking, but..."

"Did you have fun tonight?"

"In spite of everything?" she asked, glancing back

over her shoulder at the kitchen. "Even after this *talk* with Aunt Jezebel?" She dared a little smile. "I did."

"Good. Then that's where we'll leave it for now. Don't let me rush you into a decision you're not sure of. Stand your ground, Anna. I like it when you do."

"All right," she promised.

"You'll still be able to watch the children on Friday for me?"

"*Ya*. I will. Count on it. I'll come over early." She hesitated. "Will you think about taking Naomi with you?"

He smiled and shrugged. "Once you get a thing in your head, you're as stubborn as your mother. I'll think about it."

She offered him a shy smile, went back into the kitchen and closed the door firmly behind her. Inside, she found that Aunt Jezebel had already gone to bed, so she blew out the lamp and made her way up the staircase to her bedroom. The truth was, she wanted Samuel Mast for her husband. She wanted him more than anything in the world...but she still wasn't convinced that she deserved him.

Chapter Twelve

On Friday morning, Anna, Leah and Grossmama arrived at Samuel's at 7:00 a.m., just as Samuel was preparing to get into a gray van driven by an Englisher who Anna recognized. "Morning, Samuel," she called. "Morning, Rodger."

Leah reined in the horse and Samuel turned to smile at them. "You're here bright and early."

Anna saw that there were other Amish already in the van, three men and two women. Only one was a member of their church, but she knew them all, and she waved to them as well. "Told you we would be here early," Anna replied. *How fine Samuel looks,* she thought with a little thrill. Properly Plain, of course, but well dressed in solid boots, a new wool hat and a heavy coat. He looked like what he was—a solid and prosperous farmer.

Samuel walked over to the buggy. "The boys are finishing up morning chores, but the little ones are still abed. Mae had us up three times last night, with those bad dreams of hers. Screaming fit to bring the roof down. And when you wake her, she just cries and cries. Hope she's not a handful for you today."

"You go enjoy the auction," Anna assured him. "I'll look after the children."

"Don't let them burn down the house," he cautioned.

Leah chuckled. "We won't."

Samuel returned to the van, opened its sliding door, raised his thumb and forefinger to his mouth and whistled.

Naomi came flying out of the house and down the walk, boots untied, her best black bonnet in one hand and a book in the other. "Don't leave without me! I'm coming, Dat!"

"Put on your bonnet, girl," Samuel said. "What are you thinking?" She did as he bid her, and he straightened the bonnet over her white *kapp,* and tied the strings firmly under her chin. "Now, into the van. Hurry." He tempered his firm words with a grin. "Driver won't wait all day."

"So you decided to take Naomi after all?" Anna tried to suppress her satisfaction that Samuel had listened to her. "I'm so glad."

"Told you I'd think on it," he said. "Spoke to Joe, heard some other womenfolk would be there, so I thought, why not? It's a small thing to do, if it pleases you. Why not?"

"And Naomi," she reminded him. "Your daughter most of all. It's not a small matter to her." From her seat by the window, Naomi sat up tall and smiled shyly.

Leah waved and Naomi returned the wave.

"Have a good time," Anna called.

"Can't say what time this will be over," Samuel said, still looking at Anna.

"Don't worry. A hot supper will be waiting when you get here."

"Make sure the boys get to school on time."

The driver leaned toward Samuel and said something that Anna couldn't make out, and Samuel closed the sliding door and got into the front passenger seat. As the engine started, he rolled down the window and called, "I told Peter and Rudy that if there's trouble, I'll know the reason why."

"Go!" Anna said, laughing. *Men.* To make such a fuss over being away from the farm for a day. As if she couldn't manage four children. As mischievous as boys could be, compared to Grossmama, dealing with Samuel's twins was a piece of cake.

By the time Lori Ann and Mae woke and wandered down to the kitchen in their long nightgowns, Anna had apple pancakes and sausage cooking on the big gas stove, and Leah was topping mugs of hot chocolate with tiny marshmallows. Lori Ann rubbed her eyes and said, "Our dat—dat's g-g-gone away and you c-c-came to t-t-t-take care of us." Mae only stared and popped her thumb into her mouth.

"Indeed we have," Anna said. She noticed that Mae's feet were bare. Sweeping her up, she hugged her and wrapped her in a furry throw that was hanging near the cupboard, and plopped her down into Grossmama's arms. One looked as surprised as the other, but her grandmother nodded and began to rock the child and sing a lullaby to her in the old dialect.

"Mae had a—a—a b-bad dream l-l-last night," Lori Ann said. "And—and she wet her night—nightgown."

Mae hid her face in Grossmama's large bosom, but her stiff little body softened as she cuddled against the old woman. Grossmama stroked the child's back and whispered in her ear, "It's all right. Just a dream."

Anna glanced at Leah, who shrugged. Whatever the reason, Anna was glad that her grandmother had obviously taken to Mae and the little girl to her.

Anna wiped her hands on a towel and crouched down beside them. "This gown?" she asked, sniffing the material and feeling it. It felt dry, and all she could smell was the sweet scent of a clean child.

Lori Ann shook her head. "*Ne.* Naomi…she gave her a—a—a b-b-b-bath and put a-a-another nightgown on her."

Anna pursed her lips and sighed. "She's a good sister, Naomi. She takes care of her like a little mother."

"Me t-t-too," Lori Ann ventured. "I—I—I'm a—a—a g-good g-g-girl."

"*Ya,*" Anna agreed, giving the child an approving glance. "You are a very good girl, to always think about your little sister." Lori Ann straightened her shoulders and smiled. "The best," Anna said.

She was so glad that Naomi had gotten to go with Samuel today. It wasn't fair that she spend her entire childhood taking care of a house and her younger siblings. Again came the thought that Samuel really needed a mother for the five of them. Providing a home and working a farm was work enough for any man, without having to do it all alone. Maybe this was God's wish for Anna, that she care for these children, even if there would be no love in the marriage. How was she supposed to know?

"Now, you go and eat your breakfast like a good girl, Martha." Grossmama stood Mae on her feet. "And someone find some stockings and shoes for this baby before she catches the ague."

"Can you show me where her things are?" Leah asked Lori Ann. The girl nodded and the two hurried off.

Anna lifted Mae into a plastic booster seat on a chair, and slid her up to the table. Anna took a sip of the hot chocolate to see that it wasn't too hot, and then handed the cup to the child. She glanced at the clock, then went to the kitchen door, opened it and struck the iron triangle to call the boys to breakfast. Soon Rudy and Peter came charging in, Leah and Lori Ann returned with the thick stockings for Mae, and everyone, including Grossmama, gathered around the big table for breakfast.

"Look at those hands," Grossmama snapped at Rudy. "You do not eat with hands like those. To the sink, both of you." Her order encompassed a grinning Peter. "Soap. Scrub hard. You need clean hands for school." The twins went without argument, and the rest of the meal passed by without a hitch.

Anna was glad she'd offered to bring Grossmama over early with her, rather than picking her up on the way to Byler's store. Mam had looked doubtful when she'd suggested it, but Aunt Jezebel had clearly been pleased to get a few hours' respite from her sister's constant complaints. And Leah had cheerfully offered to help out Anna for the day. Instead of a problem, Grossmama had turned out to be a blessing.

Getting her grandmother up and dressed in time to get Samuel's children off to school hadn't been difficult, because Lovina had gotten up before daylight every day of her life, and saw no reason to change her routine at this age. "This is a good house," Grossmama said, after the boys left for school, leaving only the women and girls to clean up the kitchen. She waved a hand, taking in the spacious kitchen, the oak cupboards and the sturdy table that sat twelve. "I've always liked this house."

"You've never been to Samuel's before, have you?" Leah asked.

"Snickerdoodles," Grossmama snapped. "We moved here back in the spring of…well, I don't recollect the year exactly. Sometimes my mind plays tricks on me. But two of my girls were born here—and my Jonas. He was the best baby, if I do say so. Not colicky like Martha here." She indicated Mae, who returned the attention with a lopsided smile. "A fine, healthy baby, my Jonas. A little woodchopper to help his father."

Leah looked at Anna, and Anna shook her head. If Grossmama was satisfied, what good would it do to upset her by correcting her? Mae didn't seem to care that Lovina called her Martha, and Anna doubted there was much chance of winning the argument that this was Samuel's house and not Grossmama's.

"So," Anna said, when the girls were dressed, the kitchen was shining and a pot of dried butter beans were soaking in a pot on the back of the stove. "Who wants to go to Byler's?"

"Me!" Lori Ann cried. Mae nodded.

Anna smiled at them. They looked so cute in their starched white *kapps* and cornflower-blue dresses that Samuel's sister, Louise, had sewn and sent from Ohio. Anna knew it was as hard for Louise to be separated from little Mae as it was for the child to be apart from the only mother she'd even known, but Louise had a big family of her own. Sending Mae back to Samuel had been a difficult choice, but the right thing to do. When a child had a loving father, she should be with him, not only for their sakes but for Naomi, Lori Ann and the boys.

Mae's return had shaken up the household in more ways than one. Lori Ann, who was naturally shy and had a speech problem, was no longer the baby; and Naomi, who was already overworked, had even more to do. Anna's heart went out to these motherless children. If only she knew for certain that there was the possibility that Samuel could learn to love her, despite her size and lack of looks, she would have been thrilled to take on that challenge.

The back door banged open and Rudy dashed back in. "Where's our lunch?" he asked.

Anna looked at Leah. Leah grimaced. "I guess we forgot," she admitted.

"Naomi is supposed to make our lunch," Rudy said, rocking from one snowy boot to the other. He stood with the door still half open behind him.

"Shut that door," Grossmama ordered. "Were you born in a barn, Jonas?"

"I'm Rudy," he said, but he meekly pushed the door shut.

"I know who you are," Grossmama said. "You're trying to trick me, pretending there's two of you, but I know better. You're my Jonas. But if you were Bishop Ash, I'd still tell you to shut that door and not let the heat out!"

Anna scanned Samuel's spacious kitchen. On wrought iron hooks near the door, three black lunch kettles hung. She opened one after another, but all were empty. "You go on to school," she said to Rudy. "I'll make you each a lunch and drop it off in the cloak room as we go out to Byler's."

"I want bologna," Rudy said. "Two slices with cheese in the middle, and catsup on my bread. Potato chips. And cookies—six."

"You'll eat what we give you," Grossmama said, "And be glad to get it. When I was a girl, my Mam gave us boiled squirrels, still with the head and bones, and corn bread in our lunch pails and we were glad to get it. A bear killed our hogs, and all the meat we had one winter was wild game my father shot." She made a shooing motion. "Go on. You heard my Anna. Off to school with you, Jonas."

Rudy stiffened. He started to say something, then eyed Grossmama warily, thought the better of it, and ducked back out onto the porch. Anna followed him.

"Don't worry," she promised. "I'll give you plenty to eat."

He spun around suddenly. "You aren't our Mam, you know," he said in a mean voice. "And we don't like you. You're fat and ugly and Dat won't ever marry you."

Anna gasped. Hurt tightened her throat. "That's a rude thing to say, Rudy. Your father would be ashamed of you."

"We don't need you. We don't need anybody. This is our house, and we don't want you here." He turned and looked at his twin, who was standing on the sidewalk a few yards from the house. "Do we, Peter? Tell her. We don't want her here."

Peter put his fingers in the corners of his mouth, stretched his mouth wide and stuck out his tongue. "Fatty, fatty, two-by-four!" he shouted. "Can't get through the kitchen door!" And before Anna could gather her wits and think of a suitable comeback, both boys ran, leaving her standing, eyes stinging with tears, on the cold, windy back porch.

Even on a cold Friday morning in January, Byler's was bustling with Amish, Mennonites, local Englishers and a scattering of tourists with their outlandish dress and out-of-state license plates on their big fancy cars. Anna felt more at home at Byler's than she did in the Dover supermarkets or Walmarts. The Kent County folk had lived with their Plain neighbors for generations, and few stared and pointed as the strangers did.

Sometimes tourists tried to sneak pictures of the Amish. It was rude and embarrassing. Photographs were against the Ordnung. Anna had been baptized into the church when she was fifteen, and she'd never willingly permitted her snapshot to be taken. But sometimes Englishers jumped out, a flash went off in her face, and then what could she do?

Leah never seemed to get upset by the intrusions. "They don't know any better," she said. "We're lucky that no one wanders into the house like the Englishers do in Lancaster. Pauline's sister tells her that they have tourists walking in all the time. There is a sign on the far side of their property, pointing to the 'Old Amish Farm,' and people mistake their house for the showplace."

"I don't know why anyone would want to see our house anyway," Anna said. "I don't go into their homes and stare."

Leah chuckled. "Because Mam taught us better."

Anna was still smarting over the way Rudy and Peter had acted. Their cruel words hurt, but a secret voice whispered that they were right. Samuel would never marry her, and if he did he might be sorry.

Leah and Anna each took a cart and put the girls in the seats, so that they wouldn't have to chase them. "C-c-can we have i-i-ice c-cream?" Lori Ann whispered. "I l-l-l-like i-i-ice c-cream."

"You certainly can," Anna promised. "But only if you are very good."

Grossmama took a cart, as well. Anna had offered to push her in a wheelchair, but her grandmother had scoffed at riding in a moving chair. "They have motors," she confided, "like cars. They run away with you." So Grossmama pushed her own cart and happily loaded it with cinnamon, nutmeg, walnuts and oatmeal.

"That's too much," Leah murmured in Anna's ear, but Anna only smiled.

"We'll put some back later. Let her please herself. She seems to be having such a good time. And she'll get tired."

Byler's store had begun on the back porch of a local farmhouse, when the founder had started going to the city to buy staples in large amounts for his big family. Like a weed patch, it had grown and grown, until it was now a large, modern business that specialized in discount groceries. The inventory included wood stoves and a wide array of kitchen items, as well as a produce and dairy section, a bakery and a deli. Best of all, Byler's sold fresh-dipped ice-cream cones at a very reasonable price.

Soon, as Anna had guessed, Lovina's steps grew slower. "I'm tired," she said. "And I'm hungry. I want a submarine sandwich."

"And—and we want i-i-ice c-cream," Lori Ann reminded.

"I know just the place for you to eat your lunch," Anna said. She guided the family back to the entrance lobby, where the store workers had placed long wooden picnic tables. She found a seat for Grossmama next to two elderly Mennonite ladies, gave her the oversized sandwich, napkins and her orange soda pop. "We'll be glad to sit here with you, if you want," Anna offered.

"Ne, ne." Grossmama beamed, and Anna could tell that she was delighted to be sitting where she could stare to her heart's delight at all the folks coming and going.

Leah looked dubious. "You won't wander off, will you? Remember what happened when we took you to the hardware store in Ohio? You took the buggy and—"

"You hush that talk," Grossmama said. "Jonas took me home. You never mind that. I want to eat my lunch in quiet. You two finish your shopping and buy those children their ice cream."

"Don't want ice-cream cone," Mae said, stretching out her arms to Grossmama. "Want to stay *wiff* her."

"You need to come with me, honey," Anna said gently. "Grossmama wants to eat her lunch."

"Ne!" Mae stuck out her lip. "Stay *wiff* her!"

"Give the child here," Grossmama said, scooting over on the picnic bench. "Martha can help me eat my submarine. She can sit right here."

Anna looked at Leah. Their gazes locked and Leah nodded. "That will be fine," she said, lifting Mae out of her cart.

"But if…" Anna began.

Leah smiled. "Grossmama will take good care of her," she said.

"Stop your chattering, you two. Finish your shopping and let us eat," Lovina said. Mae climbed up on the bench beside her, and Grossmama tore off a piece of sandwich and handed it to the child.

Leah motioned to the sliding door that led back inside the main shopping area. "She'll be fine. Grossmama is always better when she has something to do."

Behind them, Anna heard a woman remark in a New York accent, "Look at that adorable little *Aim-ish* girl in the bonnet. Isn't she precious? Take our picture, Phil. I'm sure they won't mind."

"No pictures!" Grossmama said. "You should be ashamed of yourself! Didn't your mother teach you better? And why are you coming to Byler's in your undershift?"

Inside, Anna turned back to intervene, only to see Grossmama had pulled Mae into her lap. Mae hid her face against Lovina, and Grossmama had thrown her shawl over the girl's head. The two Mennonite women were laughing, and the Englisher lady in a very short skirt began to sputter. Before she could do more than utter a squeak, the man with her had grabbed her arm and pulled her back outside. Grossmama had picked up her sub and continued eating as though nothing had happened.

Leah dissolved into laughter. She and Anna laughed until tears ran down their faces, and Lori Ann was giggling, too. Finally, when Leah could speak again, she said, "You go on and finish the shopping. I was planning on standing here and watching them. Grossmama can't see me, but I can be sure she or Mae don't come to harm."

"You don't mind?"

"*Ne.* Rebecca and I did it all the time. It hurts her feelings if she thinks you are treating her like a child."

"I…want my ice-cream c-cone," Lori Ann said. "I was g-good, Anna."

"*Ya,* very good," Anna agreed. Still smiling, she pushed the grocery cart away toward the ice-cream counter. "What kind shall we get?"

"Make mine butter pecan," Leah called after them. "Two scoops."

The rest of the day went as smooth for Anna as cake flour sliding through her fingers. Leah drove the horse and buggy from Byler's to the Yoder home without a mishap. Rebecca and Susanna came out to help unload their purchases, and Aunt Jezebel helped Grossmama into the house. She was tired and wanted her afternoon nap. Mae was sleepy, as well, and fell asleep in Anna's arms, somewhere between Mam's house and Samuel's. She didn't wake when Anna laid her on the daybed in the kitchen, and covered her up with a soft throw.

"I—I have to g-gather the—the eggs," Lori Ann said. "It's my job."

Anna glanced at the time. Soon the boys would be home from school, and she wanted to get a start on supper. She hadn't had a minute alone with Leah, to tell her about the twins' bad behavior this morning, and she was still stinging from their taunts. She didn't doubt that she could manage these little girls if she and Samuel were to marry, but what if it was different with Rudy and Peter? What if they really didn't like her? Would it drive a wedge between Samuel and his sons?

She closed her eyes, said a quick but fervent prayer for guidance, and did what she did best—cooked. By the time Samuel and Naomi came in at 6:30, the kitchen smelled of hot biscuits, fried ham, hot applesauce and butter beans and dumplings.

Samuel walked past her, opened the oven door and grinned when he saw the bread pudding bubbling inside. "Anna, Anna," he said in his big, deep voice. "You are wonderful. Here I am, thinking it was cold ham sandwiches and canned soup for us, and you've cooked up a feast." Lori Ann ran to her father, and he popped a piece of biscuit into her mouth, picked her up and lifted her high in the air before giving her a hug.

Satisfaction filled Anna with a delicious warmth. "And how was the auction?" She didn't need to ask if Naomi had a good time. The girl's shining face told it all. "Good. Good," Samuel said, grabbing a hot biscuit and tossing it from one big hand to another before taking a bite. "How was your day? You make out okay? Looks like you did. I haven't seen the kitchen this clean in ages."

"We had a fine day, we girls." She had no intention of telling Samuel about the twins' rudeness. She'd decided that the boys were her problem to solve. "But I'd rather hear about the auction, than talk of shopping and cooking."

"Wait until you see what I bought."

"What is it?" Anna asked.

"I'm not telling," he replied. "You'll see soon enough. It's a surprise."

"Oh, a surprise?" Anna found herself truly curious.

"You'll see next week," he said with a grin. "And by the way, the weatherman is calling for eight inches of snow next week."

Chapter Thirteen

The following day, Anna rose early to start the fire in the wood-burning cook stove, to make morning biscuits, and found Grossmama already at the table drinking coffee. After greeting Lovina, Anna went to the gas stove, picked up the coffeepot and poured herself a cup. To her surprise, the coffee was excellent. "Did you make this?" she asked her grandmother.

Grossmama laughed and shook her head. "Jezzy doesn't let me use the gas stove. Thinks I'm not right in the head. She made the coffee."

At the mention of her name, Aunt Jezebel came into the kitchen from the hallway, fully dressed but with her damp hair wrapped in a towel. "We got up first. First up makes the coffee," her aunt explained.

"There!" Grossmama slapped a color brochure on the table. "I want you to see this." She looked at Anna. "See." She tapped the paper.

Anna picked up the brochure and examined it. The cover read "Maple Leaf Center. Join active seniors in your community for crafts, fellowship and education. Monday through Friday. Luncheon and transportation provided." Pictured was a one-story brick building with a red metal roof and window boxes full of flowers.

Puzzled, Anna glanced at Grossmama. "This is a place for older people to gather and visit?"

"Read it," Lovina said impatiently.

Anna unfolded the colorful brochure and looked at the photos of a library, a dining room with smiling English people sitting at round tables, a table where two women were sitting and knitting and a line of people climbing into a large sightseeing bus.

"And on the back," Grossmama insisted. "There's more on the back."

The last picture was of a group of women sitting around a quilting stand piecing together a quilt. But one woman was braiding strips of cloth. In her lap lay the beginnings of a braided rug.

"They make rugs," Grandmother said. "I want to go there. I want to ride in the red van. I make the best rugs. I can show those English women what they are doing wrong."

"I tried to tell her that this Maple Leaf place was for Englishers," Aunt Jezzy said, "but…" She spread her palms in a hopeless gesture.

"I want to go," Grossmama repeated. "I want to go tomorrow. Today, I want to go home to my house. Jonas left the door open. The kitchen will get cold."

"I tried to tell her that was Samuel's house she's thinking of, and Samuel's boy," her aunt said. "But she never listens to me."

Mam and Susanna walked into the kitchen. "Leah and Rebecca are still sleeping," Anna's mother said. "Not that I blame them on such a cold, bleak day."

"It's going to snow," Grossmama announced. "I can

always smell snow." She glared at Hannah. "I'm going home before it snows. Tell that Irwin boy to hitch up the horse."

"You're right about the snow, Lovina," Hannah said. "I turned on Jonas's radio to listen to the weather, and there was an announcement. Church will be canceled this Sunday if we get more than four inches." She smiled at Grossmama. "I hope you enjoyed your trip to Byler's yesterday."

"Martha and I had a submarine sandwich and we saw an Englisher woman in her shift."

"What?" Mam asked.

"I'll explain later," Anna promised.

"I'm going to ride in the red van," Grossmama went on. "And you can't stop me. I'm going to make braided rugs, hundreds of them. I make the best."

"Sister, let's get you dressed while Hannah and the girls make breakfast," Aunt Jezebel said, taking Lovina's arm.

"I want eggs." Grossmama pointed at Anna. "And you make them. Hannah is a terrible cook. Her eggs taste like cow pies." She narrowed her eyes and peered around the room. "She's a thief, too. She sneaks into my room at night and takes my pocketbook."

"Mam would never do such a thing," Anna defended.

"Would, too!" Grossmama said. "I had thirty-five dollars and now I have twenty-six dollars and fifteen cents."

"You bought a submarine sandwich and mints yesterday," Aunt Jezebel reminded her. "Hannah would never steal from you."

"So you say." Grossmama shuffled across the kitchen.

"You're probably in it together, taking my money while I'm asleep."

"That's not very kind of you, Lovina. And it's not kind of you to speak of Hannah's cooking that way either."

Grossmama thrust out her lower lip, but said no more.

"Anna will make your eggs just the way you like them," Hannah promised.

"How do you stand it?" Anna asked, when her grandmother and aunt had gone back to their bedroom. "She's not mean to me. You should have seen her yesterday. She was so good with Samuel's Mae, and the child adores her."

"Pray for her, Anna," her mother said with a sigh. "She's confused and far from home. She's lost her husband, her only son, her brothers and two of her daughters. And thank the Good Lord that you weren't born with Lovina's disposition. I do, every day."

By eleven o'clock that morning, heavy snow began to fall, large lacy flakes that tumbled and piled on the windowsills, and gathered in drifts around the porch. Anna and her sisters helped Irwin stable all the livestock in the barn, heaping their stalls high with bright straw and filling their water pails. It was cold, but not the usual bitter cold that came with heavy snowfalls in Delaware. And the wind, surprisingly, held little force; and the farm took on a wintery, white beauty, as snow covered the roofs and lawn and barnyard.

Anna kept busy, first with the outside chores and then in the house. Everyone was glad to gather around the table for a hearty dinner of beef stew and apple fritters. Grossmama continued to insist that she was going to Maple Leaf Center and to argue that she needed to go home before the storm got any worse. Mam had given all of them a look that told them to keep a sharp eye on their grandmother. They couldn't have her wandering out of the house in the middle of a snowstorm.

But in spite of all she did with her hands, Anna's mind remained on Samuel and his children. She wondered how were they faring today. Had Samuel had time to prepare them a hot meal? Was Naomi able to manage both small sisters and still work her way through the inside chores? And then there were the tougher questions. Did Samuel really care for her, or was she—Anna— a poor substitute for the beautiful wife he'd loved and lost? And what was she going to do about the twins? Provided, of course, that she decided that she wanted Samuel to court her. She had to make up her mind about him before she could solve the other problems.

"Where's your husband, Anna?" Grossmama asked.

It was late in the afternoon. Mam and the girls were cleaning the upstairs, and Anna was just finishing up in the kitchen. It was still snowing, and Anna had paused, a dishcloth in her hand, to stare out the window. She'd thought Grossmama was napping. Obviously, not. "I don't have a husband," she said. "I'm not married."

"Well, don't wait too long. A big girl like you. Strong and sweet. You'll make some man a good wife, Anna. Don't be too fussy, like Jezzy. You wait too long, you'll wither on the vine."

She turned toward her grandmother. "You think I'd make a good wife?" So what if Grossmama's memory failed her and she was sometimes confused? It would make Anna feel better to hear someone besides her mother say so. "You don't think I'm too...too Plain?"

"Too Plain to be a wife? No such thing! Potatoes. I like potatoes. I don't like rice." Then Grossmama paused, as if deep in thought. "My nose was too long. I was too tall and skinny. Didn't make a bit of difference to Jonas's dat. He wasn't all that much to look at either."

Anna nibbled on her lower lip. How could her grandmother be so sensible one moment, and then so confused the next? As prickly as the old woman was, Anna still loved her and wished she could find some way to ease the tensions between Grossmama and Mam.

Lovina hobbled to the window, leaned on her cane and stared out. "Hope my geese are snug in their shed." She glanced at Anna. "You need your own flock, girl, for when you marry. Every wife needs poultry. Whatever money comes from the ducks and geese and chickens, that's hers by right. Not the husband's. A woman needs her own money." She sniffed. "Especially in this house, where they're all trying to steal every penny I've got."

"You worry a lot about money, Grossmama," Anna said, touching her grandmother's arm. "You don't have to. We'll take care of you. We want to take care of you."

"Got to worry about money. Never enough. We lived on squirrels one winter when I was a girl. Did I tell you that?"

Anna nodded. "You did. Was that when you lived in the Kishacoquillas Valley?"

Lovina snorted. "Valley, nothing. We lived on the mountain. My dat was too poor to own bottomland. Rock and trees, that's what he tilled, rock and trees. Bears and wild things eating our livestock, and him with eighteen mouths to fill. I was the oldest girl. Many a day, I'd give my dinner to the little ones and go without. Never enough money. Got to get yourself a flock of geese, Anna. If you've got poultry, you'll always have a full purse."

Anna wrapped her big hand around her grandmother's bony one and tried to imagine a tall, skinny girl in a *kapp* going hungry to feed her younger brothers and sisters. She looked around Mam's kitchen and thought how fortunate she'd been to be born here in Kent County, where there were no bears to steal the winter's meat and no rocks to litter the fertile fields. Other than fasting days, Anna couldn't ever remember going hungry, and her heart went out to her brave and tough grandmother.

"I'll remember that, Grossmama," she said. "And when spring comes, I promise I'll buy some baby goslings and start my own flock."

"I'll show you how to collect the down," Grossmama said. "But your Samuel can't have the money. It's yours, and that's all there is to it."

"He isn't my Samuel," Anna said softly.

Lovina snorted again. "Of course he is. He's your husband, isn't he? And a fine man, too, to give you all those beautiful children."

"They are beautiful, but Rudy and Peter don't like me," Anna admitted. "They don't want me to marry their father."

"Not up to children," her grandmother said. "Up to the Lord. He decides."

"You really believe that?" She stroked Lovina's hand. "That God has a plan for each of us, even for me?"

"'Course He has a plan. For all of us. He wants me

to go to that Maple Leaf in the red van. I'm going to-morrow, right after I go home to Martha and Jonas."

There was no church service on Sunday. Out on the main roads, the big snowplows roared, but few cars and trucks passed the farm. By midmorning, the snowfall had trickled to tiny flakes, glittering like stars in the sunshine. Charley and Eli came up to the big house and got Irwin, and the three of them shoveled paths to the barn, chicken house and pigpen. They threw bales of hay down from the loft, and broke the ice in the water troughs, to see that all the animals had plenty to drink.

Anna was just sweeping snow off the porch when she heard the sound of bells and looked up to see Samuel's Morgan horse come around the barn, pulling a beauti-ful, old-fashioned sleigh. Anna's eyes widened in as-tonishment. "Samuel," she called to him. "Whatever are you driving?"

"Do you like it?" he asked. "This is the surprise I told you about." He reined in Smoky, and Anna saw Mae's small face peering out from a mound of blan-kets in her father's lap.

Excitement made Anna giddy. The beautiful horse, the black-and-gold sleigh that looked like something out of a storybook, took her breath away. "You bought a sleigh," she said. "I… I love it."

"The man I bought it from said he had it for years, mostly collecting dust in his shed." He grinned and of-fered his hand. "Climb up, Anna. I came to take you for a sleigh ride."

"Me?"

His laughter rang out across the yard. "What other

Anna could I be asking to ride with me on such a beautiful Sunday?"

"I…" She wanted to go. She'd never wanted anything so badly than to ride in that shining sleigh with Samuel behind a high-stepping horse. Samuel could have asked any of a dozen young women. He could have asked her sister, Leah, but he'd asked *her*.

"I… I'll have to ask my mother," she said.

"Ne." His smile lit up his whole face and his beautiful eyes sparkled. "Decide for yourself, Anna. You're a woman, full grown. Church has been cancelled, so that makes this a visiting Sunday. Come visit with me. I mean to check in on the old and sick, to be certain they have all they need." He offered his hand again. "Come away with me, Anna Yoder. Or stand here and wish you had," he teased, pulling away his hand. "Who knows when there will be another snow like this?"

Anna took a deep breath and glanced at Charley, who was still digging a space around the chicken house door. "Should I go?" she asked.

"Ne," Samuel said again. "You must decide, Anna. Are we courting or not?"

"Courting is not a promise of marriage," she answered.

"But few marriages go forward without it."

She looked back toward the house and saw Aunt Jezebel's pale face staring out. If she didn't take this chance, she might end up like her aunt, and she didn't want that.

"All right," she said, and put her hand into his. To her surprise, he leaped down out of the sleigh and helped her to climb in. She was afraid that her weight would be too much for him, but he lifted her in his strong arms, as though she were no bigger than Miriam. In two flicks of Smoky's tail, she was sitting in the deep seat, her legs and shoulders swathed in blankets.

Samuel climbed back up, picked up the leathers and shook them over the Morgan's back. With a jingle of bells, they were off across the barnyard, down the orchard lane and across the field, toward her Aunt Martha's house. Snow flew from the horse's hooves and the harness creaked. Snowflakes swirled through the air and landed on Anna's face.

Beside her, little Mae giggled and opened her mouth. "Taste good," she said.

"Do they?" Anna asked. She tilted her head back and mimicked the child. And soon Samuel was doing the same. Laughing, they bounced and slid over the deep snow, and Anna marveled at how fast they covered the distance. Eventually, Mae wiggled off her father's lap and into Anna's. She was warm and soft, and Anna felt a surge of love fill her. Maybe her grandmother was right, she thought. Maybe God did have a plan for her. And maybe, if she was lucky, Samuel would be part of it.

He leaned close. "So you admit that I'm courting you? That if we suit each other you'd be willing to become my wife?"

"I'm thinking on it."

Samuel laughed again, and the sound of his big, booming voice was like music to her ears. "You are a stubborn woman," he pronounced.

"*Ne,*" she answered. "My Aunt Martha is a stubborn woman. Something tells me that she won't be happy to see us together."

Samuel nodded. "You're right, but who better to let know our secret. By tomorrow morning, snowstorm or no snowstorm, every family in the county will know that we're walking out together." Snowflakes lodged in his beard, and Anna reached up and brushed them away.

"Was that so hard?" he asked, looking into her eyes.

"What?" She was suddenly shy. This wasn't happening to her, couldn't be. What had she done to deserve such a beau?

"To touch me, Anna? To smile at me? You don't know how many nights I've lain awake wondering what was wrong with me, wondering why you didn't want me." He draped a big arm around her shoulders and pulled her and Mae closer to him. "I love you, Anna. You may not believe it, but I do." He leaned even closer, and before she knew it, Samuel's lips brushed hers.

Anna's heart skipped and hammered against her ribs. For long seconds the snowy landscape, the sled, the horse, everything, vanished. There was nothing but the sweet sensation of Samuel's kiss. And then she realized where she was and what she'd just permitted. She pulled away just as horse and sleigh broke out of the woods' lane and into Aunt Martha's yard.

Dorcas, carrying two buckets of water to the barn, stopped gape-mouthed and stared, so surprised that she dropped her buckets. "Anna?"

Aunt Martha came out of the chicken house with a basket of eggs. She wore a denim coat of Uncle Reuben's, men's high rubber boots and a blue wool scarf over her head. "Whatever are you doing in that contraption?" Aunt Martha cried. "On a Sabbath. With Samuel Mast?" she demanded. "Reuben! Reuben! Come see this."

"Good day, Martha, Dorcas," Samuel called, merrily. "Just checking to see that you have everything you need. What with the snow and the roads blocked."

"You have Anna alone in that sleigh? With bells?"

Samuel shook his head. "The bells are on Smoky, Martha. No bells on Anna. Her mother wouldn't approve."

Anna saw Dorcas standing behind her mother, break into a grin.

"Don't worry. We have Mae with us."

Her aunt huffed. "A child? Hardly a proper chaperone." She glanced around and shouted again. "Reuben!"

"Certain you have everything you need?" Samuel asked.

"This is not right. Not proper," Aunt Martha declared.

"Then we'll be off," Samuel called with a wave. "Lots of families to visit."

"See you at church next week," Anna called, mischievously. And then they were off again, flying over the ground, charging through the snowy fields on a thrilling and heart-pounding ride.

Chapter Fourteen

The snow didn't last. The following week, a warm front moved across the state, and heavy rains washed away the accumulation of snow. Samuel's beautiful sleigh was stored in his carriage shed, covered with a tarp, to wait for another day when travel by buggy was impossible. Anna's ride with Samuel had caused quite a flutter in the community, but her mother and sisters were more than ready to support her.

"I told Lydia that Samuel couldn't find a better wife if he searched every Amish community in the county," Mam told Ruth one afternoon.

Ruth's Eli had been working late at the chair shop, so she'd walked across the field to visit with the family. She'd brought Grossmama some lovely strips of blue wool for the rug she was working on.

It was Thursday, and Mam had a school board meeting at seven, at Roman's house, so they'd planned an early supper. "It's time Anna had a little fun. Who deserves it more?"

Anna busied herself at the sink, carefully washing the battered copper pot that Grossmama had brought with her from Ohio. The pot, called a kettle, had been purchased in Philadelphia as a gift for a bride, long before Pennsylvania became one of the original thirteen colonies. It was her grandmother's most cherished possession, handed down through the family for generations.

"That kettle goes to Anna when I die," Grossmama said. "Martha will kick up a fuss, but she's not to have it. Martha couldn't make peach jam without burning it, to save her soul, and she doesn't deserve it."

"Now, sister," Aunt Jezebel interjected. "You're too hard on Martha."

"Martha's too hard on me. Like to killed me, getting born. I was in labor with her for three days. It's a wonder either of us lived." Lovina was seated in the big rocking chair near the stove, where she'd supervised the making of a batch of apple butter. "Is the van here yet? I'm waiting for the van to take me to the center."

Grossmama had been asking all day about the van that would take her to Maple Leaf.

"Couldn't we arrange for her to go to the center just once?" Anna quietly asked her mother, when Hannah had brought her a clean towel to dry the kettle. "She seems set on going."

Mam sighed. "Maple Leaf is for the English. Plain People don't go there. We provide for our older family members in our homes. We don't need the help of strangers to do what's right."

"But what harm could it do if she wants to go?" Anna persisted.

Her mother shook her head. "Bishop Atlee wouldn't allow it. It wouldn't look right."

Ruth joined them. "We are a people apart from the world, Anna."

"But why is it wrong for Grossmama to spend time with the English, if it would be good for her?"

"We must live by the Ordnung," her mother said. "Sometimes it's hard, but our faith has sustained us through trial and hardship. We can't question the ways that have kept us on God's path."

"But what if Bishop Atlee agreed?" Anna dried the kettle with the dishtowel. "If he approved, would you let her go?"

"He won't," Ruth said. "No Amish have ever gone to Maple Leaf. I know, because my friend Flo works there in the kitchen."

"Is it a nice place?" Anna asked. "Do the Englishers treat the older people kindly?"

"Ya." Ruth nodded. "Flo says that everyone there is nice. Sometimes she helps with serving the lunch and cleaning the craft room."

"I was thinking," Anna began, and Mam laughed.

"What?" Anna asked.

"You've obviously been thinking hard about a lot of things. Samuel included."

"Ah, Samuel," Ruth teased. "How long are you going to keep him dangling?"

"She told Samuel that she'd give him an answer by her birthday," Mam said.

Ruth looked unconvinced. "But you should know by now whether you want him or not."

Mam chuckled. "And you didn't keep poor Eli dangling?"

"That was different," Ruth said. "I had to be certain that he was committed to the faith. I knew how I felt about him, but I could never have married anyone who wasn't as dedicated as I was. And Anna doesn't have that concern. She and Samuel both joined the church years ago."

"I'm just not sure," Anna said. "I care for Samuel, but I don't know if we're right for each other. If it's really God's plan for us."

"Because of those kids?" Ruth asked. "They'd be a handful, especially the boys."

"Ne." Anna shook her head. "It would be easy to love them all. I think I do already. It's Samuel that troubles me. And me." She shrugged. "Look at me. Do I look like I belong with Samuel Mast?"

Her mother folded her arms and looked stern. "See how it is, Ruth? Your sister doesn't see herself as we see her—as beautiful and kind and strong. And as long as she can't love herself, she's not ready to accept the love of a man."

Anna swallowed. "You don't understand. You're my family. I know you love me. But maybe that love blinds you to who I really am?" Hanging her apron on the hook, she hurried out of the room and upstairs. Not even her mother or her sisters understood what it was like to be born ugly in a family of pretty faces. No one understood.

She hadn't even gotten to tell them about her idea for her grandmother. Next week, a truck would be bringing the rest of Aunt Jezzy and Grossmama's things. Her aunt had told her that Lovina had stacks of braided rugs that she'd made over the years. What Anna had thought was, that perhaps their sister Johanna could see if the English shops that sold her quilts would be interested in selling Grossmama's rugs. If they could sell some or all, Grossmama would have money of her own, and perhaps her mind would be at ease.

Upstairs in her room, Anna pulled her rocking chair to the window where she could catch the last of the daylight, and removed a new, pale green dress from her sewing basket. As she hemmed the dress, the tension seeped out of her shoulders and neck, and she began to softly hum an old hymn. She always felt better when her hands were busy and she felt useful.

The last time Naomi had been here, Anna had her try the dress on her, so it could be hemmed to the proper length. Samuel's sisters in Ohio kept the children in clothes, but the style wasn't always what the other children at school were wearing, and Naomi was at the age where she didn't want to look different. Anna could understand that perfectly. Surely, it wasn't vanity for Naomi to want her *kapps* and dresses to be like those of her friends. And Anna decided that she would ask Samuel when Naomi had last had her eyes checked. She spent a lot of time with her nose in a book, and it seemed to Anna that she was starting to squint. Maybe she needed a new prescription.

As Anna knotted the thread and put the last few stitches in the hem, Rudy's taunts rose in her mind, and again her stomach knotted. She would have to find a way to win over Samuel's twins, or there was no question of the two of them marrying. As Mam had said, she'd promised him an answer by her birthday, and that was only three weeks away. What if she was as undecided then as now? Would she have to refuse him? Better to say no than to say yes, and spend a lifetime doubting her choice.

"Anna?" Mam pushed open the bedroom door. "Are

you sewing? Why didn't you light a lamp? You'll go blind."

She smiled at her mother. "*Ne,* Mam, I'll not go blind. You worry too much."

Mam came to sit on the edge of the bed near her. "I'm sorry if you felt pressured about Samuel. You know we all have your best interests at heart. We want you to be happy."

Anna smoothed the wrinkles from the small, neat dress. "You want me to marry him."

Mam shook her head. "Not if you don't want to."

Anna replaced her needle in its case, and tucked the spool of thread into the basket beside the *kapp* and apron she'd finished on Tuesday. The *kapp* would need starching and ironing, but the outfit would be ready for Naomi to wear at next Sunday's services. "I'm sorry if I upset everyone," she said. "But I have to decide for myself."

"*Ya,*" Mam agreed. "You do. I know a little how you feel. When I chose your father, it was against my family's wishes. My father especially felt betrayed."

"Because you fell in love with Dat?"

Mam steepled her hands and tapped her chin gently with her fingertips. "Because, in marrying him, I chose the Old Order Amish faith over the one I was raised in."

"But you weren't turning your back on God."

"*Ne,* but my parents felt I was turning my back on the world."

"Have you ever been sorry?"

Her mother smiled, and Anna thought again how beautiful she was. "Not for a moment. It wasn't giving up life, so much as embracing it. Our way is a special blessing, and I thank God every day that this was the path He chose for me."

"You really believe that? That our Lord wanted you and Dat to marry?"

"With all my heart."

Anna sighed. "That's beautiful, Mam. It's what I want. To love someone like that. To have him love me. And to never wonder if I made the right decision."

"It's what you deserve." Mam rose and picked up Naomi's dress. "This is good work, Anna. And you've put in a deep hem. She'll start to shoot up soon. I think she will be slim like her mother, but tall like the women in her father's family. A sweet girl, Naomi. With a bright mind. She may make a teacher some day."

"I think she'd like that."

"It's good of you to take an interest in her. She's been a long time without a mother's care."

"So I told Samuel. Sometimes I think Naomi has had to grow up too quickly. She needs to be a child for a few years yet."

"It sounds to me as if you have a mother's interest in Samuel's girls."

"*Ya,* but I worry about the twins," Anna admitted. "It's clear that they don't want me to marry their father."

Mam folded Naomi's dress and laid it on the bed. "They are children still, Anna. Sometimes you have to be tough."

"You never had any boys, Mam."

"Ne?" Her mother smiled. "I had brothers. And now we have Irwin. I think he has become my son, even if he was delivered a little late in life."

"Peter and Rudy don't want a new mother, and they don't want to share their father with a wife." She wouldn't tell Mam about the hurtful things the twins had said to her. That was her problem.

"Eleven-year-old boys can be difficult, but you'll work it out. I have faith in you."

More than I do, Anna thought.

"Do you want to go with me to the school board meeting? Samuel's coming to pick me up, so that I don't have to drive. We'll be planning the winter picnic, and we could use your ideas."

Anna shook her head. "It's not my place, Mam." She could guess what Mam was about. Her mother wanted to throw her and Samuel together. Anna hadn't seen him since their thrilling sleigh ride last Sunday, and the impulsive promise she'd made to allow him to court her seemed scary. She needed more time to think. "You go. I'll see to the house and pack your lunch for tomorrow."

Her mother turned toward the door. "Very well." Anna heard her sigh. "Sometimes you remind me so much of your father. It always took him forever to make up his mind about the least thing."

"And once he had?"

Mam chuckled. "And once he had, there was no wavering. Jonas would stand by his decision until fish grew in our garden and the hens laid cabbages."

Samuel had to pass the chair shop on his way to Hannah's farm, and he couldn't resist the opportunity to stop and chat with Roman before the others arrived. As satisfying as Sunday's sleigh ride had been, and as pleased as he was about Anna finally agreeing to the courtship, he was still worried. Her birthday was fast approaching, and he was growing impatient. What if she refused him? They were the talk of the community this week, and if she wouldn't have him, he'd be an object of jest for years to come.

He could protest that he didn't care what anyone thought, but he did. He valued the judgment of his friends and neighbors, and he wanted them to be supportive. He hoped he didn't look like a fool. He knew his sons weren't happy about his courting Anna, but he wasn't certain they would have welcomed any woman as their stepmother. He was afraid that he'd spoiled them.

Finding the fine line between being a responsible father and a doting one wasn't easy, and he'd found that each of his children was different. What worked with Lori Ann was exactly the wrong thing for Naomi or Mae. Even the twins had their own separate personalities. Peter tended to follow Rudy's lead; yet, left to his own devices, he could show more maturity than his brother. Samuel had always believed that when the children were older, it would be easier to be a father, but that wasn't so. He needed a partner more than ever, a woman to talk to and confide in. Anna was his first choice; but if he couldn't have her, he'd have to make the effort to find someone else…perhaps someone older and more settled.

He tied his horse to the hitching rail and went into the shop. Roman had brought in kerosene heaters and placed gas lamps on the oval table for the meeting. The shop had electricity, but there was no need for it tonight. Fannie had made heaps of *fastnachts,* a fried donut with nutmeg, and Roman had a kettle of sweet cider heating. In the shop, the board could talk as long and late as they pleased, without disrupting Fannie's routine of getting her children ready for bed.

Roman looked up from his ledger and smiled as Samuel entered the room. "Where's Hannah? I thought you were bringing her tonight?"

"I am, shortly. Just wanted to be sure you had those receipts I sent Peter over with last week."

"Right here." Roman waved to a chair. "Heard you made quite a sight on Sunday, in that fancy sleigh of yours. Wish I'd seen it."

"You heard about it, huh?" Samuel sat down. "So you know that Anna and I are walking out together."

Roman laughed. "You'd better be. And I'd best be hearing bans read in services soon. Martha was fit to be tied. Said it was scandalous, you two flying around the county with bells on."

"She would."

Roman offered him a mug of cider, but Samuel shook his head. "So you're set on Anna, are you?" Roman removed his glasses and looked hard at him. "You're sure this is right for both of you?"

"I am, but she's still nervous."

"About you, herself, or the children?"

Samuel leaned back and folded his arms. "She keeps talking about Frieda, about how pretty she was. Anna doesn't think I'll be satisfied with her, not after Frieda. I try to tell her different, but she's stubborn."

Roman sipped his own cider. "Comes by it honest. Her mother puts the *S* in stubborn when she sets her mind to it." He hesitated.

"Say what you're thinking," Samuel urged him.

"I hope you can work this out first. Otherwise you'll spend the rest of your life trying to make her believe that you see more in her than a strong back and a Plain face. Not loving oneself can tear up a marriage. I've seen it with my cousin and his wife. She inherited a farm, and he came there as a hired man. After they married, he worked it and made a go of it, but Zekey never felt like he was good enough."

"They still together?"

"Oh, sure. He's turned Beachy Amish, got a car, but they hold to their vows. Trouble is, neither one seems happy. It's sad when a man and wife don't fit together like a hand and glove. Hard on the children."

"But Anna Yoder. You think we can be happy together?" Samuel urged his friend.

"I think so. But it's not me, it's Anna you have to convince of that," Roman said. "Whatever you decide, I'll still be there for both of you."

It was after nine when the school board finished its business and made the final plans for the winter picnic. The event would begin in Samuel's barn, Saturday evening, in two weeks. The children would put on a program demonstrating to their parents what they had learned, and then there would be a spelling bee.

Next, Samuel would auction off baskets of cookies made by unmarried women and girls. The men and boys would bid on the baskets, and all the money would go toward the school. Each eligible young woman would pack supper to go with the cookies, and at the end of the evening, the couples would spread a blanket on the straw and share the food. Afterward, there would be games and singing. It would be well chaperoned, fun for everyone and a proven moneymaker for the school.

Hannah was excited with the prospect of the frolic. "Winter's bad weather keeps our young people in their homes too much. It's so important that they have a chance to mingle with others their own age," she said on the way home in Samuel's carriage.

"I agree," Samuel said, urging Smoky toward Hannah's house at the end of her lane.

"I'm glad the children have two weeks to study their spelling. Since you've offered to donate a calf to the top speller, competition will be fierce."

Samuel chuckled. "And maybe some of the parents who don't care too much about their kids' education will take a little more interest."

"You're a good man, Samuel," Hannah said, as he reined in his horse at her back door. "You give so much to the community. I hope everyone appreciates it."

"I have three children in the school and two more to follow. Why wouldn't I help as much as I can?" He got down and helped her out of the buggy. The ground was still muddy from the melted snow.

"Come in for coffee?" she asked.

He was about to decline when he saw Anna's face at the kitchen window. Their eyes met and his heart leaped in his chest. "*Ya,*" he said, hurrying to tie the horse to the rail. "Coffee would be good, after all that sweet cider.

"I'd like to drive Anna to church this Sunday," he said. "If it's all right with you." How was it that a man his age could feel like a boy again? Just the sight of Anna's sweet face made him giddy-headed.

Hannah called over her shoulder. "You'll have to ask her."

He followed her into the house, and there was a flurry of putting away of coats and scarves and mittens. Only Anna was in the kitchen, but it wouldn't have mattered if all her sisters, her grandmother and her aunts were there. Samuel had eyes only for Anna.

"What kind of cookies will you be baking for the winter picnic?" he asked her.

"What kind do you like best?"

"Sand tarts and black walnut cookies," he answered, "but I eat them all."

"Almond slices?"

"Love them."

Anna smiled. "I'll see what I can do."

"I suppose I'll have to pay a high price for your basket. Everyone knows how well you bake."

Anna dimpled and blushed. "You can't bid on mine. You'll be the auctioneer."

"Don't care. Nobody gets your basket but me." Somehow, in the exchange, Hannah had left the kitchen. He hadn't even seen her go.

"Would you like coffee?" she asked.

He nodded. He would have drank vinegar, if it meant he got to sit here at the table, in this warm, cozy spot, with her. He took his seat at the head of the table while she brought him a steaming cup and a slice of lemon meringue pie. "Mmm," he said. "Looks delicious. If you keep on like this, I won't be able to fit through the barn door."

"*Ne,*" she said softly. "You work too hard, Samuel. You'll not get fat."

The sound of his name on her lips made him want to pull her into his arms and hug her, but he didn't dare. Instead, he took a bite of the pie. It was as good as it looked.

"I wanted to ask you a favor," Anna said, coming to

sit at the table with him. "I want you to speak to Bishop Atlee for me. It's about Grossmama."

He listened as she explained Lovina's desire to go to the English senior center. He didn't speak until she'd finished.

"I don't see what harm it would do," Anna said. "It would make her feel useful."

Samuel hated to deny Anna anything, but what was she thinking? They didn't send their old people to be cared for by the English. They kept them at home, no matter how ill or feeble they became.

"So what do you think?" she asked. "Will you speak to the bishop for me?"

"I know that you care for your grandmother more than even some of her own daughters seem to do. But this is not our way, Anna. You know that. It would be useless to take such a question to Bishop Atlee. He wouldn't permit it."

Anna stood up. "So you won't ask him for me?" Her voice was no longer sweet, but firm.

He loved her, but he couldn't allow her to force him to do something he knew wasn't right. It wouldn't do to start their marriage off by letting her think that he could be led around by the nose like a prize bull. "There would be no need," he said firmly and he left it at that.

Chapter Fifteen

On Sunday, Samuel and the children came to drive Anna to services. Anna held Mae on her lap and Lori Ann sat on the seat between them. Irwin had taken Naomi's dress and *kapp* over on Saturday, so the girl was able to wear her new outfit to church. Anna was pleased to see that it fit her so well. Being with Samuel and his family seemed right, and despite the glares she received from the twins, Anna felt comfortable as they reached the Beachy farm and were caught up in the familiar day of worship and fellowship.

As always, the hymns and preaching soothed Anna and made her feel that all was right with the world. Mae seemed content to be held, and when she and Lori Ann grew restless, Susanna was there to take the two children to the kitchen for milk and a snack. When they returned, Miriam produced a handkerchief doll from her pocket for each girl to play with, and soon Mae drifted off to sleep in Anna's arms.

Maybe, if I married Samuel, it wouldn't be so different, Anna thought. *I wouldn't be leaving my family, just stretching my arms to include more people that I* love. She knew that she loved Samuel's children, but did she love Samuel the way a woman ought to love a man? Did he love her that way? She knew there were different kinds of love. Were there different kinds of love between married couples, too?

Miriam's tug on her sleeve broke Anna from her reverie, and she realized that everyone was rising for one of the closing hymns. Mae stirred and made a soft little sigh, then nestled against her. Anna smiled down at the child as a warm surge of emotion enveloped her. *She could be mine,* Anna thought. *They could all be mine...even Samuel.*

She closed her eyes and prayed fervently for guidance.

There had been no time alone, after services and the communal Sunday meal, for Anna to try to convince Samuel to reconsider talking to the bishop for her. Samuel drove her home and then hurried to his own farm to begin the evening chores. Anna really wanted to speak with Samuel on the matter, because she didn't feel he'd given her plan fair consideration. Who could possibly believe that Grossmama wasn't being taken care of properly? Anyone who knew her should be able to see that hers was a special case, and that teaching Englishers how to make her rugs would only restore her sense of being useful.

Monday was wash day, and too busy for Anna to find time to do something about her idea, but late on Tuesday afternoon, when Grossmama was taking her nap, Anna walked across the fields to Samuel's house with a mind to plead her case to him again. She didn't see anyone in the farmyard, and she doubted that Samuel would be in the house at that time of day. Hesitantly, she pushed open the heavy barn door and called his name. "Samuel? It's Anna. Are you here?"

She heard a rustle and what sounded like a giggle, but there was no sign of Samuel. She entered the barn and pulled the door closed behind her. Light poured through a glass window at one end of the hayloft, but otherwise, it was shadowy and dark inside. Horses stood in their stalls, and the boys' pony nickered. "Samuel?"

Something flew past Anna's head. Splat! Puzzled, she turned to see a smashed egg oozing down the side of the pony's box stall. As her eyes adjusted, she caught a glimpse of a white face and blond hair before another egg came sailing down from above, out of the hayloft, and just missed her shoulder. "Rudy?" she shouted. "Is that you? You're supposed to be in school!"

"Not Rudy," Peter called from the feed room. "It's me!" He drew back his arm and hurled a dead mouse, of all things, at her. He leaped out into the passageway, stuck out his tongue and taunted, "Fatty-fatty, two by four!" Then he darted into the dark shadows again.

Anna almost laughed out loud. It was time she and the boys had a little talk, and this would be the perfect opportunity. If Peter was on the ground floor, Rudy could only be one place. The direction the second egg had come from: up. Stripping off her coat and bonnet, she dropped them onto the nearest hay bale. She might be a big girl, but she was strong, and she could move fast when she wanted to. Rudy wasn't going to escape. There was only one way out of the loft—down the ladder.

Anna strode across the barn and took the ladder, one rung at a time. Behind her, Peter was shouting, "Can't catch me, can't catch me," but she had no intentions of trying. Rudy was the main mischief maker, and if she caught him, she wouldn't have to go after his twin.

When she reached the top of the ladder, she saw Rudy climbing a stack of hay bales. Pigeons flew up and feathers and dust sprayed the boy as he climbed higher, toward the roof. He'd lost his hat, and when one pigeon dropped a smear of excrement on his head, Anna burst into laughter. Scrambling, Rudy reached the top of the hay pile, and the whole structure began to sway.

"Best you get down here and take your medicine before you fall and break your neck," Anna warned. "You know your father is going to find out you skipped school." She waited, arms folded, beside the hatch that opened to the ladder.

"Not coming down," Rudy said. He wiped at the gooey mess in his hair and grimaced. "You can't make me."

"I don't have to," Anna said. "All I have to do is wait here until your dat comes in for evening milking. Then you can explain why you're wasting good eggs, knocking down his hay bales and being rude to a guest."

"We don't like you." Peter came slowly up the ladder behind her and poked his head into the loft.

"You don't have to like me." Anna looked from one twin to the other. "You have to respect me."

"We don't want Dat to marry you," Rudy said. "Naomi says Dat is going to marry you and then you'll be our mother." His voice was tight, as if he was about to burst into tears.

"Ah," Anna said. "You two think you know better than your father, when it comes to deciding what he should do?"

"You aren't our mother." Peter walked around Anna to stand closer to his brother. "She was pretty."

"*Ya,*" Anna agreed. "Your mother was beautiful, and a good woman, a good mother. But she's in heaven now, and your father needs help with the house and with the little girls. You two are almost grown. You may not need a mother, but you might need a friend."

Rudy slid halfway down the pile. "We don't need anybody."

Anna sighed. "You must trust your father." When neither boy answered, she went on. "Tell me something. If he came to the bottom of the ladder right this minute and said 'jump'—if he held up his arms to catch you, would you trust him?"

Peter frowned.

"You would jump, wouldn't you?" she pressed. "Because you trust him to do the right thing. So you have to trust him now. If he chooses me or another woman to be his new wife, you must try to understand. He's the adult and your father, and you still live under his roof. You have to trust his decisions."

"You gonna tell on us?" Rudy asked. "Not about school. We'll tell him that. About the eggs?"

"Should I?" Anna replied.

"We'll be in big trouble," Peter said. "More than last time." Rudy slid the rest of the way down the hay. Peter looked at him and wrinkled his nose. "You stink," he said.

"Pigeon poo."

"Maybe that's fair punishment for throwing eggs at me." Anna's gaze narrowed. "Think about what I said. Think about your father and sisters, and about what's best for your family. You're growing older, both of you. Maybe you should find a way to do good instead of causing trouble. Maybe that would make your mother happy."

Rudy was red-faced, sniffing and wiping at his dirty face with the back of his hands. "Sorry," he said.

She turned her gaze on Peter. "And by the way, Peter. You're right," she said. "I am fat, but it still hurts my feelings when you call me names. It makes me cry at night. Did you like it when the other boys teased you at school for failing your spelling test?"

Peter shook his head. *"Ne."*

"At your age, you should be thinking about what kind of men you want to be when you are grown. Do you want to be someone like your dat? Because if you do, it's time to start changing your ways."

Anna stood there for a minute looking at both of them, then climbed down the ladder and put on her coat and bonnet. "I'd clean up those eggs if I were you," she hollered up to the twins. "And if you try something like that with me again, I promise you'll not get off as easily."

She was halfway back across the field toward home when she realized that she hadn't found Samuel and wasn't any closer to helping Grossmama than before. She didn't know if she'd made things worse between her and the boys or better, but she was through taking their nonsense. From now on, she would be the adult. But mature as she was, she couldn't help but take satisfaction from the memory of Rudy wiping pigeon poo out of his hair.

Twice that week Samuel and the children came to dinner at the Yoder home, and he was heartened by the way his girls ran to Anna to be hugged and fussed over. Hannah and her family treated him as though he was already family, and the twins were on their best behavior. But as much as he wished it, there was no opportunity for him to spend time alone with Anna.

He needed very much to talk to her. She was as warm and friendly as ever to him, and he couldn't have asked for anyone to be kinder to his daughters. But there was a distance between them that hadn't been there the day he'd taken her riding in the sleigh. She was obviously upset about the matter of Lovina and the English senior center, but surely Anna wouldn't allow that to come between them, would she?

He'd written to his sisters in Ohio, and told them that he was courting Anna Yoder, and that they should be expecting an invitation to a wedding soon. Normally, weddings were held in late autumn, but since he was a widower, he could marry when it was most convenient, so long as the proper bans were called and the church leaders were in agreement. Anna was young, but she was of age, and she'd never been married before. There was no reason they couldn't become a married couple before spring planting.

Sunday was a visiting day, and Samuel hoped to be able to leave the children in Hannah's care and take Anna in the buggy to visit friends in the neighborhood. Maybe then he could talk about their little disagreement and get past it. With each day, Samuel was more and more convinced that Anna was exactly the right wife for him, and that he could make her happy.

Earlier in the week, he'd ordered ice cream from a delivery truck and had it stored in the freezer at the chair shop. After dinner, he'd drive down and pick it up, so that they could all enjoy a special treat. His hogs had come back from the butcher in neat packages, and the meal the two families had shared had centered around fresh pork chops that he had brought to Hannah's the day before. Soon, he hoped to be able to have Anna's mother, sisters and extended family to his home for dinners. Other than his children, he had no relatives here in Delaware, and with Anna's help, he couldn't wait to play host.

But once again Samuel was disappointed. Anna agreed to come with him, but just when they were about to depart, Bishop Atlee, his wife and sister arrived to pay a call on the Yoders. In a buggy behind them came Martha, Dorcas and Reuben. There was no question of Samuel's leaving, and the whole group ended up spending the afternoon in Hannah's parlor. It was a pleasant time, as the bishop was known for his sense of humor, and always had a store of new jokes and news from far-off communities. But it wasn't the way Samuel would have chosen to spend the hours.

Finally, when everyone had stuffed themselves on cake and ice cream and consumed pots of strong coffee, Bishop Atlee rose and began to make his good-byes. "Oh, Samuel," he said as he reached for his coat. "You'll be pleased to know that I've come to a decision on Anna's request." His eyes were twinkling.

Confused, Samuel glanced at Anna and saw that she'd blushed a rosy red. He returned his attention to what the bishop was saying.

"Quite an unusual request, this. I can tell you that I prayed over it several nights." His expression grew serious. "You did know about Anna's coming to see me on Friday, didn't you?"

Samuel shook his head.

"But she *has* spoken to you about Lovina's request to take part in the program at the Englisher senior center?"

"*Ya*," Samuel answered, as it dawned on him that what he was talking about was that Anna had gone to the bishop herself, after Samuel had refused her. He bristled. "I told her that it wasn't our way, that we kept our old people at home."

"And who are you to say where I should go or not go?" Lovina demanded.

"Mother!" Martha admonished. "You don't talk so to the bishop."

"He's young enough to be my son, and I'll say whatever I please. I want to go and teach the Englishers how to make proper rugs."

"There, there." Bishop Atlee broke into a wide smile and raised his hand. "And so you shall, Lovina. I doubt we have to worry about you straying from the fold, do we? You might even teach the worldly folk a thing or two in the process."

He glanced back at Samuel, who didn't know what to say.

"Come, don't be such a stick-in-the-mud." The bishop grasped Samuel's arm. "We may be a conservative church, but we aren't backward. We don't turn our back on the Englisher doctors or hospitals, do we? And as Anna has so ably pointed out to me, Lovina isn't going two days a week to be cared for, but to teach and relieve the spirits of others. I think it's a fine plan, and if she wants to ride in the red van, she has my blessing."

All the way home, Samuel kept thinking about what Anna had done. Where had she gotten the spunk to go to Bishop Atlee on her own, and how had she convinced him to break with tradition and allow such a thing? A part of Samuel was annoyed; he'd been embarrassed to hear the news from the bishop first. But a part of him couldn't help but be pleased with Anna. Most women would have trusted his word as a deacon, but she'd gone to a higher authority. As was her right as a member of the church, and maybe her duty to do all she could for her grandmother.

Still, he felt a little foolish.

Was this how it would be, once they were married? Would she challenge his authority in the household? Frieda never would have. What was he getting himself into?

Unconsciously, Johanna's husband's words came back into his mind. "Hannah's too liberal. She's spoiled her girls. They don't know their place."

A man had to be the head of the house. It was the way he'd been raised and what he believed. A wife should heed her husband's advice. And he'd made it quite clear to Anna that he didn't think that sending her grandmother to the English was a good idea. Yet, she'd gone and asked the bishop herself. It stuck in his craw like a fish bone.

Anna had always seemed so sweet and easygoing. Had he misjudged her? Yet, Anna hadn't challenged him or argued. She'd simply persisted, and apparently made a good case to the bishop, good enough to get his approval. Samuel wished Reuben and Martha hadn't heard it all. It would be common knowledge in the community by tomorrow. It would be a long time before his neighbors quit calling him "stick-in-the-mud".

By the time Samuel had finished the evening milking, sent the hired man on his way and tucked Mae and Lori Ann into bed, the worst of his annoyance had passed. Anna was, after all, very young. He loved her, and this was something they could work out. She just had to understand that she had put him in a bad position, going over his head and not telling him. It was natural that a couple have some disagreements, and this would be easily mended.

She must have known that he was unhappy. He'd seen the distress in her eyes when he'd said his good-byes and left her mother's house. Doubtless, Anna was already regretting her hasty decision to go to the bishop after Samuel had been clear in his opinion on the whole matter.

Samuel knew he didn't have it in him to be harsh with Anna, but it would be best if he nipped this mis-guided independence early on. He'd stay away from the Yoder house for a few days. When he didn't come she'd know why, and she'd quickly seek him out to make things right between them.

As much as he enjoyed being with Anna, and as much as it would hurt him not to be with her, he'd have to be firm. She had to remember that he was a church deacon, that he had to set an example for other members of the community. And Anna, as his wife, would have to do likewise. It wouldn't do to have the deacon's wife running about the county, going against her husband's wishes and making him look bad.

By Saturday's school program and cookie auction next weekend, they'd both be laughing about this incident. Anna would have learned from her mistake, and nothing like this would ever happen again.

Chapter Sixteen

Samuel didn't come to visit on Monday or Tuesday, and he didn't come on Wednesday or Thursday, although his hired man stopped by in the afternoon to bring ten pounds of bacon, a fresh loin of pork, fifty pounds of potatoes and two blocks of scrapple. Leah stowed the gifts in the refrigerator as Anna continued rolling out dough for Saturday's cookie bake. "Wonder why Samuel didn't bring them himself?" Leah asked, with a twinkle in her eye.

Anna chuckled. "You know why. You saw him on Sunday afternoon, when Bishop Atlee called him a stick-in-the-mud. Samuel Mast's nose is out of joint because I persuaded the bishop to let Grossmama go to the English center."

Leah grinned. "You've hurt his manly feelings, Anna."

"All I did was check with the bishop myself," Anna replied, choosing a cookie cutter in the shape of a cow, and beginning to cut out cookies and slide them onto a baking sheet.

"You think he's angry with you for doing that?"

Anna shrugged. "I think his pride is a little bruised that I didn't take his word on the matter."

Leah brought a second cookie sheet to the table. "What if he's still upset by Saturday—what if he doesn't bid on your basket?"

"Then I'll give the cookies to the children. It was right that Grossmama got to go. She might not like the senior center once she's there, but that's up to her." Anna slapped another lump of dough on the floured board and began to roll it out with a wooden rolling pin that her father had made for her mother when they were first married. "If Samuel wants to marry me, he should know who I am. I don't have Miriam's temper or your courage out in the world, but I won't be quiet when I think I'm right. Even if I wasn't right and the bishop had said no, at least then I would know I had tried my best. I don't think Samuel would have been so annoyed if the bishop had said no."

"I think you're right," Aunt Jezebel said as she came into the kitchen. "You know, that's what I always admired most about your mother. She was a good wife to your father, but she never let him get too big for his britches." Her face flushed a delicate pink. "I didn't mean to listen in, but Lovina fell asleep, and I thought I'd come to give you a hand with the cookie baking."

Anna smiled at the little woman. "We can use your help," she said. "You always made the best black walnut cookies, and Irwin cracked and hulled two cupfuls of nuts from the big tree at the end of the garden last night."

Aunt Jezebel hesitated before coming to hug Anna. "It was a brave thing you did, speaking to your bishop. A kind thing for Lovina. It will make her feel useful.

Better for her to be out among people, sewing her rugs, than always sitting in your kitchen finding fault. I think she will be happier."

"So you don't think I was wrong to go to the bishop?" Anna asked.

Her aunt dusted a bit of flour off Anna's chin. "*Ne,* love, I don't. And I think your young man will see that, once he's had time to cool down."

"I wouldn't want him to think I was forward," Anna said. "To go against his wishes… A man should be the head of the house."

"And the woman the heart." Aunt Jezebel looked into Anna's eyes. "He's a fool if he lets you slip away. You will make Samuel Mast and his motherless children happy."

"You really think so?" Anna asked.

Her aunt pursed her lips. "What do you see when you look at your Grossmama? Do you see her wrinkles or her thinning hair?"

Anna shook her head. "I see her like she was when I was a child. She always walked so straight, and her bonnet and apron were so stiff they crinkled when she walked. I thought she was wonderfully Plain."

Aunt Jezebel smiled. "You really love my sister, don't you?"

"*Ya,*" Anna said. "I do. She can be grouchy, but inside I know she wants to be kind."

"You see Lovina that way because you have love in your heart for her. Many a fair face hides a sour disposition. You are beautiful inside, Anna. And if your Samuel can't see that, he doesn't deserve you."

"I agree." Leah slid a pan of cookies into the oven. "You always think of other people before you think of yourself. Besides, if you don't say yes, Samuel might be desperate enough to end up with Dorcas. And she wouldn't be able to manage those five kids—not to mention her biscuits." Leah giggled. "The last batch she made were so awful, Aunt Martha said the chickens wouldn't even eat them."

Saturday evening finally arrived, and containers of food and baskets of cookies had been stowed in the back of the big Yoder buggy. Irwin, Leah and Rebecca had walked over to Samuel's to help make last minute preparations for the get-together. Miriam and Charley invited Susanna to ride with them, leaving Mam, Anna, Aunt Jezebel and Grossmama to take the family buggy.

Anna had been looking forward to parents' night and the cookie auction as much as anyone, but not hearing from Samuel all week had made her nervous. She wanted him to outbid everyone for her basket, and she wanted to see his children recite their pieces, take part in the spelling bee and show what they had learned this term in class. Most of all, she wanted to sit on a blanket in the barn with Samuel and the other unmarried couples, and share laughter, as well as the contents of her picnic.

She'd been so worried that she wondered if she should walk over to Samuel's house and tell him that she was sorry. Mam had put an end to that idea.

"Are you sorry that your Grossmama is going next week in the red van?" Mam had asked. "If you had it to do over again, would you still take your case to Bishop Atlee?"

Anna had nodded slowly. "I suppose I would."

"Exactly," Mam said. "So if there's any apologizing to be done, it should be Samuel Mast who does it, not you."

Anna hadn't gone to Samuel, but neither had she slept much last night. What if he was still angry with her? What if he ignored her and bid on some other girl's basket? What if he wouldn't speak to her? Before, when she was resigned to being unmarried, she'd come to accept it. But Samuel's courting had opened up a whole armful of wanting. If she lost him forever, she didn't think she could bear it.

She looked at the clock for the third time in the last thirty minutes. "We'd best be going, hadn't we?" she asked.

Mam smiled at her. "It's early yet, but it won't hurt. Find Grossmama's black bonnet and help her into her heavy cape."

"I'm sick," Grossmama whimpered when Anna went to her room to find her. The old woman lay on her bed, her face pale, eyes fluttering weakly. "I'm having a dizzy spell. I tripped and…"

"Oh, Grossmama, did you hurt yourself? Why didn't you call us?" Anna ran to her and laid a palm on her forehead. Her grandmother's skin felt cool to the touch, but a fall could have injured her bad hip again. "Mam!" she shouted. "Come here." Anna poured water from the bedside pitcher into a glass. "Would you like a drink?"

"*Ne.* My head hurts. Let me lie here and try to sleep."

"I hate to have you miss the evening. Aunt Martha and Aunt Alma will be there."

"I couldn't go out on such a cold night. It will be the death of me. You all go to your frolic. Don't worry about me."

After her mother and Aunt Jezebel had joined Anna

at Lovina's bedside, the three withdrew to the kitchen. "What do you think?" Mam asked Jezebel. "Is she really ill?" She glanced at the clock. "As much as I'd like to, I can't stay with her. The children and their families will be arriving soon at the gathering. As their teacher, I need to be there."

"Anna!" Grossmama called in a surprisingly strong voice. "Bring me a cup of chamomile tea."

Aunt Jezebel sighed. "I'll stay. I don't know whether this is real or not. She always says she's dizzy or sick when she doesn't want to go somewhere or do something. You and Anna go on." Anna could see the disappointment on her aunt's face. She loved getting out of the house and visiting with other women in the community, and she loved watching the children recite.

"Anna!" Grossmama called. "I need you."

The sound of a glass shattering brought Aunt Jezebel to her feet. "Let me go in to her," she insisted. "I can usually calm her when she has one of her spells."

But Grossmama would have none of it, and fifteen minutes later, when the buggy rolled out of the yard, it was Mam and Aunt Jezebel who were going to the parents' night program, and Anna who was sweeping up the last of the broken glass. She'd forced a smile and insisted that she didn't mind, but inside she wanted to weep. She'd wanted so badly to be with Samuel tonight, and now she wouldn't have the chance to make everything right with him. And even if they patched up their disagreement later, tonight would be gone forever.

"Anna!" Grossmama called shrilly as Anna carried the broken glass to the kitchen trashcan. "Where's my tea?"

Anna sighed and turned to the cupboard. She took down the can of chamomile tea and carried it to the counter. Maybe it was best that she didn't go tonight, she thought. That way, if Samuel was still angry with her, she wouldn't be embarrassed in front of everyone. Besides, if she'd left her grandmother and the woman really had been ill, she'd never forgive herself.

An hour later, Grossmama's dizziness seemed to have passed, and she felt well enough to have a bowl of chicken soup, some applesauce and three oatmeal cookies leftover from the bounty that had been baked for the school program. "You're a good girl," her grandmother said, patting Anna's hand. "You're the only one who cares about me."

"That's not true," Anna replied. "Lots of people love you. Mam and Aunt Jezebel, my sisters, and…"

"Not like you," Grossmama insisted. "You're the only one who listened to me when I said I wanted to go to the Englisher center. Everyone else thinks I'm a crazy old lady…just because I get confused…forget things. You will, too, when you're my age."

Anna patted her hand. "I don't think you're crazy, and neither does Mam."

"And…" Tears welled in the elderly woman's faded blue eyes. "Because sometimes I make believe my Jonas is alive…when I know he's not."

Anna fought tears, her heart touched by her grandmother's revelation. "I can't imagine how hard it must be to have lost so many people you love. But…" She took a deep breath and said what she'd wanted to say since Grossmama had first come to stay with them. "You should try to be kinder to those who love you— to Mam, especially. She does her best to care for you and…and you…" She couldn't say more. Reverence for the elderly was too ingrained in her. It wasn't her place to lecture her grandmother, but it was so difficult to see her and Mam always at odds.

There was a long pause, and then her grandmother nodded. "*Ya, ya,* I know. Hannah is more of a daughter to me than my own blood daughters, but it isn't easy to live in a daughter-in-law's house."

"It's Dat's house, too. Your son's house."

Grossmama's mouth tightened. "And how much do I see him? He's always in the barn. Those cows must be milked dry."

Anna blinked. A moment ago her grandmother had said that she knew Dat was dead, but now... Was she pretending now, or had the fog closed in on her mind again? "Mam wants you here," she said. "We all do."

"I suppose I can try harder." Grossmama yawned. "For Jonas's sake, not Hannah's."

Anna leaned close and pulled the quilt up around the old woman's shoulders. "Sleep for a little while. I'm sure it will make you feel better."

"Don't leave me. I don't want to be alone in this big house."

"I won't leave the house. I'll be right in the kitchen."

"If Jonas comes in, tell him I want to talk to him." Her grandmother closed her eyes. Soon her breathing grew heavy. The lines in her face relaxed and she began to snore. Anna rose and quietly left the room.

In the kitchen, she washed the cup and dishes that Grossmama had eaten from and lit a gas lamp. Carefully, she carried it into the parlor and set it on the wide windowsill, taking care to tuck the curtain away from the glass chimney. "To bring you all safely home," she whispered.

The children's program would be over by now, and the bidding on the cookie baskets would be next. She wondered how Naomi had done in the spelling bee. Her spelling was quite good, but Anna wasn't sure if it was good enough to win against children who were several grades ahead of her. She'd wanted to be there for Naomi and for the twins as well. Anna hoped the talk she'd had with them in Samuel's hayloft would help. She didn't worry about the two younger girls. Susanna and Rebecca would watch over them and see they didn't miss out on anything, but Naomi could sometimes be shy around the other children in the community. It was easy for her to be overlooked. Anna should have reminded Aunt Jezebel to be sure that Naomi didn't feel neglected.

Anna glanced in on her grandmother, who seemed to be sleeping peacefully. Maybe the hectic evening and the cold night air *would* have been too much for her.

She returned to the kitchen and looked around to see if anything needed doing. The others wouldn't be home for more than an hour. It was too early for her to go to bed, and she wasn't in the mood for sewing. She took Dat's old barn coat off the hook and stepped out onto the back porch. Everything was still beneath the full, silver moon; not a sound came from the barn or the chicken house.

"Oh, Samuel," she murmured into the darkness. "I wanted to be with you tonight." Salt tears stung the backs of her eyelids and she blinked them away.

And then, just as she'd turned to go back into the house, she heard the faint sound of a horse's hooves on the frozen dirt lane. *Clippity-clop. Clippity-clop.*

Anna's pulse quickened. It was too soon for Mam, Aunt Jezebel and the girls to be coming back. Unless something had gone wrong… Was someone else ill, or had there been an accident? She hurried across the porch and down the back steps into the yard. Had she imagined the sound? No, she could definitely make out the creak of buggy wheels and the hard rhythm of a pacer coming fast.

But the horse and buggy that appeared around the corner of the house wasn't Mam's. It was Samuel's.

He reined the horse in only an arm's length from where she stood. "Anna? What are you doing out here in the cold? I nearly ran you down."

She laughed. *Samuel! Samuel was here!* He'd come to find her. "Not likely," she managed.

He climbed down out of the buggy and came toward her. He was so tall, so broad and sturdy in the moonlight. "I waited, but you didn't come," he said.

"I wanted to come," she said. Her hands were trembling so hard that she tucked them behind her back. "But Grossmama took sick and…"

"Your sisters told me." He looked down, then up again. "I was wrong, Anna, to be upset that you went to the bishop. All week I thought about it. I was wrong. You were right to talk to Bishop Atlee for your grandmother."

"I didn't mean to make you angry. I just wanted to be sure I had done all I could for Grossmama."

"As you should have. Anna, Anna. Just when I think I have you figured out, you surprise me. You're wonderful, did you know that? Wonderful."

Pleased but flustered, she took a step back, searching for a safer subject. "Naomi," she seized upon. "How did she do in the spelling bee?"

"First place," he said with a chuckle. "My own daughter won the heifer."

Anna laughed with him. "She's smart, Samuel, like her father." She swallowed the constriction in her throat. "But why are you here? The evening can't be over. Everyone must still be at your place."

"And so they are." He turned back to the buggy, returned a minute later with a blanket and two baskets. "I put your cookies up first, bid fifty dollars on them, and no one else made an offer."

"Fifty dollars?" The tears were back, but this time they were tears of happiness. "You paid fifty dollars for my cookies?"

"I would have paid more, if anyone had bid against me. And if you couldn't come to the picnic, I'm bringing the picnic to you. Come now, before we freeze out here. Take these baskets. I'll put my horse in the shed and follow you in."

She nodded, too full of excitement to speak. *Samuel had come!* He wanted to be with her. He'd left the frolic for her, and he'd bought her cookies for more money than anyone had ever paid. It might be *Hochmut,* pride, but it filled her with joy that he'd done such a thing. It couldn't be the cookies. It had to be *her* that he valued, Plain Anna Yoder. *Samuel valued her!*

They spread Samuel's blanket on the kitchen floor, opened the door to the wood stove, and built up the fire. Then, by the light of a single lamp, they laughed and talked and ate the food that she'd packed. Samuel told her about his plans for spring planting and his desire to buy horses for Peter and Rudy. "They're getting too long-legged for the pony," he explained.

"And what will you do with the pony?" Anna asked.

Despite all the goodies spread around them, she'd been too excited to eat. He must have felt the same way, because, for once, he wasn't eating much either. They were too busy talking.

"I was thinking that Naomi might like it. Not to ride astride, not for a girl."

"*Ya,*" Anna agreed. "But she could use the pony cart. It would be good for her to learn to drive. She spends too much time in the house with her books."

"I wanted to ask Lovina if she would teach Naomi to make braided rugs."

His words made her smile. "You like my grandmother, don't you? In spite of her sharp tongue?"

Samuel chuckled. "She reminds me of my Grossmama. You couldn't get away with anything around that one, I can tell you. *Ya.* I do like Lovina. And so do my girls. Despite her words sometimes, she always shows them kindness."

"I'm glad to hear you say that, because I've been thinking."

"About my proposal of marriage?" His voice grew husky. "Your birthday will be soon, Anna. You promised me an answer. Will you marry me?" He took hold of her hand and held it in his big one. "Beautiful Anna Yoder, will you do me the honor of becoming my wife?"

She opened her mouth to protest, to tell him that she wasn't beautiful, that he didn't have to say so when it wasn't true, and then all the things that Mam and Grossmama and Aunt Jezebel and her sisters had reminded her about inner beauty came rushing back. And suddenly it didn't matter that she was Plain anymore. Suddenly, she was so full of happiness that she could hardly speak.

"How much do you want to marry me?" she asked. "Enough to take my grandmother as part of the package? I want to be with you, Samuel. I want to take care of you and the children, and I want to be a good and true wife to you, so long as I live." She paused to catch her breath. "But could you…would you consider having my Grossmama come to live with us? I think she would be happier there, with the little ones. I know it's a lot to ask, but—"

"You'll have me?" He grabbed her and pulled her against him in a great bear hug, then slowly lowered his head and kissed her tenderly on the lips. "I love you, my Anna," he said. "And if you'll take me, a man with five children, you can bring a dozen grandmothers to our home if you wish. You can bring your Aunt Jezebel, your sister Susanna, even your cousin Dorcas if you want."

Mouth tingling from the kiss, Anna touched his warm cheek and found it damp with tears. "Are you crying, Samuel?"

"I am," he admitted. "But don't tell anyone."

"I won't bring Dorcas, I promise."

He chuckled, stood and caught both her hands, lifting her up. "So you will marry me?"

"I said I would, didn't I?"

"When?" he asked.

"As soon as the bans can be properly read. You are a deacon in the church. We must set a good example for the young people."

"We could be married by spring."

"Whatever you say, Samuel," she replied sweetly. Every doubt had vanished. And in her heart, she was certain that this was the path that God had planned for her all along.

Epilogue

Anna rose from the big bed she shared with Samuel, and padded barefoot, in her long, white cotton nightgown, across the thick, braided rug. In the east, the first rays of dawn would soon appear and the roosters would be crowing to welcome the new day. In the darkness, she found her nightstand, removed her nightcap and brushed out her hair. Any minute, Samuel would be up to begin the morning chores, the children would tumble sleepily out of their beds and Grossmama would wake and want her morning cup of chamomile tea.

Anna smiled. She loved this time, when all the house was silent and the day full of possibilities waited like an unopened birthday gift. This was her home, her wonderful husband, her children and her grandmother. She never expected to be this happy in her marriage. She'd hoped she might be, but the reality of life with Samuel was better than she could have dreamed.

Deftly, she rolled her long hair into a bun and pinned it at the back of her head, before reaching for her freshly starched *kapp* and covering her head with it. The sweet, rich smells of spring wafted through the open window:

plowed earth, apple blossoms, freshly cut grass and the first blooms of climbing roses.

Anna knelt and bowed her head in a moment of silent prayer, as she did every morning. God had answered all of her prayers, and her heart was full of praise for His many blessings. She knew that she and Samuel would face trials; every family did. But with each other, with faith and hard work, she was confident that they would overcome each obstacle.

As she rose to draw back the simple white curtain, Samuel called from the bed. "Anna, where are you?"

"Here, sleepyhead. Making ready for the day, as *you* should. The cows will be wanting milking and the sheep must be fed before breakfast."

"Come back to me, my sweet *kuchen*."

She heard him pat the bed beside him and she smiled. This was the teasing game they played every morning, and neither of them ever tired of it. "What, with so much to do, lazybones? It will be midmorning before I get the coffee on."

"Just for a minute, Anna."

Laughing, she returned to the high-poster bed that had been Samuel's great grandfather's and slid in beside him. Samuel put his arm around her and drew her close, and she tucked her head against his shoulder.

"Mmm," he murmured. "This is nice. Can't we just stay here all day?"

"*Ne,* we cannot." She giggled. "What would the community say if their deacon lounged in his bed while the spring day was wasted?"

"I suppose you're right." He yawned. "I've been thinking, my Anna."

"*Ya,* Samuel. I'm sure you have."

"I think there's too much for you to do in this house. Your grandmother, the children, your garden. I have the boys and the hired man, but Naomi and Lori Ann are too young to be of much help."

"Hush." She placed two fingers over his lips. "To say such a thing about your daughters. They are good girls who show great promise of being better house-wives than I am."

"No one could be a better wife or mother than you."

"Hush, Samuel. You will make me blush with such talk."

"All well, but I have decided. You must have help. My niece has more girls than her house can hold. If you agree, we'll ask her to send one or two to help you out."

Anna found his hand and squeezed it. "You are too good to me. But there's no need. If you think I need help, let's ask my sister Rebecca to come for a few hours every day. She knows the way I like things in my kitchen, and she'll be good with the children."

"You've asked her already, I suppose," he said with a chuckle.

"Of course, Samuel. But if it doesn't please you, I can—"

"It pleases me very much, Anna. And if you'd rather have your sister than one of my nieces, that's exactly what we'll do. But you will have help. I'll not have you working your hands to the bone for us."

Anna laughed. "Small chance of that. What other husband in Kent County regularly scrubs his wife's kitchen floor?" She wiggled free of his embrace and slid across the bed. "Now, get up before the twins, or they'll never let you hear the end of it." She found her night robe on the chair and put it on.

"Do I have to?" he groaned.

She rested her fists on her ample hips. "*Ya*, Samuel. You have to. As you do every day."

He sat up and halfheartedly tossed a pillow in her direction. "Have I told you that I love you, woman?"

"Every day," she answered.

"You bring joy to this house."

"And you, Samuel, bring joy to my heart."

And, as was their custom, he rose and dressed, and they went down the wide staircase together, hand in hand, like young newlyweds, which was, she supposed, exactly what they were.

* * * * *

DANGER
IN AMISH COUNTRY

* * *

FALL FROM GRACE
Marta Perry

DANGEROUS HOMECOMING
Diane Burke

RETURN TO WILLOW TRACE
Kit Wilkinson

FALL FROM GRACE

Marta Perry

This story is dedicated to my husband, as always.

But they who wait for the Lord shall renew
their strength; they shall mount up with wings
like eagles; they shall run and not be weary;
they shall walk and not faint.
—*Isaiah* 40:31

Chapter One

S ara Esch smiled as her young scholars burst out into the autumn sunshine at the end of another school day. Even the best of Amish students couldn't help showing a bit of enthusiasm when freedom arrived at three o'clock each weekday afternoon, especially on Friday.

All except one, it seemed. Seven-year-old Rachel King hung back, her small face solemn, as if reluctant to leave her desk.

Sara tried not to let concern show in her expression as she approached the motherless child. Rachel had been in Sara's one-room school for less than a month, since she and her father arrived in Beaver Creek, coming to Pennsylvania from Indiana. That meant Sara didn't know Rachel as well as she did most of the *kinner* in her school.

Sara knelt next to the child and spoke softly, knowing her words would be masked by the chatter of the two eighth-grade girls whose turn it was to wash the chalkboards.

"*Was ist letz,* Rachel?" She asked the question in dialect. She always spoke Englisch in school, but the familiar tongue of home and family might put the child at ease. "What's wrong?"

"Nothing." Rachel's round blue eyes grew rounder still, as if she was surprised that her teacher had noticed. "Nothing is wrong, Teacher Sara."

Sara sat back on her heels, studying the small face. Rachel might have been any young Amish girl, with her blue eyes, rosy cheeks, and blond hair. Her plain blue dress and black apron were like those of every other little girl, too. But something was different about Rachel King, of that Sara was certain sure.

She took the child's hands in hers. "You can tell me if anything is troubling you, Rachel. I want you to be happy here in Beaver Creek."

Rachel's lips trembled, as if she were on the verge of speech. Then she looked over Sara's shoulder, and her expression lightened.

"Daed!" She ran to the man who filled the school-house doorway.

So. Sara got slowly to her feet, mindful of Caleb King's gaze on her. His arrival meant she wouldn't hear anything more from Rachel today. But at least she could see that Rachel's problem, whatever it was, wasn't with her father. She would hate to have to deal with such an issue.

She took a step toward Caleb, smiling, and stopped when she encountered an icy glare. His face was set in severe lines above the warm chestnut of his beard, and Caleb's gaze seemed an accusation. Her heart gave an uncomfortable thump.

Caleb patted his daughter's head. "Go out and play on the swings. I need to talk to Teacher Sara."

Sara caught a swift flare of panic in the child's face at the prospect of going outside. She moved toward them.

"Perhaps Rachel could help with washing the boards," she suggested. "We might step out onto the porch to talk."

Caleb's gray-blue eyes grew steely with annoyance, probably at her interference, but he nodded. He stepped back and held the door open like a command.

Sara pushed Rachel gently toward the chalkboard. "Lily and Lovina, you'll like to have Rachel help you for a bit, ain't so?"

Lily looked a tad mulish at the prospect, but gentle Lovina seemed to take the situation in and smiled, holding out her hand to the child.

"*Ya, komm,* Rachel."

The little girl ran toward her happily enough. Satisfied, Sara stepped through the door, very aware of Caleb's looming presence behind her. He had a complaint, it seemed.

The door clicked shut.

"What has happened at school to bring my child home so upset she could not even eat her supper?" Caleb didn't give Sara time to turn around before he threw the words at her. "And to give her nightmares, as well? I don't expect this at an Amish school."

Stiffening at the implication she was at fault, Sara made an effort to keep her expression calm as she faced the man. "I noticed that Rachel seemed upset today. I was just trying to get her to tell me what was wrong when you came in."

And whatever it is, I am not to blame, she added silently. Nothing was more important to her than her scholars—they were the only *kinner* she was ever likely to have.

"You didn't scold her for anything yesterday?" Caleb didn't look mollified. "Or let another child bully her?"

"Certainly not. Bullying is not tolerated in my classroom." She took a deep breath, reminding herself not to let the man's antagonism rouse her temper. Even teachers in Amish schools had to learn to deal with troublesome parents. "I am as puzzled as you are. Maybe together we can figure out how to handle this problem."

She met his gaze steadily, and after what seemed a very long moment, she had the satisfaction of seeing some of his antagonism fade.

"Sorry. I didn't mean… *Ach,* I was worried."

Caleb seemed to realize belatedly that he still wore his black hat. He took it off, revealing hair the same chestnut as his beard. His face was lean and austere close-up, and there were fine lines around his cool eyes. He was a widower, so the rumors ran, his wife having died after a long illness. It was natural that he'd be protective of his only child. But not natural at all that he should immediately assume she was at fault.

Sara gathered her scattered wits to concentrate on the problem at hand. "I thought Rachel seemed a little reluctant to leave school yesterday. That's why I made sure the Miller children walked along with her. She didn't give you any idea of what was troubling her?"

Caleb shook his head, worry deepening the lines in his face. "When I heard her crying in the night, she sounded so afraid. The only thing she said made no sense. She said Der Alte would get her."

"The Old Man?" Relief swept through Sara. "So that's it."

"What's it?" Caleb demanded, his fists clenching. "Who is this old man who frightened my child?"

"Ach, it's not real." She put her hand on his arm in an automatic gesture of reassurance and felt taut muscle beneath the fabric of his coat. She pulled her hand away as if she'd touched something hot, realizing she was probably blushing. She'd treated him as she would one of her three brothers, but he was a stranger, despite being Amish.

"Komm." She moved quickly off the schoolhouse porch, just as glad to turn her back on him. "I'll show you."

The schoolhouse sat in the fertile Beaver Creek Valley. Amish farms stretched out on either side, while in front of the schoolhouse the long lane led to the paved county road that entered the town of Beaver Creek a bit over a mile east.

Sara turned away from the road, heading across the playground behind the school. Here the ground sloped down to the creek for which the valley was named.

On the other side of the creek the wooded ridge went sharply upward, seeming to lean over the valley protectively. No year-round houses had been built there, but the ridge was dotted with hunting cabins that would be busy during deer season.

"Where are you going?" Caleb's long strides kept up with hers. "Are you going to answer me about this old man? Does he live back here?"

"In a way." She raised her arm to point. "See that rocky outcropping? Watch what happens when we move just a little farther."

A few steps took them to the spot where the rocky cliff suddenly took on a different aspect, its sharp edges forming what a child's imagination might see as the profile of an old man.

A quick glance at Caleb's face showed that he understood. "Der Alte," she said. "The *kinner* call it that. I forgot that you wouldn't know."

Caleb stared at the rocky profile, frowning. "*Ya,* I see. But I don't understand what there is about it to frighten her so."

"Nor I." Her voice firmed. "But I mean to find out. If one of the older scholars has been telling scary stories to the young ones, that is not—" She broke off, her gaze arrested by something dark at the base of the cliff face. "Look there. That…that almost looks like—"

"A person." Caleb finished for her. "Someone is lying there."

Caleb's thoughts fled to Rachel. But his little girl was safe enough in the schoolroom, and if someone was lying hurt across the creek, he must go help.

"Go back to the *kinner*," he said shortly. "I'll see what's happened." He didn't take more than a few steps before realizing that Teacher Sara was right behind him. He swung around, exasperated. "I said—"

"If someone is hurt, it's better we both go. Then one can stay with the injured person while the other runs for help."

A look at her stubborn face told him arguing would do no good. Heaven preserve him from a headstrong woman. Not wasting his breath, he ran toward the creek.

"This way," she said, panting a little. "Stepping-stones."

He nodded and veered after her as she headed downstream. No doubt the teacher knew the area better than he did. If the man was injured badly enough to need a stretcher, she'd know the best way for emergency workers to get to him, as well as the closest telephone.

And if it was worse? He didn't have a clear line of sight now, but that dark form had been ominously still. Well, he'd tried to protect Teacher Sara from going. If she saw something bad, it was her own fault.

She was already starting across the stream, jumping lightly from one flat stone to another. He followed, but when they reached the other side, he took the lead again, brushing through the undergrowth toward the base of the cliff.

They broke through into the pebbly scree at the bottom of the cliff. Any hope he'd had that the form was an animal or fallen log vanished.

Sara reached the man first. She dropped to her knees, her skirt pooling around her, and put her fingers on his neck. Caleb could tell her that she wouldn't find a pulse. No one could still be alive when his head looked like that. The poor man didn't have a chance.

Moving quickly to her, Caleb took Sara's arm. *"Komm,"* he said, his voice gruff. "There's nothing you can do."

He helped her up, eyeing her face. If she was going to faint on him… But though her normally pink cheeks were dead white, Teacher Sara seemed to have herself in hand.

"Poor man," she murmured, and he thought she was praying silently, as he was.

"Do you know him?" He drew her back a step or two, keeping his hand on her elbow in case she was unsteady on her feet.

Sara shook her head. "Englisch," she said unnecessarily. If the man had been Amish, she'd certainly have known him. "He looks fairly young." Her tone was pitying.

Young, *ya*. The fellow wore jeans and boots, like so many young Englischers. Dark hair, with a stubble of beard on his chin. He looked... Caleb sought for the right word. He looked tough. That was it. Like someone you might not want to get on the wrong side of.

But they couldn't stand here wondering about him. "It doesn't seem right to leave the poor man alone. If I stay with him, can you see to calling the police?" Amish usually tried to steer clear of entanglement with the law, but their duty was clear in this case.

"Ya." Sara took a step back, away from the support of his hand. "There's an Englisch house not far. They'll have a phone. And then I'll stay with the *kinner*."

"My Rachel." His gaze met Sara's. "You don't think she could have seen this?" He gestured toward the body, his mind rebelling at the thought of his little girl viewing anything so gruesome.

"No." Sara seemed to push the idea away with both hands. "I don't think... Surely he hasn't been lying there since yesterday."

"It's possible." He looked up at the cliff face above them. From this angle it just looked like a jumble of rocks. "If she was standing where we stood..." He stopped, looking at Teacher Sara accusingly. "You shouldn't let the *kinner* go so far from the school."

"It is the edge of the playground," she said, a touch of anger like lightning in her green eyes. "The scholars are never out of my sight when they have recess."

"Sorry," he muttered.

He shouldn't blame Teacher Sara, when the thing that

troubled him was his own inability to get his child to confide in him. Rachel had been so distant and solemn since her mother's death, as if all Rachel's laughter had been buried with Barbara.

"I'll go now," Teacher Sara said, turning away stiffly.

He let his gaze linger on her slender figure until the undergrowth hid her from sight. No matter how long this took, he knew instinctively that she would stay with Rachel. She'd attempt to comfort his little girl.

But if Rachel really had seen this man lying dead… His thoughts stuttered to a halt as something even worse occurred to him. What if his little girl had seen the man fall?

Chapter Two

"I'm not sure what else we can tell you, Chief O'Brian." Sara tried not to think how odd it was to see the bulky, gray-haired township police chief sitting behind the teacher's desk in the Amish schoolhouse. "Neither of us knows who the man was."

She and Caleb were perched atop the first graders' desks, which were, of course, the row closest to her desk. It was not exactly comfortable, but she kept her hands folded in her lap and her feet, in their sedate black shoes, together on the wide planks of the wooden floor.

Chief O'Brian, benevolent and grandfatherly, had guided the small police presence that covered both the village of Beaver Creek and the rural township since before Sara was born. He consulted the notes he'd been making and then looked up at her.

A girlish giggle floated in from the porch, distracting him. Lily and Lovina were teaching Rachel how to play jacks under the observant gaze of a young officer. Sara felt sure that the giggle, coming from Lily, was for the benefit of the policeman.

She'd chide the girl, but she was too relieved that

they were well screened from the efforts under way across the creek, where the emergency crew was removing the body.

"Well, now." Chief O'Brian returned to the subject at hand. "I think there's just one thing that's not quite clear to me, Teacher Sara. Why exactly were you and Mr. King out there looking at the ridge to begin with?"

She opened her mouth to answer, but Caleb beat her to it.

"My little girl was telling me something I couldn't make heads or tails of about an old man," he said. "When I picked her up after school today, I asked Teacher Sara about it. She showed me the way the rock outcropping looks like a face in profile."

"Caleb and his daughter are new to Beaver Creek," Sara said, although she suspected that the police chief, like the Amish bishop, knew all there was to know about newcomers. "You know how the *kinner* talk about that face they think they see in the rocks." She turned to Caleb. "Chief O'Brian visits our school several times a year. He teaches the scholars how to be safe when they're walking along the roads. And brings them candy canes at Christmas, ain't so?"

Chief O'Brian's lined face relaxed in a smile. "Visiting the schools is my favorite part of my job. Not like this situation." He jerked his thumb in the direction of the ridge.

Caleb's explanation had made it sound as if Rachel's questions about the old man were mere curiosity. No doubt he was relieved that the chief had moved away from the topic.

"I'm sorry for the man's family to be getting news like this," she said. "Do you know who he was?"

"Not yet," Chief O'Brian said. "So you folks were just looking over that way out of idle curiosity, is that it?"

Apparently he wasn't ready to move away from the topic after all. Sara glanced at the poster above the chalkboard, which proclaimed *Visitors are the sunshine in our day* in cursive letters.

She could practically feel the intensity of Caleb's will directed toward her. For whatever reason, he didn't want her to say anything more about Rachel.

"I… I suppose so." Sara tried to sound confident, but it went against her nature even to imply something that wasn't true. She could feel her cheeks growing warm.

"I see." Chief O'Brian looked from her to Caleb, and her flush deepened. Now he was thinking exactly the wrong thing, supposing she'd made an excuse to walk with Caleb. But to say anything more would just make things worse.

Fortunately, Chief O'Brian was distracted by a gesture from the officer on the porch. He rose, very authoritative in his gray uniform.

"Well, I guess I won't be bothering you good folks any longer. Mr. King, I'm sure you want to be getting your little girl home. Sara, sorry for the disruption."

Sara murmured something, she wasn't sure what, just glad for the moment to see him leaving her classroom. He paused for a second on the porch to say something that made the girls giggle again, and then he and the young officer headed off toward the police car.

Sara swung to face Caleb. "Why didn't you tell Chief O'Brian the truth about Rachel?"

Caleb's strong-featured face tightened. "I didn't lie to the man."

"You told him only part of the truth," she snapped, keeping her voice low so that the children on the porch couldn't hear. "And you involved me in saying less than the truth, as well."

Caleb had a remarkably stubborn jaw. "My child's nightmares are not his business."

"It might be important that Rachel was so upset last night about the Old Man. It might mean…" Sara let that thought trickle to a stop, afraid of where it was going.

"Ya." His face was bleak. "It might mean that my Rachel saw something bad. And if so, it's for me to deal with. Not you. And I'm certain sure not the police."

He stalked out of the schoolhouse, leaving Sara with nothing at all to say.

The gentle clink of plates accompanied the evening routine of helping her *mamm* with the dishes. Sara, her hands in the warm, soapy water, found the chore comforting after the stresses of the day.

"I can finish up, Mamm, if you want." Her mother looked a bit tired, but she wouldn't want to hear Sara say so.

"No need." Her mother polished a plate with her usual vigor. "I don't mind. I remember when you girls used to make so much noise with washing dishes I had to get away."

Sara smiled. True enough. When she and Trudy and Ruthie did the dishes, they'd chattered and laughed and argued the whole time. But now Trudy and Ruthie were married, as well as her two oldest brothers, and Trudy had twins on the way.

Funny. Sara, the oldest, had been the first one to plan a wedding, but Tommy Brand had managed to postpone it for one reason or another for nearly five years. And when he did get married, it was to someone else.

"I'm wonderful glad Caleb King was with you when you saw that poor man." Mamm set a bowl on the shelf. "I wouldn't like to think of you finding him all alone."

Mamm didn't like to think of her doing anything alone. She was still trying to marry off her maidal daughter.

"*Ya,* I'm glad he was there, too." Sara kept her tone neutral. "Lily and Lovina had stayed after school to help, so they were there to watch his little girl."

"They're *gut* girls, even if that Lily is a bit flighty," Mamm said. "So, Caleb is a fine-looking man, ain't so? And I hear Josiah King is wonderful glad to have his nephew there to help out while he's laid up. Maybe Caleb will even decide to stay, *ya?*"

"Stop matchmaking," Sara said with mock severity. "I'm not looking for a husband."

"*Ya,* but they're nice to have, all the same." Her mother's eyes twinkled.

"And then who'd be here to help with the dishes?" Sara retorted, smiling. "If I—" She stopped at the sound of voices in the living room, where Daed had been settled in his favorite chair, reading *The Budget,* the Amish newspaper.

She exchanged glances with her mother. "That sounds like Chief O'Brian."

"You'll be wanted, then, ain't so?" Mamm handed her a towel. "Dry your hands and hurry in."

Sara touched her hair to be sure it went smoothly under her white organdy *kapp* and shook out the apron that matched her green dress. She reached the living room just as her *daed* called out for her.

"Chief O'Brian is here to talk about that poor man you found." Daed pushed his glasses up on his nose, looking as if he wished anyone else had been the finder.

"Nothing to be alarmed about, Eli," the chief said easily, maybe aware of Daed's tendency to be upset about the Englisch world intruding on their lives. "I thought you'd want to be up-to-date about what was going on."

"It's kind of you," Mamm said, a swift look at her husband reminding him to be hospitable. "You'll have some coffee and maybe a piece of apple pie, *ya?*"

"That sounds fine, Emma." Chief O'Brian's expression relaxed, something that was the usual result of Mamm's warm friendliness.

Sara gestured him to the sofa and took the rocking chair, waiting for him to begin and hoping it wouldn't be questions about Caleb or Rachel.

"Well, we identified the man who died," he said, setting his cap on his knees. "His name was Jase Kovatch."

"Kovatch." Daed pronounced the name carefully. "I can't say as I know him."

"No, don't suppose you would. The police did, and that's not exactly a recommendation," Chief O'Brian said.

"He'd been in trouble, then?" Sara asked.

The chief nodded. "Minor stuff, mostly. Drunk driving, petty pilfering. No family that we can find, and I can't see as anyone's going to miss him much except maybe some of his drinking buddies."

"That is a sad way to live." Mamm set a mug of steaming coffee and a big wedge of apple pie topped with vanilla ice cream on the end table next to him.

"Sure is." Chief O'Brian took a bite of pie and spoke

thickly around it. "I just can't figure out what he was doing up on the ridge to begin with."

"Small-game season," Daed said promptly. "Out after rabbits, maybe."

The chief shook his head. "No gun," he said succinctly.

Sara's mind chased after reasons for the man to be out there and came up empty. This time of year, people went into the woods with shotguns, looking for small game. Bird-watchers and nature lovers were sensible enough not to wander through the woods during hunting season, especially not when deer season started next month. Then all the hunting cabins would be filled to bursting.

She realized the room had fallen silent. Chief O'Brian was looking at her.

"I can't think of anything that would take the man up there," she said, hoping she hadn't missed a question.

"You haven't seen him around? Noticed anyone maybe taking an interest in the school, for instance?"

"No." She could only shake her head, perplexed. "Why?"

O'Brian shrugged. "I went up top today, along with a couple of men. We didn't find anything unexpected. But I noticed one thing about that place." He paused, looking grave. "It has the best view a person could have of your schoolhouse."

His words sank in, and alarm ricocheted along Sara's nerves. She didn't need to look around the room to know that they were all thinking the same thing.

Everyone wanted to believe that their corner of the world was safe. Unfortunately, danger was not limited to the back alleys of big cities. Even innocent schoolchildren weren't safe from evil in the world.

"Now, I don't want you folks to get all upset about it," Chief O'Brian said. "If this fellow… Well, he's dead now. But I wouldn't be doing my duty if I didn't mention it, just in case."

Sara nodded. "*Danki,* Chief O'Brian. If I see anything out of the ordinary, I'll let you know right away."

He seemed satisfied, turning back to his pie, but Sara couldn't let go of it so easily.

Tomorrow was the semiannual auction held to support the school, and every Amish person in the area, as well as plenty of Englisch, would be on the school grounds for the event. Including, she hoped, Caleb King. She had to confront him about what he hadn't told Chief O'Brian. She must make him understand that if Rachel had seen anything, she had to speak.

Chapter Three

"The playground certain sure looks different today, ain't so?" Caleb tried to keep his voice cheerful as he and Rachel neared the auction on Saturday. Auctions were a common way of raising money for Amish schools, valued as much for their fellowship as for their fund-raising.

Rachel clung a little tighter to his hand. *"Ya,"* she murmured.

"We'll bring something to Onkel Josiah when we leave, *ya?* Maybe a funnel cake or an apple dumpling." Onkel Josiah had declined to come, since he was still hobbling around on crutches and fretting over his broken leg.

Caleb's voice sounded unnatural, even to himself, but maybe Rachel didn't notice. At least she was staring, wide-eyed, at the tents and canopies that had sprung up overnight on the school grounds. Besides the auction going on inside the big tent, there were plenty of improvised stands selling food and drink, which seemed about as popular as the auction itself.

A couple of Englisch teenagers passed them, and Rachel shrank against him. He put a hand protectively on her shoulder, a wave of dread washing over him. He'd been so sure this move would be good for his Rachel. Instead, it seemed to be having the opposite effect.

Onkel Josiah's offer had seemed a godsend. Caleb had been so eager to get Rachel away from the sad memories of her mother. But instead of making things better...

The thought trailed off when he saw Teacher Sara coming toward them. She was holding the hand of a little girl who looked about Rachel's age.

Sara met his gaze and smiled, showing a dimple at the corner of her lips. With her rosy cheeks and those dancing green eyes, she looked hardly old enough to be a teacher, but he knew from Onkel Josiah that she was only a year or two younger than he was.

She and the little girl came to a stop in front of them while he was still trying to decide if her hair was blond or brown or something in between. As if aware of his thoughts, she smoothed her hair back under her *kapp* with one hand.

"Look, Becky, here's Rachel. Now you'll have someone just your age to walk around with." Sara's gaze met Caleb's. "This is my niece, Becky, my brother's girl. She's been longing for another girl to walk around with, instead of her brothers."

He nodded to the child, who had a pert, lively face and hair a shade darker than Sara's. Becky grinned at him and grabbed Rachel's hand.

"*Komm, schnell,* Rachel. Aunt Sara said she'd get me a treat but I must look at everything before I decide. You can help me."

Rachel clung to his hand a moment longer, but at an

encouraging nod from her teacher, she let go. The two girls started off together.

"Don't get too far away from us, *ya?*" Sara cautioned.

Becky nodded, already chattering away to Rachel about the relative merits of a funnel cake or an ice-cream cone.

"Danki," he said softly. "It's kind of you to think of helping Rachel get to know your niece."

"I thought Rachel might feel more at home with a friend," Sara said. "She already knows Becky a little from school. And our Becky is such a chatterbox. She talks enough to charm a turtle out of its shell."

"Rachel isn't a turtle, but she does have a shell," he admitted, impelled by a need to explain something he didn't quite understand himself. "Her mother was sick so long—" His voice seemed to stick there. "She passed not quite a year ago. Rachel hasn't had much of a childhood."

"That must have been so hard on both of you." Sara's eyes were warm with sympathy.

"Ya." He struggled to find words. "I hoped a fresh start, away from all the reminders of her *mamm,* would help her forget about the past."

"But she can't—" Sara began. Then she paused, seeming to censor what she was about to say. "I'm sorry it's been a difficult beginning for her here."

A burst of laughter came from the auction tent. Sara glanced in that direction, smiling at the sound. "Josh Davis is a fine auctioneer. He always gets the crowd into a buying mood." She turned back to him. "There's something I need to tell you."

"Ya?" They were as isolated in the noisy crowd as anywhere, he supposed. "Has something happened?"

"The chief came to our house last night. They know the man's name now." She shot a look at the girls and lowered her voice. "Jase Kovatch. The chief said he'd been in trouble with the police before."

Caleb nodded, frowning. The death of an unknown Englischer was sad, but nothing to do with them, surely.

"The worrisome thing is that the police could find no reason for him to be up there on the cliff." She took a breath, as if she didn't want to say more. "The chief says there's nothing much up there. Nothing but a good view of the school."

She didn't say any more. She didn't need to. There wasn't an Amish person alive who didn't know about the Amish schoolchildren who'd died at the hands of an Englischer.

"That's bad, that is." He fought to speak through the tightness in his throat. "But since the man is dead, there's no call to worry, *ya?*"

Sara's expression said she wasn't convinced of that. "Maybe. But we don't know for sure. If there's any danger to the *kinner*— Caleb, don't you see you must speak to the police about Rachel's fears?"

"No." His response was instantaneous. "I won't have my child involved in this."

"But—"

He cut off her protest by grabbing her wrist. He felt her pulse thunder against his palm and released her just as quickly.

"She is my child. It is for me to say. And I say no."

They stood so for a moment, their eyes challenging each other, and the noise surrounding them seemed to fade away. He felt… He wasn't sure what he felt.

Before he could decide, a voice called Sara's name.

They turned away from each other, and he wondered if Sara was as relieved as he was.

"Teacher Sara." The speaker was Silas Weaver, leader of the school board. Behind him stood another man, an older Englischer who seemed vaguely familiar.

Silas nodded to Caleb in greeting before turning to Sara. "I need a word." He made it sound like an order.

"I will keep an eye on Becky," Caleb said. "Take your time."

He moved off after the girls, just as glad to have this uncomfortable conversation interrupted. Teacher Sara seemed to have a knack for eliciting all sorts of feelings in him, and he didn't have room in his life for that.

Sara had to push down her instinctive reluctance to talk to Silas Weaver. She didn't have a choice. He was president of her school board. Unfortunately, he also possessed a stern, disapproving temperament that didn't make him easy to deal with.

She tried to manage a smile as she joined the man. "The auction is going well, ain't so?"

He grunted, casting a disapproving gaze at the tent. "We'll be lucky to end up with enough to cover our costs for a few more months. Folks don't realize how expensive it is to run a school."

Sara was well aware of Silas's reluctance to spend money on the school other than necessary repairs. She'd had more than one clash with him and come off the loser. The other two board members seemed as cowed by Silas as his own *kinner* were.

"Well, we must hope we'll realize more than expected," she said, not eager to get into another disagreement with the man.

A grunt was his only answer. He gestured to the Englischer who stood nearby. "Mr. Foster has come to me with a proposition."

Sara nodded, answering Mr. Foster's smile with one of her own and thinking she detected a bit of sympathy in his eyes.

"Mitch, please. We don't need to be formal, and I know Teacher Sara." Foster was lean and graying, with a tanned face and a ready smile. The owner of the local hardware and sporting-goods store, he was well-known for sponsoring all the local sports teams. Not that the Amish participated in those, but a person could hardly not know about it. People in a small community talked, that was certain sure.

"See, it's this way, Teacher Sara. I heard about the trouble you folks had with finding that body and all."

Silas's look turned more disapproving, if possible. "It's not proper, an Amish teacher going about finding bodies."

She could hardly expect him to approve, but Sara wasn't sure what she could have done about it. A little edge of apprehension pricked her. Silas might well seize any excuse to replace her with someone younger and more malleable.

"I'm sorry that what happened brought attention to the school," she said.

"Nonsense," Foster said bracingly. "You couldn't help what happened. You could hardly leave the poor fellow lying there. Anyway, it made me think about your school."

She nodded, not sure where this was going.

"So the long and short of it is that I noticed the playground equipment is getting a bit dilapidated. I figured

I'd like to donate the materials you need for an overhaul. Maybe add a few new pieces, as well."

Sara managed to restrain herself from jumping up and down in excitement. "That's very generous of you, Mr. Foster." She slid a look at Silas, expecting a negative reaction, and realized he was actually nodding.

"Generous," Silas echoed. "Though I'm not sure the *kinner* need all these newfangled things to play with when they should be attending to their studies."

Silas's philosophy was always that what had been good enough for him was good enough for everyone.

"Scholars seem to do better with their studies when they're able to run about and play in the middle of the day," she said. *Please,* she prayed silently.

"Sure thing," Foster said. "Everyone knows that's true. They've got to run off some of their energy. So what do you say?"

Silas gave a short nod, as if to do more would be unbecoming. "Well, if you insist, we accept. We can set up a work frolic to get the repairs done. I think Teacher Sara already has a list of what's needed, ain't so?"

Sara nodded, unable to keep a smile from her face. "*Ya,* I do." A list she'd presented to the school board at least twice with no action. "I'll get it for you."

"Fine, fine." Foster took a quick look around. "I do need to get going, but I can wait a few minutes. Or you can have your *daed* drop it off at the store."

"I'll get it right away." She spun and headed for the schoolhouse, excitement bubbling, hardly able to believe Silas had agreed to this. Maybe the thought of getting something free had outweighed his reluctance. She'd best get the list to Mr. Foster before Silas changed his mind.

She stepped inside, closing the door behind her, mind intent on the list. She took one step toward her desk and stopped, her heart giving an uncomfortable thump.

Someone stood at her desk. Not just someone—a man, Englisch, young. He wore jeans and a tight black T-shirt, and he was as out of place in an Amish schoolroom as a zebra in a henhouse.

"What are you doing here?" Nervousness lent an edge to her voice.

"Just wanted to see what the school looked like. Nothing wrong with that, is there?" His bold eyes swept over her, studying her body in a way that made her want to hold something up to shield herself from his gaze.

Sara pushed down a momentary panic. There were people, plenty of them, just a shout away. Nothing could happen to her in her own schoolroom with half the residents of Beaver Creek nearby.

"The school is closed to visitors today." She made her voice firm. "I'll have to ask you to step outside."

He sauntered toward her, his gaze never shifting. "Well, now, that's not very friendly, is it?"

"The school is closed," she repeated. She took a step back and bumped into a desk. Was it time to call out now, before he got any closer? She edged her way around the desk, feeling behind her for the door.

He smiled, as if he knew she was afraid and enjoyed it. "I know lots of ways to get friendly with a pretty girl like you." He moved to within arm's reach, and only the conviction that it would be a mistake to turn her back on him kept her from running.

"Get out of my schoolroom." She would not panic. If she made a scene… Her mind shuddered away from the thought. It would be another black mark against her in Silas's book—that was certain sure.

"Your schoolroom? So I guess that makes you the teacher, huh? Bet I could teach you some things."

He reached toward her, and panic slipped her control. She drew in a breath to scream.

Chapter Four

Caleb's first censorious thought at finding Teacher Sara alone in the school with an Englischer vanished when he saw the fear in her face. "What is going on?" He reached them in a few long strides, impelled by an alarming surge of protectiveness.

"Sara." He moved between them, forcing the other man to take a step back. He focused on Sara's strained face. *"Was ist letz?"*

Sara took a breath, some of the color coming back into her face. "I found this man in the schoolroom. He doesn't want to leave."

And he had frightened her. Caleb could read between the lines. Had he threatened her?

He fixed his glare on the man—hardly more than a teenager, but hardly an innocent. The way he'd been looking at Sara gave Caleb an urge to douse his head in the nearest water pail.

"Go. Now." He didn't waste words.

The stranger took another step back, wiping his mouth with the back of his hand. A flicker of bravado showed in his expression.

"I heard tell the Amish don't hit back. So how you gonna make me?"

"That's true enough." And he'd never had such a longing to break that taboo. "But there are plenty of Englisch outside who'd be glad to help us out."

He didn't bother to repeat his command. He stared until the man's gaze fell.

"Just having a little fun." His voice had taken on a whine. "That's all." He swaggered out the door, the effect ruined by the speed at which he disappeared.

Caleb turned to Sara, overcome with the need to comfort her. "Are you all right? You're safe now. He's gone."

She shook her head, turning toward him in an instinctive gesture, so that it seemed the most natural thing in the world to put his arm around her.

"It's all right," he said softly, just as he would soothe Rachel. "Nothing can hurt you now."

Sara gave a watery chuckle. "*Ach,* I must be *ferhoodled* to let the likes of that one upset me so." She drew back, as if aware of his arm around her.

He squeezed her arm in reassurance and let his hand fall, taking a step away. "It was sensible to be afraid, finding a stranger in here. Did he threaten you?"

She shook her head. "I don't suppose he meant any harm. He was just showing off, most likely."

Caleb's thoughts were busy with the man's reasons for being in the schoolroom, of all places. "Did you know him?"

Sara shook her head. "You don't think I'd be friends with someone like that, do you?"

"I'm glad to see your spirit is back." Although he

couldn't help but think Sara might be safer with a little less of that quality.

"Oh." Her eyes widened. "The *kinner*. Where are they? You didn't leave them on their own?"

"The girls are fine. Your brother and his wife took them to get funnel cakes. That's what I was coming to tell you." He hesitated. "Are you going to tell Chief O'Brian about what happened here?"

"I didn't think of that." The color came up in her cheeks again. "He said to tell him about anyone hanging around the school. I suppose I must."

He thought he understood her embarrassment. The Englischer had said something offensive to her—something she probably didn't want to repeat.

"*Ya,* I think you should talk to him," he said firmly.

Sara looked at him with a challenge in her green eyes. "That's a turnaround for you, isn't it?"

He stiffened. "It's an entirely different thing. My Rachel is a child, already having a difficult enough time of it. You're a grown woman." A fact of which he was uncomfortably aware.

Sara didn't speak, but he could see the stubborn disagreement in her face. Well, maybe that was a good thing. It would encourage him to keep his guard up with her.

By the time school started on Monday morning, Sara still hadn't talked to Chief O'Brian about her unwelcome visitor. Well, it wasn't her doing, was it? He'd left the auction by the time she went in search of him, and she could hardly seek out the police on the Sabbath. She'd have to do it, and soon, but at the moment, she needed to deal with all the chatter going on in her schoolroom.

She stood, and the buzzing stopped when she looked at her scholars, but she saw suppressed excitement on several faces. Well, maybe some serious schoolwork would get their thoughts off gossip, which she didn't doubt had been flying around the valley since Friday.

"We'll begin with reading for first and second graders," she announced, and the little ones obediently began pulling their desks into a circle. "Seventh and eighth graders will work on their written reports."

There were some sighs from the older boys, who'd rather do almost anything than write a report.

She went on to assign each of the other grades to work on arithmetic or practice spelling words, and then she sat down with the small group of the youngest scholars. The room was quiet except for the scratching of pencils and the murmur of spelling words as the third graders quizzed one another.

Concentrating on the eager little ones was a good antidote for her worries. She loved seeing their faces light up when they sounded out a new word or read a complete sentence in Englisch.

A teacher's sixth sense presently told Sara that something was wrong with the background noises. She looked toward the back of the room to discover that Lily was not only not working on her report, she was out of her chair and hanging over Johnny Stultzfus's desk, whispering away.

"Lily!" Sara's sharp tone had every pair of eyes in the room focused on her. "You will take your seat immediately, and you will also write one hundred times *I will not chatter in class*. Is that understood?"

Lily, her pretty face set in a pout, nodded.

She was justified, Sara told herself, but she hated to see all of her students looking at her with such dismay.

Relenting, she went to lean against her desk. "All right. Tell me what is so fascinating to all of you that you can't concentrate on your work."

"Please, Aunt Sara." Becky remembered to raise her hand, but she forgot, as always, that she was supposed to call her aunt Teacher Sara in the classroom. "Everyone is talking and wondering about the man who fell off the cliff."

"Did he really jump?" Johnny's question exploded out of him before she could react to Becky. "I heard he had a parachute."

"Not a parachute, dummy." Adam Weaver, seated next to him, gave him a light punch on the arm. "Nobody could use a parachute off a cliff."

"Adam, keep your hands to yourself," Sara said sharply.

"I heard—" someone else said, and a babble of voices spoke, all telling a different, wilder story.

Sara sighed. If anyone had hoped the *kinner* wouldn't learn about the body at the bottom of the cliff, they'd be disappointed. The only sensible thing was to tell them the truth so they'd stop making up stories.

"Enough." She held up her hand, and the room fell quiet. "Here is exactly what happened. On Friday, after school, I was showing Rachel's *daed* the cliff, where it looks like the profile of an old man."

Several heads nodded. They probably all knew that much.

"We saw someone lying at the bottom, and we went to see if he was hurt. Unfortunately…" She hesitated, but they already knew. "Unfortunately the man had passed from his injuries."

"Was there a lot of blood, Teacher?" Adam said with a certain amount of relish.

"No, there was not." She said it firmly and held his gaze for a moment, mindful of what he might likely repeat to his father. Some of the parents were bound to dislike this departure from the curriculum. Including, most likely, Caleb.

"The poor man was beyond help, so I went to Mr. Brown's farm and asked them to call the police. The emergency squad came and took the man away. And that's all that happened. Are there any questions?"

There were, of course, but she was able to answer them honestly without giving any gory details. Finally her scholars seemed to run out of queries.

"Now you know the facts," Sara said. "So you don't need to make up any stories about it." She paused. "Do any of you have anything else to say about it?"

She let her gaze rest for a moment on Rachel. It seemed she was about to speak. But the moment passed, and Rachel joined the rest of the class in a chorus of "No, Teacher Sara."

Sara felt oddly dissatisfied. There were too many questions as yet unanswered. Maybe they never would be. But as her scholars got back to work at last, she realized that the cheerful presence of the children was chasing any remaining shadows from her thoughts as well as her schoolroom.

It was raining when school ended, a steady gray drizzle that made Sara disinclined to rush out into it. She saw Caleb standing at the edge of the playground, waiting for his daughter.

Why hadn't he come to the door for her? She hadn't spoken to him since Saturday, although of course she'd seen him at worship yesterday. Maybe Caleb thought they'd gotten too close during those moments in the schoolroom on Saturday. Now he was eager to put some distance between them.

Sara settled down to grade papers, trying to dismiss the thoughts, but Caleb's frowning face kept intruding. She sighed. Caleb was so determined that Rachel should forget the past, but obviously he couldn't do that himself. And she suspected he was wrong in his approach to his daughter's grief, although she didn't think he'd want to hear it from her.

Forcing the troubling thoughts away, she set to work and had the correcting done in an hour. She glanced at the windows, startled at how dark it had become because of the thick clouds and the steady rain. She'd better head for home before Daed came looking for her.

Putting on her outer clothes, she glanced back at the schoolroom before locking the door. With the battery lamp turned off, the familiar room looked different. But not scary. Of course not. She locked up and started down the path toward home.

At least the rain was stopping now, but water still dripped from the trees, and wet branches sagged, waiting for her to walk into them. She moved quickly, hugging her jacket around her. It was only sensible to get to the warmth and light of home as soon as possible.

The path wound along the creek, where the water rushed over the stones, fed by the rain. She resolutely did not look toward the opposite side, not that she could have seen the cliff from here anyway. Still, if—

Her skin prickled. A sound, some alien noise, had

disturbed her. She was as familiar with the usual sounds along the path as she was the tone of her schoolroom. She slowed, listening, trying to identify the sound. It was the faintest murmur, but it almost sounded like footsteps on the path behind her.

Sara whirled, staring, but no one was there. *Ferhoodled,* that was what she was, letting herself imagine things. She hurried on. She wasn't frightened exactly. She'd walked this way almost every day since she was six. But the loneliest section of the path was just ahead of her now, where it dipped into the pine woods before coming out behind the barn.

It was always dark and silent in the pines. Shadowy even on a bright day, which this surely wasn't. Well, if she didn't go through the pines, she wouldn't get home, not unless she went clear back to the school and walked home along the road.

The thought of turning and walking toward the sound she thought she'd heard made her heart quail. No, it was better to go on.

She strode into the trees, trying not to imagine things in the shadows. She was perfectly all right; in a few minutes she'd be home, and it was ridiculous to let herself be spooked.

A sound came again, from behind her and to the right—like a body pushing through the undergrowth beyond the pines. Her heart jerked, and she forced herself to turn around, to call out.

"Is someone there?" The dense shadows swallowed up her voice.

No answer. But suddenly the bushes shook as if someone was forcing his way through them. In a moment he'd step into the clear space under the pines where nothing grew. She'd see him.

No. Sara spun and ran, her breath coming in ragged gasps, her schoolbag thumping against her hip. Were those footsteps behind her or the thudding of her own heart? She didn't know, and she wouldn't stop to find out.

She ran on, letting the bag slip down so that she could grasp the strap in her hand, with some vague thought of fending off an attack. An image of a body falling from the cliff filled her mind, accelerating her fear.

And then she broke through into the cleared ground behind the barn, which glowed with a welcoming light. She raced through the door and into the comforting presence of her startled father and brother.

Chapter Five

Caleb didn't stop at the end of the path as he usually did when he walked Rachel to school in the morning. The memory of her frightened cries in the middle of the night was too strong. He wouldn't relinquish her hand until they'd reached the safety of the school.

He spotted Sara almost immediately, standing by the porch, in conversation with a man he recognized as the school board head. It didn't look as if either of them were enjoying their talk.

Rachel tugged at his hand, apparently ready to join some of the other youngsters at the swings.

"Have a *gut* day." He touched her cheek lightly, wanting to hold her tight and knowing he couldn't. "Listen to Teacher Sara, *ya?*"

"I will." She hesitated. "You'll *komm* after school?"

"I'll be here," he promised. "Go on, run and play until the bell rings."

When he glanced at Sara again, she was alone and looking relieved. Catching his eye, she came toward him, smiling but not, he thought, quite as blooming as usual.

"Is something wrong?" he asked bluntly when she was close enough.

"No, not at all," she said too quickly. "How is Rachel?"

"She had another bad night." Some things he'd rather keep to himself, but if Sara were to help Rachel, she had to know. "I tried to get her to tell me what frightened her, but she wouldn't." His frustration was probably obvious.

"I'm so sorry." Distress filled Sara's face. "I hoped…" She let that trail off.

"You talked to the *kinner* about what happened, Rachel says."

Sara seemed to brace herself for his disapproval. "I felt I had to."

"*Ya,* I know," he said quickly, not liking that she expected instant criticism from him. "I understand. They'd be imagining worse if you didn't tell them."

Relief flooded her face. "I wish other parents understood that."

"Giving you a hard time, are they?"

"Not all, just a few. Silas Weaver in particular." She broke off as a buggy swung around in the lane next to them.

Her niece, little Becky, hopped down and raced off toward Rachel. Sara's brother leaned across the seat, grinning.

"Morning, Caleb. Sara, have you seen any more bogeymen since last night?"

"Very funny, Isaac." But he was already driving off.

Caleb studied her, alerted by the tension in Sara's face. "What did your brother mean?"

"It was nothing." But she rubbed her arms as if she were chilled. "I just… I went home a bit later than usual yesterday. It was such a dark day, and I thought I heard someone following me along the path."

He frowned, sensing it was more serious than she wanted to let on. "Did you see anyone?"

"Not exactly." She seemed to be trying to get it straight in her mind. "I thought I heard someone behind me, but when I looked, no one was there. Then when I reached the pine woods, I heard it again. I called out. No one answered, but the bushes moved as if someone was pushing through them. Isaac says I was imagining things. It must have been an animal."

Nothing he'd seen of Sara would make him think she was easily spooked. "An animal wouldn't sound like a person's footsteps."

She looked startled that he was taking it seriously. "No. But if it *was* a person, he had left by the time my *daed* and Isaac went out to look."

"I don't like it." His frown deepened. "Someone could have been waiting for you to leave so he could follow you. I think I'd best have a look around outside the schoolhouse, if it's all right with you."

"Ya, danki." She managed a smile. "I hadn't thought of it, but that would make me feel safer."

The school bell set up a clamor, shaken by one of the older boys who seemed to enjoy making as much noise as possible. The *kinner* came running to line up, two by two, and began walking into the schoolhouse. Sara, with a last grateful look at him, followed them inside.

Caleb waited until the school door closed behind Sara. Then he studied the building, considering. He wasn't what anyone would call a fanciful man, but he'd sensed the fear Sara felt when she talked about her walk home the previous day. The Esch farm wasn't all that far from the school, but the path was a lonely one, and it would have been dark and isolated under the trees.

He circled the schoolhouse with deliberate steps. For someone to follow Sara, he must have been hiding someplace out of sight, waiting for her to leave. A car parked near the Amish school would have been spotted instantly.

He scanned the ground beneath each of the windows, his skin crawling at the thought of someone peering in at Sara. But there was no sign of disturbance.

A windowless white frame storage shed stood behind the school building. The door was padlocked. No one could have lurked there. He began to feel foolish, prowling around the school this way, until he reached the rear of the storage shed.

Boot prints were plainly visible in the ground left muddy by yesterday's rain, and the stubs of several cigarettes littered the ground. He stared, almost wishing he could disbelieve the evidence in front of his own eyes.

But he couldn't, and he couldn't fool himself that ignoring this would make it go away.

Moving quickly, Caleb circled the schoolhouse to the door and tapped lightly before opening it. Every head swiveled toward him.

"Teacher Sara, may I have a word?"

Sara nodded, eyes widening. She gave a few quick words of instruction to her scholars before coming to join him on the porch.

"You found something?"

"*Ya.* Behind the storage shed. Footprints in the mud that look like boots. Man-size, not a child's. And cigarette butts. Someone waited there, smoking."

Sara paled, but she didn't lose her composure. "It

couldn't have been any of the scholars. Not even the older boys would do that."

The sound of a motor interrupted her, and they watched as a panel truck drove up the lane. Caleb took an instinctive step in front of Sara before realizing the truck bore the name of the local hardware store.

Mitch Foster got out and regarded them quizzically for a moment. Then he headed for them.

"Something wrong? You folks are looking upset. I was just going to get some measurements for the playground equipment materials while the kids are still inside, but if this is a bad time…"

"Not exactly." Sara looked as if she didn't know quite what to do with the man. "Maybe later would be better." She sent a questioning look toward Caleb.

He made a quick decision. "We found signs that a stranger has been lingering on school grounds. If you are going back to town, maybe you could stop at the police station for us?"

Foster looked startled but agreeable. "I can do better than that. I've got my cell phone. We'll give the chief a call right this minute."

It was done. Caleb couldn't ignore the possible danger to the other *kinner* and to Sara, no matter how little he might want to be involved. Still, it had become too serious to pretend he could. Like it or not, he'd have to tell the police chief about Rachel's nightmares.

Once again, Sara found herself and Caleb in consultation with Chief O'Brian—not in the schoolroom this time, but behind the storage shed, staring at the footprints. The muddy marks gave her too strong an image of someone standing there, watching the schoolhouse, waiting for her, and she edged a half step closer to Caleb's comfortable bulk.

"No doubt someone was here for a fair amount of time," the chief said, squatting to have a closer look. "Don't suppose it could have been one of the older boys?" He made it a question.

Sara shook her head, grateful when Caleb took it upon himself to answer.

"A scholar that age wouldn't dare. And there's not one of them would wear boots that make that kind of print. Maybe when they hit *rumspringa,* but not at this age."

For all his earlier reluctance, Caleb was clearly ready to take charge, and she was just as glad to let him. She'd hate to have to admit the hollow feeling it gave her to know her fears were justified.

The chief nodded, rising, and gestured for the young patrolman he'd brought with him to take pictures of the marks. Then he eased Sara and Caleb around the building.

Once they were seated on the steps of the porch, O'Brian pulled out a small notebook. "Now, Sara, I know this is upsetting. But did you get any glimpse of the man you say followed you last night?"

She shook her head. Did the way he phrased the question mean he didn't believe her?

"Have you seen anybody hanging around?"

"There was an Englischer in the schoolhouse on Saturday, when the auction was going on." Caleb answered again, maybe to save her embarrassment. "Sara found him. She told him to leave, but he was…" Caleb glanced at her. "He refused to leave."

The chief cast a cautious look at Sara. "Insulted you, did he?"

She nodded, hoping she wouldn't have to repeat the things the man had said.

"So how did you get rid of him?"

"I came in," Caleb said.

"I see." The chief's glance went from Caleb's stoic face to hers, which she felt quite sure was red. "So both of you got a look at him. Can you describe him?"

"I'd guess him to be early twenties," Caleb said. "He had dark hair, a thin face, a couple of those tattoos on his arms."

"He was wearing a black T-shirt," she said. "Jeans and b-boots." She looked quickly at Chief O'Brian. "He did have boots on."

The chief was frowning. "In that case, I think I know who it is. Kid by the name of Sammy Moore, it sounds like." He paused a moment. "He was a buddy of Jase Kovatch's."

Sara realized she was shaken but not really surprised. "They wore the same sort of clothes, ain't so?"

Caleb nodded. "What are you going to do?" He shot the question at O'Brian. "If Sara or the *kinner* are in danger from this man, we need to know."

O'Brian looked up at that. "Why the kids? Seems to me by the sound of things it's Sara he's interested in."

Sara held her breath. *Please, Caleb. Tell him about Rachel.*

Caleb's face was so tight it seemed the skin was stretched over the bones. "My child, Rachel, has been having nightmares about Der Alte—the cliff face. It started on Thursday night."

Chief O'Brian's face lost its usual smile. "According to the medical examiner, Kovatch died sometime Thursday afternoon."

"So." A white line formed around Caleb's lips. "My little Rachel might have seen something that day."

"What does she say about it?" O'Brian shifted his weight, looking uneasy, as if this turn of events upset him, as well.

"Not much," Caleb admitted. "All I've been able to get out of her is that she's afraid of Der Alte."

"And this started before you found the body." O'Brian sighed. "I don't like doing it, but it sounds as if I'd better talk to her."

"No," Caleb said instantly, glaring at the chief.

"She probably wouldn't open up to you," Sara said, hoping to disarm the sudden antagonism between the men. "Rachel hasn't been here long enough to get to know you, and her Englisch isn't very strong yet."

The chief looked exasperated. "What do you suggest? If the child saw something, I have to know what."

"I think Rachel might speak to Teacher Sara," Caleb said, and she could hear the reluctance in his voice.

"But I've already tried to get her to tell me what was wrong," she protested. "I failed."

"*Ya,* but that was in the schoolroom with others around." Caleb focused entirely on her, as if this were between the two of them. "I've been thinking on it. If you came to the house for supper, maybe played with her a little, even helped her get ready for bed…" Pain clouded his eyes that he had to ask for help with his child, and Sara's heart hurt for him. "That's when she always used to talk to me."

Chief O'Brian cleared his throat. "I'd be agreeable

to that," he said. "Teacher Sara's as reliable as anyone I know."

They were both looking at her, but they couldn't know her thoughts. She'd gone to her scholars' homes for supper plenty of times, but never to a home with a single father. Never with a man she found herself so attracted to as Caleb.

But there was no choice.

She nodded. "All right. *Ya,* I will do it."

Chapter Six

Caleb sat on the top step outside Rachel's bedroom that evening, listening to the sounds coming from within. So far all had gone as they'd planned. Sara had arrived in time for supper, bringing with her an apple-crumb pie.

It had been the liveliest meal they'd had around the kitchen table since he and Rachel had come to Onkel Josiah's farm. Josiah had been on his best behavior, joking with Sara and even teasing a smile from Rachel.

Afterward, Sara had insisted she and Rachel would help with the washing up. Onkel Josiah retired to his rocking chair in the living room, and Sara kept the chatter going while they washed and dried.

Now Sara was putting Rachel to bed, something Rachel had greeted with enthusiasm. He was the one who'd suggested this, so it was *ferhoodled* to feel left out and maybe even a little resentful of all the giggles coming from the room. But it had been a long time since he'd been able to make his daughter laugh.

By moving slightly, he could peer through the crack in the door and see them. Rachel was tucked in her bed, with Sara leaning against the headboard, arm around his daughter. She was reading a fanciful story about a piglet, and they both giggled over the pictures.

The story came to its happy ending, with the piglet home in its pen. His hands clenched on his knees. Now Sara would move toward the purpose of her visit.

"I like made-up stories about animals, don't you?" Sara smoothed Rachel's hair back with a gentle hand.

"Me, too." Rachel looked confidingly up at her. "Peter Rabbit especially. Daed reads it to me."

He'd read it so many times Rachel had it memorized, but she still wanted to hear it.

"True stories are fun, too," Sara said. "My *daadi* tells stories about when he was a boy and all the mischief he got into. You know the difference between a made-up story and a true one, don't you?"

Rachel wore a tiny frown, but she nodded.

"Like the story of Der Alte," Sara said, her tone casual. "The *kinner* made that up, but he's not real. It's just that the rocks look like a face, that's all."

He could see Rachel stiffen at the mention, and it took all his strength to keep from rushing in and snatching her up in his arms.

"But he is real, Teacher Sara." Rachel's voice trembled. "I saw the Old Man make the other man fall."

The words reverberated in Caleb's mind. It was what he'd suspected all along, but it was still a blow. He should have protected his little girl, but how?

Sara held Rachel snugly against her body. "Do you mean the rocks made him fall?" Her voice expressed none of the tension she must feel.

Rachel shook her head.

"Then what?" Sara stroked her hair again. "You can tell me."

For an instant he thought Rachel would clam up. Then she took a firm hold of Sara's apron. "The Old Man came to life," she whispered. "He pointed something at the other man, and the man fell over the edge." The words came out in a rush, and she buried her face in Sara's sleeve.

"Did the Old Man push the other man over the edge?"

Rachel shook her head, and relief took his breath away. At least she hadn't seen a murder. This was bad enough.

"What did the Old Man look like?" Sara asked.

Rachel seemed puzzled. "I don't know. Just like the Old Man."

"I'll tell you something I know for certain sure," Sara said. "I know it was just another person up there, not Der Alte. Maybe the two of them were friends, taking a walk. Or maybe they were arguing, and the poor man just tripped and fell. But it doesn't have anything to do with the face in the rocks."

She said it with such confidence that Rachel looked impressed. Maybe she could accept from her teacher what she couldn't from him.

"Are you sure?"

Sara nodded. "And I'll tell you why I'm sure about it. Because when my brother was younger, he climbed right up those rocks one day, clear to the top. And he didn't see anything else. Just rocks, because that's all they are. All right?"

"If you say so, Teacher Sara."

At first Caleb feared his daughter was just trying to say what she knew her teacher wanted to hear, but as Rachel leaned back on the pillow, he could see the relaxation in her face.

"Now I'm going to tell you a real story about the time I went to pick blackberries with my brother," Sara said. "And you're going to close your eyes and try to see all the things I tell you."

Sara began a story, her voice soft, the words repetitious. The tale grew slower, her tone more gentle as Rachel slid into sleep. Finally Sara eased herself off the bed. She tucked the quilt over Rachel and bent to kiss her forehead.

The simple gesture seemed to seize his heart. He got to his feet as Sara slipped from the room.

"You heard?" she whispered.

He nodded. "We'd best go downstairs and talk about it."

To say nothing of deciding what exactly they would tell Chief O'Brian.

Sara followed Caleb downstairs, her mind busy fitting the pieces together. He paused at the bottom, nodding to where his uncle slept in the rocking chair, newspaper draped across his lap.

In silent agreement, they moved into the kitchen. It was better to talk about what they'd learned from Rachel without an audience.

The kitchen was utilitarian, with no flowers blooming on the windowsills or colorful calendars on the walls. Even though the Amish didn't believe in useless ornamentation, a woman usually made her kitchen a warm, cozy place through a dozen little touches. Josiah's wife had been gone a long time now, and he wasn't one to bother with what his house looked like.

Caleb pulled out a chair for Sara at the kitchen table

and sat down opposite her. She studied his face, looking for a clue to his feelings.

"At least now we know what Rachel saw." His voice was heavy with regret. "For my child to see a person fall to his death… No wonder she's been having nightmares."

"And no wonder she didn't want to say anything. I suppose trying to talk about it made it too real. But bad as it is, it sounds as if Kovatch fell accidentally, don't you think?" Sara tried to cling to the one bright spot in the whole business.

Caleb frowned. "That's not what Rachel thinks. She said the other man pointed at him and made him fall."

"*Ya,* but…" Sara struggled to make it fit. "We know he wasn't shot. It might have been coincidental, his pointing just when Kovatch tripped."

Caleb shifted restlessly in his chair, as if possessed of the need to do something, anything, to resolve this tangle. "If that's so, why hasn't the other man come forward?"

"I can't imagine." She pressed her fingers to her forehead. "To see someone fall and not try to get help for him—that's incredible."

"If the two of them were up to no good, I suppose that might account for it," Caleb said. "At least that's for the police to figure out."

She nodded. This was one situation she'd be happy to leave to the authorities. "Chief O'Brian said he'd stop by my *daed*'s tonight to hear what I learned." She hesitated, not sure he was going to like what else she had to say. "Daed also insisted we must inform the bishop, before he hears about my being involved from someone else."

Caleb's lips tightened, but he nodded. "I can understand his wanting to explain the police being at his house. It's not what we're used to."

Nothing about this situation was remotely common in her usually quiet life, that was certain sure. "I'm sure Rachel has told all she knows, and that's what I'll say to Chief O'Brian. There's no point in his troubling her with any questions."

"*Ya. Danki,* Sara," he added.

"As for her confusing the Old Man of the cliff with the person she saw, that's probably natural at her age. Most likely she heard one of the *kinner* say something about Der Alte shortly before she saw the accident and mixed them up in her mind."

Caleb nodded, but he didn't really look relieved. She could hardly blame him.

"You did a *gut* job of reassuring her. I'm grateful to you, Sara." The bleakness of his face extended to his eyes. "I could not have done as well. I couldn't even get her to tell me."

His pain seemed to wrench her heart. He needed reassurance as much as Rachel had, it seemed. "Sometimes it's easier for a child to talk to someone other than a parent, that's all. I remember telling my *mammi* things I didn't want to tell Mamm."

"Maybe." He didn't look comforted. "My little Rachel has had so much sorrow in her life, with her *mamm* sick for so long. But at least we used to be close. Since her *mamm* died, she's been so withdrawn."

"Even when we know it's coming, death is a shock." Sara picked her words carefully. "And children get funny ideas sometimes about what caused it."

"I thought bringing her here would help her forget."

The words came out explosively, and his hands clenched into fists. "Instead I made it worse."

"*Ach,* Caleb, you mustn't blame yourself." She touched his taut fist tentatively, wanting only to comfort him. "I don't think it's possible to forget the passing of those we love, even for a child." She hesitated, afraid she might be going too far, but he needed help so badly. "Have you talked with her about it?"

He seemed to draw away. "Not much." His voice was choked. "It's too hard."

Her heart ached for him and for Rachel. "I know. But it might help Rachel heal if you could talk, even a little, about how you feel."

"No." His facial expression seemed to close and his voice grew harsh. "I won't expose her to my grief. She's only a child. Don't you see that?"

"I know. I just want to help," she said, keeping her tone gentle. If he had to be angry with someone over what had happened, it might as well be her.

"I'm sorry." He rubbed his hand over his face, as if trying to chase away the tension. "I should not have snapped at you. You are the best thing that's happened since we came here. For Rachel, I mean," he added quickly.

"She's a dear child. How could I help loving her?"

Caleb almost smiled. "You have plenty of love for your scholars. Anyone can see that. But you haven't…" He let that sentence die out, but she suspected she knew where it had been headed.

"Haven't married?" She wouldn't hide from it, as if it had been her fault. "I was supposed to be wed once. But it seemed Tommy always had something to do first— finish his apprenticeship, save some money, get experience with a job in Ohio—and then when he did marry, it was to someone else."

It was his turn to touch her hand now. "He must have been *ferhoodled*."

She shrugged. "Folks thought I should be heartbroken. But by then, I was busy with my teaching. I found my happiness with my scholars, and I didn't look for anything else."

She still didn't, did she? She was suddenly aware of how alone they were in the quiet kitchen, with Caleb's hand clasping hers so warmly.

"I... I should go home," she stammered. "They'll be wondering why I'm so long."

"Ya." He let go of her hand and stood, turning to take her jacket from the hook on the wall. "I don't like thinking of you driving back by yourself."

"Ach, the evenings are long this time of year. It's not near dark yet, and I'm going less than two miles down the road."

He glanced at the window and then nodded, holding the jacket as she slipped it on. He paused for a moment, his hands on her shoulders, and when she looked up, his face was very close to hers, his gaze warm on her face.

Her breath caught, and she couldn't have moved to save herself. They stood so for an endless moment. Then Caleb was turning away, opening the door for her, careful not to look at her.

"Good night, Caleb," she said quickly and hurried out of the house, her cheeks hot, trying to figure out what had just happened.

Chapter Seven

Sara reached the end of Caleb's lane before her brain started working again. Fortunately Star could find her way home from just about any place Sara drove her.

Small wonder her thoughts were in such a jumble. She had never felt anything like those moments when she and Caleb looked into each other's eyes. The feelings she'd once had for Tommy Miller seemed like boy-and-girl foolishness in comparison.

Sara bit her lip as she turned toward home on the narrow blacktop road. And speaking of foolish—wasn't that what she was being right this very minute? Caleb probably felt nothing more than gratitude for her help with Rachel. She couldn't build that into romance, and she certain sure couldn't let Caleb see what she felt.

Star trotted along comfortably, unconcerned with the tumult in Sara's heart. Star wouldn't blink an eye even if a car whizzed past with its horn honking, something Englisch teens sometimes did out of mischief, but there was no traffic on the road at the moment.

Sara glanced toward the western ridge. As she'd told Caleb, it wasn't really dark. The sun was just beginning to slip behind the ridge, painting the sky with a vibrant splash of pink and purple. She feasted her eyes on the sight, letting God's handiwork soothe her troubled spirit.

Whatever happened or didn't happen with Caleb would be God's will, and she would accept it. If she was meant to end her days teaching other people's *kinner,* that was still a high calling. All she could do was her humble best.

She'd nearly reached the lane to the schoolhouse when she realized that the reference book she'd intended to bring home still lay on the corner of her desk. She'd be hard put to prepare tomorrow's geography lesson for the eighth graders without it. A bright group, they constantly challenged her. She loved them for it, but she didn't want to let them get ahead of her.

With an inward sigh, she tugged on the line, signaling Star to turn into the schoolhouse lane. The flicker of Star's right ear showed the mare's annoyance at being kept any longer from her stall and her supper, but she turned obediently.

Well, this would only take a moment. Sara would still reach home well before dark. She had to admit that she'd grown a bit wary of being outside alone after dark these past few days.

The playground looked lonely without the *kinner,* but it seemed to Sara that she could almost hear the echoes of their voices. She toyed with the notion, half smiling as she thought of the generations of young ones who'd attended the Beaver Creek School. Had they all left echoes of themselves here?

Star came to a halt at the porch, and Sara slid down from the buggy seat. She patted the mare affectionately.

"I'll just be a minute, no more. Then we'll go home, *ya?*"

The mare's head moved, jingling the harness, as if nodding in agreement.

Sara had the key ready in her hand, and she unlocked the door and stepped inside, letting it swing closed behind her, her thoughts on the book. She hadn't taken more than a couple of steps toward the front of the room before she realized her mistake.

Outside, it was still plenty light, but in the schoolroom, with the shades pulled down as she always left them, the darkness was nearly complete.

She took another step and walked smack into a desk. Her breath caught. *Ach,* objects always seemed to move from their places in the dark. She felt disoriented. She'd have to feel her way back to the door and prop it open. Then she'd have enough light for her errand.

With her hand on the nearest desk, Sara made her way back down the row, stretching her hand out in front of her to feel for the door. Her fingertips touched the wooden frame, and she slid her hand down until she grasped the knob.

The door creaked a little as she pulled it open. Then she heard what sounded like a rush of feet behind her, setting her heart pounding. She spun, instinctively shielding her face with her arm. Something hard struck the side of her head, and pain exploded, taking her breath away. She stumbled a few steps and fell heavily, her outflung arm hitting a desk, adding another layer of pain.

Sara gasped for breath, curled onto her side, unable to move. But she had to move. Panic surged along her nerves. She had to move, had to try to defend herself. She couldn't lie here helpless. If he came after her—

But even as she fought her way to her hands and knees, she realized that the footsteps were receding, not coming closer. He was rushing out the door, his feet now pounding on the porch.

Sara lunged forward, determined to get at least a glimpse of him. She grabbed the door frame, her head spinning, and tried to focus her eyes.

He was running toward the patch of woods to the side of the school. In a moment he'd vanished, but not before Sara recognized him. It was the man who'd been in the schoolroom on Saturday.

Fresh fear trickled through her. She tried to stand, discovered her legs wouldn't support her, and sat down abruptly on the porch floor. Star, seeming to know something was wrong, whickered anxiously.

"I'll be all right," she said, more to hear the sound of her own voice than to reassure the mare. "He's gone."

But he could come back. Remembering how he'd looked at her brought a wave of nausea. Or maybe that was only the effect of the blow. She raised her hand to her head, vaguely surprised that she didn't seem to be bleeding. A lump had already risen on her head, but her bonnet must have protected her from the worst of it.

She couldn't just sit here, hoping he didn't come back. She had to get to safety.

Suppressing a moan, Sara clutched the railing and half crawled, half fell down the steps. Reaching the buggy, she clung to the edge of the seat, not sure how she was going to climb up. But if she didn't, if the man came back—

That was enough to propel her into the seat. She fumbled for the lines, a fresh wave of dizziness sweeping over her. Something roared in the distance.

Hold on. She had to hold on. She snapped the lines and clicked to Star. The mare started off at a trot, throwing Sara off balance so that she slid sideways on the seat. It didn't matter. She rested her throbbing head against the padded seat. Star would take her home.

The noise alerted Caleb. Not that it was strange to hear a siren on the country road—police after a speeder or an ambulance rushing to the hospital. Still, he couldn't deny that he'd had an uneasy feeling since Sara had left.

He stepped out onto the porch, looking toward the sound. His heart jolted. Flashing lights sped down the lane toward the schoolhouse.

Wheeling, he strode into the house. Onkel Josiah looked up. *"Was ist letz?"* He tossed his paper aside and reached for his crutch.

"I don't know. Something at the schoolhouse." Caleb grabbed a flashlight from the drawer. "I must go. You'll be all right with Rachel?"

"Ya, ya, fine. Go." Onkel Josiah waved a hand as if to hurry him.

Caleb was outside in less than a minute. No point in harnessing the mare—he could be there faster on foot. He set off at a jog along the path, which was shorter than going clear out to the road.

And all the while he ran, the circle of light from his flashlight bobbing ahead of him, wordless prayers lifted from his heart.

Sara. He should never have allowed Sara to go home alone. If she was in danger, hurt, even worse… His mind wouldn't allow him to go any further in that direction.

Sara would be all right. She must be. It was over an hour since she'd left his house. She should have been home in no more than ten minutes or so.

But all the logic in the world couldn't help when he burst into the clearing around the school and saw the police cars pulled up at the door, their lights circling, flashing on the school, then the playground. He thundered up the stairs to the porch and burst into the schoolroom, heedless of the young patrolman who held out an arm to stop him.

"What's happened? Sara—" Before he could say more he spotted her, standing next to her father on the other side of the room. She looked pale, shaken, but otherwise whole, thank the Lord.

Ignoring Chief O'Brian and several other men who were clustered around the teacher's desk at the front of the room, Caleb hurried to Sara.

"Are you all right? What happened?" He spared a quick nod for her father, but all his attention was on Sara. She was so pale, she looked as if she'd pass out, and his heart lurched.

"I'm safe." She tried to manage a smile, but it wasn't very successful. "Just a lump on my head and a few bruises, that's all."

"How?" He wanted to take her arm but he couldn't, not with her father right there and everyone in the schoolroom, it seemed, looking at him.

"Sara's going to be fine," Chief O'Brian said, but his ruddy face was strained. "She stopped at the school for something and interrupted an intruder." He glanced at the police photographer, who was taking pictures of the books and papers that must have been swept from Sara's desk. "A vandal, maybe."

If the chief thought this a matter of random vandalism after all that had happened, Caleb didn't think much of his intelligence. But O'Brian's warning glance suggested that he didn't want to have a conversation on this subject with an audience.

Caleb nodded slightly. Just as well not to make everything they knew public, especially since Rachel... His heart cramped at the thought of his child.

"Sara looks as if she'd be better off at home," he said.

Eli Esch broke in. "*Ya,* that is chust what I was saying, too."

"Now, folks, just take it easy. Sara agreed to come over and see if anything's missing. Isn't that right, Sara? Just as soon as the photos are done, she can take a quick check and then go off home to her *mamm*." O'Brian turned back to his officers.

"It won't be long," Sara murmured. "I can wait."

"At least you don't need to stand." Ignoring the others, Caleb seized a straight chair that stood against the wall and brought it over to her. "*Komm.* Sit."

Sara sank into the chair gratefully. *"Danki."*

"I should never have let you drive home alone," he said, keeping his voice low.

Sara shook her head and then winced. "My fault, not yours. I stopped for a book, not thinking how dark it would be inside the schoolhouse. There was someone here. He knocked me down trying to get away."

Caleb felt sure she was trying to minimize what had happened. She must have been terrified, alone here at the man's mercy. "Did you see who it was?"

"Ya." Her voice trembled a little. "Sammy Moore. The man who was in the schoolroom at the auction."

"You told the chief?"

She nodded. "He said he's been looking for the man ever since I first told him about it."

Sara's father entered the conversation. "He hasn't been

able to find him." Eli's face tightened, reminding Caleb that Sara was his daughter, and no doubt he was just as shaken by the danger to her as Caleb was about Rachel.

"Did you tell the chief what Rachel said?" Caleb asked softly. If he knew that, the chief certain sure wouldn't talk about vandalism. The Amish were used to periodic acts of vandalism against them. This was something much worse.

"Not yet. I haven't had a chance." He could see the same worry in her eyes that he knew was reflected in his.

"All right, now, Sara." Chief O'Brian waved his people away from the desk. "You just take your time looking at everything, but don't touch any more than you have to. Let me know if anything is missing."

Sara's father took her arm protectively and walked with her to the desk. She just stood there, studying everything as if making a silent inventory.

They'd have to tell O'Brian what Rachel had said. Caleb's jaw clenched. At least they could be sure now that someone had been up on the cliff with Kovatch. Most likely that someone was this fellow Moore.

Sara pulled out the drawers in her desk, her face sober. Finally she looked up.

"Only one thing is missing," she said, her pallor seeming to intensify. "The school register. The book that lists all the scholars with their ages and addresses."

Silence reined. Everyone must be thinking what Caleb was.

This was the proof, wasn't it? The man knew a child from the school had seen him that day. How long would it take him to figure out who it was?

Chapter Eight

Sara leaned back in the rocking chair, her aching head against a pillow. How much longer could this endless day last?

The farmhouse living room seemed crowded with Daed, Chief O'Brian and Caleb all here. She had been surprised when Caleb had been set on coming back to the house for this conversation. She'd have expected him to rush home to Rachel.

But Chief O'Brian had dispatched an officer to sit quietly outside his uncle's house, alert for any whisper of an intrusion. That seemed to allay some of Caleb's fear, although his strong face still showed strain around his eyes.

Small wonder. At the moment Caleb was recounting all that Rachel had told her. Daed shook his head, murmuring as if in prayer, his face filled with sympathy.

"Do you have anything to add, Sara?" O'Brian asked.

"No, I don't think so." She'd learned the inadvisability of shaking her head when pain stabbed her the last time she'd moved it. "Caleb heard everything from the hallway."

"And you're sure the little girl said Kovatch wasn't pushed?"

"Positive. I asked her that, and she said the 'Old Man' just pointed at him, and he fell."

O'Brian looked dissatisfied. "The thing is, if Sammy didn't push Kovatch, why is he going to so much trouble to find out who saw him?"

"It does not make sense." Daed pronounced the words in a tone which said that much of what he saw in the Englisch world didn't make sense.

"I agree with you there, Eli," O'Brian said. "Still, Sammy's not the brightest bulb in the pack. He could figure he's on the hook for threatening his pal and causing him to fall, even if he didn't push him."

"If his actions caused the man's death," Caleb began, but the chief interrupted him.

"The district attorney might come up with some charges in the accident, I guess, but with the only witness a seven-year-old child, I doubt he could make it stick. But now we've got Sammy on assault, theft, breaking and entering... That'll ensure he's not around to bother anyone for a good while. Then you folks can stop worrying about him."

"You must catch him first," Daed said.

"There's no problem about that. I've put out an alert to the surrounding jurisdictions. That old pickup of his is pretty easy to spot."

His words penetrated the fog in Sara's mind. "Pickup?"

"Sure, why?" Chief O'Brian glanced at her. "We have the license number and a description. He won't get far."

Sara shook her head and instantly regretted it. "I heard his vehicle start up. It was a motorcycle."

The certainty slid from the chief's face. "You sure of that?"

She thought of the roar she'd heard when she got into the buggy. "*Ya.* I couldn't mistake it."

The chief muttered something under his breath. "Guess he's smarter than I gave him credit for. I'll have to amend the alert."

Sara shivered a little. Maybe Sammy was not smart, but he was sly. And mean. It wasn't pleasant to think of the man on the loose. Still, surely he'd run away now that he knew he'd been identified. Wouldn't he? A flicker of panic stung her.

"The *kinner* must be protected. We'll have to cancel school for tomorrow." She started to rise, but Daed put a restraining hand on her arm.

"You are going to bed. We will take care of canceling school."

"Why don't I stop by the bishop's place?" Chief O'Brian said. "It's on my way back to town. I'll explain there's been a break-in, and we're not finished with the crime scene yet." He looked at her. "Nobody can blame you for that, Sara."

Like the bishop, the chief seemed to know everything that went on, probably including her clashes with her board president.

"That's wonderful kind of you, Chief. But I have to accept responsibility."

"Not all of it," Caleb said firmly. "And not tonight. Tomorrow, when you're better, will be time enough to meet with the board members. When you do, I'll be there."

His support warmed her, but Daed looked a bit ruffled. "It's not needed. Sara will have her family to back her up."

"Sara is protecting my daughter." Caleb's tone was firm. "It's only right that I be present to explain it."

Daed studied him for a long moment, as if judging his intentions. Then he gave a short nod. *"Ya. Gut."*

Nobody asked her what she thought of it, but at the moment, Sara was too weary to care. As Caleb said, tomorrow would be time enough to tackle all of her problems.

The next morning found Caleb back at the Esch farm again, with Rachel this time. Caleb touched his daughter's head lightly, not wanting to let her go after all the worries of the previous night. But she would be safe with Sara's family today, and he didn't want to leave her with just Onkel Josiah to watch over her while he was working, and Sara's *mamm* had suggested he bring her over.

"It's wonderful kind of you to have Rachel visit today."

Sara looked better for a night's sleep, and her smile seemed to banish the stress that he'd seen in her eyes. "We love having her here. My brother brought Becky over, so the two girls will keep each other amused. They're not used to being at loose ends on a school day."

Now the tension was back in her face, and he couldn't be surprised. "You're worried about the effect on the *kinner* of canceling school."

"I don't want them to be afraid." She glanced at Becky pushing Rachel on the swing that hung from the branch of an oak tree. "But it would be far worse if they were at school and something bad happened."

"Ya." He couldn't let himself dwell on that subject, or he'd never let Rachel out of his sight.

"You're afraid for Rachel," Sara said, her voice soft. "I am, as well. But the chief seems convinced that Moore has run away now that he's been identified."

"Running away would be the sensible decision. But I'm not so sure he's one who thinks things through," he said.

Sara rubbed her arms, as if the thought chilled her. "Even so, he has no way of knowing it was Rachel who saw him."

He didn't find that thought much comfort. "I guess the school board agreed with the chief's suggestion of giving the *kinner* the rest of the week off, did they?"

Sara nodded, her lips tightening. "They didn't like it, that's certain sure, but the bishop spoke to them, and they agreed."

"Sara, it would be *ferhoodled* for anyone to fault you in all this." He spoke to the worry that lay behind her words. "Surely everyone can see that you did nothing wrong."

"You'd be surprised if you think that." She managed a smile. "I've already heard from Silas Weaver. The board wants to meet with me."

"When and where?" he said instantly.

Her eyes met his, and the sunlight seemed to bring out gold flecks in the deep green. "Caleb, you don't need to get involved in this."

"I am the parent of a child in the school, so it would be my concern in any event. And everything you've done has been to protect my child. The board members need to hear that from me." He waited while Sara thought on his words.

"*Ya,* all right," she said finally. She gave a little gesture of giving in. "Silas wants to meet at the school tomorrow morning at eleven."

"I'll be there." He said it firmly enough to forestall argument.

But Sara didn't seem inclined to argue. "*Danki,* Caleb." She gave a shaky laugh. "I'll go over a little early to clear things up. The schoolroom is still a mess, and I don't want anyone to see it that way. After all, it's still my school, at least for the moment."

"They would not dream of replacing you. Where would they find a teacher who cares for the *kinner* more than you?" He touched her hand, wanting to reassure her, and couldn't seem to stop his fingers from encircling her wrist. Her skin was warm against his palm, and he felt the flutter of her pulse, light as the wings of a butterfly. His gaze met hers...met and clung. Her eyes were wide, questioning.

He let go, taking a swift step back. "I... I should get going. *Danki.*"

He drove away, not letting himself look back. What was wrong with him? He couldn't allow himself to continue like that. If anyone had noticed the way he was looking at her...

Sara was an attractive woman. A good woman. But they didn't know each other all that well, and he certain sure didn't know what his future held. He wasn't even sure if he could love again. Maybe those feelings had been deadened during the long years of Barbara's illness.

Clicking to the mare, he turned into the lane that wound up into the woods. Onkel Josiah earned a little money by looking after some of the hunting camps when their owners weren't using them. He'd been fretting about not having made his rounds since he'd been laid up, so Caleb had promised to do that today.

He smoothed out the roughly sketched map his uncle had drawn for him. Most of the cabins were along the lane that led up into the woods, easy enough to drive the buggy to. The ring of keys was carefully marked, so that he could go inside and check each one.

The lane wound around the curve of the hill, and he had a fine view of the valley spread out below. The farmhouses looked like toys from here, surrounded by golden fields of corn not yet cut for silage. There was the schoolhouse, and in the distance down the valley he could see the scattering of houses that marked the beginning of the town.

Beaver Creek Valley was a good place. If not for all that had happened, he and Rachel might have settled down and been happy here. Of course, Onkel Josiah hadn't said anything about them staying on at the farm. Once he was well, he might expect them to leave.

He could buy a small place here, Caleb supposed. Farmland wasn't as expensive as it was some places. But not if it meant that Rachel was going to go on being afraid.

Before he could explore that notion further, he came to the first cabin on his list. Stay-a-While, the signboard read. He'd noticed the Englisch seemed to like giving names to their hunting camps.

Stopping the mare, he sorted through the keys to find the right one and slid down from the buggy seat. Onkel Josiah had said to check that the windows and doors were secure and that all was as it should be inside. Some of the cabins were furnished in a way that the Amish would find fancy, as if the owners didn't want to leave their luxuries behind even when they were roughing it.

Key in hand, Caleb reached the door, and then he realized that the key wouldn't be necessary. The door stood ajar, and the lock was clearly broken.

He hesitated, as one thought took hold. Sammy Moore was running from the police. He might think this a fine place to hide out. Chief O'Brian wouldn't thank Caleb if he set the man running again, but still, he had a job to do.

He pushed the door open cautiously, not sure what to expect. He was greeted with nothing. No sound, no movement. He stepped inside and paused, looking around.

Moore wasn't here, as far as he could tell without a thorough search. But someone had been. Several pieces of furniture lay overturned on the floor, and the gun cabinet on the wall was broken.

Caleb spread out the list his uncle had given him of the cabin's more costly contents. Even a quick look convinced him. The cabin had been stripped of its valuables. It looked as if he'd discovered what Kovatch and Moore had been doing in the woods.

Chapter Nine

Sara was at the schoolhouse well before her meeting the next day, eager to set things to rights. She didn't want anyone else to see her schoolroom in such disarray.

Her schoolroom. Would it be that much longer? Possibly not, if Silas had his way. Teaching had filled all the voids in her life. What would she do if she lost that?

Ach, don't be so foolish, she scolded. Daed would be here for the meeting and her brother also. He'd talked of asking some other parents to come, as well. And Caleb would be here. She wouldn't have to confront the board on her own.

She bent to pick up several primers from the floor, forcing down queasiness at the thought of someone handling them with evil in his heart. Smoothing out the pages, she restored them to the bookshelf. It shouldn't bother her so much. No one had been hurt, other than the bump on her head. She must thank God for that and let the rest of her feelings go.

The door creaked a bit as it opened. Sara whirled, heart pumping, a pencil falling from her hand. Caleb and Rachel stood in the doorway, and he seemed to take in her reaction at a glance.

"See, Rachel, I told you Teacher Sara would be cleaning up this morning. She'll be glad of our help, ain't so?"

His cheerful voice seemed to dispel the lingering shadows in the room.

"*Ya,* that's certain sure." Sara tried to match his casual tone. "Rachel, do you think you can find all the pencils that were spilled? That would be a big help."

"I will." Rachel let go of her father's hand. She scurried along the row of desks, crawling under them to retrieve the scattered pencils.

"I didn't know you were coming so early." *And I'm sure glad to see you.* But she wouldn't say that. Caleb seemed to be successful at pretending she was nothing to him but his child's teacher, maybe because that was what he actually felt.

"We didn't have a chance to talk when I came for Rachel." He began straightening the tipped-over desks. "I thought you'd want to know the latest from Chief O'Brian."

"Does he think Sammy Moore was the one who robbed that cabin?" Caleb's discovery surely had something to do with all of this trouble.

"Not just that." He set a visitor's chair against the wall. "The chief had his men searching hunting camps. He says every one they checked had been broken into. And they found both Sammy's and Kovatch's fingerprints, so they were both in on it."

She shook her head. "I don't understand how they dared. Surely they knew it would be discovered soon, with hunting season starting."

"I don't suppose they thought that far ahead." Caleb

frowned. "Onkel Josiah is feeling bad about it, thinking it's his fault for not checking the cabins sooner. Though how he could have done it with a broken leg I don't know."

"He's not responsible for other people's evil deeds. I suppose, if the two of them were in it together, they might have been quarreling that day up on the cliff."

"That's what the chief thinks. He's called in some volunteer help to be sure all the hunting camps in the township are checked. He says they probably have most of the things they stole hidden someplace. They couldn't sell them locally—they'd have to take them to a bigger town."

"*Ya,* I guess that makes sense." She bent to pick up a book at the same time Caleb did, and they bumped heads. She couldn't help letting out a gasp as the impact seemed to ricochet through her skull.

"Easy does it." Caleb took her elbow, helping her to straighten, and the warmth of his hand penetrated the fabric of her sleeve. "You…" For an instant he seemed to lose track of what he was saying. "You probably shouldn't be bending over at all. Let Rachel and me get things off the floor."

"*Danki.*" She was light-headed, all right, but she wasn't sure it was entirely due to her injury. "I guess that is a *gut* idea."

"Sara…" His grip tightened for a moment. Then he let go and took a step back. "I just wanted to say that Rachel has been sleeping better."

"That's *gut.*" Was that really what he'd intended to say? She might never know. Caleb wasn't one to open up easily. His daughter must get that trait from him.

Rachel was absorbed in fitting the pencils back into

their box, and she didn't seem to be paying any attention to them.

"Maybe talking about what happened was enough to ease her mind," she said, keeping her voice low. "Sometimes talking about things helps."

"Sometimes." Caleb seized the broom and began sweeping the dirt that had been tracked in, both by the intruder and by the police, most likely.

Obviously he wasn't convinced. Maybe he was right, but she couldn't help feeling that talking about Rachel's mother's death would do much to resolve the gap between them.

She didn't have the right to press her views, and maybe she never would. But she couldn't help caring, for both their sakes.

The sound of a vehicle in the lane distracted her. If it was Chief O'Brian, she could only hope he'd be gone before the school board members arrived. It wouldn't help her position for them to find the police in the schoolhouse.

Sara walked to the door and stepped outside, shading her eyes against the sunlight. The approaching vehicle wasn't the township police car. The pickup from the hardware store pulled up, and Mitch Foster got out.

"Good morning, Teacher Sara. I didn't think anyone would be here this morning." He glanced toward Caleb's buggy, probably thinking it was hers. "I heard about school being canceled."

"I suppose everyone is talking about it." She could hardly expect it to be otherwise. She went down the steps to join him.

"Nothing to worry you," Foster said quickly, his smile kind. "Folks are glad to see the last of Sammy

Moore. And Jase Kovatch, for that matter. All these burglaries—" He shook his head. "Hard to believe they weren't caught before this."

"It is too bad. I hope folks are able to get their belongings back."

"Most of them are probably well insured." He seemed to shrug that off. "In any event, I brought the materials over for the playground repairs. Okay if I unload?"

"*Ya,* that's fine. It's wonderful kind of you. I'm sure the school board will set up a workday soon."

Apparently attracted by the sound of their voices, Caleb came out onto the porch, Rachel trailing behind him. "I'll be glad to help," he said.

But it wasn't Caleb who drew Sara's eyes. It was Rachel. The child had frozen, her eyes wide, her small face frightened. Slowly she raised her arm, her finger pointing at Mitch Foster.

"Der Alte," she whispered.

Caleb froze for an instant, his mind struggling to accept what he'd heard. Then he snatched Rachel up in his arms, heart pumping furiously.

Foster's expression didn't change as he reached into the bed of the pickup. He pulled out a shotgun and aimed it at Caleb.

"Come down off the porch. Now." He gestured with the weapon. "Right over there."

Obviously he wanted to keep Caleb from seeking shelter inside the schoolhouse. Could he have done that, leaving Sara standing a scant yard from the gun? He wouldn't have to find out, it seemed.

Carrying Rachel, her face buried in his shoulder, he came down the steps. His gaze was fixed on Foster's face, but he caught a movement from the corner of his eye. Sara was grabbing for the weapon.

Foster evaded her easily. "No, I don't think so, Teacher Sara. You just back up over there with your friends."

Sara backed slowly away from the barrel of the shotgun. An image filled Caleb's mind of what Rachel must have seen—Kovatch backing away from the pointed weapon, losing his balance, arms windmilling as he fell.

"You were the one on the cliff," he said. "Kovatch was trying to get away from you when he fell."

Foster winced. "It wasn't like that. Put the little girl down."

"No." His arms tightened around his child. He couldn't do much, but he wouldn't let her go while he had breath in his body.

Sara changed direction slightly, so that she was between them and the shotgun. "Tell us what happened, Mr. Foster. It was an accident, wasn't it? We know you didn't push him."

Sara sounded so calm, as if they were talking about the new playground equipment instead of a man's life. She was gaining them time, putting off the moment at which Foster would decide what he was going to do about them.

"No, of course I didn't push him." Foster's face twisted. "I wouldn't do that. He…he just wouldn't listen to sense. He kept taking more and more risks."

"You were just trying to get him to listen," Sara said, holding Foster's attention.

"That's right." He sounded relieved that she understood. "That's how it was."

Caleb shifted Rachel slightly in his arms. He couldn't

run with her. They wouldn't stand a chance that way. But if he could shove her into the buggy and slap the mare, there was a chance of getting Rachel away. *Please, God.*

"We were arguing, that was all." Foster was intent on explaining himself to Sara. "I wanted to stop. I knew it was too dangerous. At first it was so easy—just slipping a few extra items into the truck when I was shipping something out. No risk. But Jase was greedy. He didn't understand what I have to lose—my business, my good name…"

Caleb moved a cautious step closer to the buggy, measuring the distance with his eyes. Another step or two would do it.

"So his death was an accident," Sara said. She seemed to sense what Caleb was doing, and she moved slightly, keeping Foster focused on her. "You weren't to blame."

"That's right. He just fell. I wouldn't have done anything with the shotgun. I only carried it so if someone spotted me it would look as if I was out after rabbits. But he fell. I looked down, and there was nothing I could do for him. Then I saw the little girl on the playground, watching."

"You didn't know who it was," Sara said.

"They all looked alike. That was the trouble." His voice took on a complaining quality. "I wanted an excuse to be around the school so I could figure it out, so I thought up that business about the playground. But I still couldn't tell which kid it was, and I was afraid to get too close."

"You sent Sammy Moore to try to find out." Caleb could hear the strain in Sara's voice. How much longer could she hang on? He edged a little closer, lifting Rachel slightly. He didn't dare try to whisper an explanation. She'd be afraid.

"Sammy's an idiot. I should have known better than to trust him with anything. All he wanted was to scare you. I have to do everything myself."

"Not this," Sara said. She held out her hand to him, the way she would to a frightened child. "You weren't to blame for what happened to Kovatch. But if you harm a child…" Her voice shook with emotion. "Don't you see? That's not the kind of man you are. There's no going back from that. You'll have no future left at all."

It had to be now. Caleb lifted Rachel, his muscles tensing for a lunge toward the buggy.

At that moment Foster turned to them. Caleb's eyes met his, and he froze, his precious daughter still in his arms. Foster held the shotgun for a moment that seemed to last forever. Then he dropped it and buried his face in his hands, sobs shaking his frame.

All the breath went out of Caleb. He thrust Rachel into Sara's arms and grabbed the shotgun. He thrust it under the buggy seat. A moment later he had his arms around Sara and Rachel both, his mind filled with incoherent prayers.

Chapter Ten

It was Monday before classes resumed at the Beaver Creek School. Somewhat to her surprise, Sara was there to greet her scholars as they arrived.

Still, what else could have happened? Silas might have made more of a fuss with the other board members, but since he was the person who'd supported Mitch Foster's proposal about the playground, he'd apparently decided that the least said, the soonest mended.

Even as she greeted each scholar and answered parents' questions as briefly as she could, Sara realized she was watching for Caleb and Rachel.

She'd thought, in those moments when they'd held each other, that they'd expressed something more than relief that they were all still alive. But since she hadn't seen anything of Caleb since then, it appeared she'd been wrong.

"So, did you hear that the police caught up with that Sammy Moore?" Her brother helped Becky down from the buggy seat and leaned across to ask the question.

"No. Where did you hear that?" Relief chased the final remnant of apprehension from her thoughts.

"I had it from Chief O'Brian himself. He hailed me when I was coming through town and said to let you know. State police arrested him out on the interstate, he said. So you don't need to worry."

"I'm not worrying." She really wasn't. In those terrible moments of facing the shotgun, she'd known what it was to trust in God's care, living or dying. Whatever happened, it was God's will.

"Teacher Sara, might I talk with you for a moment?"

Her breath caught at the sound of Caleb's voice, and she struggled to greet him and Rachel normally. "*Ya,* of course. I'm glad to see you this morning, Rachel."

Rachel looked up at her, a smile lighting her small face. "Teacher Sara, guess what? Daed says that I can go to Becky's house to spend the night on Friday."

"*Ach,* I'll get no sleep that night for all the giggling," Isaac said, grinning at her. "We're sure glad you'll *komm,* Rachel." He snapped the lines, and his buggy rolled on. Rachel and Becky ran off, hand in hand, toward the swings.

"She is looking very happy this morning," Sara said, watching her. "Any more nightmares?"

"Not one." Caleb touched her elbow lightly. "Do you think if we walked around the side of the building we could talk while you watch the *kinner* on the playground?"

"*Ya,* of course." She tried not to speculate as to what Caleb had to say. *God's will,* she reminded herself.

They stopped in a spot where the autumn sunshine reflected off the white schoolhouse, warming them. She glanced up into his face, not sure what she was reading there.

Caleb frowned a little, studying the ground. "Rachel

and I have done a lot of talking these last few days. It was important that she understand that the bad men wouldn't be around to trouble any of us."

"*Ya,* that is important. It looks as if you were able to reassure her."

He glanced toward his daughter. "It's not just that. After everything that happened, I…well, I got to thinking maybe you were right about talking to Rachel. About her *mamm,* I mean."

Sara nodded, not sure how to respond.

"So I tried." He sucked in a long breath and turned to face her. "My little Rachel…" His voice broke. "She got it into her head that she'd done something wrong and that was why her *mamm* died. How could she think something like that? Why didn't I see?"

Her heart ached for the pain in his voice. "Maybe you were too close to it. And you had your own grief to deal with."

"You saw it. I should have."

Dismissing the talk it would cause if someone noticed, Sara clasped his hand. "You did your best, Caleb. That's all any of us can do. The rest is in God's hands."

He pressed his lips together for a moment, as if he didn't trust himself to speak. Then he gave a curt nod.

"You were right. I couldn't run away from the past by coming here. A new start wasn't the answer to our grief." He paused. "*Danki,* Sara." His voice was thick. "You helped us."

"I'm glad." She had to force herself to smile. "Does that mean you are going to move back home again?" She held her breath, not sure she wanted to hear the answer.

"We won't be going anywhere. We've found a home here." His voice was firm. "Onkel Josiah wants us to stay. He wants me to take over the farm. I think it's the right future for us."

"That's *gut*. I'm glad." Whether she was to have any part in that future or not, she would be happy for them.

Suddenly he was holding her hands in both of his, his gaze steady on her face, and it seemed she couldn't breathe at all. "I'm thinking maybe it's the right future for all of us, Sara. What do you think?"

Sara couldn't speak. She could only nod, her heart filling with love. They would not rush, she knew. They would get to know each other better and give Rachel time to get used to the idea.

But as Caleb raised her hands to his lips, she knew what the end would be. They would be together, forever.

* * * * *

DANGEROUS HOMECOMING

Diane Burke

I would like to thank Marta Perry and Kit Wilkinson
for the opportunity to share this anthology
with them, and I sincerely hope
I held up my end of the task.

I would also like to thank Tina James,
editor extraordinaire, who uses her talents
to teach me how to be a better writer.

As water reflects a face,
so a man's heart reflects the man.
—*Proverbs* 27:19

Chapter One

The paper shook in Katie Lapp's trembling fingers. She read the message. Dread crept over her like an encompassing fog.

Please, Lord! Not again.

Her eyes made a sweeping glance of the land between her white clapboard house and the barn.

Nothing out of the ordinary.

The sun, beginning to rise on this crisp autumn morning, shed light on the harvested, empty fields. Katie's eyes searched every shadow, every tree.

No one was there.

She looked back at the paper and resisted the urge to drop it like she would a poisonous snake. It had been nailed to the post of the house steps. Just like the first two.

Katie's heart hammered. Her pulse quickened. A familiar tightening seized her chest and her breathing became more difficult. She slid her hand beneath her white apron and withdrew an inhaler from the pouch she had pinned to her dress.

Calm down. Remember what the doctor said. Stress will only make your asthma worse.

She clutched the inhaler in her right hand. Her other hand, the note tightly clenched in her fist, fell to her side. Hating her dependency on this medical necessity, she tried to prevent the impending asthma attack by using mind over matter. She forced herself to slow her short gasps of air and concentrated on each and every breath.

Katie closed her eyes. Although she tried to think of nothing but pulling air into her lungs, the threatening word on this third note had branded itself on her mind.

Her chest continued to tighten. Each breath was now an effort.

Please, Lord, I need to calm myself. Grant me peace.

She had to distract her thoughts from the paper still clutched in her hand.

Katie closed her eyes and tried to picture the large pond at the edge of her property. She willed herself to remember the feel of the sun on her face. She tried to remember the feel of the breeze against her skin.

Breathe in.

Now slowly exhale.

That's right. You can do it. Again.

In...

God surrounded his children with beauty and tranquility no farther away than nature. If she could just stop being so afraid...

Out.

Katie could almost smell the clean scent of a freshly mowed field, almost hear the sound of water lapping against the shore.

Peace filled her body and the painful constriction in

her chest began to ease. Her heart no longer raced. Her lungs no longer made her fight for breath.

With God's help, all things are possible.

With a sigh of relief, Katie shoved the inhaler into her pouch along with the note, which had started the whole asthma thing in the first place. She had chores to tend to. She didn't have any more time to waste on things she couldn't do anything about.

What else could she do? Report a scrawled word on a piece of paper to the police? Somehow she didn't think they would take it seriously. Tell the bishop? She knew that was exactly what she should do, particularly after what had happened to her fields, but she couldn't bring herself to do it.

The bishop had been trying for the past year to persuade her to remarry. He did not approve of a widow living alone and trying to run a farm.

Katie glanced at the puckered skin on her left wrist. Jacob was dead and he'd never be able to hurt her again. The redness from the burn had faded over the past year; the scars, both physical and emotional, had not.

No. Marriage was not a consideration. Not ever again if she had anything to say about it.

Entering the barn, she lit three oil lamps, basking the interior in a warm yellow glow. She opened the slide latch to the stall, put a halter on the closest horse and then repeated the process for the next two horses. She gathered the leads and guided them out of the barn, turning them out into the paddock.

When she returned to the barn, Katie placed the mouth of her wheelbarrow opposite the open door to make it easier to push the load outside. Grabbing her pitchfork, she mucked out the first stall. But as hard as she worked, she couldn't draw her mind away from the note crumpled in her pouch.

Who would do such a thing? Why?

Was there any possibility it might be a teenage prank? Even in *rumspringa,* when Amish teenagers were known for their less-than-stellar behavior, it would be out of character for any of them to purposely frighten a widow. She knew all of the teenagers in her small district. She shook her head. No. None of them could do such a thing.

Besides, the destruction of her crops was not a prank. It was a warning. Fear shivered down her spine. A warning she took seriously. She just didn't know what to do about it.

A shaft of morning sunlight filtered through the open door announcing the arrival of dawn. Katie doused the lamps. As she returned to her chores, the note in her pouch called to her as surely as if it had a voice. Unable to ignore it anymore, she withdrew the wrinkled paper and read it again.

A frown pulled at the corners of her mouth. How could one simple word make her so afraid? One word chill her to the bone? She ran her fingers over the crude block letters and read the word aloud.

"'Die!'"

"I hope you don't mean that."

At the sound of his voice, Katie spun around with the speed of a toy top.

"Joshua!" Her eyes widened and she couldn't hide her surprise. "What are you doing here?"

"That wasn't exactly the greeting I expected." Joshua Miller chuckled and stepped closer. "*Guder mariye,* Katie. I'm sorry if I startled you."

The sleeves of his blue shirt were rolled up to his elbows. Blond hair poked from beneath his straw hat, fell over the back of his collar and dusted his forearms like corn silk in the fields.

"Here, let me help you." He approached with speed, placed his hat on a nail and, before she realized what had happened, he'd taken the pitchfork from her hands.

She didn't know how to react to his sudden presence in her barn or what the proper thing to say might be after he'd been gone so long, so she said the lamest thing that popped into her head.

"When did you return?"

"Last week. I'm staying with my parents," he said. "I can hardly believe how much the town has grown. The Englisch have made themselves a home in Hope's Creek. I see there are two banks now, a pharmacy, a dry cleaner. I even saw a garage at the end of Main Street that repairs their broken automobiles."

He turned his attention to mucking the stall. "What do you think of all the changes? It isn't just an Amish community anymore, is it?"

Katie shrugged. "Everyone I've met has been nice enough. We are in the world, Joshua, even if we strive not to be worldly."

She couldn't help but watch his muscles ripple beneath his blue cotton shirt as he lifted the straw and threw it into the wheelbarrow. Her cheeks flooded with heat when he caught her staring at him and grinned knowingly. Quickly, she averted her eyes.

"Are you staying or just visiting?" she asked.

Katie didn't know what surprised her more, her boldness at asking his private business or the fact that she was curious about the answer. She didn't *really* care.

She avoided men whenever possible. All men. Even a man who used to be her best friend in what felt like a lifetime ago.

The three of them, Joshua, Jacob and she, had gone everywhere together. They'd fished in the nearby pond. They'd played softball in the school yard. They'd raced buggies during *rumspringa*. And many times they'd sat together under the willow tree and shared teenage problems and secrets that they knew the adults around them just couldn't understand.

Was that only a few years ago?

When had Jacob become a drunkard and a bully? Before or after their wedding? Were the signs always there, and in her youth and the throes of first love she had simply ignored them? Could her judgment of a person's character have been so wrong? If she had made a mistake in judgment, she had paid dearly for it.

"I'm back to stay." Joshua stopped what he was doing, leaned on the handle of the pitchfork and smiled at her. "It was time for me to come home."

For just an instant, Katie couldn't tear her eyes away. His sturdy, masculine build revealed he wasn't a stranger to hard work. Joshua had left Hope's Creek, Pennsylvania, a shy, gangly teenager. He had returned a man.

"You've been gone a long time."

It was simply a statement of fact. Why had she laced her words with a disapproving tone? Maybe because selfishly there had been a hundred times in the past few years she could have used the presence of her best friend. She lowered her eyes and chided herself. Joshua didn't know the things that had happened—and never would if she could help it. It wasn't fair to blame him now for not being around to help.

"I admit it's been a long time. Three years. Can you believe it?" That familiar dimple she had always teased him about appeared in his left cheek when he grinned. "It took a lot of time for my cousin to mentor me in carpentry. He threw some furniture making into the mix. I can fix a roof, build a stall or fashion a chest. I can do a little bit of everything now, I suppose."

She smiled at the welcome sound of his laughter. How long had it been since she'd laughed?

Joshua looked at her intently, his mouth twisted into a frown.

"Is everything all right, Katie? You don't seem like yourself. You're as skittish as an unbroken mare."

"Don't be foolish. Of course I'm all right. I'm just surprised to see you, that's all."

She was glad he didn't press the issue. But he was right. She couldn't settle her nerves, not for weeks now. She constantly had that eerie feeling that someone was watching her but she didn't ever see anyone nearby. She supposed the tension was starting to show. Forcing a smile to her face, she looked up at him. Warm chocolate-brown eyes stared back at her.

"What brings you back to Hope's Creek now?"

"When Daed took ill, I came to help Mamm. But I think it was just a ruse to get me home again, because as soon as I got here, Daed got better and started tending the fields again on his own."

They both chuckled. Katie remembered how close Joshua—the only son—had been to his parents.

"I'm surprised you didn't stay on the farm in the

first place. I don't remember you ever wanting to work with wood."

Joshua shrugged and his grin slid away. An unidentifiable emotion flashed through his eyes. Apparently Joshua had secrets of his own. Wanting to alter the sudden tension in the barn, she tried to steer the conversation in a new direction.

"Which do you like better?" Katie asked. "Carpentry or furniture making?"

"Both. I have found that God's blessed me with the ability to know exactly how a piece of wood should be used."

"Prideful, Joshua?" she taunted.

"Thankful, Katie."

She colored at his gentle scolding.

"That's why I'm here," he said. "I heard Levi was looking for someone to build new stalls and make some repairs on the house."

Katie nodded to affirm his words. "*Ya*, that is true."

"I've come to ask for the job."

She tried but she couldn't give him her full attention. She couldn't shake that uneasy feeling that never seemed to leave her anymore. Her eyes darted around the barn, searching, second-guessing every shape and shadow. Was the person who left that note still here?

"Katie!" The sharp tone and puzzled expression on Joshua's face drew her attention.

"What?" She offered him a weak smile. "Were you talking to me? Sorry. My mind must have wandered."

"Who would have ever thought I'd be asking Levi for a job, heh?" Joshua's grin returned. "He was always just Jacob's pesky younger brother following us around.

Now he's helping you run the farm and I'm asking him for a job. God has a sense of humor, *ya?*"

She glanced over her shoulder. Someone *was* crouching in the shadows. Her heart pounded in her chest and fear seized her breath. She squinted her eyes and stared hard into the back corner of the stall. She could barely make out the form.

"Someone's there!" She couldn't hide the trembling in her voice.

"Where?" Joshua frowned and looked in the direction she was pointing. He stepped inside the stall and disappeared for a moment into the shadows.

Katie thought her heart was going to stop beating.

When he appeared again, he held up a large bag of oats and a metal bucket. "Is this what frightens you?"

Katie stared at the objects in his hands and embarrassment flooded her cheeks with heat. "Levi should be here shortly. You're welcome to wait and speak with him about the work if you'd like." She held out her hand for the pitchfork. "I will finish my chores now."

Joshua studied her intently. When he spoke, the timbre of his voice was calm and soothing to her already frayed nerves.

"What kind of man would I be if I sat idly by while a woman mucked out a horse's stall?"

"Nonsense. Give it to me." Katie extended her hand.

He drew his arm away. "I will gladly finish the job I started."

"I don't need a man to do chores that I am perfectly capable of doing myself." The instant the words flew out of her mouth, she knew she'd made a critical mistake. She could tell from the surprised look on Joshua's face that he hadn't expected this reaction from her. But she couldn't help it. Her eyes flew to the twisted flesh on her left wrist and her mind went to all the scars hidden beneath her clothing. She hadn't meant to snap at Joshua. Remorse filled her gut. Tears burned the back of her eyes.

But no man was going to order her around or use brute force to make her do his bidding. No man…not ever again.

Joshua stepped back in surprise. This wasn't the gentle, happy, spirited girl he remembered. Her blue eyes no longer held the sparkle of a lake on a summer's day. Now there was a darkness in them he didn't recognize. She appeared wary, suspicious…frightened?

Something was wrong. But he'd been gone a long time. It wasn't his place to push.

Katie's hands stayed in constant motion plucking at the string of her *kapp,* fiddling with the edges of her white apron, sliding up and down the handle of the pitchfork.

Joshua frowned.

This was Jacob's wife—Jacob's widow—and the three of them had once been the best of friends. What kind of friend would he be now if he turned a blind eye to her obvious distress? Whether she liked it or not, he was going to get to the bottom of things. Amish took care of their own. How could she expect him to do anything less, no matter how long he'd been away?

"Katie?" He kept his voice low and steady as he would if approaching a frightened animal. The moment he took a step toward her, he saw her entire body tense.

He was right. She *was* scared.

Of him? How could that be?

"Many things have changed in my absence," Joshua said. "But I never thought I'd see the day when the Katie I knew would lie."

She flinched as if he'd struck her and she looked away.

"You are not fine. Why do you tell me that you are?"

Maybe the stories he'd heard on the Amish gossip route had been true, that she was in danger of losing her farm. He could understand that causing her stress. But where had the fear come from?

One look at the silky blond strands of hair peeking from beneath her *kapp,* the clear, satiny smoothness of her skin, the natural blush of her cheeks and the pout of her lips, and Joshua felt all his old feelings come rushing back. He knew he should let someone else help her with her problems and he should run in the opposite direction. He remembered *everything* about their youth, and the pain still cut deep. He'd opened his heart to her once. He had told her that she was the only girl for him. He could still hear the tinkling sound of her laughter in his mind.

He knew she hadn't meant to be unkind. They'd been children, a year before their teens. She'd thought at first that he was teasing her. He remembered the look in her eyes when she'd realized that he might not be fooling around. The confusion. The sympathy. And then the pity. He could bear that least of all.

His stomach clenched as the pain of that memory flooded back.

He remembered what he had done. He had thrown his head back and laughed as loud as he could at the time. He had needed to convince her that she'd been right and that he'd been joking. It was the only way to save face and hold on to her friendship. It was the only way to erase the pity he had seen in her eyes.

A shudder raced through him.

Well, he wasn't a boy anymore. He knew better than to ever open his heart to her again—or any other woman right now. Teenage angst had been difficult enough. Now, though, he was trying to get his business off the ground and didn't have the time for courting.

He watched her gaze everywhere in the barn except at him and took the opportunity to study her profile. He smiled at the touch of color in her cheeks. He watched as her even, white teeth chewed on her lower lip. He allowed his eyes to slide down the gentle slope of her neck.

He inhaled deeply and forced himself to look away. No, he couldn't let himself have feelings for Katie. He had no desire to find out what adult rejection felt like— particularly from the girl he used to love.

As an adult he had become more adept at masking his feelings. He had to call on those skills at the moment as embarrassment and attraction rushed through his body.

He'd heard about the way Jacob had fallen to his death during a barn raising. He'd even heard the rumors racing through the Amish grapevine that Katie had been physically treated poorly by her husband. He had brushed that off as mere gossip. Jacob could never have hurt Katie. Could he?

But now he wasn't so certain when he noticed her skittishness. Her wariness and the flashes of fear he saw in her eyes.

Could the rumors hold any truth? And if they was true, then Joshua also needed to add guilt to his list of hidden feelings. Knowing the harm his actions—or inactions—had caused years ago, how could he ever ask Katie's forgiveness now? He didn't think he could bear the censure he was certain he'd see in her eyes if she ever found out.

He knew he was the last person on earth that Katie should rely upon right now but he also knew he was the last person on earth who could turn and walk away. He'd just have to keep his emotional distance. He'd have to treat her like a treasured friend, which she was and had always been, and nothing more. He was sure he'd be able to do that, and he totally ignored the warnings in his head telling him that task would be harder than he thought.

Silence stretched between them for several uncomfortable seconds.

"When I entered the barn, you seemed upset and shoved something into your pouch." Joshua nodded, his eyes connecting with her blue cotton dress. "Let's start there. What is it that has upset you? What is it that you are trying to hide?"

"It's nothing for you to concern yourself with." She hesitated for a moment as though she had realized he had done nothing to incur her curt tone, and with a soft smile and softer voice she said, *"Danki."*

He didn't want her thanks. He wanted answers to his questions.

With his left hand, he tilted her face and locked his gaze with hers. "Katie." He allowed his tone to voice his question…and his command. Without speaking another word, he turned his right palm up and waited.

She stepped away from his touch. Her eyes were filled with suspicion and wariness. Although he knew he hadn't done anything wrong and couldn't possibly be the reason for the emotion flashing in her eyes, he still felt a twinge of pain at her rebuff.

She surprised him when she reached into her pouch and placed the balled-up note in his hand.

He opened the wrinkled paper and frowned. "I don't understand. Where did you get this?"

"It was posted to the porch railing this morning."

"Do you have any idea who did it?"

Katie shook her head.

She offered a nervous laugh. "It isn't the first one. Nothing ever comes of them."

Joshua tried to keep shock from registering on his face. He kept his tone calm but inside his blood boiled. "How many of these notes have you received?"

"That is the third one in a month's time."

"What have you done about it?"

Katie shrugged her shoulders and gave him a puzzled look. "There's nothing to do."

"Come with me." He clasped her hand and pulled her behind him.

"Wait! Stop! Where are we going?"

She dug her heels into the ground. He stopped so abruptly that the change in momentum made her crash into him. His hands clasped her arms and he helped her steady herself and regain her balance.

The unexpected closeness caused a tension to hang in the air between them.

Joshua immediately released her but his stern tone left little room for objection.

"I don't know why you are fighting me. Why won't you let me help you? I am not going to go away and pretend that nothing is happening here."

Removing his hat from the nail, he put it back on his head, spread his feet and crossed his arms, prepared to do battle if necessary.

"If you do not come with me, Katie Lapp, then I will go myself."

She looked as if she was going to bolt at any moment, yet despite her vulnerability he sensed an inner strength he'd never seen in her before as she stood her ground and stared him down.

"Go where?"

"To the police."

"You seemed smarter when you were a boy, Joshua." She put her hands on her hips and assumed a stance. "When do the Amish run to the police?" she asked. "Have you been gone so long that you have forgotten our ways?"

"When something evil and beyond our control comes to our door," Joshua replied. "I am not too proud to ask for help when I need it."

"*Ya,* and I am certain the police will find a word scrawled on a piece of paper quite sinister. What are you thinking?"

"I am thinking that you are a widow living alone. You should have reported the first note and didn't. Have you told the bishop or any of the elders?"

Katie lowered her eyes.

"That's what I thought. You have done nothing to protect yourself. I am your friend, Katie. I was Jacob's friend. It is my duty to step in and help. That is what I am thinking!"

Katie watched him carefully and he noticed she rubbed her left wrist.

"Did I hurt you when I pulled your arm?" Instantly,

he crossed to her. His heart pounded in his chest and his pulse raced. Though his words had been harsh, he'd thought his touch gentle. Still, had he hurt her? How would he live with himself if he had done such a thing? Before she could move away, he took her hand in his and turned her palm up for a closer look.

His breath caught in his throat the second he saw the scars on her wrist. His eyes widened as his gaze flew to her face.

"How did this happen?"

Katie sighed deeply and lowered her eyes. "It is not important." She removed her hand from his. "It happened a very long time ago, Joshua, and I don't think about it anymore." He saw her cringe and knew her conscience was scolding her for her lie.

Joshua didn't push for more information. He knew Katie would only pull more inside herself if he tried. She would have to tell him in her own way, in her own time, and he would have to be patient.

But he was more certain than ever that Katie needed a friend.

Now he knew why God had put it so strongly on his heart to return to Hope's Creek.

Joshua needed to discover who was behind the threatening notes, even if it meant he would have to maneuver through the minefield of Katie's wariness and pride. He was determined to protect her from any danger—and that protection started now.

Chapter Two

"Joshua! I heard you were back. For once the gossip is true." Levi Lapp walked leisurely into the barn and then stopped. His eyes darted from Katie to Joshua and back again. "Am I interrupting something? Is there a problem?"

Katie could feel the intensity of Joshua's stare as he waited for her to answer her brother-in-law.

"No problem, Levi. We were just talking. Joshua really came to see you."

Levi smiled. "It is good to see you again, my friend. But if you were looking for me then why didn't you stop by my house? It would have been easier to find me, don't you think?" The smile on Levi's face did little to ease the awkwardness between the three of them.

Levi had never been Joshua's friend. He had dogged Jacob's every footstep and pushed himself into the older trio's time together with annoying regularity. But it certainly would do him no good to remind Levi of that when Joshua was here to ask for work.

"It is good to see you again, too, Levi. I was told you come every morning to help Katie with the farm.

I thought I might talk to you before you started the chores."

Levi tucked his thumbs into his suspenders. "*Ya,* 'tis true. I was surprised that Jacob left the farm in Katie's name. It is our family farm. He should have known I would have taken good care of her if anything happened to him." Levi shrugged. "And that is what I do. I split my time between the farm I purchased when Jacob inherited this land from my parents, and there is no reason I can't continue to help you." He nodded in her direction and then caught Joshua's eye. "I do not wish to be rude but there are many chores to be done and I do not have the time for idle chatter. But I am sure if you join us for church services Katie will extend an invitation for Sunday dinner."

Both men glanced her way and Katie nodded.

"*Gut.* I look forward to hearing what you have been doing these past years and you can tell us about your cousin's district."

"That is kind of you, Levi. *Ya,* I will come." He smiled. "But I came here this morning to lighten your load. I heard you are looking for a good carpenter and I am looking for work. Maybe we can be a help to each other."

Levi stared hard at Joshua for a moment before he spoke.

"*Ya,* I remember hearing that you became a carpenter and I am looking for someone." Levi clapped Joshua on the shoulder. "It will be good for us to work together. When can you start?"

"Right away."

"*Gut,* come with me and I will show you what needs to be done."

Levi led the way out of the barn. When Joshua didn't immediately follow, Levi looked back over his shoulder and shot Joshua a puzzled look.

"Katie has something she needs to tell you." Joshua looked at Katie and waited.

Levi looked her way. "Is this true?"

If she had had a pie in her hand, she might have thrown it at Joshua. Why couldn't he mind his own business?

"He is Jacob's brother, Katie. He is family. He has a right to know."

Knowing Joshua was not going to budge on this issue, she brought Levi up-to-date on all three notes.

"Why didn't you mention this to me?" Levi asked. "Particularly since it was only a short time ago that someone set fire to your fields."

Joshua looked shocked at that revelation.

"Please, Levi. I think Joshua is making it more than it is. The fire in the fields was deliberately set. It was evil and intentional. I can't believe that someone so diabolical would suddenly stoop to something so simple and childish as scrawling a word or two on a slip of paper. They are vastly different incidents and I find it hard to believe the two are connected. Still, I have not been foolish. I have been cautious and alert just in case."

"We should go to the police," Joshua said.

"The police?" Levi shook his head. "I see no reason to bring them in on this. Katie is probably right. The two incidents are most likely not related."

"You aren't going to do anything?" Joshua looked astonished.

"Of course I am. But I am not going to take it to outsiders. We can handle this situation on our own, *ya?* I will bring it to the bishop. He will decide what should be done."

Joshua nodded his acceptance.

"Now, come," Levi said. "Let me show you what needs repair."

A week passed without incident. No more notes. No more feelings of being watched. The bishop had made her promise to let him know if anything out of the ordinary happened again. When nothing did, Katie relaxed in the knowledge that she had probably been right all along. The fire in the fields had been an isolated incident, and the notes…the notes were of no importance.

Life returned to normal, if normal was having Joshua work on the farm each day.

He didn't go out of his way to talk to her or interfere in her daily chores. He simply nodded with a smile when he arrived and went straight to work in the barn. When she took him a warm cup of apple cider to cast off the autumn chill, she didn't know whether to be happy or upset that he accepted the drink, thanked her and went back to his work as if she didn't exist.

She decided she was happy that he kept his distance. She didn't want to get involved in any way with any man. Especially Joshua.

But…

She couldn't keep her eyes from straying to the barn and trying to catch a glimpse of him passing the door now and then. She couldn't keep the smile from her face when he ate the slice of pie she'd given him at lunch today as if he'd never tasted anything so good. She couldn't keep her mind from wandering to childhood days of wading in the pond and fishing and taking long walks and talking.

Reluctantly, she had to admit that she had sorely missed her friend.

But every time she allowed herself to remember how close they had once been, she would also remember Jacob, and her trip down memory lane would slam to a halt.

Standing in the yard, she had been so lost in thought she didn't hear the buggy approach and almost stepped in front of it. She pulled back not a moment too soon. Shielding her eyes against the morning sun, she tried to see who was inside.

"*Guder mariye,* Katie."

It had been a good morning until Joseph arrived. *God forgive me for my unkind thoughts.*

"*Guder mariye,* Joseph. Levi is in the field."

"I have not come to speak to Levi, Katie. I have come to speak to you." He climbed down from the buggy. "You know why I am here."

"*Ya,* Joseph, and nothing's changed. I do not wish to sell my land."

Joseph removed his black felt hat. "I thought you might have changed your mind after Levi returned from the market. I am sure you did not receive the income you expected after losing half your crops in that unfortunate fire. Have they found out who set the fire?"

Katie didn't want to be disrespectful of the older man but his presence on her land and his fake friendliness made it difficult for her to hold her tongue. She knew he only wanted to seize her property.

"You know the same as I do, Joseph. I lost more than half my crop. And no, they have no idea yet who did it."

She shifted the basket of eggs she carried to her other hip, redistributing the weight. "You'll have to excuse me, Joseph. I have baking to do."

"If you do decide to sell, I will give you a fair price. I do not want you to sell to the Englischer. Your land abuts mine. It is only right that you let me buy it. The Englischer will not farm the land. He most likely will level everything and build apartments or condominiums or, perhaps, a massive housing development. I cannot allow that to happen."

Joseph reached out and patted her forearm.

Katie startled and instantly stepped away.

His mouth twisted as though he had bitten into something distasteful and he drew his hand back. "Please… if you sell, let Amish land remain in Amish hands."

Katie looked Joseph in the eye. "I don't know how many ways to say it, Joseph. I am *not* selling my land. Not to you. Not to the Englischer."

Joseph placed his hat back on his head. "That is *gut.* I know the astonishing price the Englischer offered to me to buy my land and I've made discreet inquiries of others that also received offers for their land. If he offered you the same, then I would understand how that could appeal to a widow trying to make ends meet on her own."

"I am not alone. I have Levi, and Joshua is making repairs, and Esther buys my eggs and my pies for her bed and breakfast. And you know that Esau and Matthew helped Levi with the harvest."

"*Gut.* I am happy that you will be staying on the land." He climbed into his buggy. "But if you should change your mind..." He clicked the reins and turned his horse around.

Katie watched him leave and disturbing thoughts filled her mind.

If he really knew how much she wanted to sell...how hard it was each day to keep things afloat...how unsure and afraid she was, then he wouldn't have left so easily.

But if she sold the land, where would she go? What would she do? Her parents had left the community right after she married Jacob, and moved to the Amish retirement community in Florida. Her father said his bones protested too much with each passing winter. She certainly wasn't ready to move into a retirement village, so moving back with her parents was out.

The fire chief's words last month that the fire in her fields had been deliberately set still caused an icy chill to crawl up her spine.

Who was doing this to her and what did they want? *Die.*

The memory of the word scrawled on the last note actually made her skin crawl. She did not want to think that anyone who knew her would say such a terrible thing, let alone mean it. She was unsettled and couldn't help but wonder what might happen in the months ahead.

A shiver raced through her and she clasped her arms around her waist.

Katie continued to watch the buggy until it became nothing more than a speck on the horizon. She almost had to stop herself from racing down the lane to tell him she'd changed her mind.

"Was that Joseph King I saw?" Joshua approached

from the barn. He reached out for the hand towel hanging from her apron and wiped his hands. "If he is here to see Levi, I'm surprised he didn't stay. He will be back soon."

"He wasn't here for Levi. He came to speak with me." Katie walked toward the house and Joshua fell into step beside her.

It never ceased to amaze her that even after all these years their steps matched in stride and rhythm as if they were one.

"Whatever would he want with you? He's much too old to come courting," Joshua teased. He winked at her and she felt color flood her cheeks.

"Mind your manners, Joshua Miller, or I won't invite you in for coffee and a piece of apple pie."

Joshua paused and drew his fingers across his lips. "You draw a hard bargain, Katie Lapp, but you have a deal."

Arm brushing against arm, they climbed the porch steps.

Katie liked the way his earthy, masculine scent, laced with the fresh aroma of soap, clung to his skin and mixed with the smell of wood chips, hay and dirt that clung to his clothes. On any other man the combination might be unpleasant but not on Joshua. It was unique and masculine and made her want to breathe in the fragrance of his skin.

She liked the dimple in his cheek when he grinned and the errant wave of hair that fell across his forehead. She even liked the feeling of butterflies fluttering in her stomach whenever he came close.

What was wrong with that?

Just because she had sworn off relationships with men didn't mean she had to stop enjoying their presence.

* * *

Once Joshua settled himself at the kitchen table, Katie placed an ample slice of pie and a hot cup of coffee in front of him. She told herself that she didn't cut Joshua an extra large piece of pie just to try to please him. He was a hard worker and needed the extra calories for energy, that was all.

Joshua was on his second cup of coffee and last bite of pie when he again broached the subject of Joseph.

"I am curious, Katie. If he is not here to court you, then what could Joseph King want with you?"

"He wants to buy my land."

Joshua looked as if he'd been taken totally off guard. He spit his coffee back into his cup but not before some of the hot liquid splattered on his work shirt and the remainder of the brew spilled onto the table.

Katie grabbed a dish towel and hurried around the table. She righted his mug and sopped up the spill. Then, reacting without thought, she dabbed the towel against the splatter on Joshua's shirt.

Within seconds she realized her mistake.

She found herself standing directly in front of him, her hand moving from spot to spot across his chest, her breath close enough to flutter his hair.

A sudden intimacy hung in the air between them.

She froze.

His warm brown eyes gazed at her. They flashed with an emotion that she didn't recognize, which just as quickly disappeared. His hand shot up and stilled hers. Gently he took the towel from her hands.

"I've got this," he said.

The husky, emotional timbre of his voice wrapped around her senses and filled her with questions she didn't want to answer, thoughts she wouldn't allow herself to entertain.

She realized the inappropriateness of her actions, and heat burned her throat and cheeks. Without a word, she stepped away. Snatching the mug from the table, she hurried over to the stove.

"Let me get you a fresh cup," she said, lifting the silver percolator from the burner.

"No." He stood and tossed the towel on the table. "*Danki,* but I have to get back to work."

They stared at each other for several heartbeats.

His eyes hard, intense, challenging.

Hers wary, embarrassed, denying.

Katie turned back to the stove and didn't dare move as she heard the back door slam shut.

Joshua couldn't get out of there fast enough.

He'd been shaken to his core. He wasn't sure if it had been the thought of Katie selling her land and leaving the district or if it was the overwhelming attraction he had just felt for her in that kitchen. The price of a piece of pie and a cup of coffee had been higher than he'd ever thought he'd pay.

He had almost jumped out of his skin when Katie dabbed the hot liquid from his shirt. He had looked into those incredibly blue eyes and felt like a drowning man in a beckoning sea. Her lips had hovered mere inches from his mouth and he couldn't deny how much he had wanted to cover them with his own. Her breath had wafted across his skin and it had taken every ounce of control not to wrap his arms around her waist and pull her closer.

But he had no right.

If she knew what he had done, she would never be able to forgive him. How could she when he wasn't able to forgive himself? The Bible taught that a person must forgive another if they wished to be forgiven. When Peter asked how many times he should forgive his brother, Jesus replied "seventy times seven."

Joshua wondered what Jesus thought about forgiving oneself.

He leaned against the back wall of the barn and watched the horses grazing in the paddock. He remembered teaching Katie as a young girl how to ride bareback even though Amish girls weren't supposed to do such a thing. He remembered teaching her how to hit a ball, to bait a hook. He remembered comforting her beneath the willow tree when she'd cried because she thought Jacob did not care for her the way she cared for him.

He remembered loving her and leaving her.

He remembered his silence about so many things. He'd known about Jacob's poor choice of friends. He had known about his drinking. He'd even seen a mean streak in him once when he'd found him drunk.

But he didn't tell.

And Katie had paid the price.

The puckered scar on her wrist flashed through his mind. The memory of the wariness, hurt and fear residing in her eyes tore at his heart.

He could have saved her if he hadn't covered for Jacob...if he wasn't afraid that she might not believe him because of his declaration of love years before.

Some actions—or inactions—could result in causing others incredible pain.

Some sins—his sins—were unforgivable.

Chapter Three

Katie sat on her porch and watched the setting sun. The sky, a myriad of bright colors mirroring the reds, oranges and yellows still visible on the trees, had hues streaked across the horizon. She drew her shawl closer around her shoulders to ward off the evening chill. It was mid-November and there had not yet been even a dusting of snow. Cold air bit her cheeks and Katie knew that wouldn't be the case much longer.

She loved twilight, a time of light and shadows, a peaceful quiet at the end of a busy day. Levi and Joshua had both returned to their homes. She was alone. A smile bowed the edges of her mouth. She felt closest to the Lord when she could enjoy the silence and talk with Him in prayer.

When her evening prayers ended, Katie placed her Bible on the table beside her and stood. She'd have to remember to take it into the house once she finished her evening chores.

She had just stepped off the last step of her porch when a car roared up the lane shooting dust and dirt in its wake.

Katie grimaced. She knew who this was. There was no mistaking the black low-to-the ground sports car that she'd seen too much of these past two months. Mr. Henry Adams. The man drove as though no one else had a right to the road and traffic signs had no meaning. Many times she had to calm a skittish horse as he roared past her buggy on the way to town.

The car kicked up more dirt as the tires squealed to an abrupt stop.

Katie coughed as she inhaled the fine mist and waved her hand in front of her face to ward off most of it.

What a rude, arrogant man! Maybe she should say a prayer for him.

"Good evening. How are you this evening, ma'am?"

"I am quite well, Mr. Adams. Thank you for asking." She tried to keep her distaste for this man from showing on her face. "What can I do for you?"

"I was wondering if you had a chance to consider my most recent offer."

"There is nothing to consider, Mr. Adams. I've told you repeatedly that I have no intention of selling my land."

He moved closer, his smile wider but his eyes reminding her of the black eyes of a snake.

"My offer is more than generous, Mrs. Lapp. I have offered you the same amount as I have offered to your neighbor, Joseph King, even though your property is half the size."

"It does not sound like a good business decision to offer more than you believe something is worth."

He threw his head back and laughed. Unlike Joshua's laugh, which she never tired of hearing, this man's laugh sounded like nails on a blackboard and she could barely stand the sound.

"I am a kind man. I am willing to forego my small percentage of profit if it were to help a widow such as yourself."

The phoniness of his friendly demeanor soured her stomach. How could he convince anyone to do business with him? He certainly didn't seem trustworthy to her.

Another thought slowly seeped into her mind. Both Joseph King and Mr. Adams competed nonstop for her land. Just how badly did they want it? Bad enough to burn a field of crops? Bad enough to leave threatening notes on a stair post?

A sense of unease slid down her spine. It was hard to believe that Joseph King would do such a thing. But why not? Being Amish didn't make a person stop being human. Even Amish struggled with envy and greed and anger and a wide variety of other faults. And Henry Adams?

It was getting easier by the second to suspect him. He reminded her of a creepy, crawling insect, only larger and fatter. All Katie could think about was getting Mr. Adams to leave.

"I appreciate your kindness but I must turn you down. My land is not for sale."

The smile disappeared from his face.

"That remains to be seen, Mrs. Lapp."

"Please don't waste any more of your time. I will not change my mind."

"Never say *never*." The sinister, slick way the words fell from his mouth gave Katie pause. "I know you have had some misfortunes lately. I am offering you a way to ease that suffering."

A sinking feeling settled in her stomach.

Could I be right? Is this man responsible for my current troubles? He doesn't really want me dead, does he?

Katie fought the sudden urge to run and, instead, tried to sidestep around him. "If you'll excuse me, I have to attend to my chores."

He continued to block her path. "I know that more than half of your crops were destroyed in a fire. I also know you took a financial beating at the market."

Katie's heart pounded but she refrained from comment and moved past him.

"I also know, Mrs. Lapp, that someone has been leaving upsetting notes for you to find."

She gasped and came to an abrupt stop.

How can he know about the notes unless he wrote them?

"You are mistaken, sir." She offered a silent prayer that God would understand the reason for her lie and forgive her this transgression. "Where would you hear such a thing?"

"You should know that the gossip mill runs rampant in this town. Hang around the general store. You hear juicy tidbits on everyone and everything."

"Then you should consider your source, Mr. Adams. Gossip is usually just that—gossip. Now, if you'll excuse me, I must ask you to leave."

He shrugged his shoulders. "Everyone has their price, Mrs. Lapp. In time I will discover yours."

She watched as he climbed back into his fancy automobile and sped down her lane. She couldn't shake the feelings of disgust and unease that rose in her every time he came around. She sincerely hoped he would

tire of her constant refusals and take his offers someplace else.

Shaking off the unsettling feelings, she went about
her evening chores. She was filling the horse's troughs
with fresh water when she heard a sound behind her.

"Well, there you are." She hadn't realized she'd
been holding her breath until she let it go and then she
laughed. "I haven't seen you for a couple of days. Did
you wander off and visit your friends on other farms?"

The cat mewed loudly and, tail twitching, walked in
continuous circles.

"What's the matter, huh?" Katie stooped down and
gathered the gray striped cat to her chest. "Why are you
so upset? No fresh mice for dinner?"

The cat wouldn't rest in her arms and resisted her
attempts to pet her. Digging claws into Katie's flesh, it
meowed and tried to leap out of her grasp.

Katie bent over and released the animal.

What was wrong? She'd never been scratched before.

Katie frowned and continued watching the cat pace
in ever-widening circles. She couldn't imagine what was
upsetting the animal. Then she heard a soft mewling
coming from above her head. She looked up and had
to look again to make sure her eyes weren't deceiving
her. Four tiny faces hung over the loft edge, crying and
pacing as they tried to get down but didn't know how.

"You're a new mama! How in the world did you get
up there in the first place, mama cat? And what are you
doing down here without your babies?"

Katie's gaze shot around the barn and then it dawned
on her. Several bales of hay were always stacked on top
of each other just inside the back barn door to make it

easier to care for the horses. The cat must have used the stacks of hay as a stepladder to the loft.

Katie frowned and that uneasy feeling came rushing back.

Someone had moved the hay.

Levi would have had no reason to move those stacks and she certainly hadn't. She cast a sweeping glance around the barn and didn't see them anywhere.

Fear niggled at the corners of her mind but she refused to let it in. She had to get up to the loft and save those kittens before they fell to their deaths. She'd worry about the missing hay later.

She glanced up once more and offered a silent prayer that God would make them stay put until she could rescue them. She figured God wouldn't mind her praying for a few kittens. They were his creations, too.

Jacob had always tended to the chores that required ladders and Levi did it after Jacob's passing. Since her husband's death in a fall, Katie had had a fear of heights, but she didn't dare wait until morning when Levi would arrive. Those kittens were hungry and they saw their mother down below. Her heart skipped a beat when she thought about what could happen if she didn't get up there in a hurry.

She'd wrap the kittens in her apron and bring them down to their mother. She hoped there weren't more than four and that they didn't run away when she approached. She had no desire to be crawling around the straw looking for frightened kittens.

The large stepladder was heavier than she realized. Dragging it across the floor, she struggled to stand it upright and drop it against the edge of the loft. She climbed three of the steps and then stopped and wrapped her arms around a rung. She felt dizzy and a little bit nauseous. A sick feeling like a mass of stone formed in the pit of her stomach. Every cell in her body wanted to get back down as quickly as possible but she knew she couldn't.

With a steely resolve, she climbed the fourth step and then another.

Her head started to spin and little spots danced in front of her eyes.

Oh, Lord! Please give me strength!

She dared to glance up. She still had several feet to go.

Maybe if I close my eyes...

Clawing the edges of the ladder, she climbed a step and then another and another. Squeezing her eyes shut, she continued to climb. Suddenly the ladder shuddered beneath her and began to rock.

It all happened so fast Katie didn't even realize the danger she was in. She was too high on the ladder to do more than flatten her body against the rails and clasp the top.

Someone below pulled the ladder away from the loft. Katie clung to the final rung with all her strength. The ladder swayed in open air and then slammed against the edge of the loft. She gasped as it swayed backward and crashed forward once again.

Katie's foot slipped from one of the rungs and she screamed.

The ladder swayed from side to side, shaking her like a dog with a rag doll in its mouth. She hit her chin against a rung and her teeth bit into her lip. Blood lent a metallic taste.

Unable to hold on any longer, Katie found herself

clawing at air. She screamed as her body slammed against the dirt floor. Pain radiated through every pore and she remained still for several seconds trying to get her bearings. She rolled over onto her knees and started to stand.

A shadow appeared in her peripheral vision. It was the shadow of a man and he held a shovel over his head.

Before she could react, that shovel connected with the back of her head. She went down, her face hitting the dirt. She groaned in agony, raised her head again and touched the back of her skull. Pulling her hand away, she stared at her bloodstained palm.

Katie didn't have time to think about who had struck her or why. She simply closed her eyes and slid into oblivion.

"Katie! Open your eyes." Joshua continued to press a towel firmly to the back of her head to stanch the bleeding but he didn't dare move her until he knew if she'd broken any bones.

His heart pounded in his chest. He hadn't believed his eyes when he'd entered the barn and seen Katie sprawled on the dirt floor. One glance at the ladder standing beside her and he knew instantly what had happened. He just hoped she hadn't been too high up when she'd fallen.

"Katie! Come on, *lieb.* Don't do this to me. Wake up."

He shook her shoulder gently. "Open your eyes, Katie. You're scaring me."

Almost as if she'd heard him, he saw her eyelids flutter. She groaned and Joshua knew she was regaining consciousness.

"That's it! Wake up."

Katie's eyelids fluttered again and again, until finally he stared into the beautiful blue eyes that he adored. He felt all his efforts to stay emotionally distant fade away.

Danki, Lord.

But somehow a prayer of thanks didn't seem to be enough. She could have died and the pain that seized his heart was almost more than he could bear.

"Joshua?"

Her hoarse whisper was as welcome to his ears as a shout.

"*Ya,* Katie. It's me."

"The ladder... I... I was on the ladder..."

"That's not important right now. How are you hurt? Where is there pain?"

Gently he lowered her head to the floor, letting the towel act as a cushion against the dirt. Gingerly he ran his fingers down her arm, feeling for any breaks. Finding none, he stepped to her other side and repeated his movements. Nothing seemed to be broken.

"Can you raise your arms?"

His pulse beat wildly and he held his breath. This was the moment of truth. This would tell whether she'd broken her back or her neck or injured her spine.

A sense of relief washed over him when she lifted her arms.

"Katie, can you move your feet back and forth?" Seconds ticked by and Joshua thought he might never draw a breath again when she didn't move.

"Katie? Lift one of your legs, please."

It seemed to take her another moment to comprehend what he asked but elation raced through his every pore when she not only pumped her feet but also moved both legs. Pulling up her knees, she tried to sit up.

"Whoa! Where do you think you're going?" Joshua gently forced her shoulders back down. "You've just had a nasty spill. Give yourself a minute or two before you try to get up and walk."

Katie groaned again and lifted a hand toward her head. Joshua caught it in midair. "I know. Your head must hurt. I'll get you inside and tend to it just as soon as I'm sure I won't make things worse by moving you."

He leaned in closer and stared into Katie's eyes. He hoped she wouldn't see the tears he fought to hold at bay.

"You scared me. When I came in and found you on the floor, lying perfectly still, bleeding…" He reached down and brushed a loose tendril of hair from her cheek. The silky smoothness of her skin against his fingertips sent chills down his spine. To think that he'd almost lost her. He gritted his teeth and refused to let his emotions rule the moment.

"I should have known better. It takes more than a little spill from a ladder to stop Katie Lapp." He slid his arms beneath her. "Let's try to sit up. I'll help you." He supported her shoulders as she rose to a sitting position.

She caught her breath and clasped her head with both hands.

"What happened?" she whispered.

"I was hoping you could tell me. What were you doing climbing that ladder? There's no reason for you to be in the loft."

"Kittens. I was bringing them down to their mother."

"What?" Joshua strained his neck to look up and then glanced back at her. "Well, if the mother cat was down here, she must have clawed her way back up, because she's lying there nursing her brood without a care in the world. Unlike you, I'm afraid."

He tilted her chin to the side to get a better look at the back of her head.

"I'm surprised you fell from the ladder. The Katie I knew as a kid could hold her weight on a vine and swing out over the pond without falling." He chuckled at the memory.

"I wasn't afraid of heights when I was younger. I seem to be now." She offered a timid smile. "Besides, I didn't fall. Someone threw me off."

The laughter died in his throat. "Someone did this to you on purpose? Who would do such a thing?"

"I don't know," Katie replied. "I was too busy holding on for dear life to look below and see who it was."

"Are you sure, Katie? Maybe the ladder tipped beneath your weight."

"Then why is the ladder still standing? *Ya,* I'm sure. I don't know who and I don't know why, but I am absolutely sure of what happened."

"Enough is enough. I do not care what Levi thinks. It is time we go to the police." He slid one arm beneath her legs, the other behind her back and lifted her into his arms.

"What are you doing, Joshua? Put me down. I can walk."

"I'm not letting you walk anywhere until I tend to that head wound and make sure that you are steady on your feet." He held her tightly in his arms. She felt so tiny and light and fragile, a far cry from the little spit-fire that stood her ground the first day he'd challenged her in the barn, the one who wasn't scared of confrontation from anyone.

"Grab the oil lamp." He paused just long enough for her to do as he asked. The lamp lit their way as he walked across the darkened yard.

Katie's *kapp* brushed against his chin and he could smell the fresh fragrance of her hair mixed with the coppery scent of her blood.

He thought he was going to choke on his anger. This was no longer just a word scribbled on paper. This was sinister, evil. Someone had done this to Katie on purpose. She could have been killed.

His mind refused to even entertain the thought of a world without Katie in it.

He would find out who did this to her. He only hoped he'd be able to do it before anything worse happened to Katie.

Even through his concern, he realized that she wasn't objecting or demanding that she walk to the house on her own. Was that because she was finally letting down her guard and allowing him to help her? Or was it because her head injury was more serious than he'd thought?

For a brief instant he didn't care about the reason. It felt so good to cradle her in his arms, to protect her—even if it was just for a moment, just for this one reason.

He knew he was losing touch with the emotional distance he'd demanded of himself.

He couldn't let that happen.

It wouldn't be good for either one of them.

Katie made it quite clear she didn't want to get involved in a relationship with any man. He couldn't bear opening his heart and having her reject it again.

No. He had to get his emotions under control and retain his distance. But what would it hurt to enjoy the closeness for one more moment? He cradled her just a little bit closer, his arms and his heart aching at the thought of having to let her go.

Suddenly a thought popped into his head and dread filled his mind.

Had Katie been conscious when he'd spoken to her in the barn?

Had she heard him call her *lieb?*

She had had a bad fall and had been knocked senseless. Even if she had heard his words, she would have dismissed them as nothing more than confusion caused by her head injury.

Joshua didn't want to think about any other possibility. His mind raced as he tried to remember those first few moments in the barn and then he relaxed. He was certain everything would be fine.

There was no way that Katie could have heard him call her "love."

Chapter Four

When they reached the porch, Joshua snatched the lantern handle in his fingers, being careful not to loosen the hold he had on Katie's legs. At the door, he had her reach down and turn the knob. Kicking it open the rest of the way, he paused in the doorway. The illuminated sight inside made his blood run cold.

He placed the lamp on the nearest porch table before putting Katie in the closest chair. Not wasting another second, he crossed the floor and beat the metal triangle hanging from the eaves. The clanging sound filled the night air.

"Joshua!" She covered her ears with her hands. "What are you doing?"

She steadied herself on the edges of the chairs and planters but she made her way to him. "Stop, Joshua. What are you doing? Everyone will come."

"*Ya*, Katie. That's what I want," he said, ignoring her hand and continuing to hit the metal form.

"But why? I don't understand."

"Look inside but do not go in. Stay on the porch with me until help comes."

Katie moved toward the door. He saw her pick up the lantern and hold it high against the darkness inside. Within seconds she lowered her arm and leaned heavily against the doorjamb. Joshua could see the color drain from her face.

He knew what she saw.

Someone had ransacked the house. Broken pieces of furniture were strewn across the floor. Books ripped. Pillows emptied. A two-foot-high word clung to the wall over the fireplace—*Leave!*

Why was this happening to her? Joshua wondered. Someone had burned her fields, sent her threatening notes, pushed her off a ladder and now this…

Katie, her clothes splattered with her own blood, met Joshua's gaze. He could see the terror in her eyes. But he also saw the subtle squaring of her shoulders.

There she was! The Katie he knew. The Katie who wouldn't run, who would find the strength to get through anything God sent her way.

She looked away and bowed her head. He saw the slight movement of her lips and knew this was exactly what she needed.

Katie was praying.

The flashing strobe lights of the police cruiser and the red lights of the ambulance danced in circles across the porch.

One of the paramedics cleaned and bandaged Katie's head wound. "You're lucky," he said, squatting down to close his bag. "You could have been seriously hurt. I can't find anything more than a few bumps and bruises," he continued, "but with a head wound, we should take you to the hospital for a more thorough checkup."

"That will not be necessary," Katie said. "The good Lord protected me. I have no need to go anywhere but inside my own home. *Danki.*" She gave him a dismissive smile.

The man acknowledged her words with a nod and carried his bag back to his rig.

"How could such a terrible thing be happening here?" Amos Fischer, bishop of their small district, asked. "We are a quiet, peaceful community."

"Evil happens everywhere, Amos, even in God's country," Joseph King replied.

Several other neighbors, gathered in small groups on her porch and at the base of the steps, agreed as they watched the paramedics and the police finish their work.

"How are you feeling, Katie? Did you see who did this to you?" Levi sat down beside her. "I am grateful to Joshua for finding you when he did. I hate to think what could have happened if you had lain there all night with a bleeding head wound."

Levi looked up at Joshua, who stood behind Katie and had been silent this whole time. "Why were you here at such a late hour, Joshua?"

"I was returning home later than planned from a job I had done for Eli. I could see the barn lights from the road but there were no lights in the house. I found it strange that Katie would be in the barn at such an hour and I came to see if everything was all right. I am glad that I did."

A murmur of agreement moved through the crowd.

"You must have fallen on your head to receive such

an injury," Levi said. "I checked the barn. The ladder was still standing and there was nothing on the floor for you to hit your head on."

"She didn't hit the floor. Someone hit her from behind."

Everyone turned toward the sheriff as he walked across the yard and joined the group at the edge of the porch.

"I believe this could put a healthy dent in anyone's head. I found it tossed in the back of one of the horse's stalls." The sheriff held up a shovel covered in dried blood.

Esther, Amos Fischer's wife, gasped. "Come with me, child. You shouldn't have to see this. Let me get you inside. I'll make you a hot cup of tea while you get ready for bed."

Katie rose. She was grateful for the help. Grateful not to have to look at the shovel. Grateful not to think about who hated her so much that they swung a shovel to the back of her head.

Her eyes sought out Joshua. He leaned against the porch wall, arms crossed, listening and not saying much.

But that was the Joshua that Katie remembered. Always standing in the background. Quiet. Yet ever present.

His dark eyes stared intently at her.

"*Danki* for helping me," she whispered.

Joshua nodded. *Always, Katie,* he mouthed back.

Katie woke hearing voices coming from downstairs. She went down to investigate. When she reached the bottom of the steps, she could see several women from the district cooking in the kitchen. Others were cleaning the remnants of the mess from the night before.

Esther looked up from sweeping broken glass from the living room floor. "*Guder mariye,* Katie. Are you sure you should be up?"

Katie smiled. "*Ya.* A little headache and a couple of bumps and bruises. Nothing to worry about." She noted that someone had already scrubbed away the word that the intruder had scrawled over the fireplace. What could be salvaged of the furniture was back in place, and the delicious smell of bacon and eggs mingled with those of casseroles the women had prepared for dinner. The enticing scent wafted from the kitchen and her stomach growled.

"I appreciate everyone's efforts." Katie smiled at the women. *"Danki."*

"This is what we do," Esther said. She wrapped her arm around Katie's waist and continued talking as she led her into the kitchen. "We take care of our own."

Several *ya*s came from the other women.

Katie enjoyed the breakfast. She thanked the women for the two casseroles fresh from the oven. She was grateful for their help but right now she just wanted everyone to leave. Her physical wounds might not be severe but her emotional wounds were taking their toll.

She had barely slept last night. She had no idea why someone wanted her to leave this district, to leave her home, but suddenly Katie found herself giving serious thought to the suggestion. She had some distant cousins on her mother's side living in an Ohio district. Maybe she could go there.

Probably seeing her fatigue, the women wished Katie well and took their leave.

Esther, the only one to remain behind, invited Katie to sit down at the table, then turned to retrieve two cups from the cupboard.

"Katie!"

At the sound of her name, she turned to see Levi, obviously agitated about something, tramp through the living room and into the kitchen.

"Did you ask these men to come?" he queried, waving his hat toward the window.

"What men? I don't know what you are talking about, Levi."

She made her way to the window. One glance outside and she felt a wave of anger. Joseph King and Mr. Adams were having an animated conversation. "No, Levi. I did not ask these men to come. Could you please ask them to leave?"

"Gladly." Levi shoved his hat back onto his head and stomped out the door.

Katie watched for a moment, sighed heavily and returned to the table. She looked down at the cup Esther set in front of her.

"Chocolate, Esther? This early in the morning?" She smiled at the older woman.

"It is never too early for chocolate, child." Esther patted the seat beside her. "Come. Sit. Levi will handle whatever the problem is outside."

Katie didn't need a second invitation. She sipped her drink and then ran her tongue over the chocolate foam ringing her lips. Both women laughed.

"See," Esther said. "Chocolate can make all your problems disappear."

"I wish it was that easy."

Esther gave her a puzzled glance.

Katie took another sip of her drink before Esther asked, "And which man is going to buy your land?"

She looked up in surprise.

"This is a small community. You know that. Besides, Mr. Adams has been approaching all of us with offers for our land. Joseph surprises me but I suppose I shouldn't be surprised. Your property touches his. It makes perfect sense that he would rather expand than share a border with an *Englischer.*"

"What makes you think that I'm going to sell? Do you, too, want me to go?" Katie knew her tone was defensive and held a bristled edge, but she couldn't help it. She felt alone and unwelcome in her own community, and it hurt.

Esther simply smiled and placed a hand on top of hers. "You know better than that, child. None of us want you to leave. But what choice do you have?" She patted her hand. "It has been a year and a half since Jacob's death, *ya?* You have turned down every man who has tried to come courting. You cannot do this work all on your own."

"I am not doing it alone. Levi helps."

"You and Levi have done a fine job trying to keep the farm running. But, Katie, Levi has his own farm that he has been tending. Everyone can see it has taken a toll on him. He won't be able to help you forever, even if you are family."

Tears burned the back of Katie's eyes. "And if I choose to stay?"

Esther shrugged then picked up her mug and took a sip. "That is surely your choice." She gestured with her hand toward the fireplace easily visible from the kitchen. "But someone wants you to leave. It might be wise for you to take the money and go while you still can. Get a fresh start. Start a new life."

Katie caught Esther's eyes. "Why is someone doing this to me? Who do you think it is?"

"It must be the Englischer. I'm not particularly fond of Joseph King, but he is one of us and I cannot believe that greed would make him cross that line. But no matter who it is, I do not believe they intend to stop." Esther's eyes glistened with unshed tears. "I don't want to see anything happen to you."

Katie clasped the older woman's hands. "*Danki,* Esther. You are right. I must make a decision soon on what to do with my life." She sighed heavily. "I'll talk with Levi and see what he would advise."

"*Gut.* It is necessary to talk with family when you have to make such an important decision." She pointed her index finger toward the ceiling. "But it is best to talk to God. Let Him direct your path."

Esther took a last sip of her chocolate. A twinkle appeared in her eyes. "Of course, you would not have to sell your land if you married again. Joshua Miller, perhaps?"

Katie gasped. "Joshua? Whatever makes you say such a thing? Joshua is a childhood friend."

"*Ya.*" Esther nodded. "But he is not a child anymore. He is a grown man and from what my eyes can see he is dependable, hardworking and handsome. That cannot hurt, *ya*?"

The memory of Joshua's voice flooded back.

Katie! Come on, lieb. *Don't do this to me. Wake up.*

Esther stood and placed a hand gently on Katie's shoulder. "It seems you have many things to pray about, child. I will leave you to it."

Katie followed Esther onto the porch and waved at the buggy as she pulled away.

Levi approached from the barn. "I told both men to leave and not to come back again."

"*Danki* for handling that for me, Levi." Katie sat down. "Could you spare me a moment, please?"

Levi sat down opposite her. "What is it? Do you feel ill? Do you wish for me to take you to a doctor?"

"No." She waved her hand. "I'm fine. Just a small headache. It will go away."

"What, then?" Levi asked.

"I need your council."

Levi waited silently.

"You are Jacob's brother and you have done a wonderful job helping me after his death…."

"That is my job. The Bible says when a brother dies then the oldest should step up and take his place. I am the only brother Jacob had. It is my duty to provide for his widow."

Katie felt a twinge of guilt. Levi tended his own farm and then did his best to run hers, as well. Lately he had started hiring people when the workload became more than he could handle. People like Joshua.

Her gaze wandered to the open barn door and Katie couldn't help but wonder if Joshua had arrived and might be already working inside.

Levi frowned when he saw the direction of Katie's gaze. "I do not have time to waste." He stood. "Do you have something you wish to ask me or not?"

Katie blushed when she realized Levi knew where her eyes—and her mind—had wandered.

"I have two considerable monetary offers on the

farm, Levi. Enough money that I could leave this place and never have another financial worry."

Levi looked as if she'd slapped him. "Do not tell me that you are thinking of selling? Why, Katie? Haven't I been running things to your satisfaction? Haven't I been working hard enough?"

She jumped to her feet and put her hand on his forearm. "Levi, you have done a wonderful job. I don't know what I would have done without you. But…" Her words trailed away.

"If you want to leave, then leave. I will not try to stop you. If you need money to leave, then I will give you money." His eyes hardened. "But this is Lapp land. It does not belong to Joseph King and it certainly does not belong to an Englischer."

He turned, bolted down the steps and disappeared behind the barn.

"That didn't go well."

Katie jumped and turned toward the sound of the voice. "Where did you come from? I thought you'd be working in the barn."

Joshua hopped over the porch railing on the far side. "My work in the barn is finished. I am beginning my repairs on the house."

"You've got to stop sneaking up on me. You've scared me twice now," she scolded.

Joshua laughed. "You never used to be afraid of me."

"That's because you never sneaked up on me. I always knew you were nearby."

"How so?"

"Don't you remember?" Katie teased. "I nicknamed you The Shadow because you always seemed to be right behind me."

"And now?" Joshua stepped closer.

She could feel his breath on her face and smell the minty tang. She stared at his lips and couldn't help but wonder what those lips would feel like pressed against her own.

"Are you going to kiss me?" she whispered and then wished the words had not escaped her lips.

His expression darkened. "You are Jacob's widow. I have no right to kiss you…now or ever."

Katie colored. "I was simply teasing you, Joshua. You are standing so close and you always were so shy…." Her voice trailed off as they stared at each other.

"Make no mistake. I am not that shy teenager anymore, Katie." The huskiness in his voice held a deeper meaning. The intensity of his stare challenged her.

Joshua *wanted* to kiss her.

She could see it in his eyes. She could sense it in his tense body language.

And she wanted to kiss him back.

The thought scared her to death.

Both of them stepped away almost simultaneously.

What was happening to her? She couldn't afford to let another man into her life or her heart. She refused to forfeit control over her wants and needs and become a submissive wife again. She'd lived in silence through a bad marriage, a horribly abusive marriage. She'd kept Jacob's secret. But at what cost to herself?

No, never again.

She'd never trust another man. She'd never relinquish control. Never.

But her heart thundered in her chest when her eyes locked with Joshua's. Her stomach clenched and her pulse raced like wild horses.

She could trust Joshua, couldn't she?

Katie took another step back. Once upon a time she had thought she could trust Jacob.

"I... I have to go." She backed toward the door. "I... I have to tend to things on the stove."

Katie turned and practically ran inside.

Chapter Five

Enjoying the twilight—and the silence—Katie closed
her eyes, leaned her head back and tried to ignore the
familiar tightening in her chest. Autumn and spring
were the worst times. So many allergens triggered her
asthma during these seasons that she'd lost count of
the list of things the doctor had warned her to avoid.

Of course, stress headed the top of the list and she
had to admit she was on stress overload these days.

She practiced taking long, deep breaths through her
nose and then released the air slowly through pursed
lips.

Diaphragmatic breathing, the doctor had called it.

She didn't care what he called it. She only knew
that sometimes it helped to ease an impending attack—
that and a puff on the inhaler she carried with her at
all times.

This time the breathing wasn't helping. She still felt
as if a giant fist was inside her chest and squeezing the
air right out of her.

She withdrew the inhaler and drew a puff into her
mouth. She hated depending on medicine. She hated

showing any sign of weakness at all. She was finished being weak.

Four nights had passed since the incident in the barn. Three nights of being almost constantly under Levi's and Joshua's watch. At first, it had annoyed her. She was perfectly capable of taking care of herself. But both men seemed determined to make sure nothing and no one would hurt her again. Once she got past her pride, she was grateful for the attention and the company.

The men worked out a schedule between them. Tonight, guard duty fell to Joshua. A smile touched her lips. If Levi had any idea how dangerous her feelings were every time she was around Joshua, he would have probably provided her with a guard dog instead.

"It's good to see you smile again."

This time she didn't startle. Although she hadn't heard him approach, she was becoming accustomed to his presence. During the day, when she could hear him hammering away on the roof, she knew it wouldn't be long before the hammering would cease and he'd steal a moment to check on her before returning to his work.

It probably should have upset her—that feeling of always being spied on, the inference that she needed a man around and couldn't cope on her own.

But it didn't.

It made her feel safe. Protected.

She opened her eyes.

Joshua stood in the shadows but she hadn't had to hear his voice to know it was him. Just one glance his way would have told her. Even in shadows she knew his height, the breadth of his shoulders, the way his energy filled a room—or a porch—with his presence.

"Hello, Joshua. I didn't hear you approach."

He stepped into the yellow glow of the lantern. "Yet you didn't jump. We're making progress."

She smiled widely. She had to admit she enjoyed watching him work and particularly enjoyed when he sat with her for a while.

Almost as if he could read her mind, Joshua pulled over a chair. They sat in companionable silence for a long time, enjoying the twilight, lost in their own thoughts, yet Katie was certain their thoughts were never far from each other. There was a tension between them. An awareness that filled the air with electricity.

She could feel his eyes watching her now.

"Are you hungry? Can I fix you something to eat?" she asked.

"No." He laughed. "I'm still full from the lunch you made me. If I continue to eat your good cooking, I am going to be too fat to climb up onto the roof."

Her eyes wandered to his flat stomach. She couldn't imagine how even one pound of flesh would appear to be anything on him but solid muscle.

For some reason, he seemed reluctant to leave this evening. More so than on other nights. She could tell he had something on his mind. Something that hid behind his eyes and yet wanted to pour out.

She shot him a questioning look but remained quiet. He'd talk when he was ready. The Joshua she remembered didn't say much, but when he did his words held their own power and importance.

"Are you finished with the roof?" she asked, giving him the time he needed to say whatever it was that troubled him.

"*Ya,* it is done."

She smiled. "*Gut.* What does Levi have you working on next?"

"Nothing. I am finished. It is time for me to go."

Her eyes flew to his face. She knew she couldn't hide her disappointment. Was that what he was finding so difficult to say?

"I'm sorry to hear that, Joshua. I was getting used to having to feed you."

She smiled as she spoke the teasing words but she didn't feel lighthearted. Her heart felt heavy and sad.

"I am still your neighbor, Katie. I intend to come by and see if you need anything."

"That would be nice."

Inane words, meaning nothing but saying everything. He was telling her he would never be far away. She was telling him she wanted him near. Yet their actual words told one another nothing of importance at all.

"Katie."

The seriousness of his tone caught her attention.

"I've wanted to ask you…about Jacob."

Heat flooded her cheeks and she lowered her eyes. She'd thought she'd put the anger behind her months ago. She'd thought she could hear his name and not think the things she did or feel the way she did.

She was wrong.

She didn't know if she was ready to talk about Jacob to anyone. She didn't know if she ever could. She shrugged nonchalantly as if Joshua's words carried no weight. "What is there to say? Jacob is dead."

Joshua leaned closer but refrained from touching her. "How did he die?"

"You know how he died. He fell during a barn raising and broke his neck." Anger flashed in her eyes when she looked at him. Her tone challenged him. "You didn't come back for the funeral but I am sure you were told of his death. Your cousin's district wasn't that far away."

Empathy and something else, compassion, perhaps, shone in his gaze.

She shifted uncomfortably. "Why do you want to know about his death now? It happened over a year ago."

"*Ya,* it did." He sighed heavily. "But you haven't re-married."

"That's none of your concern, Joshua Miller." She tapped her foot in a nervous rhythm against the porch floor. Her stress level rose.

"No, you're right. It's not." He tilted her chin toward him. "But I'm asking just the same. Why haven't you been courting? It would solve your land problem."

She jumped to her feet. "Is that what you think, Joshua Miller? That poor Katie Lapp needs a man to save her? Well, I don't. I am a strong, independent woman who can fend for herself. I can make my own decisions. I don't need a man to tell me what to do. And especially not you!"

Joshua stood and clasped her forearms in his hands.

Immediately, she pushed at him and tried to pull from his grasp. "Take your hands off me!" She pulled harder. "Let me go!"

He released his hold. His stunned expression almost brought her to tears.

She tried to take a breath and almost panicked when one didn't come. She gasped and then gasped again.

"Katie!" He put his hands on her again but this time with a gentleness that touched her heart. "It's your asthma, isn't it?" He guided her into the rocking chair.

"I'd forgotten. You used to have attacks quite often when we were kids."

She pulled the inhaler out of her pouch and again drew the medication into her lungs.

Joshua squatted in front of her, waiting, watching.

When her breathing returned to a normal rhythm, Joshua locked his gaze with hers.

"Talk to me, Katie." His voice was soft and tender. "What happened to you in the years I've been gone?"

Tears burned the back of her eyes but she refused to shed even one. She couldn't answer him. She couldn't speak at all. Her pain cut too deep.

Slowly, so gently and so softly it took her breath away, he kissed her. It wasn't the kiss that did her in. It was the kindness, the tenderness, the empathy she felt in it, and the floodgates opened. She sobbed and, try as she might, she couldn't stop. It was as though years of pent-up tears finally broke through the impenetrable wall she'd built around her heart.

Joshua pulled her down onto the floor with him. Cradling her in his arms. Rocking her with his body. Comforting her with his words.

After what seemed an eternity, she stopped crying and he looked deeply into her eyes.

"Talk to me, *lieb*. Tell me what is wrong. Is it about Jacob?"

Katie nodded.

"Do you miss him that much? Even after all this time?"

Her sadness melted into anger as volatile as molten lava. "Miss him? I hated him!" Immediately her hands flew to her lips. She wished she could call back her words but, of course, she couldn't.

Joshua sat back on his legs and stared at her. "You can't mean that!"

She lowered her eyes, unable to meet his gaze. "God forgive me but it's true."

"Why, Katie?" He couldn't hide his shock or keep the mild censure from his voice. "What would make you say such a thing about Jacob?"

"Jacob wasn't Jacob. He wasn't the boy we grew up with. He wasn't the teenager I loved. He was a monster."

Seconds of silence beat between them.

Joshua reached out and took her hand. "Tell me."

Katie wanted to tell him. She needed to tell him. She'd never spoken of those days. Not even to God. She'd been too angry, too hurt…too scared that somehow it had all been her fault and she couldn't face it.

But she looked into Joshua's eyes and saw no censure there. Only compassion.

"Jacob drank alcohol and he became a different person when he did." Her eyes implored him to believe her. "I never would have married him if I had known he was bringing this sickness into our marriage."

Her fingers couldn't find rest. They pulled at the edges of her apron, fiddled with the string of her *kapp*.

"Why didn't you go to the elders?"

"Because it was Jacob." The saddest of smiles pulled at the corners of her mouth. "At first, he would cry and beg for my forgiveness. He'd promise to never do it again. For months, he would keep his word…and they'd be good months. He would bring me wildflowers from the fields. He would hold my hand and take long walks with me by the pond. We would talk of our future, of the family we both wanted. Then he would drink again. Oh, he would apologize—again. He'd stop for a while until I started to believe that this time he was free of that poison. But over time a pattern formed. I knew Jacob wouldn't stop…couldn't stop."

"When you knew he couldn't stop, why didn't you tell the elders then?"

She lowered her head and all the bravado she had shown Joshua since he'd returned was gone, all the anger emptied. All that was left was pain and self-blame.

"I was afraid of him."

"Of Jacob?" Joshua was incredulous. "How could anyone be afraid of Jacob? I would never have believed he'd raise his hand to any woman and certainly not to you."

She looked accusingly at him and he realized instantly that he'd said the wrong thing, reacted the wrong way.

"I'm sorry," he whispered. "I had no right to judge." He ran the tips of his fingers ever so gently down her cheek. "I knew Jacob as a boy. I didn't know him as a man."

"The alcohol made him different." Her voice sounded listless and empty. "He wasn't the Jacob I knew. He wasn't the Jacob anybody knew." She put out her hand and held her wrist face up. "He hurt me. He'd take delight in proving his strength, his power over me."

Joshua blanched when his gaze fell to the scars on her wrist. Although he'd seen them before, a fresh wave of rage washed over him. He clasped her wrist in his hand. "He did this to you?" He'd heard the women gossiping in the corner of the general store that things weren't right between them but he assumed it was the drinking. He never believed his friend could grow up into this kind of man.

"He promised he would do much worse than this if I ever spoke of his drinking to anyone…so I didn't. After he died, I promised myself that I would never again be a victim. That I would never again let a man control my life."

"I'm sorry, Katie. I'm so sorry." He slid his fingers across her rippled scars.

She shrugged. "You have no reason to apologize."

All of it made sense now. The hostility he sensed in her from that very first day in the barn. The edginess. The wariness in her eyes. The dullness in eyes that used to be bright. The bravado and false sense of independence. Her difficulty accepting help from anyone except Levi.

Joshua rubbed a hand over his face. To get her to go to the police that very first day, he'd grabbed her hand and pulled her behind him. She'd erupted in anger, a side of her he had never seen before. Now he understood. He must have seemed like just another bully trying to force her to do something she hadn't wanted to do. He understood it all—and it made him physically ill.

Please, God. Help me. How will she ever forgive me? Especially now.

How can I ever forgive myself?

Everything in him wanted to slink off into the cover of darkness.

But he couldn't.

No matter how she reacted—with anger, with a slap, with a vow to never speak to him again—she deserved to know the truth.

Joshua stood. He extended his hand and helped her to her feet.

"I cannot apologize enough, Katie. My heart breaks for what you have gone through."

Katie smiled up at him, such a sweet, endearing smile. She cupped the side of his face with her hand.

"You have nothing to apologize for, Joshua. You have been a good friend." Her smile widened. "It is because of you that I have the courage to speak of these things to someone. It has helped me more than you know." She stood on tiptoe and kissed his cheek. *"Danki."*

He clasped her forearms and gently moved her away. He knew from the expression on her face that she believed he couldn't accept the things she'd said. He knew he had to set things right—now—no matter what the cost.

"I have done a horrible thing."

Katie pulled her shawl tighter around her body. "I don't understand." Her confusion and perhaps a touch of fear appeared on her face. "What have you done but listen to me? Help me? Be the best friend that I have missed all these years?"

Her tears…and smiles…and questions were ripping his heart out.

"I have not been the friend to you that I should have been. I should have been here for you. I should have stopped Jacob."

Katie laughed mirthlessly. "That's nonsense, Joshua. How could you have stopped Jacob? You didn't know. Nobody knew. He hid it well."

Bile rose in his throat and at that moment he hated himself more than she ever could.

"I knew."

He watched her smile slip away. Doubt filled her eyes only to quickly fade into shock and finally realization.

"You knew?" she whispered in disbelief.

He nodded.

"I don't understand. What did you know? When did you know?" She clasped her hand to her chest and seemed to be holding her breath while she waited for his answer.

"I knew he drank, shortly after you were married. I knew right before I left for my cousin's."

Her eyes searched the ground as if she'd find answers in the dirt, answers she'd been unable to draw from him.

When she lifted her eyes, the sense of betrayal he saw in them was almost more than he could bear. "I can't believe you didn't warn me."

When she spoke again, her voice was calm, controlled. "How did you find out?"

"One night I found him by the side of the road. I helped him into my buggy and then I realized that he was drunk. He told me it was the first and only time. He had met up with some Englisch friends that he had hung out with during *rumspringa*. Foolishly he had gone with them to a local bar. Jacob assured me that he would never do it again. He told me that he could never disrespect you or your marriage. He begged me to keep silent and I did."

Katie paced in a small circle. She seemed to be trying to process this new information. "Do you have any idea what your silence cost me?" Absently she rubbed her wrists. "He hurt me, Joshua. He forced his will on me so many times. He grew to take pleasure in knowing I was powerless against him. And the worst of it?" Tears shimmered in her eyes. "He made me believe I was a terrible wife. He told me over and over that his drinking was my fault."

Joshua could not speak. What could he possibly say? The knowledge that his silence had caused her such pain felt as if someone had stabbed him in the heart.

"Why did you leave Hope's Creek? Why didn't you stay and see if Jacob could keep his word?"

"I believed him, Katie. Do you think if I knew that it was more than once, if I thought for even one moment that he was lying to me, that I would have kept silent no matter how much he begged? He was my friend. But you…you were so much more."

Katie just stood and stared at him.

He didn't know what bothered him most, that she didn't yell at him, slap him or tell him to get out of her life—or if it was the sadness and the disappointment he saw in her eyes.

"Tell me the truth, Joshua. Why did you leave? You were a farmer. I never heard you express a desire to work with wood. Not once in all the years I've known you. No one understood why you chose to leave so abruptly." She pinned him with her gaze. "Tell me now. I want to know."

And there it was—the crux of the matter.

"Because I loved you." He didn't know how he found the strength to force the words out of his mouth but she deserved to know the truth, all of it. He released a heavy sigh. "I loved you and you were married to my best friend." He threw his hands up in surrender. "How could I possibly stay?"

Tears streamed down Katie's face. "Oh, Joshua, what have you done?"

Chapter Six

Joshua stepped off the porch into the darkness. He didn't know what he'd expected. What should he expect when he'd just told the love of his life that he'd kept silent about her husband's drinking and that silence had cost her emotional pain and physical abuse for years? How could he ever look her in the eyes again?

He walked around the perimeter of her house making sure it was secure. Although he rattled windows and twisted doorknobs, he could think of nothing but the look on Katie's face just before she turned and went into the house.

She'd never forgive him.

He didn't deserve to be forgiven.

Joshua stepped into the barn. He checked every stall. He climbed the ladder and peered into the loft.

No one.

Nothing.

Katie was locked in and safe for the night.

Joshua, feeling the weight of the world on his shoulders, began the trek home. As he walked he relived the events of the evening. He could hear her voice in his mind as clearly as if she stood right beside him. His mind replayed every word. His memory burned images in his brain.

Katie smiling up at him.

Katie cupping his face.

Katie leaning into his kiss and kissing him back.

Katie crying and looking totally betrayed just moments before she walked inside the house and closed the door.

Dear heavenly Father, forgive me. Katie suffered for years because I stayed silent. How am I going to live with that?

Joshua was halfway home when he saw Levi's buggy coming his way. He sidestepped just as Levi pulled to a stop beside him.

"I thought you'd still be at Katie's."

"I made sure that no one is lurking around and that everything is locked up tight. She'll be safe until morning."

Levi nodded. "I certainly hope so. This is all becoming too much to handle. I am going to offer Katie money for the farm. I can't afford to give her what Adams and King are offering. But I believe out of respect for all the hard work that I have done, she will sell the land to me and keep it in the Lapp family where it belongs."

The thought of Katie leaving Hope's Creek permanently was more painful than the thought that she'd never speak to him again. At least if she stayed here he would still be able to see her…and he could hope that things might change. He'd stopped believing in forgiveness but he still hoped for miracles.

"I don't think tonight is a good time to broach the subject, Levi."

"That was not my intention. I will bring up the subject tomorrow at breakfast. So many things have been happening to her lately that I am sure she is more than ready to leave."

Joshua's heart sank because he believed it, too.

"Climb in. I will turn around and take you home. It will not take me more than a few minutes out of my way."

Joshua shook his head. "*Danki,* but no. I wish to walk. I need to clear my head and walking does that for me."

"As you wish." Levi said, "I will settle my account with you tomorrow."

Joshua shrugged. "No hurry."

"I am a man who pays his debts. You did good work, Joshua. I am grateful."

Joshua acknowledged the compliment with a nod. The Amish didn't waste words on compliments. It could cause the recipient to be prideful. So why did Levi do so now?

"Since the house has been repaired and the stalls finished, there will be no need for you to come over anymore." Levi smiled but there was no warmth in his eyes. If Joshua didn't know better, he would have thought it a veiled threat.

Again, his mind went to Katie. "You're right, Levi. There will be no reason for me to come out to the farm again."

"*Gut.* Then I will be certain to stop by your house in the morning and settle our account." With a nod and a crack of his whip, Levi urged his horse on.

Fifteen minutes later, Joshua reached the lane leading to home. He'd never felt this dejected or hopeless.

He'd lost Katie once because he'd been too much of a coward to tell her what was on his mind. How ironic that he'd lost her again because this time he did.

Katie sat in her bedroom in the dark and stared out the window. She didn't light her oil lamp. She wanted to just sit quietly and gaze at the stars. She didn't want to think, didn't want to feel. She just wanted to be.

The full moon cast a glow over the yard below. A movement in the shadows caught her eye. She stared hard and waited for it to move again.

The mother cat appeared out of the shadows. She was on the prowl for tonight's dinner. Katie smiled humorlessly. *And life goes on.*

She almost got up to go to bed when a movement caught her eye, a second shadow, this one larger and more cumbersome. She squinted her eyes to focus and stared harder at the shadows by the barn.

Was someone down there?

Her heart pounded. She didn't dare breathe as she stared at the spot where she thought she'd seen movement.

The shadow moved. Someone definitely moved in the darkness. Thankful for a full moon, she prayed that the person would step out of the shadows just long enough for her to see who it was.

But it didn't happen.

The person moved stealthily, carefully, hanging back in the gloom, hiding in the murkiness.

From the size of the moving mass, she felt fairly certain that her intruder was a man.

A man who was creeping into her barn!

Katie didn't know what to do. She wanted to discover who it was that tormented her. She wanted to sneak downstairs, tiptoe out to the barn and peek inside at the intruder. Once she knew who it was, she'd tell the sheriff and the elders and the whole world if need be just to be able to expose the culprit once and for all.

That was what she wanted to do.

But she wasn't stupid.

She knew she was alone in the house. She had no weapon even though she wouldn't use one if she did. Levi wouldn't be here until morning and Joshua… Joshua would probably never come out here again.

So she continued to sit in the darkness and stared at the barn door. Whoever went in had to come out. Maybe she'd see the culprit then.

Katie found that time moved exceedingly slow when a person had to wait. Seconds became minutes and every minute felt like a lifetime.

What was the person doing in the barn? Was he stealing her horses or her tack and farm equipment? Maybe this time the culprit would leave her a note lying on a bale of hay.

She was so nervous she thought she was going to jump out of her skin.

Maybe she should go downstairs. She might get a better look at who it was if she crept out onto the porch. This man wasn't the only person who could hide in the shadows.

But what if he came out of the barn while she was going downstairs? She wouldn't know and she'd lose her only opportunity to identify her tormentor.

She waited another five minutes, then ten.

Unable to stand it, she sprang to her feet. She'd take

her chances. She was going to hide on the porch. She couldn't just sit here and do nothing.

Before she could move, she saw it.

She wasn't sure at first. It was just the tiniest light and for a moment Katie thought the foolish man had actually taken a chance and lit a lantern.

But the light grew…and spread…and Katie's eyes widened with dread.

The barn was on fire!

Joshua couldn't resist stealing another glance toward the Lapp farm. He knew he wouldn't see anything in the darkness. Katie was safely in bed. There'd be no lights in either the house or the barn.

Still, he looked in that direction.

He blinked, then blinked again. His eyes must be deceiving him. It couldn't be!

"Katie!"

Without hesitation, he ran.

Flames licked at the edge of the horizon. He offered a quick prayer that Katie wouldn't foolishly rush into a burning barn. The thought that she might gave him a burst of adrenaline and he raced faster than he would have ever believed he could.

He'd reached the lane leading to the Lapp house when he heard it—the loud, ceaseless clanging of the triangle. Katie wasn't inside the barn.

Thank You, God.

When the clanging stopped, he began to worry. She wouldn't be foolish enough to try to put the flames out by herself, would she?

The horses!

Of course! Katie wouldn't hesitate to try to free the horses.

He pumped his legs harder, ignoring the painful cramping in his thighs. Katie needed him and this time he wasn't going to let her down.

Katie swung the barn door wide and rushed inside as the mama cat and her kittens bolted past her. The frantic whinny of frightened horses made her heart beat double time. Smoke obstructed her view and stole what little breath she had left after her earlier asthma attack. She coughed and bent over at the waist and coughed some more.

She knew the inside of this barn. She could describe every nook and cranny. Unable to see more than a few inches in front of her, she moved by rote to the first stall. She was careful to stand behind the heavy oak gate that Joshua had constructed, knowing that the terrified horse would stampede out of the stall the second it sensed liberty. Sure enough, the horse's thundering hooves pounded the dirt floor as it rushed to freedom. Moving as quickly as she could, she repeated the scenario at the second stall and then the third.

She coughed nonstop now. Her chest burned and she had to fight for every breath. She snatched her inhaler that was pinned to her dress. She couldn't wait until she made it outside. Her lungs felt as if they were going to explode.

She held the inhaler up to her mouth but somebody grabbed it away and pushed her to the floor. Thick smoke hung in the air above her. Katie turned her face toward the dirt and was able to suck in air instead of smoke. She rolled onto her back to face her assailant.

Levi!

Katie couldn't believe that Levi was her enemy. He must be a victim, too. Hurriedly her eyes scanned the barn. A sinking feeling settled in the pit of her stomach when she realized the truth that was staring her in the face.

"Why?" Katie choked and coughed. "Why, Levi?"

"This land has been in my family for generations. You had no right to it, you sniveling, weak-minded woman. Jacob should have left the farm to me!"

"Levi…please… I need my inhaler." She reached up her hand but clasped only empty air.

"This little thing?" By this time, Levi also choked and coughed on the smoke but he didn't even try to run out the door. "Let's see what happens if I throw this away."

"No! Don't!"

With a laugh that sounded surreal and almost evil, Levi tossed the inhaler into the nearby flames.

"Levi…we have to get out of here."

"You're staying right here where you belong." He laughed again.

Katie crawled on the ground. "We're family." Each word was punctuated with a cough and another gasp for air. Katie clutched the bottom of his pant leg.

Levi viciously kicked her away.

"My brother was family. You were the woman who ruined his life. He'd never have touched a drop of that poison if he'd been happy at home. You killed my brother and you might as well have tried to kill me. You were going to sell the only home I have ever known. I knew when I made my offer that it wasn't enough. I knew you would take one of the greater offers and I couldn't let you do it."

"Why are you burning the barn?"

"To bring down the value of the property. I hoped the other two men would go away."

"Levi, I never told you I would sell to them because I never would. The farm belongs to you."

He glared at her, a flash of uncertainty evident in his expression.

It was so difficult now to breathe that Katie couldn't even feel the crushing pressure of her lungs anymore.

"You knew?" The hoarse whisper that escaped her lips didn't even sound like her voice. "About Jacob's drinking?"

"I knew. And I hated you for it. My brother didn't deserve to die…but you do! May God have mercy on your soul."

"Levi! No! Don't leave me!"

Katie watched Levi disappear into the darkness. She tried to crawl across the floor but was too weak to save herself. Hope was gone. No one would get here in time to help her and she was too weak to save herself. She closed her eyes and surrendered her will to God. If this was His plan, so be it.

A strange heaviness started in her feet and slowly spread up her legs and through her body.

Is this what it feels like to die?

She couldn't draw one more breath.

Her last conscious thought was a deep sadness that she'd never get the chance to see Joshua again. He'd never know she'd forgiven him. She hoped that God would help him forgive himself.

Joshua reached the barn door just as Levi stumbled out of the smoke. He steadied the man and prevented his fall. "Levi, what happened? Are you all right? Where's Katie?"

Joshua glanced over his shoulder hoping he'd see Katie standing on the porch or waiting in the doorway. His heart sank when she wasn't there.

Levi coughed and sputtered and stammered unintelligibly.

"Levi! Get hold of yourself!" He shook the man then shook him again. "Pull yourself together. Where is Katie? Where is she?"

Levi laughed...a maniacal sound that made the hair on the back of Joshua's neck stand up.

"It's too late." Levi laughed again and pointed at the barn, which by now was almost completely engulfed in flames. "She's getting what she deserves."

By now, neighbors had heard the ringing and began to gather in the yard. They started a human chain gathering water from the troughs and passing it one to the other to throw on the fire.

Joshua could hear the distant sound of the fire engines.

But all that registered in his mind were Levi's words. *Katie is in the barn.*

He ripped his shirt off and dipped it into a bucket of water.

"Joshua, what are you doing? You can't go in there." Amos tried to stop him but Joshua shook his hand away.

"Katie's in there!"

Wrapping his wet shirt around his nose and mouth, he raced into the barn.

Joshua threw an arm up to protect his face. A blast of heat seared his skin.

"Katie!"

He screamed her name but all he could hear was the deafening roar of the fire.

Where was she? He moved farther into the barn. The black, thick smoke obscured his vision and threatened to choke him despite the wet rag on his face.

Where could she be?

Despite the fear that clawed at his gut and the chaos that surrounded him, a voice of reason sounded in Joshua's head. If Katie came into the barn, it would have been to save the horses. Moving quickly, he found his way to the first stall.

"Katie!"

Bending at the waist because of the racking coughs that claimed his body, he made it to the second stall, then the third.

He was about to admit defeat when he tripped over something on the floor and almost fell.

Katie!

Kneeling at her side, he lifted her head. He held two fingers against her throat to feel for a heartbeat and could barely detect one.

Joshua scooped her into his arms. Moving as quickly as he dared, he hurried toward the door. When he burst into the yard, several of the other men came running. They lifted Katie from his arms and placed her on the ground at the foot of the porch.

A few of the men slapped Joshua on the back and half carried, half dragged him to safety, as well.

The volunteer firefighters, composed of Amish and Englisch alike, fought valiantly to subdue the flames. He knew it wasn't to save the barn—that was futile at this point—but in an attempt to prevent the fire from leaping to the house.

Pushing his way through the crowd, Joshua rushed to Katie and fell to his knees beside her. The paramedics had put an oxygen mask on her face and were preparing to lift her onto a gurney.

"Is she alive?" Joshua wiped soot from his eyes and mouth.

"Barely. We gotta go," said one of the paramedics, who secured an IV bag to a pole on the gurney.

Joshua watched them lift Katie into the ambulance. Sirens rent the night air as the rig sped down the land.

Joshua watched the flashing lights disappear in the distance. He remained on his knees and prayed.

Chapter Seven

"There you are. C'mon, now. Open those eyes again."

When she did, Katie saw Esther Fischer smoothing the hair off her forehead and away from her face.

"You gave us quite a scare, you know," the bishop's wife said.

"What happened?" Katie's voice was little more than a whispered croak.

"We wanted to ask you the same thing." Joshua appeared in her line of vision. He looked drawn and tired.

"You look horrible." She summoned up a laugh that sounded almost as bad as her gravelly voice.

"*Danki,*" Joshua replied. He moved to the opposite side of the bed and clasped her hand in his. "Maybe that's because I haven't slept in two days."

"*Ya,* that's right," Esther said. "I tried to get him to leave but he's like a mule, stubborn as they come." Esther leaned down and whispered in her ear, "Now we can add loyal and heroic to Joshua Miller's fine qualities. If you don't let him come courting, I might consider asking him myself."

Katie chuckled. "You're already married. What would Amos say?"

"He'd say I was a fine judge of character." Esther patted her arm. "I'm going to go tell the doctor that you are awake."

The door had barely closed behind the woman when Katie turned her eyes toward Joshua.

"I need to tell you—"

"Katie, I—"

Both of them smiled.

"You first," Katie said. Her throat burned and her head throbbed but she'd never been so happy to be alive.

Joshua lifted her hand and pressed her fingers to his lips. Katie's breath caught in her throat when she saw tears form in his eyes.

"I've never prayed so hard in my life." He kissed her fingers again but did not let go of her hand. "I thought it was too late and I'd lost you." He clutched her hand against his chest, tears streaming freely down his face. "Forgive me, Katie, for what I did. I'll spend the rest of my life trying to make it up to you if you'll let me."

Katie lifted her free hand and wiped the tears from his cheek. "I forgive you, Joshua. You know we must forgive as God has forgiven us."

He nodded. "*Ya,* it is the Amish way. But sometimes forgiveness does not come easily."

"How can I blame you for what I was guilty of myself?"

Joshua arched an eyebrow.

"I didn't tell the bishop about Jacob's drinking. Maybe if I had, someone might have been able to help him."

"You cannot blame yourself for his drinking, Katie. It was his responsibility and no one else's fault."

"Really?"

He grinned at the irony of his words. "Like I said, sometimes forgiveness does not come easily. How fortunate we are that God loves us enough to forgive us even when we find it hard to forgive ourselves."

"And Levi?" Her heart felt like a stone in her chest. "What has happened to Levi?"

"He tried to run away. The sheriff arrested him the morning after the fire."

Katie sighed. "I feel sorry for him. To be silent all those years, harbor the belief that I was the cause of his brother's death and yet work sunup till sundown to help me save the farm."

"He was saving the farm for himself, not you, Katie. It was greed that destroyed him."

Katie tried to sit up.

"Here. Let me help you." Joshua slid his arm beneath her shoulders. He lifted her to a sitting position and straightened her pillows to support her back.

Suddenly, he stopped what he was doing. His one arm still rested beneath her shoulders. His other hand gently tilted her chin until her eyes locked with his. Without a word, he lowered his head and captured her lips. When Joshua released her, he removed his arm from her back and straightened up, but he never left her side.

"I wish you had shared your feelings, Joshua, when we were teens. If I'd known how you felt about me…" Her voice trailed off but her eyes never left his face. He didn't squirm and look away like the shy teenage boy he had once been. He stared back at her with a self-confidence she was becoming quite familiar with, an inner strength she found quite appealing.

"You only had eyes for Jacob back then." His eyes darkened with intensity. His smile was slow and lazy.

"And now? If I share my feelings with you now?"

Butterflies danced in her stomach.

"Now?" She gazed into his dark brown eyes and hoped she'd see forever in them.

He leaned his forearms on the hospital rail. "You have to know how I feel about you."

She lowered her eyes. Her heart hammered in her chest as she sensed him moving closer.

"You know I am a man of few words. Always have been. Always will be, I suppose." He tilted her chin up. "So don't listen to my words, Katie. Listen to my heart." He held her hand against his chest.

"I'm listening, Joshua." She placed her hand behind his neck. Her fingers twisted into his thick hair. She pulled him down and moved her lips against his ear. "If I stay still and I listen very hard, what might I hear your heart say?"

Joshua leaned back and grinned.

"It would tell you that I smile every day because I know you're here. It would tell you that it is impossible for me to have one single logical thought because my mind is crowded with thoughts of you."

He kissed her forehead.

"I try to imagine what it would be like to share breakfast with you every morning."

He kissed the tip of her nose.

"I think how *wunderbar* it would be after a long day of work to see you sitting across from me at the dinner table. To talk to you about my day. To listen to you tell me about yours."

His lips touched hers gently, once, twice and then again.

"My heart knows that I think of you in the evenings. In my mind I am holding your hand. I can feel the warmth of your body sitting beside me. I look into your eyes…and I see love…and I feel incredibly blessed."

He gathered her into his arms. "Now do you know how I feel about you?" His husky whisper sent chills up and down her spine. "God has granted me a second chance. I want to spend every day and every night of my life with you. I want us to live on this farm and make it our home. I want to raise a family, a large, noisy, boisterous family, together."

He picked up some strands of her hair and let them run through his fingers, looking at it in awe as though he was watching gold silk. "I hope our *kinner* will have hair as silky and bright as yours."

His expression sobered and he stared at her, his eyes revealing a hint of vulnerability.

"I want to grow old with you, Katie. And I intend to thank God every day of my life for that blessing if you'll have me."

Tears of happiness shimmered in her eyes. Real love had nothing to do with trying to control the life of another. Love was about trust and sharing and compromise. It was putting your partner's wants and needs first but not at the cost of sacrificing your own.

She looked into Joshua's face and she knew. She loved this man and she always would.

"How many *kinner* did you say we are going to have?"

A wide grin broke out on Joshua's face. "Four? Five?"

She tightened her hold on his neck and drew him closer. "Then we better not waste any more time." She kissed him with all the promise of a future she held in her heart.

"You will marry me?" Joshua asked.

Katie's heart felt as if it might burst. "Yes, Joshua. I will marry you."

Joshua let out an excited whoop. "When, Katie?"

"This is November, Joshua, is it not?"

He nodded.

"November is the month we hold our Amish weddings. The harvest is over and spring planting has not yet begun. It is the perfect time, Joshua. Don't you think?"

The look in his eyes took her breath away.

"I couldn't think of a better time, *lieb*. I love you, Katie."

"And I love you."

Beneath his kiss, Katie could feel her lips bow into a demure, satisfied smile.

It was true. Joshua Miller was a man of few words—but when he spoke from his heart, his words were indeed powerful and of great importance.

Danki, God.

* * * * *

RETURN TO WILLOW TRACE

Kit Wilkinson

To my son, Jonah, who is wise beyond his years.
May the Lord bless you with abundant love.
You and Charlie are my greatest joys.

Let love and faithfulness never leave you.
—*Proverbs* 3:3

Chapter One

"Good night, Bishop Miller. See you next week." Lydia Stoltz waved a quick goodbye with her cleaning rag. The old Amish man shuffled out the front doors of his furniture store, placing his black felt hat atop a nest of soft, silvery hair. A strong autumn wind blew against the glass doors. Lydia wrestled to get them closed, but not before a few orange and yellow leaves rolled under the skirt of her dark purple frock. An autumn storm was brewing on the western horizon. Cold north winds clashed with some lingering rain clouds. A quick, violent tempest was on the way.

She bolted the big steel lock and drew the long green shade over the length of the doors. Miller's Original Amish Furniture—Closed, it read on the other side. Bishop Miller owned and operated both a lumber mill, which his son Eli had recently taken over, and the furniture store. Together, they formed the largest Amish-owned businesses not only in Willow Trace, but in all of Lancaster County. People from all over trusted the name Miller and purchased their plain but sturdy wooden furniture from this store.

Lydia collected the leaves from the floor and resumed her work. It was the same each Wednesday. After hours, she would clean Miller's storefront, making the wood of each display piece gleam with the same care with which they'd been handcrafted in the workshop attached to the store. Afterward, she walked the short distance home, where she and her mother raised rabbits, sheep and miniature horses on a small farm that had been in her father's family for generations. It was hard work for just the two of them, and sometimes sales were low, hence the job at the furniture store. But Lydia loved the farm, and ever since her father had abandoned them, she had taken it upon herself to make sure that the beautiful place didn't slip through their fingers.

Lydia hadn't taken two steps from the doors when the dead bolt of the front door snapped open. She started, nearly dropping her cleaning rag. Again, cold air swept around her, and the strings of her white prayer *kapp* danced on her shoulders.

"I forgot to mention somethin' to ye." Old Bishop Miller craned his head through the tiny space between the double doors.

Lydia expelled the quick breath of air she'd held in and laughed at her own silly nervousness. "Oh dear. You gave me quite a fright."

"I'm sorry for that, but you should know that one of the craftsmen is still in the shop, working late. I didn't want him to frighten ye. You might hear him banging around back there."

Lydia nodded. It happened from time to time that one of the craftsmen worked late to finish a piece that had been preordered. With Christmas only two months away, she imagined there was quite a demand.

"Mr. Yoder. Joseph Yoder. I believe you know each other." A sly grin fell over the bishop's face. "Good night, Miss Lydia." He pulled the doors closed again and turned the lock over himself.

Joseph Yoder? Oh yeah. I know him, all right. She had courted him. Thankfully, for the past five years, she'd seldom heard his name. No one in her Ordnung had spoken much of him after he'd sped off to Indiana five years ago.

Lydia's heart beat heavily against her rib cage. She slung her dirty rag into the cleaning bucket, trudged to the closet and snatched up the broom. With sweeping, it was best to begin in the back corner and work across, moving with the grain of the wood floors. Her movements were sharp, fueled by her own emotions. Buried sentiments churned up like the dust that blew across the floor.

Just last week, Lydia had heard some gossip that Joseph would be back for his cousin's wedding. Perhaps if she had bothered to ask more questions she would have found out that he was crafting furniture at Miller's shop while he was home. But she hadn't. Lydia had vowed long ago that she would not allow herself to be interested in anything that had to do with Joseph Yoder.

For Lydia there were two kinds of men—the kind who kept promises and the kind who did not. Running off without so much as a word after promising to love her forever put Joseph into the latter category. Lydia knew all too well, from experience with her own unreliable father, that she would rather be alone than live a life with a man who could disappear without a word of explanation.

No, Lydia had quit thinking about Joseph's soft hazel

eyes and broad shoulders. She'd forgotten his hearty laugh and mischievous smile. She'd even courted Gideon Lapp for a short spell. And while the five years that had passed had dulled the burn of Joseph's abandonment, there were embers enough left to singe her when she thought on it for too long.

And now here he was so close. Although with the huge steel warehouse walls between them, they would stay quite separate. So why were her knees trembling and her heart palpitating as if she'd run a marathon?

Lydia swept the pile of dirt into a dustpan and dumped it into the garbage. Now, on to polishing— that was a job she quite enjoyed. She passed her oiled cloth over each surface, between every groove until all the wood shone bright and clean. She admired the work of the Amish craftsmen and agreed that those who worked for Bishop Miller were among the most skilled.

Of course, it was wrong to be prideful, but Lydia saw no fault in appreciating the useful pieces. Surely there were no others in the world that compared. She could not imagine any more functional or sturdy than the ones in this showroom.

Wind whistled around the metal warehouse and across the storefront. The storm outside had grown strong. Eerie sounds echoed through the building. The front and side windows pinged as a sudden downpour let loose. Lydia hastened her work, setting her pace to the heavy droplets as they hammered in rhythm against the building.

The sooner she got home the better. For many reasons. Already that day, she and her mother had worked hard in the stables, and her limbs trembled with fatigue. Now there was the storm, which would drench her on the way home. And last but not least, Joseph Yoder stood only a few feet away. Did he know she was there? What if he did? What if he came to talk to her?

Boom. A loud noise caused Lydia to jump. What was the matter with her? She closed her eyes and took a deep breath. It was nothing. The storm. The wind. A box or some sort of loose rubbish blown up against the front doors. She needn't be so edgy.

Lydia resumed her cleaning. But again, something crashed against the front doors and they shook. *That is some strong wind.* Perhaps Bishop Miller had not pulled the doors completely shut. She went forward to check, reaching for the key, which she kept in a small pouch attached to her wrist.

As she moved, the doors continued to rattle—loud and steady. *That* could not be the wind. She supposed she'd known that all along, but what *was* on the other side of the doors? She could not imagine.

Her hands trembled as she tugged at the big green shade. It rolled up with a snap. Lydia screamed and scrambled back. On the other side of the door, a large man pressed hard against the glass. He looked disheveled. His eyes were translucent. His long, thin face was framed with dark matted hair and stained with blood. In his hand, he grasped a black pistol, which he held pointed at her head.

He scratched the glass with the barrel of the weapon. Lydia let out another bloodcurdling scream. Clambering back again, she collided with a solid piece of furniture and fought to keep her balance.

"Open up. Come on. Now!" The look on his face was savage.

Lydia didn't move. She couldn't. Fear paralyzed

her. This was a way bigger problem than facing Joseph Yoder.

Oh dear Lord, what can I do?

Joseph Yoder laid aside the small chisel. He took up some fine sandpaper, and with long, steady strokes, he smoothed the slots he'd carved out of the surface of the large armoire he'd promise to finish for Bishop Miller.

With a grunt, he lifted the heavy door and lined up the corresponding slots to their hinges. His tired muscles quaked under the weight and he was forced to lower it back to the ground. He could not finish the armoire alone. Even if he'd managed to get the door in place, he didn't have the strength and balance to hold it up with one hand while placing the pins with the other.

He thought of Lydia on the other side of the building. Bishop Miller had mentioned she would be cleaning the storefront that evening. She could help put the pins in. Not that he would dare ask her. She wouldn't want to see him, and he didn't care to see her, either.

Joseph ran his calloused fingers over the fine armoire. *Ya,* even Lydia would approve of this work.

That is, until she found out it was his.

Joseph sighed and wiped the sweat from his brow with a clean cloth. Time for a short break. His hands shook from the long hours put in over the past three days. He needed some nourishment. Maybe food would calm the butterflies twittering in his stomach...even though he was pretty certain they were not caused by hunger.

He sat down with the fresh rolls and thick slices of smoked ham that his nana had packed for him. It was good to be home, even though it was only for a few weeks. After that, he would be anxious to get back to his uncle Toby's in Indiana. Joseph had wondered if he'd see Lydia while he was home and if he did whether she would speak to him or not. She had cut off all communication with him after he'd left Willow Trace. He had been devastated. But his family convinced him it was God's will for him to be in Indiana. Over time, he came to agree with them. Especially once he heard Lydia had so quickly moved on to court Gideon Lapp. As far as he knew, she was getting married herself this wedding season. So what did he care? One day, he would do the same once he'd settled in with his uncle's business.

The wind and rain slammed hard against the metal building. This severe of a storm had not been expected. He thought of Lydia having to walk home in all that rain. She didn't live far, but anyone would get soaked to the bone on a night like tonight. He must offer his buggy. It was the proper thing to do. The butterflies in his stomach felt more like hummingbirds as he crossed the large workshop. He knocked gently at the back door leading into the storefront. Bishop Miller had locked it, or perhaps it was locked all of the time. Maybe Lydia would have a key?

In any case, there was no answer.

He wrapped his knuckles again against the wooden door, a little louder this time.

Still, there was no answer. But Lydia had to be there. The shop's oil-powered lights were on. Their bright rays shone across the threshold and spread over the tops of his leather shoes.

"Lydia?" He shook the handle. "I don't mean to bother you. Just thought you could take my buggy home. Can you hear me? Lydia?"

He waited. At long last, he heard something, but it was not what he expected. There was movement. Scuffling. A loud shriek. Joseph swallowed hard. That scream…that was Lydia. He knew her voice, even when it was hysterical—and that was a rare thing for a woman like Lydia. He couldn't imagine what she could be screaming about. A mouse? A spider, maybe?

No. Lydia would never be frightened by a little critter. She was not the type of woman to scream over something like that. Joseph's throat sunk to his stomach.

"Lydia? Can you open the door? Please? Are you okay? Lydia?" He shook the door.

Nothing. All was silent and the door would not budge.

Panic struck through him. He would have to get into the store another way. Lydia was in trouble. And he was going to help her whether she welcomed him or not.

Chapter Two

Joseph raced into Bishop Miller's office. Surely the old man kept an extra key inside. But at seeing the multiple stacks of papers piled over cabinets and tables, Joseph decided it might take forever to find a key in that mess. The fastest way to get to Lydia was to go out the back door and run around to the front of the store.

Joseph wove his way through the maze of unfinished furniture and pushed through the heavy metal doors in back. Through pelting rain, he sprinted around the corner, his chest tight and heart pounding. His foot slipped on the loose gravel. Sharp rocks pressed into his palms as he pushed off the ground and kept moving. He turned the corner from the side of the building. A distant streetlight glowed over the facade of the store. He saw no cars in the parking lot. No traffic on the main road. Only darkness lay beyond the scope of the lights.

Joseph slowed his steps, approaching the big glass doors. Lydia's voice sounded faintly under the din of pouring rain. He froze as she came into view. She was crying. Sobbing. In front of her lurched a tall, dark-headed man. He was soaked from the rain and his coat was stained with…

Was that blood?

It looked like blood. The man jerked toward Lydia. Light reflected off something he held in his hand. Joseph flinched. It was a gun.

Please, Lord, don't let me have been too late, Joseph prayed as he pressed his way through the front doors. Lydia lifted her head. Her eyes were wide with fear.

"Put the gun away and step back, sir." Joseph spoke in a controlled voice as he entered the store and continued forward.

The man turned with great effort, groaning as he moved. Even his breath was labored. The gun fell to the floor. Then with his limp arms dangling at his sides, he closed his eyes and collapsed to the floor.

Joseph rushed forward and knelt over the fallen man. "What's happened? How did he get in here?"

"Joseph, it's okay." Lydia knelt beside him. "It's Billy Ferris. I let him in. He's hurt and confused."

Billy. The same Billy who'd been the reason Joseph had left the little town of Willow Trace. And left Lydia. Joseph clenched his teeth. He looked down at the man's face. Bruised, swollen, cut, bleeding, his features bore no resemblance to the Englisch boy he'd spent so much of his childhood with. *Could this really be Billy?*

Joseph reached forward and touched the man's shoulder. His eyes flickered. The man jerked forward again, grabbing at his belly.

"Joe…" He coughed. He looked up and attempted to smile at Joseph. Only then did Joseph believe that this wreck of a person was indeed his old friend.

Lydia leaned in and touched Joseph's shoulder. Her

whole body trembled. "He's bleeding badly. I think he has a fever, too. He keeps trying to say something but I can't understand."

Joseph turned to Lydia. Looking into her eyes for the first time in five years caused a flood of unexpected emotions to race through him. Love, tenderness, pain and betrayal. But that would all have to wait. Billy Ferris was between them, once again.

"How is he hurt?" Joseph examined his old friend limp on the floor. At his shoulder, there was a cut, more like a slash. His clothing was soaked from the ribs down with not only rain but with blood and dirt, as well. From the way he clutched at his belly, the pain there must have been most acute. Joseph lifted the tails of the bloody shirt and cringed at what had once been a tightly muscled abdomen. Billy's stomach had been cut. Lydia gasped and turned her head away.

It was no small wound. No wonder Billy was grabbing at his belly. He needed a doctor. "Is there a phone? We have to call 911."

Lydia shook her head. "I don't have one. The store doesn't have one. Bishop Miller won't allow them. He pays for an outside service to take orders for the store. Messages are hand delivered."

"I don't have one, either." Joseph sat back on his heels. What could they do? The closest place was Lydia's but he couldn't imagine moving Billy in his buggy in this condition.

"Can you get some water and rags?" he asked Lydia. "Maybe if we clean him up a bit, we will see that he's not quite so bad."

"*Ya*, okay." She hopped up and headed to the back of the store.

Joseph gazed down. "What happened to you, my friend?"

Billy murmured and coughed. His eyes looked up. The pain Joseph could see in them nearly brought him to tears. Billy clutched Joseph's wrist and tried again to speak.

"You have a phone, don't you?" *Of course he does.* Joseph searched Billy's pockets. He found a set of keys, a wallet and a plastic Baggie of pink powder. The label over the packet read Bath Salts. Joseph frowned. Bath salts must be some type of street drug. He tossed the bag aside. Looked as if Billy's bad choices had only gotten worse since Joseph went to Indiana. Now here he was cut and possibly bleeding to death.

"What happened to you, Billy?" Joseph grabbed a sheet draped over a nearby piece of furniture. He rolled it up and placed it under Billy's head in an attempt to make him more comfortable. "You should have gone to the hospital, not come here.... Why are you here?"

Billy tried again to speak. "Lydia... What's..."

Joseph frowned. *Lydia? Lydia and Billy? Friends?* A twinge of resentment flashed over him. Was that why Billy was there? To see Lydia?

Lydia returned with towels and water. She placed one towel on Billy's stomach then pressed another to the deep cut on his shoulder. Joseph helped inch Billy's arm out of the jacket so that she could get to the cut better. The patient protested with a groan.

"He said that he came here to see you?" Joseph wished he'd checked his emotions before speaking. Had he sounded jealous?

Lydia shrugged. "I guess. That's what it sounded

like he said to me, but I don't know why. I haven't laid eyes on him since—well—since that last night we all went out together."

That last night. Joseph knew all too well the night she meant. It had been the worst of his life. The night his parents sent him away to Indiana without letting him speak to Lydia.

Remembering it was like getting his own stomach cut open, although it was more like his heart that had been shred to pieces.

"Talk to us, Billy," Joseph said. "Who did this to you? How did this happen? Why? Why didn't you go to the hospital?"

Billy's lips trembled in a feverish delirium. "He knows—he knows—and he'll find you. What's... Remember Alex? Be...be careful."

He knows? Who knows? Who is Alex? Lydia was right. Billy's words made no sense. Whether his mind was affected by drugs or by the horrible pain, only a doctor could discern.

The cut on Billy's shoulder was much worse than it had appeared. Joseph rolled up the sleeve of his heavy coat to help elevate the wound. Something hard and metal was inside the sleeve. It had perhaps stopped the blade from causing further damage. Joseph groped inside the coat sleeve. He hadn't thought to check there for a pocket. Amish didn't have fancy things like pockets. He hoped it wasn't full of drugs. It wasn't. Joseph nearly smiled as he slid a high-tech touch-screen cell phone from the coat sleeve. He tapped the emergency button and held it until a dial tone sounded.

A voice answered quickly. "This is Emergency. Please state your name and location..."

Joseph and Lydia exchanged a look of hope.

Thank You, Lord. Thank You. Please let Billy live.

The next forty minutes seemed an eternity to Lydia. Bright lights flashed, sirens whistled, the rain continued to pour down. People ran here and scurried there. It was as if she were in a dream where the images were all blurred and fuzzy—a dream she wished she'd wake from, making this strange evening all go away.

Instead, she watched as the EMTs strapped Billy Ferris to a gurney. They gave him several injections and hooked him to an oxygen tank. Lydia closed her eyes, hoping to hold in the tears, which had perched on her bottom lids. Her own chest was tight and lacked sufficient air. Only adrenaline had kept her from feeling the full weight of the situation. But now that Billy was someone else's responsibility, exhaustion and confusion slammed down on her like a hammer.

And that was without even thinking about the fact that, after all these years, Joseph Yoder was back in Willow Trace and standing right beside her. So many emotions flooded through her—too many to sort. What was clear, however, was that, during his absence, Joseph had grown taller, broader and more handsome. His hands were now lined with calluses. His face had a crease or two developing around the eyes. His brown hair was still wavy and streaked with honey-blond strands. His soft hazel eyes looked as if they might take her in and swallow her up whole.

For a second, there'd been a glimpse of that same boy who'd loved her since grade school, but then Joseph's expression had become guarded. She wondered if he saw changes in her. Not that it mattered. What she and Joseph had had was gone. Forever.

"Miss Stoltz, I have just a few more questions."

Lydia turned to Detective Macy, the man addressing her. Several officers had arrived at the store, but this one seemed to be in charge. He wanted to know every detail of what had happened. The Amish, in general, didn't care much for the Englisch law enforcement— but they had to be there. Billy was, of course, Englisch. She tried to oblige Macy's unending questions, but since she and Joseph had had nothing to do with Billy, his wounds or his arrival to the store, she didn't see how anything she said was the least bit helpful.

"Did Mr. Ferris give you a reason for coming to the furniture store?" Macy asked. "Did he know that you would be here?"

"He tried to say a few things, but I cannot tell you that I understood any of it. I have no idea if he knew I worked here or not. I haven't seen him in years." Lydia thought, too, about Bishop Miller. He would not be pleased about all this transpiring at his store. He might even question her judgment in friends. Thanks to her father, she and her mother had enough to prove to the community without adding something else to it. In any case, this was going to be all over the papers and the evening news, as was anything both newsworthy and Amish.

Joseph ran his oil-stained hands over his thick hair and sighed aloud. He longed to be away from this chaos. How had this happened? He'd imagined seeing Lydia again for the first time in many different scenarios—

at his cousin's wedding, at her farmhouse, at Sunday meeting. But he had never imagined it like this.

"I didn't really understand him, either." Joseph fiddled with the straw hat between his hands. "But he was certainly trying to talk. He recognized me. He said my name. But he couldn't have known that I would be here tonight. I decided to work late just a few hours ago."

Macy tapped some notes into his electronic notepad with a tiny stylus. Then he turned back to Lydia. "So, you and Mr. Ferris were friends? He came here to see you?"

Lydia's eyes widened and her cheeks reddened. "No. We were never friends. Those two were friends." She pointed at him. "I haven't spoken to Billy Ferris since I last saw Joseph. And that was summer five years ago."

Joseph wondered if Macy could detect the bitterness in her voice. To him, it seemed unmistakable. "It's true. He was a *gut* friend...before I moved away. He is Englisch, but my family lived next door to his. We—we grew up together...so to speak. But truthfully, I haven't heard a word from him in the past five years. And like Lydia, I haven't seen him since that same night that she mentioned—the one before I moved to Indiana."

Macy scrunched his face, as if he'd tasted something sour. "So, you are both saying that you haven't seen each other or Mr. Ferris since you were all together on the very same night five years ago?"

It did sound kind of strange when he put it like that, Joseph thought.

"*Ya,* I suppose that is true." Joseph scratched his head.

"Did anything special happen on that night?" Macy looked suspicious.

Lydia tensed. For an instant, Joseph thought to reach

over and touch his hand to hers and comfort her. But those days were over. Perhaps seeing her brought old habits back to mind.

"It was back in our *rumspringa* days," Joseph said. "A long time ago. We met some Englisch kids and had some beer."

"Where did you meet?"

A bead of sweat formed on Joseph's forehead. He wiped it with his sleeve and swallowed hard. He knew Lydia didn't want to hear any of this. He didn't care to talk about it, either. "Tucker's Pond. It was mostly friends of Billy's. We were the only Amish. The two of us left pretty early on."

"And that's it?" Macy tapped more notes into his electronic tablet.

Lydia nudged her head at Joseph as if saying to go on with the rest of the story.

Joseph shifted his weight, hesitating before continuing. "So, there is a bit more. Just before we left, Billy took out some drugs. I have no idea what they were. We didn't take them, but most of the others did. After a half hour or so, one of the girls became very ill. When that happened, Billy got all agitated. He wouldn't let us help. He told us to leave so I took Lydia home."

"Agitated?"

"Angry. Excited. Worried about the girl, I think. But he was high, too. It's hard to say."

Detective Macy stared up at the ceiling for a second, as if stowing away this bit of information in case he needed it later. Then he looked at Lydia. "And this is how you remember it, too?"

Lydia nodded, her head down.

"Who was this girl? Do you remember any of their names?"

Lydia and Joseph exchanged a quick glance.

"They were Billy's friends. We didn't know them," Joseph said.

"I remember one," Lydia said. "One of the girl was named Michelle. Not the one who was sick. Another. She had been out with us before. But not the others. Do you think this has something to do with what happened tonight?"

Macy shook his head. "I doubt it. My guess is that this is all about drug sales. A deal gone bad. Your friend Mr. Ferris has been arrested several times on suspicion of selling and distribution. I have a feeling this will be connected with a more recent incident. But stay away from Tucker's Pond. It's still a high school hangout and a place to buy and sell."

"Yes, sir."

"Well...thank you." Macy looked over his notes and seemed pleased. "That will be all for now. I'll just need to know how to get in touch with you, if I have more questions."

They each rattled off their addresses. As he typed them into the pad, his phone began to ring.

"Excuse me." He took the call and began to circle the shop, moving away from them. Joseph and Lydia stood like statues at the front door until he returned.

"Bad news." Macy put his phone away. "I'm sorry to have to tell you this.... Mr. Ferris passed away on the ride to the hospital. I'll notify the next of kin. You should go on home and be very careful. Remember, unless the medical examiner thinks the cuts were self-inflicted, this is now a homicide. Neither of you should leave town without permission. Marked cars will be patrolling here on a regular basis until we know more. This is for your own safety and protection. I can arrange an escort home, if you like."

"That won't be necessary," Lydia said quickly. The detective turned away and dismissed them with a nod.

"Wait… Detective Macy, do you believe we are in danger?" Joseph asked.

Detective Macy looked back. "Do you think you are in danger, Mr. Yoder?"

"I don't know that I know what to think," Joseph said.

Despite her brave stance, Lydia was fighting an onslaught of tears. "It doesn't make any sense. None of it. But we do think Billy told us to be careful, or at least, it seemed like he was trying to say that."

"Then you should be careful, even if it makes no sense. One of the hardest parts of my job," Detective Macy said, "is to remind myself that with every senseless murder there is a killer somewhere who thinks it all makes perfect sense."

Chapter Three

Joseph and Lydia hardly spoke to one another as they locked up the store. Out back, she waited inside the buggy while Joseph hitched up his chestnut mare. *Ten minutes.* She could handle Joseph Yoder for ten more minutes. That was all it would take for him to get her home. Ten more minutes. Lydia stiffened as Joseph came around to the front of the buggy and gave her a nod.

"Thankfully, the rain has died down a bit, *ya?*" He climbed inside the vehicle. It was a four-seater, hard covered buggy—the type Amish families used to go to Sunday meeting. He tapped the reins and called gently to his horse. The mare stepped out onto the main road toward home.

The steady trotting and Joseph at her side made Lydia think of many courting nights that had started or ended in this way.

"A most unusual night," she said. "I can hardly believe any of it actually happened."

"Poor Billy. He should have stopped that business of his long ago."

"What business?"

"Selling drugs. I found some on him when I was searching for a phone. But I didn't know it had gone so far. I didn't know he had a record. What a shame. He was a good guy—I mean, inside him somewhere, he had a good heart." Joseph wiped the couple of tears that trickled down his cheek.

"*Ya*, it is sad." Lydia touched his shoulder. The contact made her suddenly aware of her natural attraction to him. She wondered how her body could betray her heart like that. "I saw you give the bag to the police.... So, you really hadn't talked to Billy since you left?" The question sounded like an accusation. She hadn't meant for it to, but he and Billy had been so close. It seemed so strange they hadn't been in touch.

"Didn't you read any of my letters?"

Lydia dropped her hand and lowered her head. No. She had not read them. It was too painful. And what was the point? He'd left without a word. Just like her father. His decision about her had been clear enough. No need to read his letters and feel the pain all over again. "I did not. You left. End of story."

Joseph let out a sigh. "It wasn't like that. It wasn't like that at all."

So, what was it like? There was a sadness in his voice, but she ignored it. "Why are we even talking about that? After all that has happened tonight? We should be praying for Billy's family. We should be asking ourselves why God chose us to be with Billy in his last moments. I feel some sort of responsibility in this, don't you?"

"You are right, Lydia." Joseph tilted his head, as if reflecting on her questions. "But it's all so strange. If neither of us has seen nor heard from him in all this time, it makes me wonder if he wasn't wounded near the store and stumbled into the first place he passed. Doesn't that make more sense than him actually looking for you or for me? Maybe what Billy was mumbling had no meaning or purpose at all?"

Lydia's mind flashed over the moment she'd pulled up the shade and seen this half-dead person clinging so desperately to the front doors. "I know. It's so strange that he was there. How did he get there? There was no car."

"No. I didn't see a car, either."

She nodded. "Do you think Macy will ask us more questions?"

Joseph shrugged. "I don't see why. We told him everything we know. I think he will concentrate on Billy's drug connections."

A cold chill passed down Lydia's spine. She pulled her wool shawl tighter around her shoulders. "This is such a tragedy. It will bring grief to the whole community."

After ten long minutes, they passed over the small bridge and up Holly Hill to the farmhouse where she and her mother lived. He slowed the buggy as they approached the old gray-stone-and-white-clapboard house. He halted the mare and hopped out. She jumped out, too. She did not want Joseph Yoder walking her up to the porch. It was too much like a visit to the past, too much like reliving their outings in Joseph's old courting buggy.

But she wasn't quick enough. There he was, standing at the passenger side with an umbrella in hand. He held it over her head as they walked together up the front stairs. His shoulder brushed against hers and she tensed.

When they reached the top stair, the front porch illuminated, flooding them in soft yellow light. Like most Amish farms in Willow Trace, Holly Hill used an oil-powered generator to run a refrigerator, some other small appliances and a few overhead lights. Her mother's silhouette appeared at the screen door. Naomi had been waiting up, probably surprised to hear the sounds of a buggy in her gravel drive.

"Hello, Mrs. Stoltz. *Gut* to see you. I'm seeing Lydia home in the rain. We had a bit of an—"

"Joseph Yoder!" Naomi flew onto the porch. "Now, if you aren't a sight for sore eyes. Come give this old woman a hug."

Lydia sighed. She was afraid the enthusiasm might encourage Joseph to stay longer. She certainly didn't want that.

"Please come in. Have some cake and hot tea before heading home," her mother said.

Lydia grunted silently in protest. She did not want to spend any more time than necessary in the presence of Joseph Yoder.

He, on the other hand, seemed pleased enough. "That would be just fine. I haven't had much to eat since lunch."

Mrs. Stoltz cut generous slices of pumpkin bread and poured steaming-hot cinnamon-spiced tea for each of them. They gathered around the small kitchen table, holding hands, and prayed for their food.

Joseph slid out a chair at the head of the table.

"Not there," her *mamm* said. "That's Jonathan's place."

"Oh, yes. I'm sorry." Joseph's eyes searched Lydia's as he moved quickly to another spot at the table.

Heat rushed to Lydia's cheeks. While she admired her mother's capability to forgive and to hope, she felt only anger toward her father. Where the gesture was an expression of Naomi's love and her faith in God to sustain her, for Lydia, the empty place at the table was a reminder of her pain.

As was seeing Joseph again. Which was exactly why she would maintain her distance during his visit. She had hoped to avoid him altogether, but with him working for Bishop Miller and with the evening's tragedy, who knew how much they might be forced to be together?

Lydia swallowed away the lump of emotion in her throat. She turned to her mother and provided details of their encounter with Billy Ferris and what occurred afterward.

"I can't believe it." Her *mamm* shook her head. "Such a young man. And so well liked by everyone."

"*Ya.* Who would want to kill him?" Lydia said.

"The detective seemed to think it related to his selling drugs." Joseph rinsed his cake down with a cup of tea.

"Oh dear." Her mother let out a deep sigh. "Well, it is all business for the Englisch to deal with. You must put it behind you. Let the past be passed."

Her mother patted Joseph's hand and looked at both of them in turn. There was nothing subtle in her message, which was not about Billy's death. "At least it's nice to see the two of you together again. After all these years."

Joseph stood abruptly. "I should be getting home now. It's late. Thank you, Mrs. Stoltz. Lydia."

He took his hat from the wooden pin on the wall where he'd hung it earlier. He placed it on his head. "I'll let you know when the funeral arrangements have been made."

Lydia stared at the floor as Joseph left through the kitchen door. Then, in the shadows of the dining room window, she watched him climb into the buggy and set off down the lane. It was a little ritual from their courting days. Filled with warm and tender love, she'd watch him disappear over Holly Hill.

Tonight there was no tender warmth. She felt only the memory of heartache cutting through her.

There were a couple of reasons why Lydia returned to the furniture store on Friday afternoon. For one, she had not been back to complete her cleaning. Now that the police had finish their work, the storefront really needed a scrubbing. But also Lydia had thought that by coming earlier in the day she could avoid running into Joseph. He would be busy in the back and not even know she was there. In any case, she'd see him soon enough when he drove her to Billy's funeral the following day.

"I didn't expect you, Miss Lydia." Bishop Miller stepped up to the front of the shop when the little bell rang over the front door.

"I'm just finishing up my cleaning from Wednesday. Mamm and I got our chores done early today, so I hope you don't mind. I know it must need a thorough going-over."

"Of course not. Should I let Mr. Yoder know that you're here?" The old man gave her his sly grin again.

Lydia forced a frown and shook her head. "I don't think that will be necessary. I won't be staying long."

It was hard wiping away the remaining traces of blood where poor Billy had spent some of his last moments. In a way, the act of cleansing wasn't merely physical; it helped to process the terrifying events of that evening. Then tomorrow she would face her sorrow at the funeral. *The Lord gives, and the Lord takes away. Blessed be the name of the Lord.* Life's events didn't always make sense, but as she'd been taught, she accepted them as the will of the Lord.

Lydia was running her cloth over the last few pieces of furniture and humming when the bell over the shop door rang. She stopped and looked up.

"Mr. Bowman." Bishop Miller offered his hand. "What business brings you here today?"

"Please, Levi, we've known each other for years. Call me Hank." They shook hands. Lydia turned away and went back to her work.

"Well, first I came to say that Mr. Ferris was my restaurant manager and a good friend," the large man said.

Lydia couldn't help but overhear.

"I'm very sorry for your loss," Bishop Miller said. "Such a sad, sad business."

"Billy was a good man. I don't know what happened to him getting involved in drugs. If there were any damages to your store, I am happy to cover the cost."

"That won't be necessary. But I thank ye for the offer."

"I also heard that some of your employees were here and had to deal with him. Please pass on my gratitude for calling 911 and trying to help him. It must have been terrifying for them to see a man in such a state."

Lydia ducked behind a large piece of furniture. She didn't want to talk again about what had happened that night and she feared the Bishop might call her over for an introduction.

"Well, they knew Mr. Ferris." The Bishop's voice filled the room. "Lydia and Joseph. Would you like to speak to them?"

"Oh, no, no. That's not necessary. If they were his friends, then I'll see them tomorrow at the funeral. I do have one other order of business, however. Billy used an Amish furniture maker to build all the tables we have in the restaurant front. I'd like to order twenty more for our back room."

"I'm afraid Mr. Ferris didn't order them from here," Bishop Miller said.

"Well, I like to buy local when I can, and of course, you're local and original."

Miller nodded. "Then I'll send one of my craftsmen over and you can show him what you would like. First thing Monday morning."

Bowman shook the Bishop's hand again and left the store. Then he called Joseph to the storefront. Lydia put away her cleaning. Her first encounter with Joseph had been so difficult. She need not put herself through more than necessary.

But he was too quick. She sensed him enter the showroom. She looked up as he approach the bishop.

His face glistened with hard work and the front of his trousers was sprinkled with sawdust. He had never looked more handsome. He smiled at her and her pulse raced. Lydia nodded to them both then escaped through the front doors. She scurried across the parking lot, crossed the highway and fled into the woods. She would take the long way home following an old path that led to her stable. The fresh air and exercise would set her right.

Joseph listened halfheartedly to Bishop Miller as he asked again about his uncle's furniture business in Indiana, about the mess with Billy Ferris the other night and then about making tables for some restaurant in town. But most of his thoughts were on Lydia. She had just grabbed her shawl and headed out of the store. His eyes followed her petite figure to the edge of the woods across the street. With a smile, he remembered many times walking alongside her, relaxing in the low afternoon sun. Now it was only tension that seemed to live between them.

"I have done some tables like this before," Joseph answered the bishop. "But I won't have time to make twenty of them before I go back to Indiana. Better put one of your other craftsmen on it."

"*Ach.* They won't want to do it, either." Bishop Miller slapped Joseph on the shoulder and let out a loud chuckle. "I'll tell Mr. Bowman that it will have to wait until after the Christmas rush. But we will not worry about that now. But you, young man, it's Friday afternoon. Put down your tools and go home. You're buried in work. You're too young fer that. You should be thinking about marriage and family—not just furniture, my boy."

He wasn't positive, but the old man seemed to be looking out the window toward Lydia's place as he spoke. Or was that his imagination? Joseph nodded and turned back toward his workstation.

* * *

Lydia stopped and turned in a circle on the forest path. The wind blew hard, and small animals scurried over the leaf-covered ground. She had walked through these woods a million times, played in them, even hidden there from her parents on occasion when she was younger. She loved the forest. She felt close to God, breathing in the fresh air, listening to the quick waters of the brook and watching the intermittent rays of sunlight dancing through the trees. Today, the walk had been so invigorating that she'd passed her farmhouse and taken a second path, which led to her fields on the far side of the farm. This section was sadly overgrown and made for difficult walking. After a few hundred yards, Lydia decided to turn around and go back to the stable path. As she swung around, a large shadow floated over the path then disappeared. It was the shadow of a man. A twig snapped. The sound had been close. Lydia froze and swallowed hard. Nervously, she glanced around. Was someone following her? She saw nothing but trees and leaves. Perhaps she was more tired than she had realized.

Whatever the case, she turned back again and continued to trek up to the fields. The terrain might be more difficult, but she was closer to that opening than to the stable. She walked on, increasing her pace. Again, there was movement behind her. Leaves crunched, more twigs snapped. Lydia sucked in a quick breath. She paused and listened. Were those footsteps she heard? She wasn't sure but something was behind her. She could sense it. *Oh dear Lord, let me find my way home.*

Chapter Four

At his workstation, Joseph found a folded note that had been placed next to his tools. Someone must have left it there while he was chatting with Bishop Miller. He opened it and read the computer-printed message.

If you're smart you'll disappear back to Indiana and take your girlfriend with you. If you're not smart, I'll help you both disappear.

Joseph searched the work space. Only one other craftsman remained this late on a Friday afternoon.

"Did you see anyone come in?" Joseph asked him.

The man shook his head. He was busy sanding, which was noisy. So someone could have slipped in through the back doors, which were open for ventilation, left a note for him then slipped back out unseen.

Joseph read the message again. Girlfriend? Could it mean Lydia?

Lydia, who'd gone home alone through the woods. His heart began to pound. He didn't waste a second. He was probably overreacting but he wasn't taking any chances. He ran out the back, around to the parking lot and across the street then tore down the old footpath that Lydia had taken.

By now, she should have reached the farmhouse or at least her stable. But he called to her anyway. There was no answer. But he could see her footprints in the muddy path.

He reached the creek—the halfway point—and crossed. The mud was thicker on this side, but strangely Lydia had left no prints. The path was clean. It was as if she had disappeared. Shock and panic pumped through Joseph's veins. He hurried on, calling her name with every other step.

Running hard, he reached the farm quickly. The stable was just ahead. He scanned the open area, panting, his leg muscles aching with lactic acid. "Lydia… Lydia."

A couple of miniature ponies lifted their heads from the grass, then, seeing it was him, went back to their grazing. Joseph checked toward the house. No one. Could she still be in those woods? An uneasy feeling took hold of him. The words *make you disappear* in the message were ever present in his frantic mind.

Joseph paced the edge of the forest. He could go back in and try to find the spot where her footprints had ended. But by that time she could be even farther away. He hated the thought. Once again, Joseph scanned the fields and gardens around the farmhouse and the stable, calling for Lydia. Finally, he saw movement at the house, but before he sighed with relief, he realized that it wasn't Lydia but Naomi Stoltz running out to join him.

Naomi wiped her hands on her apron as she hurried toward him. "Joseph, what is it? Where is Lydia?"

"Lydia's not in the house?"

Naomi shook her head.

"I should have passed her on the path through the woods. She should be home. She left the store a while ago. I think she's still in the woods."

"You seem worried."

"I am. She should have been home by now." He thought it best not to mention the threatening note at this time.

"Go look for her, Joseph," she said. "I'll ring the bell and call for help."

Mrs. Stoltz fled to the big bell in the front of the farmhouse. Whenever anyone in the Amish community rang a bell, neighbors knew someone needed a hand. Friends would come from all over. It was the Amish call for assistance. Joseph rushed back to the edge of the woods, searching and praying. *Please, Lord, let the bell call her home.*

Benjamin Zook and his three burley sons rolled up to the farmhouse in their open wagon only minutes after the bell sounded. They must have been close by the hill on the main road. When Joseph saw them, he ran across the far fields to the other side of the woods. Maybe she had missed the path at the creek and gone on to the fields…maybe…

Lydia's legs churned as fast as she could make them. Uphill. The wet leaves and muddy earth made for slick ground. She slipped and struggled to make her way. It seemed that whatever was behind her was only getting closer and closer. Nervously, she looked back.

He was there. A dark figure. A man. He wore black

clothing and a dark cap, which shaded the whole of his face. Like a ghost, he vanished behind a tree.

Sharp tremors rattled her. She could not ignore what all her senses were telling her. Someone was there. She'd been foolish to stop. Each time, he had only moved closer.

As fast as she could, Lydia ran up the second half of the hill. But his footsteps were close. Gaining. At last, she rounded the peak and finally she saw a break in the thick of forest trees.

If only she could make it out into the open. *Please, Lord...*

Lydia had barely started her prayer when a bell sounded. Like manna from heaven, she followed the sweet ringing over the ridge of the hill and into a small clearing. She was almost home.

"Lydia! Lih-dee-yah!" Her name echoed across the enclosure. It was Joseph.

Lydia's figure appeared at the far west end of her property. She scrambled out of the woods at an alarming speed. Her blond locks fell loose around her face, which was twisted with fear. Her white apron had bits of leaves and mud from the forest. She glanced more than once over her shoulder before running into his arms.

"Thank God, you are safe." He pulled her tight to his chest.

"Someone...someone was chasing me." She trembled.

"Someone was following you? Did you see who it was?" He wiped the tears from her face with his thumb.

"No, I couldn't see his face. But he was big. It had to be a man. Oh, Joseph, I was so scared..."

"Shh. It's okay now. You're okay." Joseph scanned the edges of the forest at the spot where she'd come out. He didn't see any movement. Of course, with a loud bell ringing out across the countryside, even a fool would know he'd better run in the other direction.

For a long moment, Joseph held on to Lydia, drinking in the feel of her weight against his shoulder. He had forgotten how nicely she fit against him. How good she smelled. Then she pulled away and he remembered the note and Billy's death. And he remembered how Lydia had forgotten him the second he'd gone to Indiana.

He patted her shoulder. "Let's go back to the house. Your mother is so worried. We'll get you cleaned up and warm again. And we'll need to call Detective Macy. Someone left us a threatening note."

Joseph didn't spend any more time with Lydia that evening. Her mother hovered over her, then Detective Macy arrived. By that time, Lydia was tired and had begun to downplay her fears and suspicions.

The police searched the woods, but they quickly had business to attend to elsewhere, which took precedence. Detective Macy left them, saying he would up the number of patrol cars that passed by and that he thought no one should be out traveling alone.

Mr. Zook instructed his three sons to sleep in the Stoltzes' living room that night and offered Joseph a ride back to his parents' place. He left disappointed, worried and confused. He was not looking forward to Billy's funeral, which was merely hours away.

Early the next morning, Joseph drove Cherry, his chestnut Morgan, once again up Holly Hill to the Stoltzes' quaint farmhouse. The sun peeked across the eastern sky, casting pale light over the lush green fields framed by the white fencing and bright gray stones. Lydia waited, leaning against a wooden post on the front porch, slender and petite like a china doll. Her pink lips and dark eyes offered the only contrast to her milky skin.

It would be a long journey to the church where Billy's funeral was to be held. Like him, she'd probably been up for hours, tending to her animals. Of course, there were no traces of farm on her now. She was dressed in a fine frock, with a crisp white apron pinned over top. Her dark blond hair had been parted down the middle, brushed smooth then twisted in a bun and tucked under a white prayer *kapp,* which concealed from the world most of its beauty. Joseph, however, could easily imagine her locks reached far down her back and still held the same wavy curls they had when she was a girl.

"It's a fine day for a long buggy ride." He slowed the vehicle at the end of the front walk. She floated down the stairs and helped herself into the buggy before he could get out and assist her like a proper gentleman.

"I thank ye for offering a ride. The Zook boys were kind enough to take care of my chores this morning." She folded her hands neatly in her lap, sat tall and looked straight ahead.

Joseph clicked to Cherry. The mare took off at a nice steady trot. "How are things at the farm?"

"Fine."

"Fine?" Joseph said. "That's not what I hear."

Lydia stiffened. "What do you hear?"

"I heard that you and your *mamm* were running things better than any of the Stoltz men could have ever dreamed."

"I don't like being compared to my *dat*."

Lydia didn't like anyone mentioning her *dat*. As close as they'd been, she'd never opened up to him about her father and why he'd left. He supposed now she never would. "So, I didn't really get to speak to you last night. What did Macy have to say?"

She shrugged. "He asked a lot more questions. Frankly, it was all a bit overwhelming. What did he say to you?"

"I gave him the note that I told you about. He didn't say much about it. I thought he would. Then again, the more I think on all this, the less sense it makes."

"How can anyone make sense of murder?"

"True." Joseph shifted positions. "Macy asked me again about the old days."

Lydia exhaled a sharp breath. "*Ya*, me, too. But I had nothing to say. Like my mother said, the past is passed."

Joseph knew that her words extended beyond the situation with Billy Ferris. She meant that she didn't want to talk about their past, either. But he might not let her off so easy. After seeing her again, he wanted some answers. He wanted to know why—no, how she'd let go of everything without any explanation. Why didn't she read his letters or write back to him? "Today might not be the day, Lydia. But we will talk about the past. Our past. I think we must."

Lydia nearly turned her back to him. "It will change nothing. What's done is done."

Joseph saw no reason to press her. There was already so much emotion in the air. "Did Macy tell you about the red Camaro?"

"A car? No, I didn't hear about that."

"Billy drove a red sports car. The police found it

abandoned in the woods near Miller's store. Billy's blood was in the car and so was the murder weapon, a hunting knife. But there were no prints. Whoever killed Billy wiped the car clean."

Slowly, Lydia looked his way. "How near?"

"Near enough that the store was in view."

Lydia narrowed her eyes on him. "What are you not telling me?"

Joseph took a deep breath. "The police think that Billy knew who attacked him. They think it was someone he trusted and possibly allowed into his car."

"But once this person attacked Billy, why would he let him get away and go to Miller's store?"

"I asked the same question," Joseph said. "Macy thinks it could be one of two possibilities. Billy could have hurt his attacker and got away. He did have a gun in his hands. Although forensic testing showed it had not been fired."

"What's the other possibility?"

"The killer allowed Billy to leave. He wanted to see where Billy would go. Maybe he followed him to the store to see who he would talk to. Or he sent Billy to us with a message on purpose."

"That would mean we *are* somehow involved."

"*Ya.* Well, at this point, it seems we are, no?"

"What do you think?"

"I think Billy knew the killer, got away from him and came to us with or without a real message. Then the killer probably followed him, and in that case, he knows Billy talked to us before he died."

"But Billy didn't tell us anything."

"No, he didn't. But the killer doesn't know that."

Chapter Five

Joseph pulled the buggy into the parking lot of Lancaster First Community Church. It was time to pay respects to an old friend.

Joseph recognized many faces at the small gathering, including Billy's family. Kind words were shared about the playful and happy side that Billy often showed to others. His father and his little sister, Anna, spoke about their memories of Billy. At the end of the service, Anna played a five-minute video slide show of Billy with family and friends over the years. Joseph was surprised to find himself in three or four of the photos that shone on the big white screen at the front of the church.

Thou shalt not make unto thee any graven image... Joseph recalled the verse from Exodus, which many Amish brethren held to the letter. His shame in being photographed was a sharp reminder of the many careless decisions of his youth.

Joseph was thankful for a forgiving God.

After the service, Billy's father made a point to speak to them. Joseph supposed they were pretty easy to spot in the crowd because of their plain dress.

"It's been a long time." Mr. Ferris gave Joseph's hand a hearty shake and nodded to Lydia. "You look well. Indiana air must agree with you."

"*Ya,* I suppose so...." He cast a furtive glance at Lydia. "I'm very sorry about what happened to your son."

"I understand you were with him just before he died." Mr. Ferris struggled with his words. "Did—did he suffer greatly?"

"I'm sorry, Mr. Ferris," Joseph said. "I'm afraid he suffered a great deal. But I don't know how conscious he was. I'm sorry we could not have done more." *I'm sorry we couldn't save him.* But it was not the Lord's will.

"He was with people who loved him. I'm thankful for that.... Come. I have something for you." Mr. Ferris motioned for them to follow. They cut through the center of the sanctuary to a private room that had been stocked with pastries and other things for the mourning family members. He offered them coffee and biscuits, which they declined. Then he retrieved a small wooden box from a bag in the corner. It was quite plain, made of maple and opened with a simple pin hinge. Joseph recognized it immediately.

"I made that for Billy." He smiled. To see the piece again after all these years brought him a sense of sweet nostalgia. "It's a valet box, one of my first pieces."

Mr. Ferris placed the box in his hands. "Billy moved out a few years ago, but he left this behind. He said he didn't want anything to happen to it because one day he would give it back to you so that...well, so that you would remember the old days."

"Did he?" Joseph nodded, turning the little container over in his hands.

"Billy bought many of your pieces online. Had them shipped all the way from Indiana. Your tables are in the restaurant. He admired them so. He was very proud of you…loved you like a brother."

"And I loved him. Thank you for this." Joseph raised the small box. "This means a lot."

Mr. Ferris gave Joseph's shoulder a firm touch then turned back to face the crowd awaiting him at the front of the church.

Lydia could see the tears building in the corners of Joseph's eyes. He was struggling. As was she. The past few days had dredged up so many difficult memories and emotions. Right now, Lydia just wanted to get back to the farm and be with her animals, where she felt more in control of things. She pressed her way through the lines of people waiting to see Billy's family. Joseph struggled to keep up.

"Slow down." He got close enough to reach her shoulder from behind. "There's no fire."

Lydia cut her eyes toward the warm, strong hand resting on her shoulder. She glanced behind at Joseph. "Okay, slower."

But now she couldn't move at all. A large man had blocked the exit. It was all she could do not to barrel straight into him.

"Excuse me." She stepped back, embarrassed. It was Mr. Bowman, the restaurant owner who'd come to the shop the day before.

"Hello." He wore a fine wool suit, one of the fanciest Lydia had ever seen. He looked straight at Joseph. "Aren't you Jason? You used to wash dishes with Billy, right?"

Joseph gave Lydia's shoulder another squeeze. It must have been quite obvious how uncomfortable and upset she was.

"Mr. Bowman." Joseph shook the man's hand. "Actually… I'm Joseph and this is Lydia. And yes, yes, I did work for you."

"Of course, Joseph and Lydia." He stared at the wooden box in Joseph's hands. Lydia could see the top of his shiny bald head. Slowly, she tried to scoot away, but another, younger man came and flanked her on the left.

"I understand you were with Billy at Miller's store the night he died," Bowman said.

"Yes, sir." Joseph tipped his head in an abbreviated nod.

"So sad." Bowman's words were flat and rehearsed. "Ferris sure knew how to run that restaurant. Kevin here will have some pretty big shoes to fill." He motioned to the man on the other side of Lydia.

"Hi. Kevin Watson." The young man shook both their hands. Lydia noticed that, he, too eyed the small valet box, which Joseph kept in his left hand. "I worked with Billy for years at the restaurant. Please come by. Have dinner on the house."

"Thank you. That's a kind offer. But for now we must be off." Much to Lydia's relief, Joseph tipped his black felt hat and turned to leave. Grabbing her hand, he led her through the exit. Apparently, Joseph wanted out of there as badly as she did. As they hurried off, Lydia couldn't shake the sensation that Mr. Bowman and Mr. Watson were watching them. It gave her an uneasy feeling, but she resisted the temptation to turn around and see if her assumption was correct.

Soon, the clip-clop of the horse's trot steadied Lydia's unbalanced emotions. She prayed silently for her own strength to get past this tragedy and the memories it had stirred.

It didn't help, either, that the more time she was in the presence of Joseph Yoder the more difficult it became to ignore her attraction to him and his changes—this new calmness and maturity that he now possessed. She supposed it was only natural that he'd grown up at some point. Then again, she reminded herself that even maturity didn't make up for his leaving her.

Joseph whistled to his mare to pick up speed. "I guess I didn't realize that Billy was still working for Mr. Bowman."

"He startled me. I had not seen him there. I guess he came in after it started."

"I saw him. He was in the back playing with his cell phone though most of the service."

"How rude. Why even bother coming? I know it sounds like I am judging but he did sound so phony yesterday when he came to the store to order more furniture. I think he just wanted to see where Billy had died. It may be wrong to say so but he gives me the creeps."

"*Ya,* that's why I quit my job at the Amish Smorgasbord. Remember? Billy and I were dishwashers there a few nights a week. Good tips."

"I remember. Even then, Mr. Bowman would tell us to eat lunch for free." Lydia gave a half laugh. "Like any of us would want to eat *that* food. I'm afraid the only thing Amish about that restaurant is the name."

"And apparently, the tables." Joseph gave a teasing grin. They both had a laugh, which felt good and natural. But as quickly as the connection was made and felt, they fell into an awkward silence.

After a few minutes, Lydia picked up the valet box that Mr. Ferris had given to Joseph. She studied the plain style of it, then stopped as she felt Joseph's gaze on her hands. "Oh, I'm sorry. I should have asked. Do you mind if I look it over?"

"No, please." He smiled. "Open it."

Despite the cool autumn air against her cheeks, Lydia blushed. She turned the box over and studied the rounded edges and clean lines. "It is very sturdy. Perhaps you remember that you made one for me, as well."

"Of course I remember. I made yours first and I spent a lot more time on it." If Lydia didn't know better she would have said there was a hint of pride on his smiling face.

"It keeps all my sewing needles, scissors and thread. It is very useful." Usefulness was the highest compliment she could give his work. Saying it was beautiful or better than another's would sound like praise, and praise was something the Amish did not indulge in for fear of truly becoming proud.

Lydia unlocked the pin in front and opened the lid of the maple box. The insides were rough and unfinished. "It's empty."

"Were you expecting something?" he teased her. "A golden treasure or jewels perhaps?"

"Don't be silly, Joseph Yoder," she protested. "It just seems a shame that something so suitable was given no purpose."

A large sky-blue pickup truck had dashed around and in front of them, then slammed on its brakes to make a left turn. Tires screeched across the road. A blur of blue swirled around Lydia.

"Whoa." Joseph pulled back hard on the reins.

The truck had allowed almost no space between it and the chestnut mare, which was traveling along at a nice clip.

Cherry broke her gait and pressed down hard to slow herself and the buggy. Her metal shoes slid on the slick, oily asphalt. Joseph applied the hydraulic brakes, common in a buggy of such size. But nothing seemed to slow their forward momentum.

Joseph's eyes went wide. He pumped the pedal again and again. The buggy was not slowing down and all of its weight pressed against the backside of the poor mare.

"The brakes are gone." Joseph stretched an arm across in front of Lydia hoping to keep her from slamming into the windshield, but she was just out of his reach.

Lydia braced for the crash. At the same time, the mare turned to the side to avoid crashing into the truck. The buggy, of course, turned, too. The torque pulled Lydia from her seat. Lydia felt herself slipping.

Joseph reached again for her. The tips of his fingers caught the sleeve of her frock. But it was not enough to hold her in. The thin garment pulled from his grasp. And the momentum of the turn threw Lydia from the vehicle.

The buggy jolted, tipped as it turned, then landed back on all four wheels. It was still settling when Joseph leaped from his seat and ran to where Lydia lay on the asphalt. "Are you okay? Lydia? Lydia?"

Lydia did not move. She lay lifeless in the middle of

the highway, face up, eyes closed. The valet box was smashed to pieces on the street beside her.

An unrelenting tightness grabbed hold of Joseph's lungs. His heart seemed to stop. He couldn't breathe but he didn't care. The only thing that mattered was Lydia.

"Please, someone call 911." Joseph sensed other cars had stopped around his buggy along the side of the highway. Someone was holding Cherry by the reins. Another person shouted they had a cell phone. Another said they'd written down the license-plate numbers of the truck that had cut in front of them.

Joseph knelt and scooped Lydia's head and shoulders into his arms and held her close. She was warm against his skin and he could feel her pulse, slow and steady at her throat. She did not wake. She did not respond. No matter how he stroked her cheek or whispered to her, she was limp in his arms.

Please, Lord. Please. Not Lydia. Please don't take Lydia...

Joseph only opened his eyes when two EMTs pulled Lydia from his embrace. He had no idea how much time had passed, but he didn't want to let go of her. As Joseph felt the separation, he realized what he had done. By going to Indiana, he had abandoned her just like her father. And for that, she would never forgive him.

Chapter Six

Lydia awoke to familiar comforts—the smell of her mother's yeast rolls rising in the oven, the softness of their old blue couch underneath her and the sound of Joseph's voice. Her eyes flickered open. His handsome face broke into a smile over her.

"Look who's back among the living." His announcement grabbed the attention of her mother, who ran over from the kitchen and planted a kiss on the forehead.

"What happened? Last thing I remember we were on our way home from the funeral."

Joseph helped her up into a sitting position. As she rose, a throbbing in the back of her head shot across her skull. She remembered the blue truck and Joseph reaching for her.

"You were thrown from the buggy."

"Ya." She rubbed the bump on the back of her head. "A truck pulled in front of us. I slipped from the buggy. The rest of it I don't remember. How did we get here?"

"The emergency crew brought us. Detective Macy and a whole team of police came to the scene. I told them about the brakes not working. They are looking into it. Inspecting the buggy. A man came with a horse trailer and took Cherry back to my parents' place."

"I'm so thankful you are okay," her mother said before heading back to the stove. By the warm, delicious smells floating through the air, Lydia guessed her mother had baked quite a dinner. She must have been sleeping for hours.

"How do you feel?" Joseph asked.

"My stomach's growling. I'm thinking that's a good sign." She invited him to sit beside her. The concerned look in his eyes warmed her from head to toe. Yesterday, she would not have welcomed it. *Be careful, Lydia,* she warned herself.

"You gave me quite a scare, Miss Stoltz. Two days in a row. You have to stop doing this to me." He took her hand in his own. He held tightly to her. Lydia filled with emotion at the tenderness of his touch. Her cheeks felt warm. "Macy will be here soon to talk to us again. Are you up for that?"

She nodded. "I think so. Really I just have a bit of headache. I'm sure I'll feel fine as soon as I eat."

His soft hazel eyes held her gaze for a long moment. Her pulse raced as she saw in him that boy who'd loved her so. It would be easy to fall for him all over again. But she couldn't. He'd had his chance and he'd made his choice. She turned her head away. "So, when do you go back to Indiana?"

Joseph's expression darkened and he sighed. "You know very well I'm staying for my cousin's wedding. That's not for three weeks. Anyway, I can't go anywhere until Macy gives his permission, and I'm guessing that won't be until this mess with Billy is resolved."

"Right, I'm sorry. I suppose I'm not thinking straight

after the bump on the head.... But I think I could use a cup of tea. You?" Lydia began to stand.

"You stay put. I'll go." Joseph grabbed her arm and kept her down.

While he fetched the tea, Detective Macy and another officer knocked at the front door. Her mother led them into the modest living area, where they each took a seat in a plain wooden chair.

"I hope you're feeling better, Miss Stoltz." Macy's voice and expression, which had always been stern and serious, seemed even more ominous.

Joseph returned with a large mug of hot tea for her. He greeted the officers and set the tea beside her.

"I'll go pour two more cups," her mother said.

"That won't be necessary." Detective Macy shook his head. "We won't stay long." He turned to the man who'd accompanied him. "This is Detective Mason. He inspected your vehicle, Mr. Yoder."

"How's the buggy?" Joseph asked.

"It's a little bumped up, but the biggest concern is the brakes. When was the last time you remember using them?" Detective Mason asked him.

"They didn't work at the accident, but I'm certain that they worked earlier. I'd used them on the ride out to the church. They seemed fine. What happened?"

Macy and Mason exchanged a serious look. "It seems someone removed your entire brake system. It wasn't that they didn't work. You didn't have any. If you remember using them earlier today, then the removal must have been done during the service."

"Why would anyone do that?" Lydia felt her eyes go wide.

"We don't know. Perhaps in hopes that you or Joseph or both of you would be injured. Detained. Scared. Killed." Detective Macy handed Joseph a small envelope.

"What's this?" Joseph took it.

"One of the witnesses to the accident picked up a couple of things that had blown out of Lydia's hands."

"Oh no." Lydia remembered the valet box had been in her hands as she fell. "The box broke. I'm sorry, Joseph. It was all you had from Billy."

Joseph turned his head toward her. "If that's all that was damaged, then I have everything to be thankful for. God's hand was truly on us."

"Amen," her mother added.

Lydia studied the small envelope Joseph held. "So, there must have been something inside the valet box after all."

"*Ya.* Perhaps tucked up in the lid." Joseph placed the envelope on the sofa. "Let's look at it later. I want to hear more about the accident." He turned back to Detective Macy. "What about the truck that tried to run us off the road? Were you able to locate it?"

"No. Those plate numbers were phony. The truck could be stolen. We won't be able to trace it."

With that, Macy stood and Detective Mason followed his example.

"I'm going to increase the amount of patrol cars circling around here," Macy continued. "I think the two of you should continue to play it safe. Stay in numbers. Don't go anywhere alone.

"With your brakes having been removed, we cannot write off this accident as coincidence. I think we must assume that someone or some group of people wish to harm you. A logical conclusion is that it is connected to Billy Ferris's death. Possibly someone—maybe a killer—knows that Billy went to talk to you both after he was injured. He or she may think that Billy gave you something of value or told you something that could incriminate him.

"If you think of anything, let me know...especially if you can remember exactly what Billy said to you before he died. Please call. I'll be in touch soon."

Joseph stood to see the officers out, then sat beside her again, picking up the envelope and holding it in his hand. "You know, Macy is right. We both knew that Billy said to be careful. Well, that accident scared me enough to think we'd better find out why. I've already talked it over with your mother and sent word to my family. I'll be staying here with you and your *mamm* for a few days. That way I can help out with the farm, since you need to rest that head. And I won't have to worry about you two women out here on this isolated farm by yourselves."

He studied her, obviously trying to gauge her feelings, but she made sure her face showed neither happiness nor discontentment. Anyway, it wasn't far from the truth. She wasn't sure how she felt about Joseph staying so close.

He lifted the envelope and took out the contents. "Pictures? Let's take a look."

He handed her what he had pulled from the envelope. Lydia smiled, taking the photos and separating them in her hands. "There are two. Billy is in both of them."

In the first, Billy had his arm around the shoulders of another guy in a pal-like sort of way. The other boy was tall, like Billy, and they both had long hair.

"I don't think I know this guy." Joseph leaned in to study the photo more closely. "This one looks like it was taken when Billy was in high school."

Lydia turned to the second photo but quickly dropped

it away from her face. This was not a picture she wanted to see. Her stomach churned.

"What? What is it?" He reached across her lap for the second picture.

"It's nothing, Joseph. Just so many memories all at once…"

He touched her hand, lifting the photo up again so that he could see it. "Oh…yeah….this must have been taken that last night when we were all together…at Tucker's Pond. All those girls were sitting together in our—in my old courtin' buggy."

She handed the second picture to him. A small piece of paper slipped from the back of the photo and fluttered to the floor. Lydia bent over to retrieve it, then she held it between them so that they could read the words together.

And you shall know the truth, and the truth shall make you free.

"A Scripture from John. Maybe it was his favorite verse?" Lydia said.

"I don't think so."

"Why not?"

"Billy wasn't too into the Bible. I'm thinking he meant something by having it stuck to the back of this photo." Joseph turned the photos over in his hands. A deep frown darkened his face. The pictures, the memories of what had passed that night, obviously affected him, too.

"Put these back in the envelope, please." He handed the pictures back to her.

"Why does everything keep going back to that night?" Joseph stood and paced the length of the room.

His frustration growing, he felt powerless, caught in this mess Billy had pulled them into. "I know you don't want to talk about the past, but I'm going to say this anyway. I hate that night. Lydia, I hate it. I exposed you to evil. I should have protected you. I should have taken better care of you. I was so stupid back then. So childish and naive. I never thought about the ripple effects of my decisions. But that night scared me.

"When that girl got sick, after I got you home, I told my parents that they were right. That I needed to get away from Billy. Away from his influence. They were more than happy to hear it. They didn't waste any time. My *daed* set me off the next morning to Indiana. They said it was best if I didn't see you first. They were afraid I'd change my mind. I had planned to come back after a year. To join the church here and be with you but you'd taken up with Gideon and my uncle needed me. I wish you'd read my letters."

"I was childish, too. And hurt." A sad smile passed over her lips. "Anyway, so much time has passed. It is all forgotten."

"No, not all of it is forgotten...." He leaned close to her and again touched her hand. How he hoped she would not pull it away. "Lydia, surely not all of what we shared is forgotten. When you spend so much time with someone, doesn't that person become—"

Lydia's face washed white with his words. Joseph dropped his head. What was he thinking bringing this up now? She had a head injury, poor thing.

Anyway, there was no future for them. Not together. She would never leave her mother alone with the farm and he'd promised his uncle to return to Indiana. He needed to be thankful for this time to repair their friendship, not keep pushing for something he couldn't have. Something that Lydia clearly did not want.

"Dinner!" Lydia's mother yelled from the kitchen.

Joseph gave thanks for the food and for God's saving them on the road that very afternoon. Then dinner passed quietly.

Lydia ate little and spoke even less. She and her mother discussed the accident and the warning from Detective Macy. Joseph couldn't get his mind off the photos and the Bible verse. What had Billy meant by leaving them in the valet box for him? Could it possibly have anything to do with who killed him?

"I wonder what happened to the people in the photos that were inside the valet box. Do you remember any of them?" he asked.

"No." Lydia shook her head.

"What if we could find out what happened to them? Maybe we could ask them about what happened after we left that night. Or maybe they know something about Billy that would be helpful to us. Maybe then we could figure out if any of this really has to do with us."

"We'd have to remember their names for that," Lydia pointed out.

"Were they all students at Willow Trace High with Billy?" her mother said.

"I believe so. Why?"

"Because then you can look through the school's yearbooks for the years that Billy was in high school. You're bound to find at least one picture of each of them."

Joseph smiled. "When does the library open?"

Chapter Seven

Monday morning after chores, Lydia and her mother drove up the main highway in their pony cart. A bright yellow sun warmed their faces. A thick wool blanket kept their legs warm. Joseph had left earlier for Miller's shop to work. The bishop himself had stopped by to escort him and to check on everyone. Her mother had some shopping to do, while Lydia planned to meet Joseph at the library. They hoped that there they might learn something about the people in Billy's photos. And from that, they hoped to find out why Billy had come to them that night he died.

"I didn't want you to go to town alone," Lydia's mother said, turning toward her. "But I came along for another reason."

Oh boy. Advice in the pony cart. Her mother hadn't pulled this trick on her since her *rumspringa* days.

"You want to talk?" Lydia smiled.

"I do," her mother said. "Lydia…"

A long moment passed and her mother had yet to begin. "What is it, Mamm?"

"Well, this is harder than I thought." Naomi wiped a tear from her cheek. "I'm worried about you, Lydia."

"Why? From that little bump on the head? Don't. I'm fine."

"No, it's not the head. It's not even this tragedy about Billy Ferris. It's just you. Lydia, you aren't fine. You work too hard. You hardly ever spend time with your girlfriends, Kate and Miriam. You haven't been to a quilting in I don't know when. You cringe every time someone mentions the word *marriage*."

"That's not so." Lydia kept the smile on her face even though her mother's harsh accusations hurt. Every word her mother said was true. "Kate and Miriam don't have much time for me now that they're married. And the last few times I visited Kate, she could not stop talking about her time coming with the baby. I didn't know what to say. I certainly don't cringe when marriage is mentioned. I have nothing against marriage. I'm just all nervous about this business with Billy Ferris."

"This has nothing to do with Billy Ferris and you know it. I'm talking about why you aren't courting. You've had plenty of callers, but you keep turning them away. They've all but quit coming. They're afraid of getting rejected."

"You don't want me to get married to just anyone, do you? I have to wait for the right man."

"Your being choosy has nothing to do with it." Her mother's voice had taken an angrier, disappointed tone.

Lydia had not fooled Naomi with the phony smile and silly explanations. She frowned as she mulled over her mother's words. "I don't know why I don't get out much anymore. I'm older than most of the girls at the barn singings. There is a lot of work to do on the farm.

But I'll make a better effort, Mamm. I will. Anyway, how can you bring that up with all of this horrible Billy Ferris business?"

"Because this Billy Ferris business is what made me realize what I've allowed you to get away with for the past few years." Her mother frowned. "And I've realized why you gave up on courting and love and men."

Lydia swallowed hard. "I didn't give it up. I—"

"First of all, you're afraid of men because your father upped and left us. Darling Lydia, your father is— was—a good man, but the Amish life was hard for him. He left us because he wasn't able to cope with the Amish ways. I pray every day that he is safe and happy. Maybe he will come home one day. Maybe he won't. But I will never judge another human based on his weaknesses and shortcomings."

"Did you want to go with Daed when he left?"

Naomi shook her head slowly. "I miss him, but my first vow is to God. I never had a doubt about that."

Lydia sighed. She did not understand her mother's complacency. "You aren't angry? You don't feel like you got a raw deal?"

Naomi shook her head and smiled. "How can I be angry about a relationship that gave you to me?"

"You're so forgiving, Mamm. I am not like you. I try but—"

"It's fear that keeps you from letting go of all this pain. The Scripture says that "you shall not be afraid." Try it, Lydia. Cast away the fear, and then the forgiveness and the love will come. And with that, you will have peace."

Lydia hoped one day to be the strong woman of

God that her mother was. "*Danki*. I will try. I will try harder."

"Wait. I'm not finished."

"You're not?" Lydia sank down in her seat.

"No, and I think you know what I'm going to say." Her mother eyed her with a knowing stare.

"Actually, I don't."

"Lydia, you are still in love with Joseph Yoder," her mother said.

"No, It is good to see him again and repair that childhood friendship. But I'm not in love with him."

She put her arm around Lydia's shoulders and pulled her near. "Take care, Lydia, that you do not lose something that could bring you joy and happiness in this life. There is so much God has for you. Don't be afraid of it."

Lydia could hardly breathe at the thought of losing the farm or leaving her mother. And Joseph she had already lost. As soon as he could, he would be going back to Indiana. Even if she did still love him, there was nothing good to come of it.

Her mother remained quiet for the rest of the ride into town, and Lydia tried hard not to dwell on their conversation. But it kept replaying in her mind. She was grateful when they pulled up to the library.

Joseph was waiting for her. She climbed out of the cart and gave her mother a kiss goodbye. Her *mamm* had certainly given her a lot to think about. But first to find out about Billy and his friends.

Joseph leaned over Lydia's shoulder, passing her the Willow Trace High School yearbooks he'd pulled from the shelves. It was nice to be so close that he could feel the warmth radiating from her skin. He liked being with

Lydia. Staying with her over the past two days, sleeping on her couch, driving her and her *mamm* to Sunday meeting, taking meals with them, it had renewed and repaired their friendship.

If only the shadow of Billy's murder didn't hover over them constantly... Joseph really hoped they would find something useful that they could pass on to Detective Macy. He was ready to get them out of harm's way. He was also ready to really talk to Lydia about her feelings.

"What should we do first?" He whispered low and close to her ear even though they seemed to be the only patrons in the library.

"First, I think we should find the names of Billy's friends who are in those photos." She handed him a couple of annuals. "Here. You take these two. I'll take the others and that will cover all four years Billy was at Willow High."

Joseph took his two volumes and sat across the broad wooden table from Lydia. Several minutes passed while they flipped through page after page in the yearbooks. Joseph split his attention equally between the photo scanning and staring across the table at Lydia. She was so beautiful, even more so now than when he'd left five years ago. There was more gold in her eyes. Her lips a darker shade of rose, her cheeks higher, more pronounced.

"What?" She looked up suddenly and caught him staring.

Joseph gave her a quick smile. Was this his chance to finish asking Lydia why her feelings for him had changed? He would have to ease into the subject. "I—I was just thinking...well, I'm surprised you're not married."

"*Ya,* I'm an old maid. *Danki.* My mother just said the same thing to me on the way here. Now, get back to the pictures."

Joseph dropped his head back to the yearbook. After he'd inspected about three more pages, Lydia swung her edition around to him.

"Look." She pointed at a class photo in the middle of the page. "This is Michelle. She was in the picture and at the pond that night."

"*Ya.* I think Billy and she were sort of together at one point."

"Maybe the others will be nearby."

Lydia marked the page, then they went back to searching the individual albums. Joseph almost immediately came across a picture of Billy in a baseball uniform. He was standing next to another boy dressed the same. This time he turned his yearbook around to share. "Look at this one. I'd almost forgotten that Billy played baseball. And that guy next to him—he worked at the restaurant with us."

"That's the same guy in the picture from the valet box. What's his name?" There was excitement and hope in Lydia's voice.

"You're right. I'm surprised I didn't recognize him. I guess after the accident I wasn't thinking too clearly." Joseph read the caption under the photo. "'Bill Ferris and Kevin 'Wats' Watson pitch Willow High's first ever no-hitter.'"

Kevin Watson?

"Oh, Lydia. Remember? Billy said 'what's' to us that night he died. Maybe Billy wasn't saying 'what' *w-h-a-t.*" He thought out loud. "He was trying to say 'Wats' *W-a-t-s?* As in Kevin Watson, the guy that took over his job at the restaurant? Wasn't that the name of the new manager? The one we met at the funeral."

"It was. You're right. And you did say he looked familiar," Lydia agreed. "What do you remember about him?"

"Not much." Joseph shrugged. "He was a year or two younger than Billy and me. At the restaurant, he would tag along after Mr. Bowman. You know, trying to impress him. Billy, I remember, thought he was a pain."

"I don't remember him being at Tucker's Pond that night. Do you?"

"No." He turned the book back around to face himself on the tabletop.

"Wait." Lydia hurried around to his side of the table and touched a photo on the opposing page. "Look at that!"

He smiled up at her. "There are all the girls from Billy's photo. They're all at a baseball game."

Joseph moved his finger to the caption under the photo, his hand brushing against hers. A tingling sensation traveled up his arm. "'Cheering on the regional champions to their final victory—Michelle Adams, Kelly Newport and Alexandra Nivens.'"

"Alexandra! Alex!" Lydia fell into the chair beside him, shaking her head. "We didn't imagine Billy saying that name, Joseph. He really said it. And he was talking about this girl." Her voice quivered. "The girl who became sick from the drugs. The one we left. We have to find out what happened to her after we left."

"Why don't we use the computers now and see if we

can find something on the internet about any of them…
especially Alex?" Lydia said.

Joseph and Lydia both stood so fast they met each
other face-to-face and toe-to-toe. Joseph froze. The
proximity of her filled his senses. He breathed in her
scent and felt the warmth of her breath. She was ach-
ingly close. He touched her soft face with his fingertips. "Oh, Lydia."

He was so close, Lydia held her breath. A strange and
overwhelming energy filled her every fiber. Every word
her mother had said in the pony cart screamed through
her head. *Joseph is not your* daed…. *You shall not be
afraid…. You're still in love with Joseph….*

Was she? Was she still in love with him? And was
it only fear that had kept her from reading his letters?
Was it fear that, right this moment, kept her from falling into his arms and telling him she'd been wrong.

Lydia lowered her head and stepped back, her heart
pounding. With a quick step, she walked to the computers. Joseph followed at her heels. He placed his hand on
her shoulder and whispered her name. The warmth of
his hand flowed from the tips of his fingers down her
back. She was moved, excited and scared. Too scared
to turn and say what was in her heart. If she let Joseph
in, even the tiniest bit, he might leave her again. And
from that she would never recover.

She pulled away again. "Let's just find out what happened to Alex and this can all be over."

She chose the first computer station. Taped next to
the big screen was a set of easy-to-follow steps for the
Amish patrons and others who weren't familiar with the
web searches. Lydia had used the internet a few times

during her *rumspringa*. Without much difficulty, she opened the browser and typed in *Alexandra Nivens*.

"Wow. There must be a hundred articles with her name." Joseph pulled a chair up alongside her.

He was silent for the moment, but Lydia feared he would try again to speak of his feelings. But really, what was the point? He was going back to Indiana. She shook the troublesome thoughts from her head. They had to focus on Billy's death.

"I don't know why there are so many articles. Let's see." She scrolled down, reading aloud the titles. "'High School Student Goes Missing,' 'Last Seen,' 'Unsolved Case,' 'Missing Person,' 'Nivens Missing'…"

"Alexandra Nivens is a missing person."

Chapter Eight

Lydia clicked on one of the links to an article. He and Lydia began to skim the article silently, when he noticed the publication date.

"This is just a couple of days after that night at the pond. Here's a quote from Billy and Michelle. 'Last time we saw her was at school.'"

They exchanged a knowing glance. They both knew that wasn't true.

"School was out, wasn't it? The last time they would have seen her would have been at the pond with us. Or do I remember it all wrong?"

"No. You are right." Joseph touched his hand to his forehead. He swallowed hard. "That was the reason for the party. It was the last day of school. So Billy and Michelle lied to the newspaper."

"What would make them lie?"

"I don't know. Because of the drugs that night, maybe?"

Lydia couldn't quite wrap her head around the concept of lying, but she did not like where any of this was going. She turned back to the screen. "Here's another article. This one is from just last year."

"It's another missing-persons case from Lancaster," Joseph said, reading along with her. "A more recent one. Another teenage girl, Melissa. And two others in the year before following similar patterns. Look, it mentions Alexandra Nivens here... as an unsolved case."

He pointed to the screen. Lydia scrolled down, reading as fast as she could. "Alexandra has never been found, but read this."

Joseph followed her finger to the paragraph that she pointed out on the bright screen.

Melissa Roan was found dead three days after she went missing. Cause of death: overdose of designer drugs. Forensic scientists do not have enough evidence to trace the drugs to a particular dealer. Police profilers, however, suspect it is a local operation and are wondering if the Nivens missing-persons case and several others could be related to this crime. All girls fit similar description, age, size and situation.

"Come on," Joseph said quickly. "We have to get to Detective Macy and tell him that Billy tried to talk to us about Alex and Kevin the night he died."

Joseph stood and offered his hand to help her up. Until now, he had not seen her tears, but it was clear she had been crying as he'd read. Joseph held out his arms. Lydia stepped into his embrace and lowered her head to his shoulder. "I'm glad you have been here. I couldn't have gone through this without you."

Joseph's heart filled with emotion. He whispered into her ear and held her tight until she was calm again.

"I'm so sorry I took you there that night, Lydia. So sorry. This is all my fault. I got us involved in whatever this is. If I could, there are so many things I would have done differently in the past. And none of them would include hurting you."

He wasn't sure Lydia had heard a word of what he'd said, but her arms were tight around him and he wished they could stay like that forever.

Lydia and Joseph called Detective Macy from a public phone in the lobby of the library. It didn't take long to explain to him what they'd learned from the pictures and internet. The detective explained that Kevin Watson had already been on his radar for Billy's murder. Kevin had shown signs of distress and confusion when police had questioned him as a rival employee of Billy's. Upon further investigation, it was discovered that Watson had played a significant role in Billy's drug business, which he also coveted and wanted to take away from Billy. At that very moment there were police cars on their way to Kevin's home and to the restaurant to make an arrest. Macy promised to be in touch, but he hoped that this was the end of it.

Somehow, Lydia felt little relief at this discovery. Even as they walked home and heard the sirens whirring in the distance—the very ones on their way to the restaurant to arrest Kevin—it still felt unresolved. Kind of like her feelings for Joseph?

They had gone about a third of their hour to walk Holly Hill when Mr. Zook happened to pass them in his open buggy. He stopped to ask them about the sirens that had sounded earlier. When he realized they were walking all the way to Holly Hill, he insisted on giving them a ride. Joseph offered Lydia the bench seat next to Mr. Zook, but she preferred to stretch out in the cart and leave Joseph to answer all of Mr. Zook's questions.

Lydia must have been more exhausted than she thought. The next thing she knew, the buggy had stopped and she was home. She climbed down from with a yawn. Her mother was waving from the front porch.

"Thanks for the ride, Mr. Zook," she said, realizing Joseph was no longer with them.

"I let Joseph out at Miller's store." Mr. Zook must have sensed her confusion. "He said he had some business to take care of and that he wanted to update the bishop on the police making an arrest in Billy's murder."

She waved to Mr. Zook as he rode off in his open buggy and she walked up the steps to join her mother.

"Well, I'm glad to hear the whole affair is over. What a relief." Naomi put her arm around Lydia's shoulders and they moved toward the front door. "I fixed a ton of dinner. I thought Joseph would be with you. Where is he?"

Lydia shrugged. "Mr. Zook just told me he only rode to Miller's store. Said he had some business."

Her mother gave a doubting look. "Probably afraid you're going to send him back to Indiana without one kind word."

Lydia sighed. She was too tired to make a reply. She followed her mother to the kitchen and helped with the meal. "It does seem a bit quiet without Joseph or the Zook boys, doesn't it?"

Lydia ignored the strange emotions twisting in-

side of her. She also ignored her mother's I-told-you-
so looks. She caught herself more than once peering
out the kitchen window to see if Joseph was walking
up the path.

The third time she peered out, she did see something moving. It wasn't Joseph. It was Candy, her larger
pony, trotting down the gravel path. "Now, what is she
doing out?"

"What's that?" her mother asked.

"Candy. She's gotten out of the stable. I'll be right
back." Lydia hurried out of the house with an apple in
her hand.

She ran down the front lane. A few whistles and the
sweet fruit had the little pony at her side in no time.
Lydia led Candy to the stable and locked her back inside
her stall. How had she gotten out? Perhaps her mother
had not shut the latch properly, but even then Candy
would have had to slide the door to the stall. None of
her ponies knew how to do that. Something wasn't right.

Lydia decided to check each of the ponies and the
stalls. She tested the latches and made certain that the
stalls were secure. She found nothing out of order. And
yet, there was a nagging feeling that she had overlooked
something.

Lydia marched back up the aisle once again, her eyes
fixed on the feed room in the very back. The door had
been left open—that was it. She headed over to the dark
corner to pull it closed. Leaving the feed room open
was the same as sending out party invitations to every
unwanted critter in the vicinity. She couldn't imagine
her mom had left it opened.

An empty bucket lay in front of the door. That, too,
was strange. Her mother liked everything neat and or-

derly. A bad feeling washed over Lydia as she reached down and picked up the bucket from the dirt floor. Before she could stand again, a horse blanket came over her head and something or someone pressed her down to the ground. For a few seconds she tried to fight back and pull the blanket from her face. But her efforts were useless.

A second later, she took a hard blow to the head. Even with the cushion of the horse blanket, it sent pain ringing through her skull. Her limbs went limp. Darkness overtook her.

Chapter Nine

Joseph hummed a quick tune as he painted the last coat of stain across the top of a special piece of furniture he'd been working on. He'd started the chest when he'd first arrived in Willow Trace, thinking he could turn it over as a quick tourist item. But today, he'd decided to make it a gift to Lydia. He wasn't sure how he would present it to her. Just as he wasn't sure how he would ask for her forgiveness. But he had to try. And the chest wasn't the only reason he'd stopped at Miller's store. He'd wanted to talk to Bishop Miller about some major life choices. Afterward, they had prayed together and written to his uncle. The rest would be up to Lydia.

Joseph straightened up his workstation and headed out of the store toward Holly Hill. He had barely walked across the parking lot when Lydia's mother came running out of the woods.

"Joseph! Help, Joseph!" Naomi ran across the parking lot, waving her hands in the air. "She's gone. Lydia."

Joseph raced across the gravel lot to meet her. "What do mean, she's gone? Where?"

"I don't know. I don't know." Her voice cracked with emotion.

"It's okay, Mrs. Stoltz. It's okay. Tell me what happened."

"Lydia went out to catch Candy. The pony had gotten out. I saw her walk the pony back to the stable. But then she was gone for so long…"

"How long?"

She shook her head. "I don't know. But it was too long. I went outside to call her. And a van was driving away down the hill."

Gasping for air, Naomi's face twisted with grief and worry. "I didn't know what to do. I just started running here. Lydia said you were here."

"It's okay. It's okay, Mrs. Stoltz. We're going to find her." Joseph took Naomi's hands in his. She was hysterical, and even though he was close to feeling that way himself, he wanted her to tell him as much as she could. "Are you saying you think that Lydia went somewhere in a van? What van?"

"It was small. A little delivery van. White and gray. It was going so fast I couldn't see inside. I went to the stable as fast as I could…but I was too late. There was a huge mess in the aisles. Stuff everywhere. But Lydia was gone."

"A mess?" Joseph clenched his teeth. Lydia kept everything as neat as a pin. She would not have left the stable in disorder unless… "Someone took her."

Naomi covered her mouth. The tears slid down her cheeks. "I wouldn't have let her go outside alone, but I thought the murderer was caught. I thought this was all over."

"Me, too. We all thought it was over." Joseph put

an arm around Lydia's mother and steered her inside the shop.

"Bishop Miller?" He called out. "I think I'm going to need that prepaid cell phone you got the other day in case of an emergency."

Seconds later, the old bishop was running forward with his new phone in hand.

With trembling fingers, Joseph dialed Macy's direct number, which he remembered from the library. Macy answered on the first ring.

Joseph explained as quickly as possible what Naomi had told him.

"It's not Kevin Watson," Macy said over the line. "He is right here with me. But I think I know who it is. I'll send a patrol car for you. Where are you?"

"At the furniture store," Joseph said. "But why? Do you know where Lydia is? Who has her? Is she okay?"

"No, she's not okay. Maybe Bowman has her. I'll explain everything when I see you. But don't worry. Mr. Watson is going to cooperate and help us get Lydia back. Stay right where you are, Joseph."

"Hello? Hello?"

Macy had disconnected. Joseph looked at Bishop Miller and Mrs. Stoltz. What could he say that wouldn't send Naomi into the absolute frenzy that his mind was already in? "Detective Macy is sending a car over to pick us up. He says everything's going to be fine."

And Joseph prayed that it would. He prayed so hard.

Lydia came to with a start. One look around the smelly van she'd been thrown into and she knew it was a service truck. She tried to sit up but she had been bound at the wrists and ankles with heavy-duty plastic zip ties.

The van traveled fast and made sharp turns. She fought in vain to keep upright, but mostly, she struggled to keep from hurting herself against the bread racks and other storage areas.

With some difficulty, she peeked through the small glass window between the front cab and the back of the van. Mr. Bowman, the restaurant owner, was at the wheel.

Lydia slid back against the side of the van. Mr. Bowman? What could he possibly want with her?

All afternoon, everyone had hoped the terror was over with the arrest of Kevin Watson. Did they have it all wrong? Lydia prayed and she prayed hard.

She should have been trembling. But for the first time in a long time, she felt peace. She thought of her mother, and of Joseph, and of all this time she'd closed herself off—afraid of her own feelings, afraid of loving again, afraid of being hurt. Tears of release spilled onto her cheeks.

Lydia lowered her head between her bound hands. *Whatever happens today, I have learned this lesson— I am not afraid. God, You have taken all my fear. And if I ever see Joseph again, I will tell him. I will tell him that I love him and that I'm not afraid. It won't matter if he loves me back or not.*

Lydia knew God would take care of her. Of course, she'd known it all along, but she hadn't felt it. She hadn't lived it. Her mother had been right. Her fears had stopped her. But no more.

Suddenly, the van came to a screeching halt. Mr. Bowman got out and walked around to the back.

"Hello again, pretty lady." He opened the back doors,

grabbed her by the wrists and dragged her out of the vehicle.

Lydia hit the ground hard. And she knew exactly where she was. She'd been there five years ago on the worst night of her life. Tucker's Pond.

"Why have you brought me here? What do you want?"

"I want to get rid of you before you ruin everything. Just like Billy. Stupid ingrate. After all I did for him. I made him rich. He had girls. He made a fortune selling my drugs. He had anything he wanted." Bowman picked her up again, carried her to the edge of the pond and tossed her down in the grass.

"We thought it was Kevin who killed Billy. But all along it was you?"

"Kevin? That little twit would do anything I told him to. But he's a weakling. Good riddance. I thought he could be like Billy. But they all turn on you in the end."

"Why would you tell Kevin to kill Billy? What did Billy do to you?"

"He found out about my— Oh, stop with all of your stupid questions. You're giving me a headache. You'll figure it out soon enough." He turned back to the van. A moment later he came back with a bottle of water, a small brown lunch bag, and a set of large dumbbells and a rope.

Fear and darkness tried to surround her again. But Lydia fought it away. She looked up and faced him.

"You know Billy didn't tell us anything the night he died? You've been running around scaring us half to death for no reason at all. We don't know anything."

"For someone who doesn't know anything, you sure do talk a lot." He sat down on the ground next to her and pulled a plastic bag filled with powder from the brown sack. He paused for a quick moment and looked into her eyes. Lydia could see that same savage look that Billy had had the night he died. "You're going to feel so good, Amish girl," he said. "Just like the others. I made them feel so good. The first time wasn't planned, of course. Billy called me. Scared to death asking me what to do about Alexandra. He had made her sick with too much alcohol and one of those party drugs. I came here. I gave her something that made her feel all better. I loved watching her find that place of peace. My mother always told me when young girls were troubled, I should help them. Help end their suffering before they grow up. You're troubled, too, aren't you?"

"No. I am not troubled." Lydia jerked away from his hand that tried to stroke her on the wrist. "I'm perfectly fine."

"Now, you aren't telling the truth, young lady." He shook his head in a scolding manner. "I know your father left you. I know that Joseph Yoder left you. You might be the most troubled of them all. Well, don't worry. Today, I'll take all of that away." He touched her face and smiled. Them he poured the powder into the bottle of water and shook to mix it.

He was right. There was no mistaking his plan. His actions were rehearsed, memorized, habitual. He was going to drug her and send her to the bottom of the pond. He'd done it before. It sickened Lydia to think of it.

She turned away. If God willed her to be at the bottom of that pond, then so be it. It was only the flesh. Her spirit would live on. "I'm not afraid of you. You can't hurt me. But I do have a question."

"Another question? What's that?"

"If Billy knew all along that you killed Alexandra after the overdose, why did you wait to kill him five years later?"

"You're smarter than you look." He laughed. "Billy didn't know about Alexandra until a month ago. He thought I gave her a bunch of money and that she ran away from home. But then he found my—he found one of my keepsakes." He took the prayer *kapp* from her head. He held it gently in his hands. "Like this. From you, I will keep this. This is perfect."

"How many others, Mr. Bowman? How many women's lives did you steal?"

"I didn't steal their lives. I saved them."

"Only God can save."

"Drink the water." She had angered him to the edge now. He stood and forced the drugged water into her mouth.

Lydia turned and pressed herself facedown on the ground. It knocked the water from his hands.

He fumed. He grabbed the bottle from the grass, turned her over and forced the drink back to her lips. "You will drink this."

"I will not foul my body with your drugs, Mr. Bowman." She spit the drink from her mouth.

"You…" He lifted his hand to strike her but stopped. There was a sound in the distance.

A very familiar sound—a siren. Help was on the way! Lydia closed her eyes and thanked God.

Mr. Bowman cursed under his breath and, with one last look at her, turned and made a run for the van. He sped away, his tires spitting dirt and gravel back at her face. She watched as he drove like a madman to the far edge of the woods. A dark sedan pulled up and blocked his path. He slammed hard on his brakes then hopped out of his van and made a run for the woods. Lydia wanted to scream. But as if placed there by God's hands, Macy and his men came from behind the trees. They were on him and toppled him to the ground.

Joseph fled from the patrol car as soon as it stopped. Macy and his men had Mr. Bowman at the edge of the woods. But where was Lydia?

He ran to the back of the service van, but it was empty. Were they too late?

Joseph's eyes scanned the woods to the shoreline of the pond. At long last, he saw a blur of blue and white near the water. Lydia. She had worn a blue frock today.

Joseph ran to her as fast as his legs could go. He fell to his knees beside her at the water's edge. A bottle of water lay spilled out at her side. "Lydia, please be okay…"

She turned to his voice. A beautiful smile covered her face. "How did you know where to find me?"

"Kevin. He told Macy about it all. Billy had just found out, too. That's why—"

"I know. Mr. Bowman thought Billy told us, too."

Joseph nodded. He loosened the bindings around her hands and feet and tore them away. He pulled her up. His arms went around her waist and he hugged her close. It was perfect. She was perfect. He would never let go of her again. "It's all over now. We are safe."

"I don't want you to leave again, Joseph." She was crying and clung tight to his shoulders. "I want people to stay in my life. I want you to stay in my life, however that may be. I love you. I have always loved you. I was just afraid. But I'm not anymore. Can you forgive me for not reading your letters nor trying to understand why you left?"

He placed his hand on her chin and lifted her face to his. "If you can forgive me for leaving without talking to you first."

"I already have." She smiled. "I love you, Joseph. Even if you go back to Indiana, I will still love you."

"I love you, too." He leaned down and placed a soft kiss on her lips. "And I won't ever let go of you again, Lydia. That is, if you'll have me. Will you marry me, Lydia Stoltz?"

"Yes, yes, I will. I will marry you."

He kissed her forehead. He kissed her cheeks. He couldn't stop the huge smile that covered his face. But Lydia pulled away.

Her head dropped and the elated look from her eyes turned pensive and strained. Joseph's heart sank. Had she already changed her mind?

"I suppose we could sell the farm," she said.

"And why would you do that?" Joseph pressed his forehead against hers the way he used to do when they were young. He rubbed his nose against hers. "I want to stay here, don't you?"

"But I thought you had to—"

"No. It's all settled. I'm going to work for Bishop Miller."

Lydia looked fast into his eyes, as if she could not believe his words. "And when were you going to tell me this?"

He smiled and pulled her tighter. "As soon as you remembered that you are in love with me."

Beautiful happy tears streamed over her cheeks. He kissed each one.

"I'll never leave you, Lydia. I never did, you know. My heart was right here all along."

She nodded. "Oh, Joseph. Yours was here and mine was with you. I think they are better off together."

"Me, too."

"So, kiss me again, Joseph Yoder."

And he did. He kissed his Lydia softly and promised both her and God that he would kiss her every day in just this way and remember this moment when God brought them back together.

* * * * *

Love Inspired®

Save $1.00

on the purchase of any
Love Inspired®,
Love Inspired® Suspense or
Love Inspired® Historical book.

Available wherever books are sold, including
most bookstores, supermarkets, drugstores
and discount stores.

Save $1.00

on the purchase of any Love Inspired®, Love Inspired® Suspense
or Love Inspired® Historical book.

Coupon valid until August 31, 2017. Redeemable at participating retail outlets in the
U.S. and Canada only. Limit one coupon per customer.

52614851

Canadian Retailers: Harlequin Enterprises Limited will pay the face value of this coupon plus 10.25¢ if submitted by customer for this product only. Any other use constitutes fraud. Coupon is nonassignable. Void if taxed, prohibited or restricted by law. Consumer must pay any government taxes. Void if copied. Inmar Promotional Services ("IPS") customers submit coupons and proof of sales to Harlequin Enterprises Limited, P.O. Box 3000, Saint John, NB E2L 4L3, Canada. Non-IPS retailer—for reimbursement submit coupons and proof of sales directly to Harlequin Enterprises Limited, Retail Marketing Department, 225 Duncan Mill Rd., Don Mills, ON M3B 3K9, Canada.

U.S. Retailers: Harlequin Enterprises Limited will pay the face value of this coupon plus 8¢ if submitted by customer for this product only. Any other use constitutes fraud. Coupon is nonassignable. Void if taxed, prohibited or restricted by law. Consumer must pay any government taxes. Void if copied. For reimbursement submit coupons and proof of sales directly to Harlequin Enterprises, Ltd 482, NCH Marketing Services, P.O. Box 880001, El Paso, TX 88588-0001, U.S.A. Cash value 1/100 cents.

5 65373 00076 2   (8100)0 12282

® and ™ are trademarks owned and used by the trademark owner and/or its licensee.

© 2017 Harlequin Enterprises Limited

LIINCICOUP0517

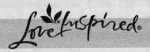
"Noah, where are you? I need to speak to you."

Working near the back of his father's barn, Noah Bowman dropped the hoof of his buggy horse Willy, took the last nail out of his mouth and stood upright to stare over his horse's back. Fannie Erb, his neighbor's youngest daughter, came hurrying down the wide center aisle, checking each stall as she passed. Her white *kapp* hung off the back of her head dangling by a single bobby pin. Her curly red hair was still in a bun, but it was windblown and lopsided. No doubt, it would be completely undone before she got home. Fannie was always in a rush.

"What's up, *karotte oben*?" He picked up his horse's hoof again, positioned it between his knees and drove in the last nail of the new shoe.

Fannie stopped outside the stall gate and fisted her hands on her hips. "You know I hate being called a carrot top."

"Sorry." Noah grinned.

He wasn't sorry a bit. He liked the way her unusual violet eyes darkened and flashed when she was annoyed. Annoying Fannie had been one of his favorite pastimes when they were schoolchildren.

Framed as she was in a rectangle of light cast by the early-morning sun shining through the open top of a Dutch door, dust motes danced around Fannie's head like fireflies drawn to the fire in her hair. The summer sun had expanded the freckles on her upturned nose and given her skin a healthy glow, but Fannie didn't tan the way most women did. Her skin always looked cool and creamy. As usual, she was wearing blue jeans and riding boots under her plain green dress and black apron.

"What you need, Fannie? Did your hot temper spark a fire and you want me to put it out?" He chuckled at his own wit. He along with his four brothers were volunteer members of the local fire department.

"This isn't a joke, Noah. I need to get engaged, and quickly. Will you help me?"

Don't miss
THEIR PRETEND AMISH COURTSHIP
by Patricia Davids, available June 2017 wherever
Love Inspired® books and ebooks are sold.

www.LoveInspired.com

Get 2 Free Books,
Plus 2 Free Gifts—
just for trying the Reader Service!

Love Inspired®

LI17R

Get 2 Free Books,
Plus 2 Free Gifts—
just for trying the Reader Service!

LIS17R